SHE SLIPPED OUT OF HER CHEMISE AND STOCKINGS . . .

She held her breath and slid down under the water to rinse out her hair. When she came back up for air, she sensed something was different.

Other than the slight luminescence of the waterfall, the cave was pitch black, and she could discern no shapes or movement within it. But something was in the cave. She knew it by the tingling, hair-standing-up-on-the-back-of-her-neck sensation throughout her body. She stayed still in hopes that whatever it was would go on its way.

But whatever it was, it was in here with her. Her heart froze when she felt hands grip her hipbones.

"Settle down. It's only me."

She stopped moving for a moment. "Leon?"

He answered by pulling her back through the water until she was cradled in his arms. Merciful Mary, he was stark naked! But then so was she. This was shameful, positively shameful.

"Leon, I don't think—"

"Stop thinking, darlin'," he said and began to kiss the side of her face and down her neck.

☆ ☆ ☆ ☆ ☆

"First-rate novel, full of humor and heart."
—Janet Evanovich

LUCKY STARS

PATRICIA ROY

✷✷✷

LUCKY STARS

WARNER BOOKS EDITION

Cover illustration ...
Hand lettering ...

Warner Books, Inc.
1271 Avenue of the Americas
New York, NY 10020

Visit our Web site at
http://warnerbooks.com

W A Time Warner Company

Printed in the United States of America

First Printing: June ...

10 9 8 7 6 5 4 3 2 1

WARNER BOOKS

A Time Warner Company

WARNER BOOKS EDITION

Cover illustration by Mike Racz
Hand lettering by David Gatti

Warner Books, Inc.
1271 Avenue of the Americas
New York, NY 10020

Visit our Web site at
http://warnerbooks.com

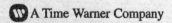 A Time Warner Company

Printed in the United States of America

First Printing: June, 1998

10 9 8 7 6 5 4 3 2 1

For my parents, Harriet and Roy, who've known all along that there's a lot more to romance than candelight and kissing.

Prologue

December 24, 1854

*L*eon watched Christmas through a window that year. With the snow swirling around his worn-down boots, he stood and stared through the glass at a kid going for a wild ride on a wooden rocking horse. He pushed away the sudden ache to be in there whooping and hollering alongside that little guy. Hell, he was nearly fifteen years old, way too big to get caught up in such foolishness.

Besides, he was heading off on his own adventures. The old-timer who ran the livery over in Harrisburg said he could stay there if he wanted and help out, and that's just what Leon intended to do. By next New Year's, he'd probably be riding his own horse. That'd show his pa he was more than just a worthless nuisance, maybe even make his stepma sit up and take notice—if she was still around, that is.

But this was no time to be dwelling on the dismal, not with what was taking place right in front of his very eyes. It was a wonder that kid didn't tip right over. He'd pull way back until the horse was straight up and down, then pitch forward until he nearly fell over the front, yelling and waving his arms in the air, having a fine time.

The boy's pa was leaning against a brick fireplace, and,

now and again, he'd rest his pipe on the mantelpiece and go over and drag the boy and his bucking bronco away from the Christmas tree.

It was the tree that'd caught Leon's eye in the first place. That beauty was thirty feet tall if it was an inch and all covered in candles. There was an angel at the very top and candle flames flickered all over her skirt of green branches. Leon was not easily amazed, but he couldn't recall ever seeing anything quite like it.

It wasn't just the tree and the little kid that drew him, it was the whole family. It was the mama rocking her baby to sleep. It was the papa tapping his pipe over the flaming logs.

Leon figured there must be something wrong with the window glass. Everything looked curvy, like he'd dreamed it up or was looking through waves of heat on a sweltering day. Leon was pretty sure he wasn't dreaming and darn sure it wasn't hot. In fact, the wind was so bitter cold it was making his eyes water.

He wiped the moisture away with the sleeve of his coat, tucked his hands under his armpits to warm them, and looked up at the night sky. The stars hung just above the treetops. It was going to be a clear, cold night all right.

Going to be? He was standing in every stitch he owned and was still shivering. No doubt it was plenty warm in there by the fire. But he wasn't in there, so he might as well give that thought a rest.

He must've ridden around like that kid when he was younger because whenever the horse tilted back and came to a halt with its nose in the air, Leon could feel a tug on his own elbows and shoulders.

But nothing good ever lasted. The way that kid was skittering all over the room, barely missing toes and table legs, this was bound to come to an end before long. Sure enough, it did.

The kid crashed into the Christmas tree and knocked it over on its side.

Everyone froze for a second. Then the man threw his pipe

down and stomped across the room. The woman let out a yell, tucked the baby in a cradle, and followed her husband over to the tree.

Leon expected it all to go up in flames. For a moment, he thought about rushing in and offering to help, but before he could get his feet moving, half a dozen servants were swarming all over that tree. Within a few minutes, the situation seemed under control.

Here it comes. The kid'll get beat and his wonderful wooden horse will get stomped apart and pitched in the fireplace.

Instead, the woman swooped the little guy up in her arms and whirled him around the room, singing some song that Leon couldn't make out even when he moved as close as he dared to the window.

If a person could ever put a moment in a bottle and save it for later, this is the moment he'd choose. He'd give anything to be that kid, dancing around the room in his mama's arms.

He was so wrapped up in watching the two of them that it was a while before he remembered the man. With his belly tightening into a knot, Leon scanned the room, and there he was, circling the tree, making sure every one of those candles was snuffed out. Then he turned around.

Here it comes. Leon stopped breathing, squeezed his eyes shut, and turned his head to the side as if the blows were going to land on him.

When he didn't hear any shouting and swearing, he turned back to look and had to blink twice to make sure he wasn't just seeing things. The kid was back riding his rocking horse and his folks were dancing around the room as if they didn't have a care in the world.

Try as he might, Leon just could not imagine ever being inside, ever dancing around like that with a laughing woman in his arms. Some people had all the luck, and others were just born to be on the outside looking in at it.

He knew which group he belonged to.

1

Hope Springs, Colorado Territory, Spring of 1869

Leon stepped into the Lucky Lady Saloon and Dance Hall, looking for a stiff drink and a loose woman. Waiting for his eyes to adjust from the afternoon sunshine outside to the dim light inside, he filled his lungs with the smell of damp sawdust, stale booze, and lingering tobacco smoke. He wondered when the dancing would start up and if the woman sitting in the middle of the room all dressed in black was the dancing gal.

Not likely, he decided, giving her the once-over, not with her hair skinned back in a bun and her hands twisting on that hankie. No doubt she was on the lookout for a wayward husband. He was glad he wasn't the fellow she was waiting for. She had a stern look about her, and Leon bet that some poor devil was in for a time of it when he finally showed his face.

As he walked over to the bar, Leon checked out the rest of the room. The only other people in the place were four cowboys playing poker and bragging to one another about how they would sooner work for Satan himself than that son of a bitch Irwin. Leon took note of that.

"We got applejack, corn liquor, and whiskey," said a nearby voice. "What's your poison, mister?"

Leon glanced down, and there behind the bar was the shortest man he'd ever seen outside of a circus.

"Bottle of whiskey and a glass of water, Shorty." If his name wasn't Shorty, it ought to be. The man'd need an apple box to see out a window.

"Name's Rooster," the bartender replied, pointing to his crop of red hair. He reached over and dipped out a glass of water from a burlap-covered crock.

Leon nodded to let him know he wouldn't be making that mistake again. Then he turned to look the place over. Since the woman in black was staring straight at him, he gave her one of his come-on-darlin' smiles. To Leon's disappointment, she didn't even come close to smiling back.

"Here's your whiskey," Rooster said, setting a bottle down next to the glass of water.

He drank the water and handed the glass back to the bartender to fill again. It was pure and cold and so thirst-quenching he didn't even really want the whiskey. But a man couldn't walk into a bar and just drink water. He knew that much.

"Is she waiting for her husband?" Leon asked, indicating the woman with a tilt of his head.

"Miss Marjorie?" Rooster acted as if the saloon was filled with females, and he was trying to make out just which one Leon was making inquiries about.

Leon nodded. As far as he could tell, she was the only woman in the place.

"No, indeed," Rooster said. "Not hardly." He refilled Leon's water glass, then was called away by the arguing poker players.

Leon turned his attention back to Miss Marjorie, who was not married but *was* sitting in the middle of a saloon. Putting two and two together, he reached the conclusion that she must be a lady of the evening. He wondered why in the world she was wearing that old black dress. It covered everything but her head and her hands. That gal needed to wear something a bit more enticing if she intended to make a living in this line of work.

On second thought, maybe not. Women were few and far between out here in the Territories. Hell, she could probably sit here huddled under a horse blanket and attract all the attention she wanted.

With a sideways nod, Miss Marjorie indicated she'd like him to occupy the chair next to hers.

Leon's hopes rose. Picking up his whiskey bottle and water glass, he strolled over. She was sitting ramrod straight, with her head and shoulders pulled way back like a schoolmarm's. He hoped she wouldn't ask him to phrase a sentence or run through his times tables.

"Mind if I join you, ma'am?" he asked, just to be polite.

"Please do," she answered, dipping her head as if she was granting him a favor.

Which, in a way, she was. Leon wished she wasn't so standoffish. Miss Marjorie wasn't a bad-looking woman. For a slender gal, she had plenty on top. Though that black dress covered her clear up, it fit snug so a man could get a fair idea of what was hidden underneath. She appeared to be curved in all the right places. In the dim light, it was hard to make out the color of her eyes, but they were soft and innocent, like a doe's.

He couldn't help but notice that her lips were drawn in a tight line, as if she disapproved of him. He didn't know what to make of that. Last he'd heard, it was still legal for a man to be in a saloon.

"Can I buy you a drink, ma'am?" he asked.

"No," she replied firmly, "but I appreciate your asking." Her eyes dropped to the lace-edged handkerchief she was fooling with in her lap. He judged her pleasant enough to look at even if she was a touch on the plain side. She didn't appear to be wearing any of the colored powders most saloon women wore. That probably made a difference.

Leon finished his glass of water, poured it half-full of whiskey, and tried to think of something else to say.

Nothing came to mind. He'd ridden for two weeks on the promise of a job, only to be told that he wasn't wanted and he'd have to ride on. Then his horse pulled up lame.

But there was no sense in going into all of that now. He'd been curled up around a campfire for way too long and was looking forward to a few nights in a soft bed. Some company in that bed wouldn't be too hard to take either.

She certainly seemed shy for a soiled dove. He briefly wondered what it'd be like with her. It was difficult to imagine. Every time a thought came to him, he let go of it. He was pretty sure a woman dressed all in black wouldn't be in favor of most of the things he had in mind.

Miss Marjorie ought to take up knitting to pass the time. The way her hands were twisting on that hankie, she could probably turn out socks about as fast as a man could pull them on his feet.

He sure wished she'd say a few words. At this rate they'd still be sitting right where they were when the sun came up tomorrow.

He glanced around in search of something that would spark a conversation. The Lucky Lady looked like every other saloon he'd been in over the past fifteen years. Lanterns hung from the ceiling, and spittoons were scattered here and there. A scarred mahogany bar ran along one wall and up above it hung a picture of a woman tied to the back of a horse. She didn't have a stitch on, just a swatch of yard goods draped across her and not enough of that to dust a fiddle. Somehow, it didn't seem right to make mention of a nearly naked woman to a lady dressed all in black.

He wondered if the black dress meant she was grieving. He hoped not. To his way of thinking, there was no sense carrying on about somebody who was already gone. As far as Leon was concerned, life was short, a person ought to live it up while he still could. Make the most of what comes along and the least of what goes. He could never understand why church folks got so upset over people dying. Much as they talked about heaven, you'd think they'd be happy to see their loved ones go there.

That thought stopped him cold. Was she a missionary? Was she about to lecture on the evils of liquor and urge him to repent of his wicked ways while there was still time? What a disturbing thought. He eyed her lap carefully to see if there was a Bible hidden under that hankie. There didn't appear to be one.

With a sigh of relief, Leon realized that no missionary would have stayed quiet this long. He was safe.

But there was still the problem of how to get things rolling between them. He guessed he could say something about the stuff on the walls. There was a broken pick and a gold pan, two crossed branding irons, and a couple dozen mounted animal heads, mostly antelope, deer, and buffalo. He'd never understood this business of hanging stuffed heads on the wall. Who wanted to drink with a buffalo looking over your shoulder anyway?

There was a piano back near the cowboys who were fussing over whether deuces were wild or not. He considered asking her if she played the piano but decided that was a poor idea. You couldn't very well sit around in a saloon and pretend like you were sparking in a parlor.

But he'd best think of something. Sooner or later some fancy talker would come strolling in and flash a roll of bills in her direction. The next thing you know, she'd be gone and he'd be back there arguing with the cowboys. Much as he loved a game of chance, now wasn't the time.

"Leon McCoy," was all he could think of to say as he reached over and grabbed her hand.

"Pleased to meet you, Mr. McCoy," she answered. She

gave him a couple of quick shakes and dropped her hand back in her lap.

He gave her a slow wink and let his hand fall with hers. His fingertips brushed across the top of her leg as he pulled his hand back. Her eyes flew open, and she looked sort of startled. She was playing this schoolteacher routine for all it was worth.

He once had a gal who'd dressed up like Little Bo Peep. Now she was a wild one, parading across the bar in her underdrawers, calling for her little lost sheep. Whoee! That brought back some memories. He'd been with a few other ladies over the years who liked to play dress-up. It didn't bother him none, long as they didn't want him to get all decked out too. Leon drew the line at that. But this was the first time he'd ever run across a whore who was playing hard to get. This was a new one on him, and here he thought he had seen it all.

"And you are?" Leon paused, waiting for her answer.

"Oh, yes. Certainly. I'm Marjorie Bascom." She let loose of the hankie, reached over, and shook his hand again. "Pleased to meet you."

He pulled her hand up to his lips and gave her a peck on the knuckles. He'd seen a gambler in New Orleans do that and the ladies just fell all over him. It wasn't Leon's usual style, but he figured it couldn't hurt. Still, he hoped none of the poker players had noticed.

Miss Marjorie jerked her hand away, acting like he'd done something indecent.

She was a shy one all right. He was curious as to how she got started in this business. She didn't seem the type.

"I take it you're a traveling man, Mr. McCoy?" she blurted out, a little on the loud side, considering how close they were sitting.

"Why, yes, ma'am," he replied. "I guess I do a bit of traveling. I've always been interested in seeing what's over the next rise, what excitement might be right around the bend."

"What brings you to Hope Springs?" she asked.

"Just passing through, Miss Bascom," he answered. "I'm on my way to the Northwest Territories. An old partner of mine is in the timbering business out there. Thought I'd go see what he was up to these days."

Leon didn't think he needed to mention that he was looking for work. It was unlikely she had a job to offer him, and he didn't feel like going into how he'd ridden two weeks only to have that Jarveson fellow tell him he'd sold the ranch and didn't want him after all.

"Could I buy you dinner, Miss Bascom?" He was hungry and figured food might get things rolling between them.

She looked him over like she was trying to decide if he had enough money to pay for the meal.

"I need to wash off some of the trail dust first, ma'am," Leon said quickly. "Then I'll be right back for you."

"That won't be necessary, Mr. McCoy. I'll meet you in front of Ruby Richmond's Hotel and Boardinghouse, right across the street. Shall we say an hour from now?"

He wondered whether it was such a good idea to let her out of his sight. Plain or not, she appeared to be the only available woman around.

She stood and offered him her hand again. He'd shaken hands more times in the last five minutes than he had in the last five years. His chair scraped along the floor as he stood and took her hand in his. He intended to kiss the back of her hand again, but she pulled it away before he got the chance.

"I look forward to doing business with you, Mr. McCoy," she said out of the clear blue.

It seemed a little cold talking about it that way, but Leon guessed that it was indeed a business arrangement, so what was the point of beating around the bush. Still, if she could pretend to be a schoolmarm, he could pretend to be smitten with her, couldn't he?

"Looking forward to it myself, darlin'." He winked at her as he tipped his hat, noticing that she smelled of lilac water. He'd always liked that scent on a woman.

Without so much as an encouraging smile, Miss Bascom turned and headed for the doorway. Her wide skirt swished from side to side in the sawdust. For being so prim and proper, the woman certainly had an enticing walk.

His worries about her finding someone else before he had a chance to get cleaned up were lessened by knowing that at least she wasn't going to wait for him here in the saloon.

As she pushed through the swinging doors, his eyes traveled up to the bun in the back of her head. Her hair was coppery-colored, like an old penny. He wondered if it fell all the way to her waist and if she'd take it down for him.

As far as Leon was concerned, things were coming along just right. He hadn't been this worked up over being with a gal since he was a kid. Usually, once he'd decided on one, they'd just go upstairs and get on with it. Generally, the money was on the dresser and he was heading out the door before he had a chance to build up much in the way of excitement.

Mostly, he just did without women. They were costly and a ton of trouble as far as he could see. The way they were always wanting just a little bit more was irksome. A woman living in a one-room cabin would carry on about how she had to have another room until her man threw up a lean-to. Then she'd start complaining about needing a new stove or wanting a window.

There was no satisfying a woman. You could work yourself into the ground trying to please one, and then she'd up and run off with a peddler or else take up with a man she met in church. No thank you. He liked his free and easy ways. Every once in a while he could do with a little comforting for a night or two. But Leon couldn't see any use of stretching it out beyond that.

The unwelcome thought crossed his mind that what with

the hankie and all, perhaps Miss Marjorie Bascom was not a loose woman. If she wasn't, then what was she doing sitting in a saloon arranging to conduct business with a stranger at a hotel?

No, she was a lady of the night all right. He just hoped he could afford her.

2

"You're planning to marry a stranger you met just a few minutes ago at the Lucky Lady?" Marjorie's aunt Ruby looked as if she thought her niece had lost her mind. "What in the world were you doing there in the first place? A respectable woman has no business being in a saloon."

Before Marjorie could defend herself, Ruby continued, "And the ruffians that hang out there are hardly what I would consider suitable matrimonial prospects."

"He appears to be a nice enough man," Marjorie said in defense of her decision, "and if he isn't, he will be long gone before he can cause all that much trouble. He's a wandering man. If he stays around a month, I'll be surprised."

Marjorie stood next to the huge, black cookstove, stirring a simmering pot of beef chunks. She acted like they'd had this discussion a dozen times already and she was growing rather bored discussing it again—even though this was, in fact, the first time she'd broached the subject with her aunt. Tasting a little of the soup stock, she decided it was on the bland side and added a heaping spoonful of dried thyme leaves.

"If you're so set on getting married, what about Charles

Irwin, or Jake Jarveson, or even Rooster, for heaven sakes?"
Ruby's plump hands hovered above a bowl of bread dough
as if she didn't quite know what to do next.

Dismayed by her aunt's suggestions, Marjorie stopped
stirring and turned to look at her.

"There is absolutely no way I could bear a lifetime of listening to Charles Irwin and his never-ending talk about becoming the governor." She picked up a paring knife and
began peeling onions with a vengeance.

"And despite his denials and feeble excuses, as far as I
know, Jake Jarveson is still married." What had possessed
her aunt to even suggest she consider marrying that lying
scoundrel? That man was nothing but misery.

"Well, what about Rooster?"

"What about Rooster?" Marjorie asked, sounding sharper
than she'd intended. "I will admit that he's the best of the lot,
but I refuse to marry a man who stands bosom high and runs
a saloon. Besides," she said in an attempt at lightheartedness,
"he's the Justice of the Peace. If he were the groom, who
would marry us?"

"Well, at least he has a steady job," Ruby pointed out.

"I don't want a steady man," Marjorie insisted. "I want
one who will sign his name on those homesteading papers
and then clear out."

"Oh, honey, you shouldn't marry a man just to get 160
acres," Ruby pleaded with her.

"I shouldn't marry anyone at all, and if it wasn't for that
arrogant land clerk, I wouldn't have to." Marjorie took a vicious whack at an onion and nearly sliced off the end of her
finger.

She stopped chopping onions and pretended to peer at
Ruby over the top of imaginary spectacles. Pursing her lips,
she imitated the pretentious land clerk's pompous voice as
she said, "The law is quite specific, Miss Bascom. Only
Heads of Households are permitted to file land claims. As a
single woman, you do not meet the qualifications."

Picking up another onion, she continued in her natural tone, "When I pointed out that if I were a single man I would qualify, he had the nerve to tell me that if a frog had wings it wouldn't bump its butt. Can you imagine?" She didn't mention the indecent suggestion he'd made about how he might see his way clear to make an exception to the rule if she would behave in a friendlier fashion to him. The very idea!

"Whatever's possessed you to be so set on homesteading all of a sudden?" Ruby wanted to know. While staring at Marjorie, she absentmindedly pulled off a chunk of dough, rolled it between the palms of her hands, and twisted it into a knot. "I just don't understand what's happened to make you want to leave us." Her voice quivered as she spoke.

Marjorie dropped the knife on the cutting board, turned around, and put her arms around her aunt's ample shoulders.

"Nothing's happened. I just know that you and Uncle Hank will be moving on one of these days, and I'm tired of moving. I've moved around my whole life, and I want to settle down in a place of my own. I want to plant tulip bulbs in the fall and know I'll be there in the spring to see them push through the ground." Not wanting to hurt her feelings, but still knowing it needed to be said, she hesitatingly added, "It'll be a place you and the kids can come stay if you need to."

Her aunt Ruby didn't say a word, but she stiffened and pulled away, so Marjorie let her arms drop.

"I could save that $20 a month the school board pays me from now until doomsday and still not have enough to buy much more than a burial plot," Marjorie said, swiftly filling the uneasiness between them with words. "Homesteading is the only chance I have for a home of my own. When I found out about that Circle I cowboy not proving up and getting the title to his land before he died, I decided that God must have meant that sweet place for me."

"But there are men aplenty out here. Surely, someone we

know would be a better marriage prospect than a total stranger," said Ruby.

"Now that I think of it, there were four Lazy J hands playing cards in the Lucky Lady this afternoon. I guess I could choose one of them," Marjorie said. She bent over, opened the door to the cookstove firebox, and shifted the chunks of wood around with a poker. The smell of woodsmoke twined around the aroma of the stew.

"Oh, honey. You don't want to marry a saddle tramp." Ruby was clearly appalled at the very idea. "With all the men out here in the Territories, surely you could find a more suitable husband than that."

"Name one," she said as she straightened up. "The country may be covered with men, but they're all wandering from place to place, grumbling about their misfortunes and bragging about the gold strike or the cattle operation that's going to make them filthy rich one of these days." Marjorie slammed the firebox door shut with more force than was absolutely necessary. "Why in the world would I want a worthless dreamer hanging around?"

"There are stable, steady men to be had." Her aunt placed another knot of bread dough on the tin baking sheet.

That brought back bitter memories. "Like the one I was betrothed to for five years?" she asked, noticing how just the thought of Oliver's betrayal made her teeth clench and her jaws ache. "The one who wanted me to wait for marriage until he was well situated and then spent every penny the two of us had managed to save on that foolhardy shipping scheme?"

She hadn't cried then, and she wouldn't cry now. The sudden wetness in her eyes was due entirely to the onions she was chopping. Before there was a chance of tears forming, she wiped the moisture away with the back of her hand. "No, thank you. I prefer a life of independence, if you don't mind."

"But that's such a lonely way to live," Ruby said as she filled up one baking sheet and started on another.

"There are a lot of things worse than being lonely." Like being married to a man who left for years at a time, Marjorie thought, or moving hither and yon trying to follow some will-o'-the-wisp man around. But if her aunt was satisfied with her lot in life, far be it from Marjorie Bascom to point out how much better Ruby's life would be without that restless husband of hers.

"Is it necessary to rush into this marriage?" Ruby asked.

Marjorie was astounded that her aunt even questioned this. "It certainly is," Marjorie assured her. "That self-important land clerk has probably already telegraphed Charles Irwin regarding my attempt to file homestead papers. As interested as Charles is in expanding his holdings, I have no doubt but that he'll send another one of his cowboys to that Denver land office. Time is of the essence."

"Well, I must admit, Marjorie, I find this whole scheme rather shocking."

"I do, too, Aunt Ruby," she said, wiping her hands on her apron. "I do, too."

They worked alongside one another in silence for a few minutes before Marjorie attempted to explain why this particular piece of land was so important to her. "There's a high meadow with a creek running through it—a perfect spot for a garden," she said. "Along the back is a blind canyon that I could fence off to keep a milk cow and perhaps a few steers for a little cash money. I would continue to teach, of course, but with my own place, I would have no need to depend on the generosity of a tight-fisted school board."

She decided not to mention the hot springs cavern hidden behind the canyon waterfall. Last fall, she'd stopped to water her mare and was surprised to find warm water trickling down the edge of the waterfall. She'd followed it back and ended up ducking through the cascading water. Soaked to the skin, she found steaming water bubbling from the back of a secluded cave. It flowed into a pool in the middle of the chamber, then drained down the rocks.

Later, she'd read that there were hot springs all through the Rockies, left over from the ancient volcanoes that had formed this range of mountains. For all she knew, every ranch around had half a dozen. That didn't make any difference to her. She'd found this one and she planned to soak her arthritis away in it when the time came.

"What I don't understand is why didn't Charles file on it himself?" Ruby asked.

"He's already laid claim to as much land as he legally can. Since this piece adjoined his ranch, he sent one of his hired hands to file on it. Charles intended to buy the place from him once he'd obtained a clear title. He would've if the poor man hadn't gotten himself hanged first."

Marjorie didn't feel it necessary to go into how Jake's men had come across the cowboy herding a bunch of Lazy J steers off. It was a wonder Jake hadn't gone after Charles himself. But since there was no way to prove that Charles was actually behind the theft, Jake had let it go.

In any case, the cowboy's demise had gotten Marjorie's hopes up, and she'd used some of her precious savings to take the stage to Denver. She was discouraged at having spent all that money on nothing but an exchange of rude remarks.

Desperate times call for desperate measures. Getting married was the best plan she could come up with. She wished she'd thought of it in Denver instead of on the stage ride home. There was a much wider selection of suitors in Denver. The men around Hope Springs were terribly poor prospects. Most were either married, shiftless, hopeless drunks, or some combination of all three.

Charles Irwin was single and settled, but he was also a braggart and a bully. He'd come courting a year ago when they'd first moved to Hope Springs, and Marjorie had spent some tedious evenings with him on the back porch swing. It didn't take her long to decide that she would rather live and die in her aunt Ruby's boardinghouse than devote one more minute listening to him expound on how his daddy was a New York senator and how he was destined to be the governor of the Colorado Territory one of these days. She didn't care whether he became governor or not, she just didn't want to hear any more about it. Fortunately, he'd decided to winter in Denver to pursue his political ambitions.

Around Christmas, Jake Jarveson had called upon her a few times. Though he was better company than Charles, his marital status was a drawback. Jake's wife had left him last fall. He told everyone that she'd gone back East to be with her family, how she just couldn't stand the loneliness and the cold winters and so on. More than likely she couldn't stand Jake. He was known to have a temper as well as a fondness for hard liquor. According to her aunt Ruby, Susanna Jarveson boarded the stage with a split lip, a bitter expression, and a one-way ticket to Philadelphia. She'd made no mention of returning.

Jake claimed she came from a wealthy family and had gotten a divorce. But since no one in town knew of any letters or telegrams arriving from her, there was some question regarding that matter.

Marjorie told Jake that she didn't feel right about keeping company with a married man and asked to see the certificate of divorce. He stormed and stomped around and accused her of not trusting him, but he'd never produced any divorce documents.

At various times, her uncle Hank had offered to put a stop to the two of them calling on her. She declined, preferring to discourage their attentions herself. Since Jake and Charles were just about the only paying customers Hank had, she hated to get him embroiled in a dispute with them. Besides, though they were odd, they were still neighbors and, if things worked out, next-door neighbors. It was never a good idea to fuss with neighbors.

When Charles returned from Denver and found out about Jake calling on her, he was furious. As far as he was concerned, Marjorie was his chosen woman.

The next Sunday morning, Charles and Jake fought in the middle of the street over who was going to accompany her to church. Jake won, but it was a moot point, as Marjorie was appalled at their behavior and wanted nothing to do with either of them.

Jake apologized and expressed the hope that they could continue to be friends. Marjorie disregarded his suggestion as she had an aversion to friends who lied to her.

Charles continued to behave as if waiting for her to recover from a temporary snit so that he could pursue his courtship in earnest.

When she made it clear that she had no interest in marrying him whatsoever, Charles informed her that if she wouldn't marry him, he'd see that she didn't marry anyone at all.

Marjorie wasn't too concerned. She had a pretty dim view of marriage, and nothing she'd seen lately had led her to change her mind on the subject. At twenty-three, she was feeling set in her ways and seriously doubted that marriage was in her future.

Over the years, she and her aunt Ruby had discussed Marjorie's views on marriage countless times. They had no need to go over it again.

Marjorie had no illusions about the financial security for which many married. Marriage was certainly a gamble in that sense. For every woman she could think of who moved up a notch in life, she could bring to mind three more who labored sunup to sundown to avoid starvation because they'd followed some man's half-baked schemes.

She'd watched her mother work until she dropped, trying to feed her and her sister. Every time they managed to get themselves halfway situated, her father would reappear, full of excitement about the possibilities just down the road. What they couldn't carry with them, they'd sell for a little bit of nothing and start all over again someplace else. They wouldn't be there long until off he'd go, promising to send for them as soon as he got established. She didn't know which she hated more—getting left behind to struggle on their own or watching her mother stare down the road, pitifully waiting for him to return.

One day her mother simply collapsed from it all. She was carrying a shoulder yoke with a bucket of water on each end when she sank to the ground and never got up again. Her heart just gave out on her.

The worst of it was, not two months before, they'd moved from a place with a water pump in the kitchen and a stream running through the garden. Her mother had died because the man who'd promised to protect and provide for her had hauled her out to the middle of nowhere and left her to fend on her own.

Marjorie and her sister Kathleen had come to live with Ruby and Hank. Though they both swore they were never going to repeat their mother's mistake, within a year, Kathleen had married a shiftless character who was later killed in a dispute over a horse race. He didn't even leave Kathleen enough money to bury him. She had to borrow the fifteen dollars from Marjorie. Four months later, Kathleen died giving birth to the second of her two little girls. With her last breath, she'd called out for that man who'd ruined her life.

Marjorie and her aunt worked silently side by side, wrapped in the warmth of the kitchen and offering one another what comfort they could in a world where women just made the best of things while the men did whatever struck their fancy.

At ten of five, with the dinner preparations completed, Marjorie waited under the Richmond's Hotel and Boardinghouse sign in her blue-serge, second-best dress. Seeing Mr. McCoy crossing the street, she took as deep a breath as her corset would allow and stepped forward to greet him. *She who hesitates is lost,* she told herself, in an attempt to calm the butterflies beating back and forth in her chest.

"Right on time, I see," she said, extending her hand and placing it on his arm.

"Wouldn't want to keep a lady waiting," he said, smiling down at her.

He was certainly tall, well over six feet, with shoulders broad enough to come in handy should he decide to take up timbering. The shave had improved his appearance considerably, and she was glad he'd kept the walrus mustache. It gave him a rugged, just this side of handsome, appearance. She remembered what he'd looked like from behind while he was leaning up against the bar this afternoon, and she felt a heated flush creep up behind her ears. In an attempt to get her mind off the image of his backside, she tried to see what color his eyes were. Blue-green she decided, like a clear, cold, deep lake.

They stepped inside the dining room, and Leon removed his hat. Black, wavy hair rested on his shoulders. It gave him an uncivilized appearance that she didn't particularly care for. If there was time later, she'd give him a haircut.

The room was not overly large, and the two small tables and one long one were all crowded in together. As it was early, they had the place to themselves. She led the way to one of the small tables and sat down on the chair on the far side. He remained standing.

"Do you mind if we switch seats, ma'am?" he asked.

"Why, not at all," she answered, getting up. He held the other chair for her as she sat down.

"I'd rather sit where I can keep an eye on things," he explained.

"That's certainly understandable, Mr. McCoy," she said, looking pointedly at the pistol and the holster strapped to his leg. "Are you a gunman, Mr. McCoy?" she asked after they were seated.

"Just a precaution, ma'am."

He didn't offer any further explanation, and she reasoned that it wasn't all that unusual to be armed, especially while traveling.

She decided it would be best to wait until after they'd eaten to broach the subject of marriage. Now really didn't seem like the time or place to bring it up. Perhaps an after-dinner stroll along Clear Creek would be more conducive to such a conversation.

It was difficult to think of what to talk about in the meantime. She seriously doubted that a man who'd seen as much of the world as Mr. McCoy had would be interested in the goings-on of Hope Springs. They traded comments about the weather, and both agreed that it'd been a nice day and a mild spring.

Marjorie was relieved when Janey entered the dining room to take their order. She introduced Janey as her cousin and one of her best pupils. Leon seemed amazed to hear she was a schoolteacher. Who did he think she was, the town trollop?

When she introduced him to Janey as an old friend from Massachusetts who had just arrived in town, his forehead pinched together in puzzlement. She shook her head in one brief back-and-forth movement to let him know that this was not the time to go into any details. She could hardly introduce him as a man she'd just met in the saloon. Janey was fifteen and highly impressionable.

Janey flipped a blond braid back over her shoulder and, unaware of their silent exchange, announced that they could select either beef stew or beef tips in gravy with vegetables. Leon asked what the difference was between the two and Janey replied that there was none, but people liked to have a choice, so she always offered one. For dessert, there was gingerbread or ginger cake. Leon and Marjorie both requested the beef stew and the gingerbread.

When Janey disappeared into the kitchen, Marjorie leaned across the table. Cupping a hand around her mouth to keep from being overheard, she whispered, "Later." She just barely had time to sit back in her chair before Janey returned with a bowl of knotted rolls and a crock of butter.

"I don't often get a chance to eat bread fresh out of the oven," he said. "I believe I could fill up on dinner rolls alone." Leon took a slow, deep breath and closed his eyes to better savor the aroma.

Oh my. For a moment, she had the wildest urge to just lean across the table and press her lips on his. Just a brief kiss. Just to see what it would be like. Fortunately, she had the presence of mind to grab on to her chair and steady herself before she'd embarrassed them both. Whatever had gotten into her? She wasn't prone to having lascivious thoughts about perfect strangers even if they did have wonderful walrus mustaches.

"Later." He said it so softly he hardly made a sound, but that was definitely the word his lips formed.

Good heavens. Was she that transparent? To hide her shame, she ducked her head and began furiously buttering a roll.

Fortunately, Janey returned with a tray containing two bowls of stew, two plates of gingerbread, and a cup of whipped cream. She tried to think of some way to engage Janey in conversation so she would stay, but her mind was running every which way. Before she could form a rational sentence, Janey was gone.

My, it's hot in this room.

"Sometimes that old cookstove just pours out the heat," she commented, raising her eyes to meet his.

He gave her a slow wink and opened his lips ever so slightly.

Mercy.

Marjorie jumped out of her chair and grabbed on to the window. If she didn't get some fresh air, she feared she would swoon right then and there. But try as she might, the window wouldn't budge. No doubt the recent rains had caused the wood to swell. She struggled with the frame, relieved to have something to think about besides Leon's lips.

All of a sudden, his lips were the least of her worries.

His arms closed around her, and she felt the entire length of him press up against the back of her.

What in the world?

She should turn around and demand that he behave like a gentleman. She would've, if she thought her legs would support her. She didn't seem to have an ounce of strength left. It was all she could do to keep from slipping to the floor as it was.

She stared at his hands in front of her—huge, strong, workingman's hands, with dark blue veins standing in ridges above his sun-beaten skin. Next to them, hers looked like doll's hands, pale, delicate, and useless. She recalled the feel of his fingers wrapped around hers when they'd shaken earlier in the afternoon and stood entranced as he bumped the window frame with his palms. It glided open, and he held it there. It took her a minute to remember to prop it up with the stick stored at the bottom of the windowsill.

The cool air was just what she needed. Still, she could barely catch her breath. If she'd been up in her room, she'd have undressed and loosened her corset strings. Whatever had brought that thought to mind, especially standing here with his arms surrounding her? She knew they should return to their seats, but she wasn't sure she had the strength—or the desire.

She cleared her throat. "Mr. McCoy, really."

"Really what, darlin'?" he asked. His voice was soft and low, and his breath brushed across her ear.

She clung to the windowsill for support, suddenly aware that he smelled of bay rum and that he had dark hair where his shirtsleeve had pulled back from his wrists.

"I think we should finish our meal." Her voice sounded high-pitched and shaky. She stopped to clear her throat again and made a conscious effort to lower her tone. "Before proceeding with matters." This time her voice sounded breathy, and she decided she'd better hush up before she made a fool of herself.

"That's fine by me, darlin'," he whispered, pressing a kiss to the top of her head before stepping away.

Sweet heavens. She really must do something before this got out of hand.

But right now, standing was all she could seem to manage. As she turned, she braced herself on the table for fear that her legs would give out before she could get seated.

"This is your first time, isn't it?" he asked, once she was settled.

This was proving to be more embarrassing than she'd ever imagined. Not trusting her voice, she put her finger to her lips to warn him to be quiet. For some odd reason, he seemed amused by her gesture.

"Miss Bascom, I think it'd be best if I just walked you home," he said. A barely contained grin pulled at the corners of his mouth. "As much as I've been looking forward to this evening, I just can't see myself leading any woman down the road to ruin."

"Can't we continue this discussion later?" she asked in a forced whisper.

"Continue discussing what? We've hardly traded a dozen words."

With Janey likely to reappear at any moment, she was in no position to be more specific.

"You know," she said under her breath, leaning forward so that her words would travel to his ears but no farther, "conduct business."

"Conduct business?" he repeated, loud enough to be heard in the kitchen if not clear out on the street.

A movement caught the corner of her eye and Marjorie glanced over in time to see Lucille Herner enter the dining room with Evie Sanderson right behind her. *Wouldn't you know?* As if this wasn't humiliating enough, now she had the town busybody and her faithful companion to contend with. She was grateful to see that Lucille's and Evie's husbands were with them. Perhaps they would provide some distraction.

Acting as if nothing were amiss, she forced a bright smile of greeting in their direction.

"Goodness, would you hush," she pleaded between clenched teeth.

"Fine by me, ma'am."

They ate the remainder of their meal in silence. Marjorie ignored Lucille's and Evie's stares and was ever so grateful when Leon finally finished his gingerbread and whipped cream and pushed back his chair.

"Are you ready to go?" he asked.

She assured him she was, and they walked to the door. Marjorie told him that he didn't owe anything since this was her aunt's establishment. But Leon said that he'd invited her to dinner and he would pay for their meal. Which he did.

Stepping out onto the boardwalk, they both paused to fill their lungs with that heady aroma of dry earth turning to damp that comes at the start of rain. It was only sprinkling, but from the looks of the dark clouds rolling in from the west, it wouldn't be long before the heavens opened up.

Marjorie realized that a leisurely stroll down by the creek was out of the question.

"Drat," she said, clenching her fists in frustration. "I was hoping we could go for a walk and discuss matters."

"Ma'am, the only thing left to talk about is whether it's going to rain or not, and from the looks of things, that'd be a mighty short conversation."

"Perhaps we could talk in the lobby of the hotel," she suggested, not deterred in the least by his comments.

"That'd be fine by me," he said, although he didn't sound at all certain about the matter.

They stepped into the lobby and were met by the sight of her two nieces and Ruby's youngest daughter playing with their dolls on the settee. Marjorie turned and pushed Leon back out the door. This was hardly a conversation one could conduct in front of children.

"Ma'am, I think it'd be best if I just walked you on home," Leon offered.

"Do you have a room, Mr. McCoy?" she demanded to know. Then, deciding to take a less forceful approach, added, "Perhaps it would be a good idea to go there to talk." She'd gotten this far, she wasn't about to back down now.

"I don't think that's anywhere near a good idea, ma'am," he said firmly. "I say we just forget about this whole thing and call it a night."

"Absolutely not." She grabbed Leon's hand and led him around to the back stairs like a reluctant schoolboy. Picking up her skirts, she dashed up the steps, glancing back to make sure no one had seen them. He followed at a somewhat slower pace.

"Which room is yours?" she asked breathlessly when they had entered the upstairs hallway.

"Ma'am, I don't know about this," he said. "You seem eager enough now, but what if you change your mind afterward. Fathers and brothers can be mighty small-minded about such situations. I've lived too long to get shot over this sort of foolishness."

"Which room is yours?" she repeated, ignoring his reservations about their being together. "I don't want anyone to catch us out here in the hallway."

"Miss Bascom, I don't know how you plan to carry on in a town this size without someone catching on sooner or later."

She paid no mind to his muttering, but rather, insisted that he open the door before they were observed.

Reluctantly, he pulled the key out of his pocket and opened the door to room six. She rushed past him and over to the window. No one was standing in the street shrieking "Harlot" and pointing up at them, so she assumed they were safe. Since there wasn't a chair in the room, she had a choice of sitting on the bureau or the bed. She chose the bed.

"Now let's get down to business, Mr. McCoy," she said, folding her hands in her lap.

"Without even drawing the shades?" Leon asked.

"There's really no need," she said. "That would only look suspicious. As long as we don't light a lamp, no one will be able to see us."

"Would you care for something to drink?" he offered as he tossed his hat on the bureau, unbuckled his gun belt, and slung it, pistol and all, over a bedpost.

"No, thank you," she replied, relaxing a little now that he was no longer armed.

He went over to the bureau, poured a half glass of whiskey from the bottle sitting on the top, and sat down next to her on the bed.

"You sure?" he asked, handing her the glass. "This evening might go a little smoother if you'd loosen up a bit. You seem on the nervous side."

"Well, all right," she agreed. There was no harm in being sociable. "Maybe just a sip." He handed the glass to her and she took two swallows.

"Good gracious," she exclaimed as the amber liquid seared its way to her stomach. She handed the glass back. "I believe I've had plenty. Thank you." She sucked air down in an attempt to soothe her throat. It didn't taste at all like blackberry cordial. How in the world could he drink this stuff?

"Miss Bascom," he began. "I don't know quite how to say this." He paused and looked around the room as if he might find the words he was looking for written on the walls. "But you don't seem cut out for this life."

What was he talking about? She couldn't live out West just because she didn't care for the taste of whiskey? There was no making sense of what men said. It was best to ignore a good deal of it.

"About our arrangement, Mr. McCoy," she began. She paused, wishing she hadn't partaken of his refreshments. Her thoughts were muddled now, and she'd forgotten completely how she'd intended to start this conversation out.

My heavens, he smelled good. She'd always liked the aroma of bay rum.

"Please, call me Leon," he said.

"No, I think it would be best if we did not get too familiar, Mr. McCoy."

"Fine with me," he agreed, as he took a drink. She was amazed to see that he didn't so much as grimace.

"Now about the money," she said, deciding that it might be best to get him interested in the money before telling him what he'd have to do to obtain it. "How does $125 sound?"

"Sounds a little steep, if you ask me," Leon said, clearing his throat. "I'm not certain I got that much on me, ma'am."

"No, silly, I'll pay you," she said. "But I'd expect you to work for it."

It took a moment for that comment to settle in.

"You mean you intend to pay me?" he asked slowly as if he couldn't quite grasp the meaning of her words. "Now that's different."

"Why, of course, I don't expect you to do it for nothing," she answered.

"Ma'am, I will admit I can be plenty comforting when I set my mind to it. I doubt you'd be disappointed. But I don't believe the experience would be worth $125." He sat the glass of whiskey down on the windowsill.

"Well, how about a hundred dollars then?" she suggested.

"Ma'am, you don't have to pay me anything at all," he gallantly offered. "I'll do it for free."

"You don't know how much I appreciate this, Mr. McCoy."

"Pleasure's all mine, ma'am," he said. "Well, that's not entirely true," he added, and brushed the ends of his mustache with his knuckles and raised one eyebrow as if she would know what he meant. She didn't.

After putting the whiskey glass back on the bureau, he sat down next to her on the bed, put his arms around her waist, and drew her close to him. "I reckon a woman is just as curious as a man about the pleasures of life, and I imagine it would be hard in a small town like this, what with you being the schoolmarm and worried about your reputation and all."

"That's part of it," she began. She needed to explain more, but he was kissing the side of her neck, and she couldn't seem to get her thoughts in order.

"Leon McCoy to the rescue," he murmured as he kissed behind her ear.

Mercy.

Marjorie felt she was melting in his arms like butter on the back of the stove. She closed her eyes, remembering that lazy, lopsided smile he gave her when he first saw her at the Lucky Lady. For a moment, she actually considered what it would be like to just let go and follow him.

Follow him where? In the end, he'd be on his merry way and she'd be stuck holding the bag, or the babe more likely. No thank you. She stiffened up and pulled back.

"That's enough," she gasped, her eyes flying open. "That's it."

"No darlin', that ain't it by a long sight," he said in a low, rumbling voice.

Merciful heavens. Was he sucking on her earlobe?

This had gone far enough.

"Stop that," she ordered, pushing him away from her. "I want you to marry me."

"Don't you think you're rushing things a mite, ma'am?" Leon reached his arm around and began kneading the side of her left bosom. She pushed his hand away only to find he was repeating the motion on the right side. Grabbing both of his hands was the only way to get him to cease his fondling of her person. Shocking as it was, she couldn't help but be aware that there was a certain pleasantness to his touch.

Not pleasant enough to allow him to continue, however.

"After we get to know each other a little better, darlin', we could talk about getting hitched," he suggested with a wink.

"I don't want to get to know you any better," she replied firmly. "I don't need a bed partner, I need a husband. That's why I am willing to pay." She said this as if explaining how two plus two always equals four to a youngster a little slow to catch on.

"Well, ma'am, while $125 may be a bit much for a night of loving, it seems a tad shy for a lifetime of devotion," he pointed out.

"I realize that's an impossibility," she said with a sigh. "I'm not asking for a lifetime, only a month or two." She pushed his hands down and away from her.

He looked at her as if she'd let loose of her senses, so she hurried on with the explanation.

"There's a place near here that I wish to homestead, but, unfortunately, I have to have a husband in order to file the claim on it. I could also use a hand fixing up the cabin, putting in a crop, and laying up wood for the winter. Although that's not absolutely necessary, it would be helpful. You'd be free to take off as soon as I was situated. You would be leaving with my gratitude and $125 to travel on."

He appeared to be considering her offer.

"Ma'am, I'd be glad to give you a hand with your cabin and all, but I don't believe it would be right to marry you," he said.

"And just why is that?" she wanted to know.

"Because I have no intention of sticking around," he said. "None at all. I've got places to go and things to do."

"Good. Then you'll do just fine," she said with a firm nod.

"Ma'am, you don't understand. Regardless of how well we get along this summer, I'll be leaving you high and dry come fall."

"Then you're no different than any other man I ever ran across, Mr. McCoy," she said. "Except most aren't as honest. In spite of all their promises, the first time someone waves a flag or a skirt or a chunk of gold in front of their faces, they're gone, leaving their wives behind to make out the best they can. They always promise to come back, of course. And some do. Usually just long enough to leave another little one before they're off again."

"Now, not all men are like that," Leon said in defense of his half of the human race.

"That's true enough," she agreed. "Some stick around, spending their money on liquor and loose women and beating their wives and children for sport."

"Since you're so sure it's a sorry situation, why get married at all?" he asked.

"Because I don't want to live out my years on the edge of somebody else's family," she answered, finding herself upset just thinking about it. "I don't want to spend my life as the maiden aunt everyone feels sorry for and makes an effort to remember at Christmas with yet another bottle of scented water. I don't want to pass on to my reward in the back bedroom of a boardinghouse." She felt herself getting worked up and stopped for a moment to regain control of her emotions.

"I have come to terms with being a spinster, Mr. McCoy. That no longer bothers me," she assured him. "But I want to belong somewhere. When I watch the geese fly south for the last time, I intend to be sitting on my own front porch. And in the territory, I need a husband's signature on the filing papers to do that."

"I feel for your situation, and I do appreciate the offer, ma'am, but I'm not the marrying kind," he said, leaving no room for doubt. "You're barkin' at a knot as far as I'm concerned." He picked up his glass of whiskey and finished it off.

"Thank you anyway, Mr. McCoy." She sighed, feeling her shoulders slump and not willing to put forth the effort to straighten them up as she knew she should. "It was kind of you to buy me dinner. I'm sorry the evening turned out so poorly."

Marjorie sat and stared at her empty hands. She'd left her handkerchief behind on purpose so she wouldn't end up twisting on it like a ninny.

Now what? She'd made a fool of herself and was at a loss as to how to proceed.

"Don't worry, Miss Bascom," he assured her, as if he sensed her discomfort. "I've had better evenings, but I've had worse." He reached over and lifted her chin up. "I'd like to help you out, but getting married is asking just too much."

"It's all right. Don't worry about it." Her eyes were stinging, and she closed them, hoping to avoid an overflow of tears. That's all she needed now.

"Come on, darlin'. Cheer up. Things can't be all that bad," he said.

"You don't know the half of it." She felt a wave of sadness overtake her. "I live in a room about this size, fixing meals and cleaning up after strangers for my keep. Seven months out of the year, I teach children to read and write and do their sums, for which I get paid twenty dollars a month—when the school board manages to raise the money."

She wiped the moisture from the edge of her eyes with her fingertips. She wished she'd brought that handkerchief.

Leon pulled her to his chest and patted her on the back. "Now, now. It'll be all right," he murmured.

It was sweet of him to attempt to comfort her. She turned and watched the rain through the window. Lightning flashed across the sky, and while she waited for the thunder she wondered how she'd gotten herself in this predicament.

"I apologize, Mr. McCoy. I guess I just built my hopes up and—" She had to stop to get her emotions under control or she'd soon be crying and that would never do.

This was going from bad to worse.

She felt him kiss the top of her head and heard him say,

"No problem. I started out the day in hopes of spending the evening with a beautiful woman in my arms."

She'd just bet he hadn't imagined that woman would be boring him with the sad story of her life. She appreciated his attempt to lighten up the situation and leaned into him ever so slightly.

He ran his arms down her back, inadvertently rubbing his forearms up against the side of her bosoms. She had to admit, the pressure felt nice. For some reason she seemed to be fairly bursting out the top of her chemise. She'd probably pulled her corset cords too tight, she decided.

Lord a mercy. I simply must get my mind off my undergarments. These immodest notions about loosening her corset were hardly appropriate thoughts, especially now. Whatever had gotten into her?

Suddenly, she realized that his hands had strayed to where they had no business being, and she jerked back. "What in the world are you doing?" she wanted to know.

"Just trying to take your mind off your troubles," he explained.

"If you want to take my mind off my troubles," she said with a sniff, "go with me to Denver and help me file on my land, but don't try to seduce me. That's not going to help any."

"Listen, lady, I don't care how upset you are, I'm not going to marry you," he said. "Let's get that straight right from the get go."

"Why not?" she demanded.

"I hardly know you."

"I hardly know you, and I'm willing to marry you," she pointed out.

"Well, I'm in no position to provide for a wife."

"I'm not asking you to provide anything more than a signature on a piece of paper. I'll continue teaching school and provide for myself."

"Well, what if come fall I want to stay around?" he asked. "What then?"

"Then I'll run you off with a shotgun. I don't need, and I don't want, a worthless drifter hanging around."

"A black widow spider's got nothing on you, lady," Leon said, sounding offended. "I might be a drifter, but I'm not worthless."

"If you're not worthless, why won't you give me a helping hand?" she demanded.

"Maybe I don't want to give you a helping hand." He splashed more whiskey in the glass and took another drink.

"Just plain worthless," she pronounced, emphasizing her statement with a sharp nod and a firm crossing of her arms.

Leon took another swallow.

"Stop that, right now," Marjorie ordered, reaching for his glass.

Leon pulled back, holding her off with one hand while gulping down his drink with the other.

"Don't you dare get drunk until we get this settled," she warned.

"Far as I'm concerned, it is settled." He tipped up the glass to get the last few drops and set it firmly on the bureau. Marjorie reached around him and grabbed the glass. He seized the bottle and started drinking straight out of it. It was going down his throat so fast she could hear it gurgle.

"Becoming intoxicated is not going to help matters any, Mr. McCoy," Marjorie said.

"Well, it beats the hell out of sitting here while you rub up against me and slap my hands away," he said. "That's for damn sure."

"I most certainly did not rub up against you," she said. *What an appalling comment. What possessed him to say that?*

"Did too," he said, and resumed drinking.

"Did not."

The conversation was going nowhere, so Marjorie switched the subject.

"Won't you reconsider my offer, Mr. McCoy?" she asked.

"Won't you reconsider mine?" A smile tickled the corners of his mustache, and Marjorie knew what it must feel like to be held in the gaze of a rattlesnake—knowing what was coming yet helpless to make a move.

"I don't recall you making an offer," was all she could think of to say, and even that sounded silly.

"Well, not in so many words," he admitted.

She had to get out of this room, there was no question about it. But how was she going to do that? She didn't have the will to stand up, let alone walk over to the door.

"What about your gallant offer to walk me home?" she blurted out.

"I think it's a little late for that, don't you? You should've taken me up on my offer when you had the chance."

Never taking his eyes off of her, he moved back up against the headboard and sprawled his legs out in front of him. The air seemed thick as taffy between them. She half expected to be pulled along with him.

But when he tipped the bottle up for another sip, she realized that he was behaving like a naughty boy, and it called to the schoolmarm in her.

"Stop drinking out of that bottle," she ordered, hoping she didn't sound as flustered as she felt.

"I'm generally not a drinking man," Leon said, slurring his words ever so slightly. "But you, Miss Marjorie, could change me."

She was alarmed by the amount of alcohol he was consuming.

"I'm serious, Mr. McCoy. You could get quite ill from drinking like this."

"No woman tells Leon McCoy what he can or cannot do." Leon carefully pronounced each word, then took another sip before setting the half-empty bottle on top of the bureau. It tipped over, rolled off, and fell to the floor. Shards of glass scattered in every direction. The smell of liquor permeated the room as the whiskey soaked into the floorboards.

"Now look what you've done," she said.

Leon locked his hands behind his head and leaned back. He didn't appear to be the least bit embarrassed by his clumsy mishap.

"I don't usually drink like this, ma'am," he said slowly. "I generally like to savor my pleasures."

"I assure you, that's no concern of mine."

Though it would probably be up to her to clean up the mess, she was grateful the bottle had broken. Not only had it put a stop to his drinking, but it had put an end to the disconcerting spell he'd cast over her.

"Come here, sweet thing," he said as he reached out for her.

"Absolutely not," she replied in her best sit-down-and-behave voice.

He didn't even come close to touching her. By now, he was probably seeing double and had no doubt extended his hand toward her image rather than her person.

"Don't play hard to get, darlin'," he coaxed in a deep, soft voice.

"I'm not your darlin', and I'm not playing hard to get," she said. "I am hard to get.'

Neither one commented on why she was sitting on his bed in his hotel room yet claiming to be hard to get.

"Have I said something to offend you?" he asked, sounding innocent and just a bit bewildered.

"No," she answered. She could feel her control beginning to slip again.

"Well, if I did, I'm sorry," he offered in apology.

"Oh, it's not your fault," she said, trying to keep a grip on her emotions. She had no intention of blubbering out her sorrows to this stranger. "Nothing ever turns out right for me anyway. Why would I think this insane scheme would work out any better than anything else ever has?"

He leaned over, put his arms around her, and attempted to pull her back against him.

"This will never work," she told him, drawing away from him.

"Sure it will, darlin'. Just give it time."

Disregarding her passive resistence, he hauled her up the bed until she was resting lightly against his chest. Even in his less-than-sober state, his movements were strong and sure. She found herself nestled between his outstretched legs, his arms folded around her, his hands enclosing hers.

"Snuggle in, darlin'," he softly suggested. "I won't hurt you. I just want to hold you for a while."

She relaxed against him, feeling, for the moment at least, safe in his arms. He didn't say anything, and neither did she. Gradually, his hold on Marjorie relaxed.

Cradled in Leon's body, she began to think again about why women marry in spite of all the work and worry. She felt safe and protected, though she hadn't a clue why. Should someone break down the door, Mr. McCoy was certainly in no condition to defend them. Indeed, the only source of danger she could imagine was Leon himself. Even now, should he suddenly decide to have his way with her, there was little she could do about it. Just the thought of that sent a prickle of fear running through her.

Still, there was a comfort in being wrapped in his arms that she hadn't imagined before. And then, of course, there were the pleasures of marital relations to be considered. From time to time, Marjorie had been curious about exactly what went on between a man and a woman. Not curious enough to risk the consequences, but curious nonetheless. She wondered what it would feel like now without the barrier of clothes between them, then immediately slapped that thought away.

Noticing that Leon's breathing had slowed to the steady pace of slumber, Marjorie settled back against him and began revising her plan. The straightforward approach had not been particularly successful. It was time to devise a more round-about one.

Dozing off and on, she remained wrapped in his arms until the pitch-black night gently gave way to the morning twilight. She hated to leave the warm nest his body made for hers, but if she was to get to Denver with a husband in tow, she'd best get going.

She tiptoed around to the end of the bed, grasped one boot with both hands, and gave a firm tug. It came right off. She tried the same strategy with the other one. It came flying off and hit her in the chin. She lost her balance and plopped on the floor.

"What the hell?" Leon woke with a start, his arms flailing out as if to grab on to something for support.

"Shhhh. Shhhh. It's all right," she murmured over and over. When his breathing slowed, she gently unbuttoned his trousers and tugged them off. He made a few groaning noises, but didn't wake up. She pulled his shirt off over his head but couldn't figure out how to get his long underwear off without a lot of fuss, so she left them on.

Relieved that this part of the plan was completed, she cautiously made her way down and across to her own room. She pulled her carpetbag valise from under the bed and folded and placed her good black dress in the bottom of it. On top, she packed her gray-flannel nightgown, a fresh chemise, a pair of pantalettes, a hairbrush, and a book she was planning to read to her students in the fall. Before closing the bag, she dabbed a bit of lilac water behind her ears.

She looked around at the little room that had been her home for the past year—the bureau with the shabby dresser scarf, the scarred humpback trunk, and the single bed covered by the Lucky Stars quilt that her aunt Ruby had helped her and Kathleen make that dreadful summer after their mother died. She would miss this place, but the yearning for a home of her own was too strong to be denied.

She carried her valise down to the kitchen and started a fire in the cookstove before dashing out to the privy. The ground was slippery, and the air smelled pure and clean after last night's rain. Puddles were already starting to dry up in the early-morning sunshine. She hoped it wouldn't turn hot and make the journey to Denver unpleasant.

By the time her aunt Ruby stepped into the kitchen, Marjorie had coffee brewing, biscuits browning in the oven, and ham gravy bubbling on top of the stove.

"You're up early," Ruby noted as she shuffled over to pour herself a cup of coffee.

"I've got a lot to get done today," Marjorie said.

"You're not still set on marrying that drifter are you?" Ruby tied a front apron around her ample middle and started stacking dishes on a tray.

"I apologize for taking off on such short notice," Marjorie said, ignoring her aunt's question as she vigorously stirred the ham gravy, "but if I intend to get my name on those homestead papers, I dare not dillydally around."

"Are you certain about this?" Ruby asked. She turned toward Marjorie, her forehead wrinkled in concern.

"Positive," said Marjorie, sounding considerably more assured than she felt.

"You know you can always live here," said Ruby.

"But you might not always be here," Marjorie gently reminded her. "Hank may decide to move to Montana tomorrow. As much as I love all of you, I'm ready to settle down. I want to belong someplace. I want a place that belongs to me."

"I know, honey," Ruby said. "Do you think I find it all that appealing to start over again every other year?" Ruby bent down and opened the oven door to check on the biscuits. "But what choice do I have?"

"You could tell him you and the kids are staying here," Marjorie said, doubting Ruby would ever put her foot down with her restless husband.

"And raise the kids alone?" Ruby raised her eyebrows in question. Both of them knew she would sooner start dealing faro over at the Lucky Lady than refuse to follow Hank on one of his wild-goose chases.

"We each have to do what we think best, and I think this is the best move for me. I've found the place, and now I need a husband to get the title to it. Are you going to help me or not?"

"What do you want me to do?" Ruby sighed. "I'll go get my wedding dress down and we can spend the morning taking it in. I'll send Janey and the girls out to gather up eggs, and we can set to baking a cake. Let me see. We could move the tables over and have it right here in the dining room. I'll have—"

Marjorie interrupted her. "There's no time for all of that. We've got to take the morning stage to Denver before someone else files on my land."

Ruby looked so disappointed that Marjorie added, "But maybe we could have a nice reception when we get back. How about that?" Avoiding her aunt's eyes, she untied her apron and hung it on a wall peg.

"For now, would you go wake up Hank and Rooster? I'd appreciate it if the three of you could meet us in the hotel lobby as soon as possible."

"Now?" Ruby asked skeptically. "Isn't this awful early for a wedding?"

"I've always wanted a sunrise ceremony, Aunt Ruby," she said with as much gaiety as she could manage. "Ask Rooster to hunt up a marriage license, then meet us in the lobby," she repeated. She was out the door before Ruby could ask any more questions.

Within minutes, Marjorie was easing back into Leon's room. He didn't appear to have moved an inch. She quickly slipped out of her dress and corset and draped them over the footboard, making certain that the corset was completely covered. It wouldn't do to have it visible for everyone to ogle. She rubbed at the itchy corset lines along her sides, then eased herself down on the bed. She unbuttoned her shoes and placed them on the floor near Leon's boots. Then, in her chemise and stockings, she crawled back into the nest she'd left nearly an hour ago.

Settling in quietly, she turned the plan over in her mind until she heard her aunt's voice coming up the stairs.

"She said to meet her right here in the lobby, but I don't see either one of them," Ruby said.

"Ruby, if this is another one of your niece's screwball schemes," her uncle Hank warned.

Marjorie crossed her fingers, murmured a quick prayer, and jabbed her elbow back into Leon's ribs.

3

"What the hell?" Leon shook himself out of a sound sleep. Had somebody stabbed him in the side? Out of habit, he reached up for his gun. He stopped when he realized there was a woman lying on top of him, and she was causing all the trouble.

"You get your hands off of me," the woman shrieked, digging that damned elbow into his ribs again. "Where am I?"

"Sh," Leon whispered. "You'll wake everyone up."

"You leave me alone," she continued in a voice that could be heard halfway to hell. That woman had some set of lungs.

Footsteps pounded up the stairway and down the hall. Leon leaned back against the headboard. He had a sinking feeling it would be some time before things settled down.

"Honey, is that you?" a woman's voice yelled from the other side of the door. "What are you doing in there?"

That was a question Leon wanted the answer to himself.

The woman scrambled to the foot of the bed, grabbed the quilt, and held it up in front of her. Though her front side might be covered, her backside was quite visible in the early-morning light. She looked familiar but he sure couldn't recall bedding the woman. In fact, now that he thought of it, he was sure he hadn't. Her hair was still slicked back in a bun, and she was still wearing her shimmy.

"What's going on in there?" This time it was a man's voice demanding answers.

"Help," the woman at the end of the bed hollered. She was carrying on like her audience was out in the street instead of on the other side of the door. "Uncle Hank. Help."

The sound of splintering wood was followed by the sight of the town blacksmith. Leon recalled leaving his horse Ulysses with him yesterday. Somehow, the man looked larger standing in the doorway than he had in the livery stable. With a sinking feeling, Leon noticed how he had to duck and turn sideways just to get in the room.

"Hell's bells, what's going on in here?" The blacksmith's voice boomed loud enough to shake the windows.

"All I remember is taking just the slightest sip of whiskey with Mr. McCoy and, and—" She let out a wail that made the hair stand up on the back of Leon's neck. "And now I'm ruined." She buried her head in her hands and began bawling. Between sobs, she managed to get out, "I've been compromised, Uncle Hank. I've been compromised."

Bewildered by her performance, Leon sat up and peered at the people in the doorway. On one side of the blacksmith was a stout woman in an apron and on the other side was the pint-sized bartender.

"Why I oughta—" Her uncle Hank raised up a fist the size of a ham.

The heavyset woman and the bartender each grabbed on to an arm as if holding him back. Leon doubted this was anything more than a gesture. The man was built like an oak tree. If he had a mind to move, he'd just shake those two off like ripe acorns.

"Now, now. Let's just see what this young man has to say for himself," Rooster kept repeating.

But Leon had no idea what to say for himself. He couldn't make heads nor tails of what was going on. Why was this woman shouting and sobbing at the end of his bed? Why was a man who looked as if he could hunt bear with a broomstick threatening to beat him up? Where were his pants?

Pants. He needed to get his pants on. It would be easier to get this whole thing straightened out if he wasn't lying here in his longhandles.

Leon leaped out of bed and grabbed his pants off the bureau. He shoved his right foot through one pant leg and was doing the same with his left foot when he realized something didn't feel quite right. It felt like he'd stepped on a nail.

Sitting down on the edge of the bed, he examined the sole of his left foot. The jagged bottom of the whiskey bottle was embedded in his heel. He jerked it out and watched in dismay as the blood spread across his foot and dripped on the floor.

He looked over at the woman. The sight of blood flowing over his hands had brought a halt to her bawling.

"Don't hurt him, Uncle Hank," she pleaded. "I've got to marry him."

"Is this your intended?" asked the hefty woman clinging to the blacksmith's arm.

"Aunt Ruby, Uncle Hank, Rooster, I'd like you to meet Leon McCoy," the woman on the bed said. "Leon, this is my aunt Ruby and my uncle Hank Richmond and Rooster Jackson, whom I believe you've already met."

"Pleased to meet you," he said, touching the brim of the hat he wasn't wearing either.

As long as she was making introductions, he wished she'd introduce herself. For the life of him, he couldn't recall her name. He regretted drinking so much whiskey the night before that he couldn't remember what he'd done or who he'd done it with. But that was water under the bridge now.

While stanching the flow of blood with his wadded-up pants, Leon tried to figure out what to do next.

"What's going on here?" her uncle Hank demanded again.

"I'd like an answer to that question myself," Leon muttered. His head was pounding, his foot was bleeding, and these looked like the least of his worries.

"We have to get married," the woman insisted. "My virtue has been sullied."

"Could we talk about that after I get my foot bandaged up?" Leon asked.

If he could only recall who she was. Her name was on the tip of his tongue. M something—Maribelle, or Marianne, or maybe Marian? Martha, that was it, Martha. He was almost certain her name was Martha. But he decided it'd be best not to say it out loud. He knew from experience that a woman would get touchy as a teased snake if you called her by the wrong name, and this woman seemed excited enough as it was.

"I won't be able to hold my head up in Hope Springs once word of this gets around," she insisted as she reached over to push his pants firmly down on his heel. "There, it's stopped bleeding. Let's start the wedding ceremony."

Leon found her constant talk of marriage irritating.

The bartender let go of the blacksmith's arm and pulled a ragged piece of paper out of his back pocket. He unfolded it and began, "Dearly beloved. We are gathered together in the presence of God and these witnesses," he said hesitantly, looking around the sparsely furnished room like he was waiting for someone to call a halt to this silliness.

Leon felt he ought to say something, but "Are you sure it was me?" seemed ungentlemanly, so he remained silent.

If looks could kill, Leon would be a dead man. Of course it was him, their accusing stares said. Who else was there in bed with her?

When no one said a word, the bartender continued, "to unite this man"—he looked over at Leon—"and this woman"—he glanced briefly at the bride, still clutching the quilt to her chin to cover her nakedness—"in holy matrimony."

"Sweet Jesus," Leon finally said, looking around. "Are you

all loony? I don't even know this woman." That wasn't alto-gether true. He knew she smelled like lilacs and he recalled sitting across a table from her. But surely you had to have more than that to get married over.

"I resent that," the woman determined to be his bride said. He wondered how she could act so high-and-mighty with her backside exposed like it was. Leon let his eyes travel down to the stocking feet peeking out from her lace-edged pantaloons. She was a tempting sight all right. He had to lean over and cover himself with his arms or else risk embarrassment. He wished his longhandles were looser-fitting.

Enough of those kind of thoughts. He needed to call a halt to this foolishness before it got out of hand.

"You can't just have a bartender say a few words over you and call it good," he said. "That isn't how it works."

"I'll have you know, young man, I am the Justice of the Peace in Hope Springs," Rooster informed him. "And I can perform both weddings and burials. Only thing I can't do is baptize a baby. You don't have a baby do you?"

"Not that I know of," Leon said bitterly. So that's what this was about. She was in the family way and needed a husband in a hurry. He had the worst luck.

He stared at her waist, trying to see if she appeared to be carrying. If she was, she sure wasn't showing any signs yet. She curved in just where a man would expect. No doubt about it, bun or no bun, this woman was flat enticing.

"Hush up, you two," she said, sounding like a schoolmarm calling her class to order. "Keep going, Rooster."

"I've lost my place now," the bartender complained, look-ing up and down his paper. Unable to find where he'd left off, he began all over. "Dearly beloved, we are gathered here in the presence of God and these witnesses, to unite this man and this woman in holy matrimony."

"Looks like they've been doing some uniting already," her uncle Hank grumbled.

"Shhh," the two women hissed at the same time.

"Lord, I need a drink," Leon muttered.

"Appears that drink has been your downfall, young man," the plump woman pointed out.

"Will you two be quiet?" demanded the woman whose name was probably Martha. "You are ruining my wedding."

"There is not going to be any wedding," insisted Leon. "I am not a marrying man." He didn't know how to make it any plainer than that.

"You're just a poke-'em-and-go-Joe, right?" said her uncle Hank. His wife turned to stare at him.

"All of you, hush up," the woman screeched.

Rooster's mouth had been hanging open. He snapped it shut.

"Not you," she ordered. "Proceed with the ceremony. Just keep it to the essentials, if that's possible."

"Do you Marjorie Bascom take this man as your lawful wedded husband, to love, honor, and obey, to have and to hold from this day forward, in sickness and in health, until death do you part?" asked Rooster, all in one breath.

Marjorie, that was her name, Marjorie. Leon felt a rush of relief. It was short-lived.

"I do," she answered, strong, clear, and determined. "All but the obey part."

"And do you?" Rooster stopped and looked straight at him. "What's your name anyway?"

Leon decided not to answer. Maybe if he refused to give them his name, they'd give up on this marriage business.

"Leon McCoy," Marjorie answered for him.

"Leon McCoy," Rooster continued, hardly missing a beat. "Do you take this woman to be your lawful wedded wife, to love, honor, and cherish, to have and to hold from this day forward, in sickness and in health, until death do you part?"

"Absolutely not," Leon answered.

"Do you or do you not want to live to see the sun set today?" said her uncle Hank as he stepped forward and raised his fist in the air again.

"I do," Leon replied, realizing his error a second too late.

"I now pronounce you man and wife," Rooster said quickly. "You may kiss the bride."

"Maybe later." Leon was in no mood for kissing at the moment. He felt like a fool for being so easily tricked.

"If you all will excuse us," Marjorie said, "we've a long journey ahead of us. We'd best get ready."

"I say we honeymoon right here," Leon snarled.

"No, we've got to be on our way to Denver as soon as possible," she explained, cheerily. "Time is of the essence."

"Listen, lady," he said, "I'm feeling a bit under the weather. My foot needs doctoring, and the only pair of pants I own is covered in blood. I'm not going to Denver or anywhere else today."

"You can borrow a pair of mine," offered Rooster in an attempt to be helpful.

"Thanks anyway, but I believe I'll rinse mine out after I get my foot fixed up," Leon replied. Rooster was not only a good two feet shorter but probably outweighed him by better than a hundred pounds. He'd as soon go around in his longhandles as wear pants that hit him at the knees and had to be held up with a rope.

"But I'd appreciate a bottle of iodine and some bandages if it wouldn't trouble you too much," he said.

"Coming right up." Rooster turned and headed out the door.

"Come on, Ruby," Hank said. "We're wasting daylight."

The aunt just stood there staring, first at Marjorie and then at Leon. He could tell from the look in her eyes that she didn't care much for what they'd been up to.

Well, she needn't be looking at him like that. He'd swear on a stack of Bibles he hadn't touched the woman. But now that they were married, that situation was about to change.

His brand-new wife turned to him, and said, "We'd best get going ourselves. The stage to Denver will be leaving within the hour."

"I'm not taking the stage to Denver today," Leon said, and that was that.

"Since you're in no condition to ride, how else do you suppose that we'll get there?" she asked.

"I don't suppose I'll be going at all," he said, "not today at least. A few days one way or the other isn't going to make any big difference in getting to Denver. I imagine it'll still be there next week."

"I'm not setting up married life in this hotel room, and that's final," Marjorie said. "If we don't get to Denver and file on my land, someone else will, and then where will I live, I ask you?"

Leon just shook his head. It didn't make a bit of difference to him where she lived.

"All right," she agreed. "First things first." She turned back to Hank and Ruby, who were still standing there staring at them.

"May we borrow a pair of pants for a few days?" she asked them.

"Why certainly," Ruby said. "I'll go find some and be right back."

She and Hank took turns getting through the doorway.

As soon as they left, Rooster returned, carrying a roll of bandages, a short, square bottle of iodine, and a tall, round bottle of whiskey.

Leon reached for the whiskey.

"Thanks, partner," he said. "I could sure use a little something to steady my nerves."

"If you will excuse us, Mr. Jackson," Marjorie looked pointedly at Rooster. She still had the quilt clutched in front of her.

"Oh my," he said, as if he had just stepped into the room by mistake. "Just holler if you need anything." He closed the door behind him.

"Can you get the wedding license ready?" she yelled after him. "We'll be needing it within the hour."

"Close your eyes," she told Leon as she squirmed around on the bed to face him.

"Why?" he asked. "We're married now. I guess I'm allowed to see you in your shimmy."

"You're determined to humiliate me, aren't you?" she said.

He shook his head. "You're not playing with a full deck, are you?" He tipped the whiskey bottle up to his mouth and swallowed.

"What's that supposed to mean?"

"Nothing. Just forget it." His head was pounding, his foot was throbbing, and he was in no mood to argue with a crazy woman. He took another pull of whiskey.

"I hope you are not a drinking man, Mr. McCoy," she said, wiggling around on the bed in an attempt to cover more of herself with the quilt.

"If I wasn't, you're the woman who'd drive me to it, that's for damn sure," he said, and tipped the bottle up again. He was slow to anger, but he could feel it coming on.

"I wish you wouldn't curse, Mr. McCoy," she said, prim as an old maid.

He swore under his breath and continued sipping and staring at her. What kind of woman would trick a stranger into marriage?

Apparently her desire to get on that stage overcame her modesty. With a dignified set to her shoulders, she turned away from him, let loose of the quilt, and pulled her dress over her head. After fiddling around with her buttons and then tucking something under the quilt, she scooted off the bed, picked up her shoes, and put them on.

Watching her dress had gotten all sorts of ideas swirling through his head. And why not? She was a fine figure of a woman, and they were married now.

Without buttoning her shoes, she slid over next to him. "Let me see your foot." She pulled the pants away and ran her fingers lightly up and down, checking for more glass. Her fooling around with his foot like this felt downright peculiar.

It was pleasant, but odd. He couldn't recall anyone else ever touching one of his feet before, and he was just a bit disappointed when she let loose. He was still lost in thought when he felt a sharp burning on the cut and jerked back.

"Good Lord, woman," he hollered at her. "You ought to at least give a man some warning." He was embarrassed to look down and see that all she'd done was pour iodine on his cut. It'd felt like kerosene.

"Well, what did you think I was going to do?" she asked. "Kiss it all better?"

His thoughts had been running in that direction all right.

She wrapped a length of bandage around his foot and tucked in the end.

"There, that'll do," she said. "I'll go see what's keeping Ruby."

She stood and, on her way out, picked up his bloodied pants and pulled something white out from under the quilt, most likely her corset.

"I'll be right back," she said. He had no doubts about that.

As soon as she closed the door, he hopped on his good foot over to the chamber pot. He'd been meaning to mention his need for a moment of privacy earlier, but there hadn't been a break in the action since he opened his eyes.

The sun was barely up and he was already half-lit and married to a crazy woman. Leon hoped the rest of the day would improve, but he wasn't going to bet on it.

4

*M*arjorie found Ruby in the storage room on her hands and knees, pulling folded clothes out of a brass-hinged trunk. From the scowl on her face to the way she was slapping clothes down in stacks around her on the floor, Marjorie knew she was upset.

"I'm certainly glad that you married a blacksmith and not a bookkeeper," Marjorie said in an attempt to lighten her mood.

"Trapping that poor man into marriage. Trading your virtue for a piece of paper." Ruby shook her head back and forth. "I hope you're satisfied, young lady."

"I will be once I get my name on those papers," Marjorie assured her. Her aunt was a stickler for following the rules, for doing things the way they were supposed to be done. Marjorie had known Ruby wouldn't approve, but she had no idea her marriage would cause her aunt this much distress.

"I just don't understand why you are so set on moving out," said Ruby, turning to stare at her. "I thought you liked living with us."

Marjorie could see the tears floating in her aunt's eyes. She felt like crying herself, but what good would that do? She put her arms around her aunt's shoulders. Ruby shrugged them off and turned away from her.

"Aunt Ruby, I love you, I love living with you, and I plan on coming back here in the winter if you'll let me."

"You're always welcome here, and you know that," said Ruby, but she didn't turn to look at her.

"And you are always welcome wherever I live," said Marjorie, her voice trembling. "But I'm twenty-three. I need to build a life of my own, and I want to build it here. I've moved around ever since I can remember, and I'm sick and tired of it. I want to belong someplace. I like it here in Hope Springs, Aunt Ruby. I want to stay. I want to grow old around people who know more about me than where I came from."

"That's a natural desire," her aunt said. "Every woman wants that."

"Then why don't we get it?"

"Because life just doesn't always work out the way we want it to," Ruby said, turning to look at her.

"And why's that?" Marjorie had her own idea on why that was, but wanted to hear what her aunt would say.

"Things come up, I guess," her aunt said, hedging the issue.

"Men." There was no uncertainty in Marjorie's mind. "That's why we don't get it. Men." She pointed to the open trunk lid. "You've packed that chest and followed him so many times your name should be Ruth instead of Ruby."

"It's always worked out," said her aunt defensively.

"Because you've made it work out, and you know, as well as I do, that's the only reason," insisted Marjorie. "Who's the one who runs this boardinghouse? Who went after the Overland Stage contract to put up their passengers and horses for the night? And who's the one that's going to announce one of these days that he's heard there are better opportunities for blacksmiths in Timbuktu, and it's time to pack up and move on?"

"We have a good marriage," insisted Ruby. "Hank's a good man."

"I know he's a good man. He only drinks occasionally, never hits you or the kids, and works steady even if most of it is on credit. But you and I both know that the reason there's food on the table and a roof over your heads is because of this boardinghouse you run."

Quiet settled between them as Marjorie realized she'd already said enough, probably too much. Her uncle Hank had been good to her, and she didn't mean to run him down.

After a time she added, "I just don't find marriage all that appealing, and fortunately, neither does Mr. McCoy."

"Well, it does seem to be a match made in heaven," said Ruby.

Marjorie decided to ignore the scorn in her aunt's voice and change the subject to the folded white dress Ruby was holding. "Is that your wedding gown?" she asked.

"In a manner of speaking." Her aunt smoothed the material with her hand and quietly visited with her memories for a moment. "I guess you could say I was wearing this when our marriage was made."

She passed the gown to Marjorie, who stood up and unfurled a long white muslin nightgown. Purple French knot lilacs were stitched around the scoop neck and down the full gathered sleeves.

"Your mother made this for me," she said. "I want to give it to you as a wedding present."

Marjorie's mind filled with the scene of playing on the floor with her baby sister while watching her mother wind purple thread around an embroidery needle. Was she just imagining this or had she actually seen her mother work the lilacs on this gown? For years she'd pushed memories of her mother away. The pain was a bottomless well, and she feared immersing herself in it, afraid there would be no stopping, no coming back out. She'd go down deeper and deeper until she ended up as one of those witless women who wander from relative to relative, asking odd questions.

It'd been nearly seven years now since she'd stood next to

that ugly coffin, hanging on to Kathleen's hand and knowing that she'd have to hold her tears in until she and her younger sister were situated somehow.

Marjorie buried her face in the gown and inhaled the scent of cedar and dried lavender.

How can it still hurt so much? Isn't it supposed to get better over time? Why doesn't it?

Ruby stood, pulled her close and patted her on the back as if she was calming a child. "I know, honey. I know," she murmured. "I miss her, too."

I have to stop. I have to stop right now. She put her mind to slow breathing, and within a few whooshing breaths, she was light-headed and tingly and able to keep the tears from forming. The storm had passed.

"You are just like her, so smart and so strong"—Ruby paused to kiss Marjorie on the forehead before adding—"and so stubborn."

Ruby's voice quivered, but she wasn't crying. Marjorie was grateful for that.

She pulled the gown from Marjorie's fingers, folded it into a square bundle, and handed it back to her. "Here, honey, you take this with you to Denver."

"It's beautiful," Marjorie said, holding it reverently. "But I can't take it."

"Nonsense," her aunt said. "It was made to be worn by a bride on her wedding night."

"No," she said, trying to hand it back. "You keep it. We won't be having that kind of marriage."

"You just take this nightgown anyway. You never know how things might work out between you two." Her aunt winked at her as if the two of them were sharing a secret. The blink formed a tear that dripped down Ruby's cheek. She wiped it away with her fingers. Both of them pretended not to notice.

"I wouldn't get my hopes up if I were you, Aunt Ruby,"

Marjorie said dismally. "I doubt the man even remembers my name."

"Sure he does. It's Mrs. McCoy," her aunt reminded her. "Look. I found a pair of pants that used to fit Hank," Ruby said, leaning into the trunk, "but I can't find a belt or suspenders. Maybe Hank's got a piece of rope that'll work."

Ruby handed the folded pants to Marjorie.

"Thank you," she said. "I left Leon's pants soaking in one of the washtubs. Would you mind rinsing them out and hanging them up to dry?" There were plenty of matters to occupy a person's thoughts. One needn't focus on the dismal.

"I'd be glad to," said Ruby.

"Imagine traveling with only one pair of pants," said Marjorie.

"Guess he figures he's only got one pair of legs."

Five minutes later, Marjorie was looking at those legs. Leon was stretched out on the bed, staring at the ceiling, when she walked back into the room. Blood hadn't soaked through the bandage on his foot. That was a good sign.

Even in his baggy long underwear, Marjorie could easily make out the shape of his calves and then his thighs. When she got that far, she jerked her eyes up to his face. What in the world had gotten into her to stand here and stare at his person? Flustered, she dropped her valise and tried to hand him the pair of pants and a piece of rope. He made no attempt to take them or to hide his amusement at her discomfort.

"You can wear these, until yours dry out," she said, giving the folded pants a little shake to call his attention to them.

"I'll just stay right here until mine dry out," he replied. He clasped his hands behind his head as if he hadn't a care in the world.

"I wish that were possible, but the stage will be leaving in ten minutes, and I've already purchased our tickets." She laid the pants down next to him on the bed.

"Get a refund," he told her. "I'm not leaving this room until I feel better." He closed his eyes as if intending to take a nap.

Marjorie marched to the head of the bed where his gun belt was still draped over the bedpost. She pulled his pistol out of its holster and pointed the gun straight at his heart.

"If you don't get dressed and get on that stage," she announced, "I'm going to shoot you."

He opened one eye just barely enough to see that she was serious. "Shot or not, I have no intention of getting out of this bed in the near future. Now unless you care to climb in here with me, I suggest you put my pistol back and go on about your business."

"I'm serious," she said, using both hands to keep the gun pointed in the direction of his chest.

"I am, too, darlin'."

"If you don't get up by the time I count to three, I'm going to pull the trigger," she warned.

"I take it that you're planning on dragging my dead body all the way to Denver?" He opened his eyes about halfway, causing a quiver to run the length of her.

"That won't be necessary," she insisted, doing her best to keep her attention on the subject at hand. "As I understand it, the widow McCoy would be classified as the head of a household in the Colorado Territories."

"You're not going to shoot me, darlin'." He gazed into her eyes with such intensity that she had to lean against the wall for support. It was that or collapse in a heap on the floor. It should be illegal to make a person feel as weak as this.

"Maybe not," she managed to get out, "but I will shoot your horse, burn up your saddlebags, and then come back and give you a piece of my mind for being too worthless to give me a helping hand."

"Sweet Jesus, I might as well get on with it. I can see you aren't going to give me a moment's peace until I do."

He threw his legs over the edge of the bed, stood up, pulled the pants on, and buttoned up the front. Though they may have been too small for Hank, they were far too large for Leon's lanky body.

"Here," she said, handing him a piece of rope. "You'll need this."

"I think I can manage." Holding the pants up with one hand, he lifted the gun belt off the bedpost and strapped it on. He readjusted the baggy pants over the top of the gun belt and tied the thong at the bottom of the holster around his thigh.

"Now the boots," she said, motioning with the gun.

Though he managed to get his right boot on, the left one wouldn't fit over the bandages, so he carried it.

He hobbled down the stairs, leaning on the banister. Rooster stopped them at the bottom with the marriage license. When Marjorie set the pistol down on the counter to sign her name, Leon slipped it back in his holster.

After they'd both signed, Rooster rolled the blotter over it. Then Marjorie folded the document and tucked it in her reticule.

"I feel like a fool," Leon muttered as they crossed the lobby.

"You look just fine," she assured him, though indeed he did look ridiculous, limping along in those droopy britches, clutching his boot in his left hand and a bottle of whiskey in his right.

She'd tried her best to convince him to leave the whiskey behind, but he'd refused. In fact, he'd attempted to purchase another bottle from Rooster while they were signing their marriage license. Mercifully, the noisy arrival of the stage had distracted him.

When they stepped out onto the boardwalk, Marjorie's heart sank. Who should be standing there but Charles Irwin.

Charles was looking dapper today. He wore a brand-new hat and a new leather vest. His boots hadn't seen much use either. One thing you could say about Charles, he kept up appearances.

"Well, good morning, Miss Marjorie," he said, tipping his

hat and giving Leon the once-over. "Doing a little missionary work today, are we?"

"Good morning, Charles," she said, ignoring both his uncalled-for comment as well as the snarl on Leon's face. "What brings you to town so early in the day?"

"I came to send a message to the marshal that we needed a deputy out here."

"Really?" No doubt he and Jake Jarveson were involved in yet another of their endless disputes over steers, but she was hard-pressed to imagine what a deputy could do about that.

Charles puffed on the stub of a cheroot while staring straight at Marjorie's chest. You'd think someone who had his heart set on being governor would cease such annoying behavior.

"Then I thought I'd pay an early-morning call on you, little lady." He raised his eyebrows and smoothed one end of his skinny mustache. Apparently, he thought she was impressed by this display. She was not.

"How charming. But I'm afraid that won't be possible. I'm taking the stage to Denver for a few days."

"Doing a little shopping, eh?" Charles's gaze traveled down to her boots and back up again. "I like to see women in the latest fashions." He reached into his pocket and pulled out a handful of twenty-dollar gold pieces and tried to hand them to her.

"No, really, Charles," she said, pulling back. "I don't want your money."

"Oh, go ahead, sugar. If I can't buy a few pretties for my woman, what's the point of it all, I ask you?"

She could have sworn she heard Leon growl. Surely not.

"Charles, for the last time, I am not your woman." She stated this as firmly as she knew how and tried desperately to think of some way to get Leon on that stage before unpleasantries broke out.

Charles hadn't even heard her. "I can see it all now, Marjorie, the two of us in the governor's mansion, maids and butlers waiting on us hand and foot."

Marjorie could feel Leon's weight pressing heavier and heavier against her side. She planted her feet firmly to avoid both of them toppling over into the dirt.

"Listen, mister," Charles said, "if you know what's good for you, you'll step away from my fiancée."

This had gone far enough. Too far, really.

"Charles Irwin, I would like you to meet my husband, Leon McCoy."

"Your husband?" Charles stared at Leon as if he was covered in lice. "When did you get married?"

"Recently," she informed him, "quite recently. Now if you'll excuse us, we must be on our way." Out of the corner of her eye, Marjorie saw Leon slip the whiskey bottle in his boot.

"You passed up being the wife of the future governor of the Colorado Territory to marry this—" his upper lip quivered in disgust as he surveyed Leon's disheveled state "—this down-on-his-luck drifter?" Charles reached out and grabbed Marjorie by the shoulder as if he were going to shake some sense into her.

"Let loose of me, Charles," she demanded, jerking away. "You're making a spectacle of yourself." It was probably too late to avoid a scene, but she thought she at least ought to try. She glanced around. Wouldn't you know, Lucille Herner was standing in front of the dry-goods store, taking it all in.

"Let her go." Leon sounded as if he meant business.

"Either shut your mouth, or I'll shut it for you," Charles said as he let loose of Marjorie and reached down to his side.

In a blink, Leon had his gun out and pointing steadily in Charles's direction. Charles's hand froze in midair.

"I don't know who you are, and I don't care," Leon said, "but you touch that gun and they'll be carving your name on a tombstone."

"Let's not get excited now," Charles said, pulling his hands back with the palms facing outward. "I didn't mean anything by it."

"I've had one hell of a morning, and I'm in no mood for any foolishness," Leon said. "Now get out of here."

The air around them practically crackled. If lightning struck, it wouldn't have surprised Marjorie.

"This isn't over between the two of us, not by a long shot." Charles took a step back. "There'll be another day," he warned.

"I don't doubt that a bit," said Leon.

"Marjorie," Charles ordered, "step away from this ruffian."

If she did, Leon would fall flat over, she was certain of it. "Why don't you just go, Charles? We can discuss this later."

"I'm not comfortable leaving you with him, Marjorie," he insisted. "What kind of man would I be to leave you in the grip of a gunfighter?"

"If you don't do it, you'll be a dead man," Leon said. "Now get the hell out of here while I'm still in a good mood."

"You wouldn't kill an unarmed man, would you?" Charles asked, waving his hands in the air to demonstrate that they were empty.

"Maybe not, but I wouldn't have any trouble winging one."

The click of the hammer prompted Charles to disappear around the edge of the stage depot.

As soon as he was out of sight, Leon turned on Marjorie. "Why didn't you marry him?" he asked. "He seems a sight more eager about this marriage business than I am."

"Charles and I are not compatible."

"You don't say."

"If you two are finished jawing, would you mind getting in the stage," said the driver. "I've got a schedule to meet."

Leon holstered his pistol and leaned against Marjorie for support. She put her arm around his waist to help steady him and marveled at the feel of his side through his muslin shirt.

Good heavens, what have I gotten myself into? It appeared she had married a gunfighter, and all she could think about was what he looked like in his long underwear or felt like under his shirt.

Between his tender foot and his less-than-sober condition, getting Leon up into the stage was a struggle. This seemed odd to Marjorie. He'd been steady enough during that set-to with Charles. Now he fumbled about like an old man, weaving and grabbing on to her. She wondered what had gotten into him but decided she'd worry about that once they were on their way to Denver.

She let out a sigh of relief when she finally managed to push Leon inside. He slumped over in the corner of the backwards-facing seat and let out a moan.

Marjorie climbed in and shoved her valise under her feet. "My husband's not feeling well," she explained to the two in the forward-facing seats.

A man wearing a striped suit and derby hat puckered up at the sight of Leon and his baggy pants and rag-wrapped foot.

"Feeling a little under the weather are we, love?" asked the other passenger, a woman in a low-cut, tight, green-taffeta dress.

"You remember to tell the marshal about that murder," Charles shouted at the driver.

Marjorie stuck her head out the window. With Leon inside the stage, Charles had apparently worked up the courage to come out from behind the depot.

"What murder?" she asked in amazement. Why hadn't he mentioned something about that instead of fussing with her and Leon?

"Jake Jarveson was killed," Charles answered. "Yesterday afternoon."

Jake Jarveson murdered! What in the world? She was stunned.

Marjorie would've liked more information, but the stage started up with a lurch, sending Leon sprawling across the man in the striped suit.

"Oh, for pity sakes," he said, shoving Leon off of him and

back into his own seat. Then the stage made the sharp turn out of town and Marjorie had to grab Leon to keep him from slipping to the floor.

Why, she'd just seen Jake a few days ago. What could've happened? He did tend to bully people. Perhaps he'd pushed one of his hired hands too far. Though Jake was hardly her favorite person in the world, she hated to see anyone in the community come to such a sad end. She closed her eyes for a moment of prayer but opened them immediately at the sound of Leon gagging.

"Best get his head out the window, love," suggested the woman across from them. "He looks a little peaked."

She helped Marjorie maneuver Leon so that he was leaning out the window by the time he began to retch in earnest. As he hadn't eaten anything since dinner the night before, he was soon down to the dry heaves. That continued off and on for miles, much to the disgust of their well-dressed traveling companion. He sat with his hands resting atop an umbrella held upright between his legs. He had the appearance of a man patiently awaiting an appointment instead of one hurtling across the countryside in the confines of a stagecoach.

As soon as he was able, Leon leaned back in his seat, pulled the cork out of the whiskey bottle, and tipped it up to his lips.

"Surely, you've had plenty of that by now," Marjorie hissed.

"Lady," Leon said when he'd finished swallowing, "I don't believe there's enough whiskey in the West to get me through this day." He tipped it up again.

The other man sneered. The woman gave Marjorie one of those looks of silent understanding that passes between long-suffering women. Leon leaned out the window and began retching again. The dust billowed in.

"I'm so sorry," Marjorie apologized. "My husband's been feeling rather poorly today."

Leon felt poorly the rest of the journey. During one bout of nausea, their gentleman traveling companion snatched Leon's bottle and pitched it out the window.

Leon attempted to strike him for interfering in his business but the stagecoach hit a chuckhole and threw him off-balance. He ended up punching Belle, the woman in the green-taffeta dress. She kicked him where it would do the most good, bringing on another bout of nausea. By this time, Marjorie had ceased apologizing and was reciting Bible verses to herself.

Every once in a while, she rolled up the leather side curtains, in hopes that the sight of trees and mountains would help settle Leon's stomach. But with a window uncovered, the dust rolled in, making it difficult to breathe. It got in their eyes and sifted through their clothes. In the long run, it was easier just to leave the side curtains rolled down.

The four of them jolted along in the dim, dusty heat. Crossing the entire country in this conveyance must be a nightmare. Marjorie wondered how people survived weeks of this incessant jostling about. Even if a person avoided broken bones, surely there'd be some ill effects on one's internal organs. There was very little padding on the seats and none at all along the sides, where she was regularly slammed as the stage lurched and careened one way and the next.

This was her third trip in five days, and she was beginning to find it wearing. Time and again, she wished she'd thought of marrying someone while she was still in Denver. She could've concluded her business at the land office without the wear and tear, as well as the expense, of another journey.

They made brief stops along the way, just long enough to pick up and drop off mail bags and parcels and switch teams. Early in the afternoon, the driver pulled to a halt at an isolated stage station and announced a half-hour layover for lunch.

The rest stop was a grim disappointment. The meal they'd been promised turned out to be cold, burnt cornbread served by two incredibly filthy men. Inasmuch as they'd forgotten to fix the beans, the men offered to share their jug of corn liquor with the passengers. Belle took a sip. Marjorie and the gentleman declined. The driver and Leon did not.

While the four men stood in the shade of the cabin, passing the brown jug from one to another, Marjorie and the other two passengers rested beneath a nearby tree, sharing a fruit jar of cold well water. Remembering this way station from her last trip, Marjorie had had the foresight to pack some biscuits and ham in her valise. Though covered in dust, she shared these with her fellow travelers. All too soon it was time to pack up and continue their journey.

Harnessing the fresh team turned out to be a more challenging task than anyone had anticipated. It appeared that the horses were not broken to harness. Marjorie was pleasantly surprised to see Leon direct the men in hobbling the horses' legs so that they could get the collars and rigging on. Obviously her new husband was skilled with horses as well as guns.

Once they were all back in the stage, the two filthy men jerked the rope hobbles loose. As soon as their legs were unfettered, the horses took off at a reckless pace.

Inside the stagecoach, the four of them bounced about like beans in a baby's rattle. To avoid being thrown out of the coach completely, they clung to one another and braced themselves against the sides. The gentleman in the derby got a split lip when his head whipped down and hit the top of his own umbrella. Leon slammed into the edge of a window and got a nasty gash over one eye. Belle's green taffeta was torn in a dozen places, and Marjorie dreaded what she'd find when she looked in a mirror.

It was only through the grace of God that a wheel didn't fall off and drag them to their deaths. Eventually, the horses wore themselves out and slowed down to a steady gallop. After that wild ride, the regular jostling seemed almost tolerable.

Belle spent the remainder of the afternoon singing "My Old Kentucky Home" with tears pooling in her eyes. Actually, she confided to Marjorie, she'd grown up in Tennessee, but it was a lovely song and the sentiments were the same. She had a job waiting for her as a singer in a Denver saloon called Pair of Dukes. Marjorie hoped the people there liked hearing about Kentucky.

Leon whiled the hours away by hanging on to a side strap and muttering to no one in particular. Marjorie attempted to engage him in conversation by offering him a penny for his thoughts, but he assured her that she didn't want to know what was going through his mind so she let the matter drop.

After thinking it over, she decided that his ease with a gun during that unpleasant encounter with Charles was merely a chance event. She'd observed little else to indicate that Leon had the character of a gunfighter. Though he'd been drinking off and on all day, he'd not attempted to intimidate anyone else. It had been her observation that the consumption of alcohol brought out the bully in a man. But as far as she could tell, it didn't have that effect on Leon. She was left to surmise that the incident this morning was not a regular aspect of her bridegroom's behavior. She found comfort in believing that he was merely being protective of her.

Even if nothing else came of this marriage, at least it would force Charles to turn his attentions elsewhere for a bride. He was forever telling Marjorie how much he admired her education and her love of books. He believed this to be an essential quality in a governor's wife. Educated women were few and far between out here. No doubt he was disappointed that it wasn't just a matter of her coming to her senses before they were wed. She looked over at Leon and hoped she hadn't jumped from the frying pan into the fire.

Jake Jarveson's murder weighed heavily on her mind. Though he could be charming when he put his mind to it, Jake was a difficult person to get along with. He'd had disagreements with practically everyone in Hope Springs.

Nonetheless, she couldn't imagine any of her neighbors, not even Charles, murdering him. The two of them were forever fussing over stray steers grazing in the wrong pastures.

But it didn't make sense for Charles to kill Jake, then call for an investigation. Besides, murdering Jake might ruin Charles's chances of ever being governor. That alone ruled him out in Marjorie's mind.

As the afternoon wore on, she considered who else might have killed Jake. Perhaps he'd gotten into a dispute with one of his hired hands. But Charles and his men would've handled that with a rope and a convenient tree; they wouldn't need to send for a deputy for that.

Surely Jake's wife hadn't returned seeking revenge. Mrs. Jarveson had kept to herself a great deal, so Marjorie was not certain just what she was capable of. However, it seemed a little far-fetched to imagine she'd returned from Philadelphia to kill her husband over a black eye and a split lip.

Though she pondered the matter off and on most of the day, nothing made any sense, and she finally just decided to turn her mind to other concerns.

They pulled into Denver late in the afternoon. Marjorie staggered down the stage steps and made an attempt to beat off the dust that'd settled over her. Leon was sound asleep, and she required assistance in getting him off the stage. She considered dragging him over to the land office right then and there, but decided that first thing in the morning would be soon enough.

With Leon limping alongside of her, they crossed slowly to the Denver Hotel, where Marjorie asked for a first-floor room. The desk clerk offered to give her a hand with Leon. On the way to the room, he informed her that the room came with a pitcher of water, but a hot tub bath would be four bits extra. Marjorie told him she'd think about it.

"Good Lord," Leon said as he collapsed onto the bed. "What a day." He groaned, closed his eyes, and appeared to fall asleep.

Even with all the grit and dirt covering the bandage, it was clear to see that the wound had been seeping. Marjorie asked the desk clerk if he would bring her a bottle of iodine and some clean strips of sheeting. He said that would be two bits extra, and she paid him.

After the clerk left, she unwound the soiled bandages and dropped them near the door. She poured the cool water in the washbasin, rinsed the dirt off Leon's face, and cleaned up the gash over his eye, before moving down to bathe his foot. She gently scrubbed the dried blood from his heel, then, while wiping the damp cloth over the rest of his foot, ran her fingers down the protruding bones that led to his toes. His feet were as long and lean as the rest of his body, and his toes curved where hers lay flat. Touching his feet seemed such an intimate thing to do that she jumped back and flushed with embarrassment when she heard the door handle rattle.

It was the desk clerk, returning with a bottle of iodine, some clean strips of sheeting, and a pitcher of hot water. He assisted her in undressing Leon down to his long underwear bottoms. He didn't mention how much that would cost, and she didn't ask. Leaving with the pile of dirty bandages, he said to just holler if she needed any more help.

There was no doubt that she needed help, but just what kind of help was beyond her at the moment. She dabbed iodine on his cut and rewrapped his foot with the clean bandages. If he moved, she didn't see it. He was so quiet, she laid her hands on his chest once just to make sure he was still breathing.

"Leon," she whispered softly next to his ear, "are you hungry? Would you like a bite to eat?"

He didn't stir. His cheeks were covered in whisker stubble, and she hesitantly ran her fingertips up one cheek and then across his thick mustache just to compare how they felt. The mustache was soft, while the whiskers were rough against the pads of her fingers. Although his face remained relaxed, she thought she heard a catch in his breath and quickly pulled her hand away.

His shoulders seemed broader than she remembered. The sheet had slipped down his bare chest, and she stared at the mounded muscles covered with short, wavy black hair. She didn't detect any changes in the slow, steady rhythm of his breathing when she touched his neck or ran her fingers over the silky hair at the top of his chest. She wondered how far down it went. From time to time she'd caught a glimpse of men washing up before they ate and wondered about that swirly, dark V that disappeared into their belts. She quickly dismissed the thought of pulling down the sheet to investigate further. *Goodness, what if he should awaken?* She blushed at the very thought of it.

But she kept thinking about what it would be like to lie next to him, imagining the feel of him pressed against her, wondering how things would be if this was a real marriage.

Enough of this, she admonished herself. She'd been engaged for five years and never once had she sat around touching Oliver's naked body. Of course, they'd kissed—chaste, good-night kisses after an evening of reading aloud to one another. Such kisses were certainly to be expected between an affianced couple. At one point Oliver had made it quite clear that he was interested in far more than kissing, but she had informed him in no uncertain terms that she was not that kind of woman, and furthermore, if he persisted in his unwanted advances, she would have no choice but to break off their engagement. They'd been engaged for three more years after that tawdry incident and never once had he made another unseemly suggestion.

Now here she was, turning into a hussy at the sight of a bare chest.

Instead of sitting here staring at this unsuspecting man, she really should see to their supper. She picked up her reticule and left in search of a bite to eat.

Twenty minutes later, she was back with a large bowl of chicken soup and a plate of biscuits. She considered purchasing two servings, but decided that she could always go out for more. No sense wasting money if he wasn't up to eating.

She leaned over and whispered in his ear, "Leon, there's some soup here for you." He gave no indication that he'd heard her. She briefly considered kissing him behind the ear like he'd kissed her the previous evening, but the thought passed quickly, and she went on to dwell on other matters.

A bath would feel heavenly, she thought, imagining herself soaking away her aches and pains in a tub of hot water. But why pay fifty cents when she could do that at home for free? The three round-trip tickets to Denver had taken a considerable portion of her savings, and she would be wise to watch her expenses. A possible bath would just have to do for now.

A soft breeze fluttered at the edge of the once-white lace curtains as Marjorie blew out the oil lamp. No sense making a spectacle of herself against the shades. Her eyes readjusted to the moonlight as she unbuttoned her dress and hung it on the bedstead. After checking to be certain that Leon was still sleeping, she unlaced her corset and rubbed at the itchy lines left by the whalebone stays. There wasn't enough water to wash her hair, so she decided to give it a good brushing to get out as much dirt as she could. She pulled the pins out of her bun and let her hair fall loose, bending over at the waist to brush the dust and dirt out onto the floor. Then she wound it to top of her head and pinned it back in place.

She slipped off her stockings, chemise, and cotton drawers, rinsed the washcloth out, and ran it over her face and down her neck. Her mother used to call this a possible bath. You start with your face and wash down as far as possible. Then you go to your toes and wash up as far as possible. Then you wash possible.

When she got to the possible part, she lingered longer than usual. Her flow must be coming soon, she decided. She felt full, heavy, and achy.

She ached all over, for that matter. All that wild jostling and bouncing about had covered her body with bruises from one end to the other.

Marjorie reached in her valise and pulled out the white nightgown with the lilacs along the neck. It really was too pretty to wear. But she guessed that was probably the whole point of it.

No, her gray-flannel nightgown would do just fine. She tugged it over her head. Almost wistfully, she wondered what a real wedding night might be like.

That thought brought her to the question of where she was going to sleep. She could, of course, crawl into the bed. There was room for two. But what if he should wake up and get ideas? Her only other choices were paying for another room or sleeping on the floor. Both were out of the question, given the state of her finances and the condition of her body after that stage ride.

The bed was the logical choice. She decided she'd just sleep on top of the covers. It would be like bundling, where courting couples covered themselves with blankets to keep warm but kept a board between them for propriety's sake, only she and Leon would be using the blankets in place of the board.

After checking to be certain that the door was locked, Marjorie padded over in her bare feet and lay down on top of the covers.

Leon, who hadn't so much as twitched since lying down, suddenly began thrashing about and wrapped his arms around her. She attempted to disengage herself, but that only brought on more restless behavior on his part, and she finally settled into a position in which she was turned on her side, away from him. As long as the blankets were between them, what difference did it make how they slept?

She closed her eyes and softly recited her evening prayer, adding Leon to the list of people she asked God to bless and watch over. Exhaustion overtook her before she got to "Amen."

The next morning, she untangled herself from his arms and sat on the edge of the bed. Though his eyes were closed, there was a faint flutter to his eyelashes, and his breathing didn't have that slow, deep cadence of slumber. Taking advantage of his pretense of sleep, she tiptoed to the other side of the bed and pulled on her stockings and slipped her chemise on under her nightgown. It took her a few minutes to get her corset adjusted and tied, then she quickly pulled her gown off and her dress on. Fortunately, he continued to give her the privacy she needed. Using her buttonhook, she fastened her boots before attempting to wake him.

"Mr. McCoy," she said, gently shaking his shoulder. "Mr. McCoy. Time to get up."

He moaned and rolled over, covering his head with the blanket.

"Please," she implored, "I need your help."

He pulled the covers down and squinted up at her as if she'd lost her mind.

"Lady, I don't know what you're planning to do that I could lend you a hand with," he said. "I'm weak as a kitten, my foot's so sore I doubt I could stand on it, and I ache all over." He paused for a moment. "You didn't kick me recently, did you?" he asked. "In a delicate area?"

"No," she said, "You hit a woman on the stage, and she kicked you."

"I've got to cut down on my drinking," he said. "What else have I done the last few days that I should know about? I know I haven't eaten anything. I'm so hungry my stomach thinks my throat's been cut."

"Here," she said, passing him a biscuit left over from the night before. "I'll find you a cup of coffee while you get dressed."

Ten minutes later, she was back with the coffee and two bowls of cornmeal mush and molasses. He was still in bed.

"Why aren't you up and dressed?" she asked.

"Can't," he answered.

"Why not?"

"I don't have any pants to wear." He said this as if the situation should be as obvious to her as it was to him.

"Can't you wear the ones you wore yesterday?" she asked, gesturing to the pair hanging over a chair. "Surely you don't change pants every day." She knew for a fact that he only traveled with one pair, so why this sudden insistence on clean ones today?

"I'd rather wear my own pants," he said.

"Well, that's impossible. We left them behind. They were all soaked in blood and needed to be washed."

"Listen, I can't go walking around Denver in this getup. I'd be taken for a fool. My hat's all smashed in. I can only get one boot on, and those pants are big enough for you and me both. If you had any pride at all, you'd be ashamed to be seen with me."

"You either get out of that bed," she said in no uncertain terms, "or I'm going to shoot you."

"Go ahead," he offered. "I don't have the strength or the will to resist."

Defeated, she sat down next to him. "Won't you please help me? If I don't get my name on this piece of land, I am doomed to spend the rest of my born days moving from one place to the next like a gypsy. I love teaching, but twenty dollars a month and the opportunity to board around with families is just about all they ever pay. I'm fortunate that I can live at my aunt's boardinghouse. But it won't be long before her husband decides it's time to search out a more prosperous community, and I'll have to pack up again. I just want to settle down somewhere. Is that too much to ask?"

"What do I get out of this deal?"

To come this far, be this close, and then have him refuse to budge was beyond bearing. She was willing to promise him just about anything if only he'd get out of that bed and walk with her down to the land office.

"Well, what do you want?" she asked, exasperated.

Leon folded his hands behind his head and smiled up at her while considering the possibilities.

"Are you refusing to help me, your own wife?" She didn't know what made her say that. It just jumped out.

"Not refusing," he said. "Negotiating."

"Negotiate a little faster if you don't mind. For all I know, while you're lying abed, Charles Irwin could be getting his hands on my land."

"First I have to figure out what I want to bargain for," said Leon, with a devilish grin.

She was so nervous she was about to jump out of her skin. There was no time for this dillydallying. Didn't he realize that?

"I'll pay you two hundred dollars if you'll stop this foolishness and go with me right now." That was close to everything she had in this world, but it would be worth it.

"Maybe money isn't what I want."

"What do you want?" she all but shouted.

"Calm down, darlin'. Give me a minute to think."

"I don't have a minute. Please," she pleaded, desperate to get him out of that bed. Already she could hear the hustle and bustle of people going about their business outside the window. The land office would be open any minute, if it wasn't already.

"I know what I don't want," he said, as if he had all day to consider the possibilities. "I sure don't want to be tied down to any farm."

"I am not expecting you to be tied down," she insisted. "You are free to go anytime after you sign those papers."

"What if I decide I don't want to go?"

"You can stay then, anything you want, it's yours." He had her over a barrel, and he knew it. If he'd just get going, they could work out the details later.

"Anything?" said Leon, grinning from ear to ear.

"Anything," agreed Marjorie. As soon as she'd said it, she knew she should call those words back, but it was too late now.

"Wait outside the door, darlin'," Leon said as he swung his legs over the edge of the bed. "I'll be with you in two shakes."

When the clerk at the land office unlocked his door, Marjorie marched right in and Leon limped along after her. The clerk recognized Marjorie from her previous visit and his "Why, good morning, Miss Bascom," was accompanied by a smarmy I-knew-you'd-be-back-to-take-me-up-on-my-offer expression.

His condescending smirk faded as he surveyed Leon from the beat-up hat and disheveled hair down to the baggy britches and rag-wrapped foot.

"And who might you be?" the clerk inquired. His lips were pursed so tightly it was a wonder he was able to get the words out at all.

"I might be John Wilkes Booth," Leon said, not bothering to hide his low opinion of the clerk. "Lucky for you, I'm not."

"This is my husband, Leon McCoy," Marjorie quickly explained, hoping to get their business completed before things turned unpleasant between the two men. "We are here to sign the homestead papers."

"How do I know you two are really married?" the clerk asked, pulling his head back so he could peer over the top of his spectacles at the two of them. "Perhaps you are a common drunkard that Miss Bascom has hired to impersonate a husband."

Leon grabbed the man by the front of his shirt and shoved him up against the wall. "How do we know you're not impersonating a land-office clerk, you beady-eyed bastard," he growled.

"Really, Leon," Marjorie said, attempting to pry his fingers off of the clerk, who had thrown his hands up and let out a frightened squeak. His eyes were opened so wide they appeared almost normal size. "Is this really necessary?" she asked.

Leon gave the clerk a firm slam against the wall before he let loose of him.

"Guess I don't feel like a lot of small talk this morning," he said. "It's annoying."

"I have the marriage certificate with me if you would like to see it," Marjorie offered. She pulled it out of her reticule and unfolded it, but the man did not appear interested any longer.

"No, no. That won't be necessary," the clerk assured her, scurrying around to stand behind his huge oak desk. "Let me see, that paperwork should be here somewhere." He shuffled nervously through a pile of papers on a credenza behind him.

Leon sat down in one of three wooden chairs lined up against the wall. He leaned back, stretched his legs out in front of him, and crossed his feet at the ankles, with his injured foot on top.

"There," said the clerk, pulling out a sheaf of papers. "I believe this is what we need."

He handed the papers to Marjorie, who examined them carefully.

"These appear to be in order," she said finally.

Marjorie laid the papers down on the neatly arranged desk and the clerk dipped a pen into an inkwell.

"We require the signature of the Head of the Household," he said, nervously looking in Leon's direction.

"Just show me where you want me to sign." Leon pushed himself out of the chair and limped over to the desk. The clerk indicated the bottom of one page. Leon tapped the pen on the inkwell, carefully signed on the line, and then laid the pen down.

The clerk waved the paper back and forth in the air to dry the ink.

"I'm afraid there are a few more places we need your signature, sir," he said, pointing hesitantly to the bottom of another document.

Leon dipped the pen, tapped it, and then carefully signed again. The clerk repeated the waving operation and indicated yet another spot to sign.

"How many of these papers have you got?" Leon asked. "It's 160 acres, not the Louisiana Purchase."

"I don't make the laws. I merely make certain that they're followed," said the clerk, his voice rising in pitch. "Everything needs to be legal, you know."

"It better be," Leon said, "or I'm coming back and you can bet I won't be in nearly as good a mood next time."

"No, I assure you, everything will be properly taken care of," the clerk said quickly. "There will be no reason for you to return until you are ready to prove up on your claim and file for your deed of ownership."

Leon signed once more and then sat down while the clerk signed and stamped all the papers. The poor man's hands were trembling so that he kept dropping blobs of ink out of the pen and having to blot them up.

"You're not ruining anything there, are you?" Leon growled at the man.

"No, no, Mr. McCoy. I assure you everything, everything is in perfect order," he stammered. "There is, however," he hesitated for a moment and cringed as if he was afraid to continue, "the matter of the ten-dollar filing fee."

While Marjorie was opening her reticule, Leon handed him the money.

"Think of it as a wedding present," he told her.

For once Marjorie didn't know what to say. There were a lot of surprising sides to this new husband of hers.

"This paper will be sent to Washington," the clerk said. "This one will remain in this office, and this is yours to keep." He extended a paper to Leon, who indicated with a wave of his hand that Marjorie was the one he should be giving it to.

"Be certain that you understand the terms of the Homestead Act regarding the number of acres under cultivation, the five-year residency requirement, and the construction of a dwelling. This building must be at least twelve by twelve and it must contain a window. Fraudulent situations will be investigated, and land claims will be denied on the basis of these inquiries." He looked pointedly at Marjorie. "The law is quite clear with regard to these matters."

"Rest assured," Marjorie said, "that the requirements will be met." She folded the paper over and placed it in her reticule.

"What does the law say about me being gone from time to time?" Leon said. "I have business interests back East which may require my attention occasionally."

The clerk gave Leon a look of skepticism but didn't utter a word. Marjorie knew he was asking himself just what sort of business interest a man who looked like Leon could possibly have. Prizefighting, perhaps?

Marjorie quickly added, "However, I will remain behind to watch the stock. One of us will always be there."

"As long as you construct a dwelling, put the specified portion of the land under cultivation, and at least one of you actually resides for six months and a day on the property every year, you will be able to get a clear title to the land five years from today."

"What about if something happens to one of us?" Leon asked.

"Since you have signed this in both your names, the right of survivorship applies."

Marjorie looked at where the clerk was pointing to the bottom of one of the documents. When she realized that Leon had written Leon and Marjorie McCoy, she was so proud and grateful that if it hadn't been for the clerk, she would have hugged Leon right then and there.

"Now what?" Leon asked as they stepped out into the bright morning sun. He didn't sound as if he was excited about the possibilities.

The thrill of actually having her own place had her mind in such a whirl that she hadn't given any thought beyond the land-office visit. The stage back to Hope Springs didn't leave until the next morning, so they had the whole day ahead of them. She looked at Leon, and the first thing that came to mind was his disgust at having to wear those ridiculous pants. She wanted to thank him somehow, and buying him a pair of pants seemed a practical way to do so.

"Let's see," she said. "If I remember right, there's a dry-goods store down the street. We could see if they have any trousers in your size." She'd hoped this suggestion would bring about a change in his sullen attitude, but it didn't appear to.

"And we should see a physician about your foot," she continued. "I hope it doesn't get infected."

"You'd be a fun one at a funeral," Leon muttered.

"What's that supposed to mean?" she asked.

"Just that you're always looking on the bleak side of things."

"I do not," she said. "I'm quite optimistic about any number of things."

"Like what?"

"Like homesteading my land, for example," she said with a self-satisfied set to her shoulders.

"Well that's the one thing you ought to be more cautious about," he said. "Do you have any idea how much work and trouble you're getting yourself into?"

"How would you know?"

"I know about trouble and hard work," he said. "Believe you me, if there's anything I'm familiar with, it's trouble and hard work."

He started limping toward a doorway that even at this hour had piano music pouring out of it.

"Mr. McCoy," she said, grabbing him by the shoulder, "you cannot drown your sorrows in liquor. Sorrows can swim, you know."

"You don't say."

"I do say," she responded. "Sooner or later, you simply must sober up and face reality."

"Why would I want to face reality?" he said, not bothering

to hide the bitterness in his voice. "As near as I can recall, I'm married to a woman who believes I'm a worthless no-account and I've just signed up to be a sodbuster. Why not add hopeless drunk to the list?"

"Talk about seeing the bleak side," said Marjorie.

Before she could continue, Leon grabbed her and gave her a kiss that made her knees dissolve. If he hadn't been holding on to her, she would've fallen right on the ground.

My, but this was an intriguing way to end an argument. For indeed, within seconds, she'd completely forgotten what they'd been fussing about. She was trembling all over. Kissing Oliver had never been like this.

"That land-office rat is staring straight at us," Leon murmured against her lips. "Probably best that we don't give him any reason to be suspicious."

What was he saying? His voice sounded so far off, and though she heard the words, she was having some difficulty making out their meaning.

Then it hit her. Good gracious, she was standing in the middle of the street, carrying on like a floozy.

"Oh, for heaven's sake, let loose of me," she implored him.

He let go, but when she went to take a step, she stumbled. If Leon hadn't grabbed her arm, she would have fallen flat on her face.

"Might I escort you to the dry-goods store, Mrs. McCoy?" he asked, polite as you please.

Not trusting her voice, she nodded yes.

My, that man can kiss.

He held her by the elbow. Before they took a step, they both turned inward and looked back over their shoulders at the land clerk.

"Smile, darlin'," she heard Leon say.

She looked up at him. He was grinning from ear to ear. She stretched up the edges of her mouth, but she knew she didn't come anywhere near the satisfaction and pure happiness on Leon's face. Even his mustache seemed to turn up at the ends.

Her knees started to give way again, and she was grateful when he slipped his arm around her waist. Following Leon's gaze, she found the land clerk staring at them, his mouth as pinched in as his eyes.

Without another glance, Leon turned around and guided her down the walk and into the mercantile. The long, narrow store was crammed full of everything from saddles and guns to sacks of flour and shoes. Tins of tobacco and steel traps were stacked on top of stoves and kegs of nails. Bolts of calico shared counter space with cans of coal oil. There were dry goods hanging from the walls, sitting on shelves, displayed in glass cases, and resting on the floor. The less popular or more expensive items were covered in a layer of dust.

A tall, boot-faced woman shuffled back and forth stacking items on a display case as a man in a sheepskin coat consulted his list. The woman invited the two of them to look around and said she'd be with them in a minute.

Look was about all they could do, since moving about was certainly out of the question. Leon managed to work his way over to a counter stacked with rifles, and Marjorie examined a cookstove next to her. It had a warming shelf on top and a hot-water reservoir to the side. It wasn't as big as Ruby's, but the firebox door fit snug, and the oven would hold a small roasting pan or a sheet of biscuits with no trouble. She wished she could see the top of the stove but it was piled with stacks of iron skillets, tin plates, and china bowls. Maybe in a year or two she could sell some steers and buy one of these stoves for herself.

A rocking chair covered in wool coats sat next to the stove. She moved the coats to the top of a nearby crate and sat down. It was built for a much larger person. When she put her elbows on the armrests, her shoulders were hunched up around her neck. Her feet barely touched the floorboards. Had there been room to rock, they would've left the floor completely.

She looked over at Leon as he sighted down the barrel of a rifle, and, just for a moment, like a little girl playing make-believe, she pretended that this was a real marriage. She wondered what it would be like to grow old with this man, to share life's trials and tribulations. She couldn't picture it. She didn't know if it was because she couldn't imagine herself putting up with all the hard work and heartache that marriage involved or whether she couldn't imagine Leon growing old. Probably a little of both.

She was pulled out of her reverie by the gravelly-voiced woman asking if she wanted the rocking chair.

"No," she replied. "It's far too big." Marjorie noticed that the customer in the sheepskin coat was pushing his way out the door.

"But we would like—" she started to say.

"We'd like to see some wedding rings," Leon announced before Marjorie had a chance to finish.

The woman turned to search through a pile of boxes behind her.

Marjorie felt as if she was still daydreaming. How sweet of him to offer to buy her a ring. She couldn't accept, of course. A ring would be far too expensive, and Leon was obviously not a man of means. Nonetheless, it was kind of him to offer.

"I appreciate the thought," Marjorie whispered to him, "but truly, a ring is not necessary."

"I think it is," he said. "Whether I'm around or not, a ring will let folks know what your situation is."

She wondered just exactly what her situation was. Things had taken quite a turn within the last hour. Was Leon feeling the same way she was? Or was this all due to the emotional relief of finally signing those papers? Things were just not as clear as they'd been before.

"Please, Leon," she whispered. "I can't afford a ring right now. Perhaps in a year or so, once things are situated, I'll get one."

"I think I've got enough on me to buy my wife a ring," he said.

There was no reason to embarrass him by arguing, so she

stood quietly while they watched the woman move and stack things around. She finally pulled out a wooden case, cleared a section of countertop to set it on, and opened the lid. There were rings of every description piled inside. Leon watched Marjorie try on a number of plain gold bands before he pulled out a ring with five small blue stones set across the top.

"To match your eyes," he mumbled self-consciously.

When had he noticed what color her eyes were?

He slid the ring on her finger. It fit perfectly. She looked up at him and, for a moment, it was as if the world around them had ceased to exist. Pulling her gaze back to the ring, she marveled at the delicate stones and wondered aloud what they were.

"Lapis lazuli," the woman said in answer to her question. "If you sleep with them under your pillow, your dreams will come true."

Marjorie didn't think she needed the ring; her dreams were already coming true.

"We'll take it," Leon said.

Despite his rough exterior, Leon was a charmer. She'd better watch herself, or she was going to fall flat in love with this man, and that was definitely not part of the plan.

"I suspect you're looking for britches as well," the woman said. "Just got in a box of them pants made with rivets. You want to try a pair on?"

She pushed her way over to an open wooden crate, dug through it, and handed a stack of pants to Leon. "Here," she said, shoving him behind the counter. "You go on in the back room and see which ones fit."

Leon walked around behind the display cases and disappeared through the back door.

The woman turned to Marjorie. "You two just get hitched?" she asked.

"How did you know?"

"The ring helped, but the dead giveaway is how he keeps looking at you like he's ready to throw you down right here on the floor and how you keep looking back like you're ready to let him."

Marjorie was afraid to reply for fear of what this brash woman would say next.

"Don't mind me," she continued. "I can be blunt as a cob if I don't watch myself." She patted Marjorie on the hand and moved over to a counter stacked with magazines. She dug through the piles until she found what she wanted. "Here," she said, handing her a pamphlet, "you might find this useful."

The pamphlet was titled *Guide for the New Bride: Information and Instructions on the Art of Marriage.* As curious as Marjorie was about the subject, she certainly was not going to purchase anything with a title like this in Leon's presence. Talk about giving a man ideas.

She handed the pamphlet back. "I appreciate your thoughtfulness, but I don't think so."

The woman pulled her hands up, displaying her open palms in refusal. "You just tuck that away," she told her. "It's my wedding present to the two of you."

Leon reappeared just then, and Marjorie murmured a fast "Thank you," as she tucked the pamphlet into her reticule. He looked a great deal better in his new pants.

He'd obviously had to unwrap and rewrap the bandage to get the pants on, and, without even being asked, the woman informed them that they could find Doc Simmons at the top of the back stairs.

Leon maintained that the cut on his foot didn't amount to much, but Marjorie insisted that they at least should have the doctor take a look at it. They went back and forth on this topic while Marjorie selected garden seeds, spices, and a bundle of stick candy.

In the end, he hobbled up the stairs behind the store, muttering about why in the world a doctor would have an office where patients had to climb a flight of stairs. Maybe it was a method of weeding out the ones who weren't going to make it anyway.

The sign on the door said to come in, so they did. The room they stepped into was a jumble of papers, opened books, baskets, bottles, and jars of every size, shape, and color. The top of a massive oak desk was completely covered, as were a credenza, a windowsill, and what might have been an examination table. From the overcrowded appearance of the room, Marjorie decided the doctor must be some relation to the woman who ran the store downstairs.

Marjorie called out "anybody here" at least a half a dozen times before an older, white-haired gentleman ambled in, seeming somewhat surprised to see them. When Marjorie explained about wanting him to take a look at Leon's foot, he moved a tray of metal instruments from the only chair in the room and indicated that Leon should sit down. He pushed aside a stack of papers on his desk, propped Leon's foot up on the cleared space, and unwrapped the rags and bandages.

"Looks like you're going to need a few stitches, young man. Here," he said, handing a bottle to Leon, "you better . . ." He didn't finish his sentence, just turned and began rummaging through the tray of instruments he'd set on the windowsill.

Leon lifted the cork and sniffed the contents. Marjorie grabbed the bottle from him and held it out of his reach.

"There," the doc said. "Found it. Now where's that . . ."

He pulled a short stool over with his foot. There was a white enameled basin sitting on it that he placed on the floor. He retrieved a square blue bottle from the disarray on his desk, pulled out the cork, and sat down on the stool. Holding Leon's foot over the basin, he doused it with a good deal of the contents of the blue bottle. Leon jerked back, but the doctor hung on.

"Got to get the poison out," he said, "or else . . ." His mind wandered on to another thought. He picked up a threaded needle and pushed it into Leon's foot.

Leon jumped right off the chair, pulling his foot out of the doctor's grasp.

"Sweet Jesus," he said. "Doesn't anyone believe in giving a man some warning before inflicting pain?"

"Let him have another nip," the doctor said, pointing to the bottle that Marjorie was holding. "That ought to . . ." She reluctantly handed the bottle to Leon and watched disapprovingly as he took three long drinks. Then he sat back down and extended his foot again.

"Go to it," Leon said.

The doctor placed Leon's foot in his lap and set to sewing.

Leon grabbed the arms of the chair and held his breath, but he kept his foot still. He looked just like a little boy trying to be brave while a splinter was removed. Marjorie reached out to smooth his forehead, but somehow that seemed too personal a gesture, so she placed her hand over his on the chair. Even that seemed overly intimate. A tingly warmth crept up her arm. Leon looked at her, and the tingling spread throughout her torso. She felt a hot flush begin behind her ears and spread across her cheeks.

Leon winced occasionally but never took his eyes off her as the doctor continued his work. Marjorie felt as light-headed as she had when he'd kissed her on the street. It was the oddest sensation, as if the building could fall in on them, and they'd still be staring at one another.

"There you go, young man," the doctor said, putting Leon's foot on the stool as he got up. "You need to . . ." He rummaged around for a few minutes. "Here," he said, handing her a string-wrapped packet. She closed her hand around it without taking her eyes off Leon. "Soak his foot in hot salt water and make a poultice of this." He shuffled out of the room before Marjorie realized that this was the first sentence she'd heard him complete.

Marjorie's thoughts were as jumbled as the room around her. Bewildered, she stood there with one hand holding on to the packet and the other one holding on to Leon.

Leon rose to his feet and, pulling her hand behind him, bent to kiss her. Just as his lips were about to brush across hers, the doctor shuffled back in and loudly cleared his throat. They drew away from one another, both behaving as if they'd done something they ought to be guilty about.

"You need to stay off that foot, young man," he ordered, thrusting a crutch in their direction. "Can't find the other one, but you should stay in bed for a couple of . . ."

"How much do I owe you?" Leon asked, pulling himself away from her.

"A buck ought to do it," the old doctor answered. "You should get those stitches taken out in a week or so or they will . . ." His attention was drawn to a book lying open on his desk. He picked it up and thumbed through the pages in the back.

Leon left a dollar on the edge of the desk. He hiked the crutch under one armpit, grasped Marjorie with the other arm, and hobbled out the door. Marjorie called out a "Thank you" from the doorway. The old man waved absentmindedly but never looked up.

Marjorie hung on to the railing as she walked behind Leon down the stairs. She had been feeling so unusual lately, woozy and loose-limbed, that she didn't trust her sense of balance. What if she faltered and fell into him? Leon definitely looked better in his new pants, she decided, but beyond that she couldn't get her thoughts in order.

Except for her ring, they'd left their purchases by the door downstairs. They stopped back in to pick up their bundles. The woman who'd waited on them was unpacking a crate of boots in the middle of that whole mess. They thanked her and went on their way.

"Did you ever see such a hodgepodge?" asked Marjorie. "It was all I could do not to offer my assistance in straightening things up."

"If it weren't for the floorboards, I'd have guessed a couple of freight wagons just dumped their loads, and they built the store around it," he said.

They passed in front of a daguerreotype studio, and she was about to comment on the pictures on display in the window when Leon suddenly announced he'd forgotten something and he'd be right back. Marjorie turned to follow, but he told her not to bother as it would just take him a minute. It would certainly be easier for her to walk back than it would be for him, but he was determined to go himself, so she stood there holding their parcels wondering what the mystery was all about. She wanted to warn Leon not to go spending money on anything for her but decided that sounded presumptuous and stopped herself before the words got out. Most likely, he was buying men's underdrawers or some personal item he didn't care to talk about in front of her.

It wasn't long until he was back. Since he wasn't carrying a package of any sort, she decided the dry-goods store must not have had what he was looking for. That was hard to imagine, given the array of goods in the place.

After briefly discussing the pictures in the window, they made their way along the boardwalk back to the hotel.

Leon stopped at the desk and asked the clerk if he could have his hat brushed and steamed and if he would arrange for a bath for the two of them.

"Will you be wanting adjoining or separate bathtubs, sir?" the clerk asked in all seriousness.

"Adjoining tubs sure sounds appealing, don't it, darlin'?" He smiled at Marjorie as if she might actually go along with this outlandish suggestion.

"I don't think so," said Marjorie. *Heavens, what went through that man's mind?*

"Loosen up a little, sweetheart," Leon suggested. He threw the arm that was not holding on to the crutch around her shoulders.

"I'm as loose as I ever expect to be," she said. The intense connection she'd experienced earlier in the doctor's office had been replaced by the need to put some distance between the two of them.

"Come on, we're in the big city. We might as well enjoy ourselves while we got the chance." Leon was still grinning as if he thought he was close to persuading her to bathe with him. He could put that silly notion to rest.

"I hardly think that would be appropriate," she said in exasperation as she turned away to avoid discussing the matter any further.

"Hey, we're in Denver, darlin'. We can do anything we want. It says so in the Bible."

Her eyes rolled heavenward. "Oh, that's just ridiculous. The Bible makes no mention whatsoever about bathing together just because you're in Denver."

The slack-jawed clerk was taking this all in, no doubt to regale his cohorts with as soon as they were out of sight. She would never be able to show herself in this hotel again. She was torn between the desire to get Leon out of there before the situation became any more humiliating and the reluctance to be alone with him in the hotel room.

"Well, I'll just bet the Bible doesn't say one word about not bathing together in Denver," he said, continuing his outrageous remarks. "It's against nearly everything else. I figure, since it doesn't mention not bathing together in Denver, it must be in favor of it."

"Stop this immediately," she insisted. She turned around and lowered her voice in an attempt to keep their conversation from carrying throughout the entire lobby. "You are making a spectacle of yourself, and me as well."

"Darlin', I'll show you a spectacle," he said in a teasing manner.

"You do, and I'll never speak to you again," she vowed, setting off immediately for their room. Let him stand around and make a fool of himself in front of the hired help. She didn't intend to be a party to it.

"Why do I doubt that?" he called after her.

She was wrapping her good black gown around her fresh underthings in preparation for a bath when she heard the door open and shut and his footsteps coming up slowly behind her. On the pretext of picking up her hairbrush from the dresser, she moved away from him.

"Don't be mad, darlin'," he drawled in such a soft, low voice that it almost worked.

"I don't appreciate being the butt of your jokes, Mr. McCoy," she said, keeping her face towards the wall.

"Leon, if you don't mind," he said. "I think, given what we've been through the past few days, you could at least call me by my first name."

"Leon, this has been a most unusual experience for me," she said, not knowing quite how to proceed. She turned to face him and was astonished to see him looking almost contrite.

"Believe you me, nothing like this ever happened to me before either," he assured her. "Absolutely nothing," he repeated.

"I'm sure that once I sort things through, I'll be able to think more clearly, but right now I'd appreciate it if you didn't attempt to confuse matters."

"And you think bathing together would confuse matters?"

"It most certainly would," she said firmly. "I can't imagine what was going through your mind even to suggest it."

"What would you think if I suggested we get our photograph taken back at that picture place?"

"Why?" she asked. The man was a spendthrift. First the ring and now a photograph, and all over a pretend marriage. It was fortunate they were leaving tomorrow, or he wouldn't have a nickel to his name.

"Why not?" he replied. "More than likely, this is the only time I'll ever get married. It may not mean a blessed thing to you, lady, but it does to me, and I'd like a remembrance."

"When you put it that way . . ." she said in an attempt to smooth his suddenly ruffled feathers.

They bathed and dressed, separately of course. Afterward, Leon went to a nearby barbershop for a shave and a haircut, while Marjorie spent the time drying and pinning up her hair.

By early afternoon they were admiring their reflection in the daguerreotype studio mirror. They made a handsome couple, if she did say so herself. Marjorie sat in a velvet chair, and Leon stood behind her with his hand on her shoulder. While the photographer fiddled with his equipment, Leon brushed the back of his fingers up and down beneath her ears. At least four times she hissed at him to stop it. She finally had to slap his hand away to get him to quit fooling around.

Just before the photographer lit the flash powder, Leon whispered an indecent suggestion. Fortunately, she had the presence of mind to ignore him. Wouldn't that have been just dandy, her with mouth wide-open, scolding him in their wedding photograph?

The photographer said that he would have their picture ready by six o'clock that night. He even offered to drop it by the hotel on his way home. That settled, Leon paid him, and they returned for an early dinner in the hotel dining room.

Over dessert, Leon announced that using the crutch was no easy matter and that he was flat worn out with all the walking they'd done today. Much as he would enjoy seeing the sights, he suggested they make an early evening of it. Marjorie had reservations about agreeing to go back to the room with him but saw no alternative to doing so. She could hardly expect him to hobble up and down the streets of Denver just because she was uneasy in his presence.

Before leaving the dining room, she prevailed upon the kitchen staff for some salt and a pan of hot water. Back in their room, she soaked the herbs from the doctor in the hot water and put Leon's foot in the washbasin full of warm salt water. Later, after drying his foot, she packed the squeezed-out poultice next to his wound and rewrapped the sheeting strips over the mixture.

"There, that ought to do it," she said, tucking the ends of

the bandage around his foot. She placed a towel underneath his foot to soak up the dark green water that slowly oozed out. Leon leaned back against the headboard and watched her fuss over him.

"What a way to start a honeymoon," he said. Another one of his easygoing smiles spread across his face. "Confined to bed for who knows how long." He extended an arm. "Come here, darlin'."

"You may be confined to your bed," she said, "but I certainly am not."

"We are married, and if I recall correctly, earlier today you did promise me anything I wanted." From the look on his face, there was no doubt about what he wanted.

How had she gotten into this predicament and, more to the point, how could she get out? She felt herself becoming frantic. Like a rabbit caught in a parlor, she ran from idea to idea, trying to find one that would get her out of this mess.

"In name only," she reminded him. "You have misconstrued our conversations if you believe otherwise. I have not the slightest intention of joining you beneath the sheets."

If he kept looking at her this way, she'd be needing crutches herself to get around.

She did the only thing she could think of. She ran out of the room while her legs were still functional. When she turned the corner in the hallway, she leaned back against the wall and tried to collect her wits. It was nearly dark, and if the shops weren't already closed, they soon would be. She could hardly walk up and down the halls of the Denver Hotel all night. Perhaps she could sit in the lobby.

No, that would never do. There were really very few places that a woman alone could go at night that didn't put her reputation, if not her very person, at peril. Perhaps she should just go ahead and pay for another room. The way things had been progressing today, all he'd have to do is give her one more slow smile, and she'd be in his arms. The cost of a room would be a small price to pay to avoid that catastrophe.

What she needed was some time to think things through. A porch extended around the back side of the hotel. Perhaps she could find some peace and quiet there. She headed in that direction and found not only privacy but a large swing with an afghan thrown over the back. Now wasn't that a thoughtful touch?

She curled up in the end of the swing, wrapped herself in the afghan, and waited for the darkness to settle in around her. The street sounds gradually changed from the hustle and bustle of the day to the more leisurely pace of the evening. People were either heading home to dinner or already there.

She'd always enjoyed this time of day, watching the stars come out. No matter where she lived, she would look for the Big Dipper and follow the two pointers up to the North Star. Across to the right, the lopsided W that was Cassiopeia, the mother, awaited her. She found comfort in finding her stars before she went to sleep. Somehow, it made the world seem safer, less topsy-turvy. Usually, she made a wish on her lucky stars. She wondered what she would wish for tonight.

The evening breeze carried a child's voice calling, "Ready or not, here I come," and the sounds of little feet scurrying this way and that.

Had life ever been that carefree for her? Surely there must have been a time when all she had to worry over was whether she could find a good hiding place in time. Wasn't it strange that was what life was all about—finding a good hiding place, getting home free. She'd known that truth since she was a little girl.

Obviously, *this* was not a good hiding place, or at least not good enough. She heard the clunk of his bootheel on the boards, followed by the muffled sound of his padded foot.

He stopped behind her, and she waited for him to say the first word. When he didn't, she pulled her legs up close to her and said, "There's room for two if you'd care to join me."

"Don't mind if I do," he said, walking around to sit in the spot she'd created. She wrapped her arms around her knees.

It was a schoolgirl position, certainly not the way a grown woman should sit. But if she placed her feet on the porch, it was as much as inviting him to put his arm around her, and she thought it best to avoid any possibility of that right now.

"How's your foot doing?" she asked.

"Oh, I expect I'll live," he answered.

He shoved off, and they swung back and forth to the tune of the rope's steady creaking as it rubbed against the hooks above them. Even though her lucky stars weren't visible yet, Marjorie closed her eyes and made a wish on them. *Please let me explain things in a way that won't hurt him,* she silently asked. *He's a fine man. It's just that I can't bear to love someone who's not going to be around. It's not better to have loved and lost than never to have loved at all. Whoever thought that one up didn't know a thing about it.* Longing was far worse than never loving in the first place. She knew that for a fact.

How to explain that she just couldn't go through with this morning's bargain? The words wouldn't come.

"I'm sorry if I scared you," he said finally, turning to look at her. "I didn't mean to."

"I wasn't scared," she lied. "I just needed some time to think about things. A lot has happened lately."

"I'll say so," he readily agreed. "I don't believe I've ever packed quite as much into two days before."

"And here I thought you were a man who liked a bit of excitement," she gently teased him.

"There's a limit to how much excitement a body can stand, darlin'."

She wondered what that limit was. She felt taxed near to the breaking point herself.

"Margie," he asked quietly, "have you thought about what your intentions are?"

"Yes," she said, just as softly. "I intend to get on the stagecoach tomorrow morning, spend the night at my aunt Ruby's, and the rest of my life on my land."

"Just like that?" he asked.

"Just like that," she answered with as much firmness as she could manage. No sense giving him the idea that this morning's kiss meant anything more to her than a way to impress the land clerk.

"What about me?" he asked carefully.

"What about you?" she replied. He needn't look so forlorn. She was not a cold woman, but neither was there any reason to lead the man on.

"What am I supposed to do?" he asked.

"What were you doing when you met me?" she asked right back. She switched her focus to the stars appearing above them. It was too hard to keep looking at him. It made her heart hurt.

"Well, if you must know, I was looking to get drunk and get laid," he said.

"I hardly think one can build a life around those two pursuits," she said. Even to her own ears, she sounded like an old-maid schoolteacher.

"I'll bet you've never even been kissed before," he taunted her.

The nerve of that man. Did he think she was so unattractive that she'd never had suitors? She pulled her head up and announced self-righteously, "Not that it's any of your business, Mr. McCoy, but I have indeed been kissed before. For your information, I was engaged for five years."

"You were engaged for five years!" he said in amazement.

"Yes," she said firmly. "And though we kissed upon occasion, I assure you he was a perfect gentleman when he was with me."

"Where is he now?"

"That really is none of your concern," she informed him.

"I'd say it was. What if he turns up tomorrow and insists on taking up where the two of you left off? He might want me out of the way." He spoke lightly of the matter, as if that possibility were so remote it was not to be taken seriously.

What did the man find so amusing about this situation? She

realized she was no great beauty. Her features were on the plain side, her hair rather unruly at times, and she had long since given up tugging on her corset ties firmly enough to pull in that wasp waist men found so attractive. It simply wasn't worth the effort. But she had her appealing qualities. She could cook a decent meal and run a smooth household. Surely it couldn't be all that difficult to imagine that someone would have grown to care enough for her to ask for her hand in marriage.

"Well, are you going to tell me what happened?" he asked.

"If you must know, he became involved in a foolhardy shipping scheme, and we came to a parting of the ways." And that was all she intended to say about the matter. She saw no need to mention how Oliver had absconded with her life's savings.

"I've been thrown over myself," Leon said, as if it lessened the disagreeableness of her experience by finding out it'd happened to him as well.

"Really?" she responded, preparing herself for some tale of how he'd been spurned by a barroom hussy.

"It was during the war," he said.

She glanced over and saw that he, too, was staring off into space.

"Sugar wouldn't melt in that woman's mouth, she was so sweet on me. I was sending her money every chance I got. She said she was tucking it away so we'd have a little nest egg once the war was over." He stopped talking, took in a deep breath of air and let it out with a sigh. "I led reconnaissance patrols for the Union army, scouting ahead so that General Grant could plan his next move. It wasn't all that easy getting a pass, but whenever I could get back home, we'd go sparking and Charlotte would giggle and carry on behind that black lace fan of hers."

Marjorie waited for him to finish. She could see that it was not a topic he enjoyed discussing. But still, he'd brought it up, and as his wife, she felt entitled to know some of the circumstances of his life. When he didn't elaborate, she asked, "What happened?"

He turned and looked at her, the hurt and anger apparent in his eyes and in the controlled way he held his mouth. "About a year before the war ended, I got a chance to go home on leave and found Charlotte tapping that damn lace fan on some other sucker's shoulder." He paused as if considering whether to continue or not. He leaned back and stared up at the sky. "Turns out she had half a dozen of us on the string. I cut myself loose from the bunch right then and there."

"How shocking," she said, and she meant it. It'd been dreadful when Oliver announced he was leaving to seek his fortune elsewhere, but at least he'd broken off with her in an honorable manner. She'd even kept his note promising to pay her investment back with interest, though she'd no hope at all of ever seeing a penny of that money again.

"I should've seen it coming," he said.

"How, pray tell? You could hardly be expected to read her mind."

"I'd seen a bunch of my stepmas do the same thing to my pa," he said, giving the swing a good shove.

"How many stepmothers did you have?" she asked out of curiosity.

"Fifteen or so that I remember, and a few more that I've forgot," he added in a matter-of-fact tone. "Maybe twenty some altogether."

"Twenty?" She was astounded. Could he be making this up?

"Around twenty, I guess, give or take a few." He shrugged his shoulders as if it were of little concern to him.

"My," she said in amazement. "Your father must have been a busy man."

"He was at that. He'd take up with just about any woman who'd agree to look out for me."

"What happened?" She'd heard of men having four or five different wives, but twenty?

"He was a railroad engineer, and he was gone a lot. When he'd come home, often as not his latest woman would've found someone else she liked better and already left. If she was still around, the two of them would get in a fuss, and she'd pack up and go back to her kin. Whatever the reason, it all worked out about the same."

"How heartbreaking." To think of going through that twenty times.

"I don't believe he cared much one way or the other," Leon said.

"I was thinking of how hard that must have been for you," said Marjorie, imagining Leon as a little boy watching another temporary mother leave him behind.

"I wouldn't worry about it," he said with a wave of his hand. "I was glad to see them go. They generally already had a pack of kids, and I was nothing but a nuisance." He shrugged his shoulders as if to emphasize how little it mattered to him. "Most of them didn't care one way or the other whether I was around."

He pulled out a sack of Bull Durham tobacco and some papers from his vest pocket. "That's not altogether true," he continued, and she heard the bitterness behind the nonchalant attitude. "If they had any dirty jobs that needed doing or were looking for someone to blame, they remembered me quick enough." He stopped himself, then asked, "Do you mind if I smoke?"

"No, go right ahead," she answered. "What happened to your mother?" She didn't want to ask, but she couldn't stop herself.

"Don't rightly know. I expect she died, or I'd have been with her." His attention was focused on holding the rolling paper in between his two first fingers and spreading the tobacco evenly along the length of it.

"Your father didn't tell you anything about her?" To never have known a mother's love was inconceivable to Marjorie.

"My old man and I never talked all that much. Mostly I

stayed out of his way if I could." Leon licked the edge of the paper and ran his thumb across the top to press it together.

What a sad way to grow up. The urge to reach out and hold him was almost overwhelming.

"Where is he now?" she asked, watching as he struck a match on the sole of his boot, lit the end of his cigarette, and sucked on the burning tobacco.

"Who knows?" He let out a stream of smoke. "I took off the winter I was fourteen, and I never went back."

"Where did you go?"

"I went to work for a guy cleaning out horse stalls. I found I liked working with horses, and when the war came along, I joined the cavalry." He inhaled and puffed out a string of smoke rings. "Those were some wild times," he continued. "It got to be a sorry situation toward the end. I was glad when it was all over and done with." He sucked in and let out another stream.

"I often wonder what my old running buddies are up to these days. I was planning on heading out to see one who'd settled in the Northwest when I ran across that Jarveson in Abilene. He offered me a job breaking a string of horses, and I decided I wouldn't mind making a little traveling money, so I said sure."

"What happened?" she asked.

"Once I got there, he said he wouldn't be needing me since he'd sold his spread," he answered.

"Jake sold the Lazy J?" This was the first she'd heard about him selling out.

"That's what the man said."

"Who'd he sell to?"

"I believe he said he'd sold out to that Irwin fellow that seemed so taken with you."

"That's odd," she said. "Last fall, Charles was trying to sell Jake the Circle I in order to raise money to finance his campaign for governor. I wonder why he changed his mind?"

"How should I know?" Leon asked. "All I know is that this

Jarveson said he'd sold his spread and I'd have to go talk to Irwin if I still wanted a job."

"In a way, that was probably a stroke of good fortune," she said. "Jake Jarveson is, or rather was, a liar and a bully."

"You're right," Leon said. "It's probably better that I starve to death than work for a liar and a bully."

"Oh, you won't starve to death," she said. "What a ridiculous thing to say."

"I will if you're as stingy with your food as you are with your affection," he said.

"I promise you'll be well fed until you're ready to depart," she said. "You needn't worry about that."

"What about the affection?" he asked.

"You'd best put that thought to rest right now. An affectionate relationship would mean so much more to me than it ever would to you. I could not bear the heartbreak," she said with an air of drama.

"What?" he asked, as if he hadn't given this a moment's thought.

"For you, I would be just one more in a long series of encounters. But it'd be different for me. If we were to engage in marital relations, I'd spend the rest of my life longing for you, looking out the window, wondering when or if I'd ever see you again. I know what that does to a woman, and I want no part of it."

"I think you're afraid," he said.

"Afraid of what?" *This was ridiculous.*

"Afraid that you might actually enjoy it. Afraid that if you loosened up, you'd find that this spinster business isn't all it's cracked up to be."

"Oh, for crying in the night. Of course there are unpleasant aspects to being an unmarried woman. I am sure there are features about being a drifter that are less than pleasant."

"You've no call to look down your nose at me for being a wandering man. I'm honest and hardworking. I put in a day's work for a day's pay. Nobody has any complaints about Leon

McCoy not carrying his share of the load." He threw his cigarette butt down and angrily ground it out with his bootheel.

"I never said I doubted that," she said, in an attempt to calm him down.

"Where would our country be if everybody just stayed in the same spot they landed?" He was getting worked up now. "I've about had it with this notion of yours that I don't amount to a bucket of spit."

"I never said—" she began, but he interrupted her without so much as a "Pardon me."

"What if everybody stayed rooted to the spot where they were born? What if not one living soul was curious about what was over the next hill?" he asked. Then, before she had a chance to answer, he said, "Why, people'd be stacked up like cordwood all along the coast. Hell, according to your theory, they should've stayed back in the old country instead of sailing across the ocean like a bunch of tramps."

He'd worked up a full head of steam by now.

"Who do you think settled this country anyhow?" he asked. "Men of adventure, that's who. Men who wanted to see what was around the bend. Come to think of it, how did you get so far from Philadelphia?"

"Mr. McCoy, there's really no call for you to—" she started, but he cut her off again.

"Call me Leon," he growled between gritted teeth. "Even if you do think I'm as worthless as bosoms on a boar, I'm still your husband."

"Please, Mr.—" she caught herself. "Please, Leon, you're getting all upset over nothing. I assure you that I never meant to imply—" she said, before he stopped her in midsentence.

"Imply, hell," he thundered. "You've as much as come right out and called me worthless and no-account. You're so certain I'm a drunk that you'll hardly allow me any medicine to ease the pain in my damn foot."

"Mr. McCoy," she said, "there's no call to get unpleasant."

"Leon," he roared. "The least you can do is remember my name."

"Really," came a high-pitched, indignant voice next to them.

They turned to see two older ladies standing beside them. Obviously, they'd been listening in on the conversation. Marjorie swung her legs down and planted her feet firmly on the porch.

"We're newlyweds," Leon explained. "You think this is loud, you ought to hear what goes on during the making up."

Marjorie wanted to hide her face in her hands. What in the world had gotten into him?

"Well, I never," said one of the outraged ladies.

"I don't doubt that," Leon responded.

This situation was becoming impossible, but Marjorie could think of no way to smooth things over. She watched the two women whirl around, march back the length of the porch, and disappear into the hotel.

"Whatever possessed you to say that?" she asked.

"Loosen up a little," he recommended, clasping his hands behind his head and stretching his legs out. "If you're not careful, you'll end up like those old biddies."

Since he was closer to the truth than she cared to admit, she decided just to ignore him and think about her homestead. She wondered whether it would be better to have her garden near the creek in case of a dry spell or up near the cabin where she might be better able to keep the rabbits and the deer out.

They rocked back and forth, listening to the frogs' evening chorus and swatting at the occasional mosquito as it buzzed by.

"So where's your family?" he asked.

"In Hope Springs," she said simply.

"Your ma and pa, too?"

"No, my mother passed on seven years ago." It was surprising how easy that was to say. "Like you, I'm uncertain as to the present whereabouts of my father."

"He's a wandering man." Leon said this as if now he understood what was going on.

"He's a dreamer," she corrected him, a dreamer being a step above wanderer in her mind. "He was always certain that the next big adventure was going to make us all rich."

"Maybe it will."

"It might," she said, "but I'll have no way of knowing. I've not seen him in nearly eight years. The news of the gold rush in the Black Hills has no doubt drawn him to the Dakotas. However, I've no intention of searching for him, and we've moved so often, I doubt he'd ever be able to find me."

"Any brothers and sisters?" he asked.

The pain was so sharp and quick that he might as well have stabbed her. She tightened her chest against the sudden ache and let out a long breath before answering.

"I had a younger sister, Kathleen. She succumbed to childbirth fever three years ago." Had it already been three years since that horrifying experience? Where did the time go? "She left Maggie and Mary Beth for us to raise. You remember the three little girls playing in the hotel lobby in Hope Springs?"

He nodded yes.

"The oldest one is Ruby's Emma, and the younger two are my sister's daughters. I dread the day Hank decides it's time to move on. Difficult as it will be to see the rest of them go, I don't believe I could bear parting with Maggie and Mary Beth. I'll have to insist they remain with me." In answer to the unspoken question of where their father was in all this, she added, "Kathleen was married to a wanderer."

"Not all men are as careless of their commitments," Leon said plainly.

"Perhaps not," she said. "But I grew up watching my mother stare out the window, praying that today would be the day he'd come riding up the road. I watched my sister Kathleen examine every passing stranger in hopes that this one would be her husband. I want something more solid than that." Now was as good a time as any to make things clear to him.

"It's not that I don't find you appealing," she said earnestly. "You are a very charming man. But should I give in to your charms, sooner or later you would be on your merry way, and I would be left with little more than jagged edges on my heart." She stopped, deciding this needed more explanation. "Every time you lose someone you love, it pulls your heart apart and leaves these jagged edges. When you try to put it back together, nothing fits right anymore, and it hurts too much to keep trying."

"I imagine you're right about that," he admitted.

"I do appreciate your traveling all this way to sign my land papers. I intend to pay you the $125 that I promised. As soon as we return to Hope Springs, you can take that and be on your way."

"I don't mind helping you get settled in, Marjorie. I haven't seen my partner in better than three years. I guess another few months won't make all that much difference."

"I truly think it would be better if you left. Hank and Ruby's boys will help get me situated. As much as I hate to admit it, I find myself growing rather fond of you, and I fear the consequences of that." She stopped herself. There was that grin playing at the corners of his bushy mustache. That man had the most disarming way about him.

"Furthermore," she continued, "I think it might be best if we arranged for separate rooms tonight." She swatted at a mosquito that had attached itself to the back of her hand.

"Separate rooms?" he asked, raising his eyebrows as if to be certain he'd heard correctly.

"That thought has crossed my mind," she said, smashing another mosquito.

"Well, cross it off," he said. "If that rat-eyed land clerk ever finds out we are not living together as man and wife, he'll tear those papers up and throw 'em to the wind."

"I suppose you're right," she said, resigning herself to the situation. "I imagine I could sleep in a chair for one night."

Leon didn't seem to be troubled by the mosquitoes, but she was slapping at them left and right. As much as she dreaded it, she feared it was time to retire for the evening.

"Maybe we'd best go in," he suggested, and she nodded in agreement.

On the way through the lobby, they stopped at the front desk. Sure enough, the photographer had left a package for them.

Dreading the thought of sleeping slumped over in a chair, Marjorie explained to the desk clerk that due to his injured foot, her husband had difficulty sleeping. Would the clerk kindly set up a cot in their room. He agreed to see that it was done and didn't mention anything about how much it would cost. Marjorie didn't ask, but whatever it was, it'd be worth it.

"What was that all about?" Leon asked as they walked down the hallway.

"You needn't worry. I'll sleep on the cot," she reassured him.

"As I recall, we slept in the same bed last night, and neither of us objected."

"The situation has changed." Surely, he understood. Last night, she was exhausted, and he was passed out cold. Not only were they wide-awake tonight, they'd spent a pleasant day together. Another kiss like that one on the boardwalk this morning, and her virtue was done for.

Back in their room, they unwrapped the package. Just as they'd requested, the photographer had printed up a larger portrait for her and a smaller one for him. He had done a fine job and had even caught that devil-may-care look of Leon's.

They were still admiring themselves when two boys about twelve or so came struggling in with a fold-out cot. They managed to bump into everything in the room at least once before they finally got it set up. Then they'd forgotten to bring a blanket and had to go back for that and then back again for a pitcher of hot water.

Their fumbling this way and that gave Marjorie time to plan how to go about getting ready for bed with a modicum of decency. When the boys had left for the last time, she pulled the book out of her valise and sat down on the edge of the cot. Leon sat on the bed facing her.

"What have you got there?" he asked.

"*The Last of the Mohicans.* I thought it might pass the time."

"I could think of other things we could do to pass the time," he suggested. She didn't have to look up to know he was winking.

"I'm sure that you could. However, this is the only activity I am willing to participate in."

He reached over and caressed the top of her hand. She picked his hand up and placed it back on the bed.

"Mr. McCoy," she began.

"Leon," he corrected her.

"Leon," she said. "Unless you prefer to remain in this room all alone, I suggest you keep your hands to yourself."

"As you wish, but you're missing out on a good time."

"Did our talk on the porch mean nothing to you?" She'd had schoolboys who'd caught on quicker than this grown man.

"Some honeymoon this turned out to be," he grumbled as if to himself, but loud enough for her to hear.

"What is the matter with you? Are you deranged?" she asked. She could feel her forehead pucker up as she tried to puzzle out his persistence in the face of her continued refusals. "We're not on our honeymoon."

"Unless I'm mistaken," Leon said, "we were married yesterday morning. That means we're newlyweds, and this is our honeymoon journey. And if I recall correctly, just this morning you promised to do anything I wanted." He certainly had a self-satisfied air about him. "I never mentioned a thing about wanting to read a book tonight."

"Oh fine," she said, standing up and slapping her hands down to her sides. "Far be it from me to insist that you behave like a gentleman. Go ahead. Do it." She closed her eyes and held her breath.

"Do what?" he asked.

"The consummation of the marriage," she said. "Go ahead. Do it."

"I appreciate your eagerness here, but I don't have the slightest idea of how to go about doing 'it' standing up," he admitted, "especially with you stiff as a fence post."

"I thought you'd been around," she said, disgusted.

"I have, some," he admitted. "But I've never done it standing up before. Would you mind lying down this first time? Later on I'd be willing to give it a go standing up."

"Oh," she said, frustrated beyond belief. "How did I ever get myself into this mess?"

Their attention was drawn to the sound of someone pounding on the wall behind Leon.

"Would you two pipe down in there?" a voice shouted from the next room. "I'm trying to get some sleep. I don't care if you do 'it' hanging from your heels, just shut up about it."

Marjorie was mortified. How much humiliation could one woman endure?

"Now see what you've done," she hissed at him.

"Me?" He had the nerve to act astounded.

"If you hadn't—" she started to say.

"You're the one who—" he responded.

"If you two don't shut up," the voice from the next room shouted, "I'm going to start shooting through this wall, and I don't care who I hit."

"Rein yourself in, cowboy," Marjorie advised in her best settle-down-in-the-back-row teacher's voice. "I'm leaving." Under her breath, she added, "While I still have a shred of dignity left."

She whispered to Leon she'd be back directly, and she hoped that by then he'd be settled down enough that she could read for a while.

By the time she was back from her trip to the necessary, Leon was in bed with the blanket pulled up to the middle of his bare chest. The sight of him had the same flushing effect on her as it had had last night. She turned her eyes away and cautioned herself to avoid looking at him.

"*The Last of the Mohicans* by James Fenimore Cooper," she said as she sat down on the edge of the cot and opened up her book. "It's a story about a man of adventure, a man much like yourself, I imagine."

"Sounds all right by me. There's only one thing I like more than listening to a good story," Leon said with a broad wink in her direction.

"Oh, for heaven sakes," said Marjorie. The man was positively exasperating. She opened the book, and began, "Mine ear is open, and my heart prepared: The worst is worldly loss though canst unfold: Say is my kingdom lost?" She looked over at Leon, who appeared bewildered. "That was written by Shakespeare," she explained.

"I thought you said the book was written by a James Cooper?"

"It was, but he uses passages from Shakespeare to introduce each chapter."

"I see."

She began to read, "It was a feature peculiar to the colonial wars of North America, that the toils and dangers of the wilderness were to be encountered before the adverse hosts could meet."

She peered over the book and saw that Leon's eyelids were drifting down. By the second page, he was making little snoring sounds with every breath. Marjorie shut the book. She'd been planning to read this to her class in the fall, but if they didn't pay more attention than Leon, why bother?

She looked with envy at the bed he was sprawled across.

Soreness was always worse on the second day. The thought of stretching out on that mattress held a great deal more appeal than sleeping on this canvas cot.

But that was not to be. She walked over to the lamp and lowered the wick until the flame was extinguished. She wondered if there was a name for this brief moment when the light was out but the room was not yet dark. Whatever the word was, she could probably apply it to herself as well. She was both excited and reluctant at the same time, like when you're ready to jump but know you better not. She didn't know how much was due to the tasks facing her as a homesteader and how much was due to the in-between place she was at with Leon.

The sensible course of action would be to stay as far away from him as possible. The danger in what she felt was clear. When their eyes held each other's this morning at the doctor's office, there was a sense of belonging, of understanding that had no rational basis. If he had asked at that moment, she would've followed him to the edge of the earth or waited for him until the end of time.

Where did men get that power over women? What could she do to protect herself from it?

Nothing came to mind.

As she undressed and put on her gray-flannel nightgown, she wondered what it would be like if he was watching. Would she have that same power over him?

After washing her face and hands, she laid her head on the pillow, pulled the blanket up, and squirmed around until she got comfortable on the cot. She listened carefully to his breathing and tried to match hers to his steady, slow rhythm. She quietly mouthed her evening prayer and realized that from now on Leon's name would remain on her blessing list. It was a comforting thought.

She soon drifted off to that place between awake and asleep, where images float by like clouds on a summer sky.

"Margie," she heard him say in the quiet darkness. "I'm a

man of my word. I promised to love, honor, and cherish you, and I'll do that."

"Thank you, Leon," she murmured back.

"And if I ever tell you I'll be staying around," he said, and Marjorie held her breath, hoping this wasn't just a dream yet praying it was, "you can count on that, too."

The word that hung in the air was "if."

5

*L*eon woke with a start. *Someone was kicking in the door.* He
pulled out his gun and pointed it in the direction of the doorway. Though the room was close to pitch-black, as far as he
could tell, the door was still shut. The man must have closed
it behind himself, as Leon could hear him thrashing about on
the floor.

"Whoever you are, stand up and keep your hands where I
can see them," he ordered. It didn't make much difference
where the fellow put his hands, Leon wouldn't be able to see
them anyhow. The room was dark enough to slow down a bat.

"Leon, it's me," came the muffled response.

That woman was a mess. Who knew from one moment to
the next what she'd be up to? "What in the hell are you doing
on the floor?" he asked.

"I think the cot collapsed," she said, sounding as if she
couldn't quite believe it herself.

"Well, get up here," he said wearily.

"I don't think that would be such a good idea."

"As much as I'd love to kiss the starch out of you, woman,
I doubt I have the strength or the stamina to do it," he said. "I

haven't had a good night's sleep since I can't remember when. Trust me, you're safe tonight, darlin'."

"My mama always said never trust a man who said 'trust me.' "

Despite her reluctant talk, Leon could hear her making her way to the bed. He put his pistol back in its holster.

"Your mama was probably right, but climb on in here anyway." He held up the covers and slid over to give her room. She lay down on the far side, taking care not to touch him.

"I won't bite, you know," he said, letting the covers settle over them.

"Biting is not what I'm worried about."

He was wide-awake now and realized they would just lie here all night staring at the ceiling unless somebody did something. He had a fair idea of what a woman wanted in bed, but he was a little hazy on the details of seduction. The women he'd been with hadn't needed all that much enticing. If the truth be known, most of them had seen him for the sucker he was and seduced him. Except for Charlotte, of course. She'd seen him for a sucker, but there'd been damn little seduction involved.

If only Marjorie would let him show her how fine it could be between a man and a woman. He dimly remembered one of his stepmothers trying to get him to eat rutabagas by saying, "How do you know you don't like it until you try it?" He couldn't remember whether he ate the rutabagas or not, but he doubted that this approach would work on his wife.

His wife. Now that had an unusual ring to it. But then she was an unusual woman. He'd never met a lady quite like Marjorie before. Though he didn't go along with how she'd tricked him with this marriage business, he had to admit she had more sand than a lot of men he'd run across.

No doubt about it, spending the night loving Marjorie would be something to remember. He couldn't begin to imagine what a lifetime with her would be like.

This last thought hit him like a boot to the gut. He knew

what it would be like all right, a lifetime of plowing and planting and listening to her complain about how he never did enough. He couldn't spend his life like that, and she'd made it clear she wasn't about to settle for anything less.

She probably had a point about passing up on the loving. They were missing a good time, but in the long run, it might be best. One of his shortcomings was living for today and forgetting about what lay ahead. But it sure was a shame to be so worried about next year that you missed out on tonight.

Well, who's to say he was missing out tonight? He was stretched out next to a good woman in a soft, warm bed. There were plenty of times he'd have thanked his lucky stars to be in this very situation.

He reached over, found her arm, and ran his hand down until it met hers.

"Leon," she warned.

"Just wanted to hold your hand in case you fell out of bed again, darlin'."

She started laughing, and, for no reason at all, he laughed along with her. When they settled down, she moved in closer. They lay side by side, holding hands and staring up into the darkness.

"Sweet dreams, Leon," she finally said.

"Same to you, Margie."

The next thing he knew, the room was lighting up with the dawn. It didn't take him long to figure out where he was and who he was holding. Silky hair fanned out around his face and filled his lungs with the scent of lilac water. Marjorie was nestled in his arms, sweet as you please. He felt his body come to life, especially the part that was snuggled in next to her rear end.

Now what to do? He hated to let an opportunity like this pass by. On the other hand, he was fairly certain that once she was fully awake, the cuddling would come to a screeching halt.

For now, he began gently stroking her from her neck to her

knees with his left hand. He nuzzled his face through her hair and kissed the back of her head, all the while staying alert for any changes in her breathing. Though it was downright peculiar to be loving on a sound-asleep woman, if he could sort of ease her into it, maybe she would wake up in an affectionate mood and nature would take its course.

Knowing how opposed Marjorie was to having relations, Leon felt a bit guilty going about it this way. But she was the one who tricked him into marriage. Why should he feel bad about tricking her into enjoying what few pleasures marriage had to offer?

She let out a sigh and arched back into him. Amazed by his good fortune, Leon continued the soft stroking. While he was considering what to do next, he detected a change in her breathing. It'd stopped.

"What in the world?" She scrambled off the bed. "Just what were you attempting to do?"

She was a sight all right, standing there in her nightie, hands on her hips, fire in her eyes.

"Well, that ought to be clear enough," he answered. "I'm trying to get a honeymoon going. We are newlyweds, as I recall."

"Then recall the part about you keeping your hands to yourself."

Lord, she looked gorgeous, her hair all tumbled down, her cheeks flushed, and her eyes aglow. Leon didn't believe he'd ever wanted a woman more than he wanted her at this moment.

"Sit down here," he said, patting a spot next to him on the bed as he tried to calm himself and her at the same time. "We'll talk about it." Her hair did come to her waist. He'd thought so.

"We can talk about it from right here," she said, her voice rising on the last word. She folded her arms firmly in front of her.

"All right," he said. "Look me in the eye and tell me that you were not enjoying that."

"That part was fine," she said. "It's what comes afterward that'll be less enjoyable."

"No need to worry," he assured her. "Believe me, it only gets better."

"For you, maybe," she said, clearly not buying his reassurances. She reached back and began to twist her hair in a knot. This made her bosoms stand out and his mind turn to mush.

"No fooling," he said, sitting up with his feet over the edge of the bed, "if you liked what we were just doing, you're going to love what comes next." He reached for her, but she backed away.

"Am I going to love what comes in nine months?"

"I've got that all figured out," he assured her.

"Really," she said, clearly not convinced. She quickly stepped forward, reached down beside him, and snatched her hairpins off the pillow.

"Really," he said, trying to reassure her. "As long as I am careful not to, ah, hmm, how could I say this without shocking you?"

"I believe it's a little late to worry about shocking me." As hard as she was jabbing those hairpins in, it was a wonder she didn't poke them right through her scalp.

"Well, ah, you see, ah . . ." he stammered.

"Spit it out. You sound like a schoolboy with a sorry excuse for some misbehavior."

"As long as I don't finish up inside of you," he said, hoping he sounded convincing, "you'll be safe."

Marjorie was quiet for a moment. Leon's hopes rose.

"I can only imagine the number of women you've fooled with that tawdry promise."

The morning went downhill from there. She made him turn around while she dressed. Then she tucked both photographs in her book, packed up her valise, and marched out the door. Before slamming it shut, she told him she would meet him in the dining room, on the stagecoach, or in hell, she didn't care which.

Breakfast was a quiet affair. As they waited to board the stage, she expressed hope that there would be no more unpleasantness between them.

Leon apologized for his behavior. They agreed that it would be best if he left as soon as his foot was healed up enough to ride. With the stitches to hold the wound closed, he should be able to get his boot back on before long. Of course, it depended on when his horse recovered as well, but that shouldn't be more than a few days.

The stage ride back to Hope Springs was uneventful. They shared the coach with a bank teller, who talked of the mining operations in the territory. Though the gold rush of '59 had long since petered out, there was still some prospecting going on. However, the remaining gold was held captive in the rocks, and few had the equipment and resources to extract it.

Marjorie related how she had moved from Ohio to Hope Springs a year ago with her uncle Hank and aunt Ruby. They'd purchased the boardinghouse, the livery, and the blacksmith shop for $425. It was the only offer the man had. He'd thrown in the furniture and all the tools and equipment for another $75.

There were people ranching and farming all around Hope Springs, but without the gold mining it would never be the bustling town it once was.

The bank teller described a dreadful experience he'd had in which the coach hit a boulder and tipped over on its side. The driver was thrown off, and the horses dragged the stage for a considerable distance before the deadweight of it finally brought them to a halt. Amazingly, everything and everyone was more or less intact. The bank teller allowed as how one trip like that was enough to last a man a lifetime. Leon agreed.

Marjorie said she remembered her uncle Hank working all night to repair that coach. It was a small world.

From time to time, one of them would roll up the leather

side curtains to see out. But the dust boiled up from the wheels and the horses' hooves and made it hard to breathe. It got in their eyes, sifted down through their clothes, and worked its way into the food that Marjorie had asked the dining-room waitress to pack for them.

At noontime, they gamely ate the gritty biscuits and cheese. They shared with the driver and the bank teller since the men who operated the halfway station had neglected to fix any food. Remembering the burnt corn bread, Leon did not count this as any great loss. They didn't offer to share their liquor this time, and he didn't ask. His foot wasn't feeling all that bad today, and there was no doubt in his mind that Marjorie would not take kindly to his drinking. No sense in riling his new bride unnecessarily.

The bank teller left them at a town called Buffalo Creek. As they had the coach to themselves for the rest of the way, they were able to get a few things straightened out. Marjorie said she was pleased to see he'd given up drinking. He decided there was no point in telling her that this was only a temporary situation.

Though he'd like to at least ride out and see this 160 acres she was so set on, he agreed that it'd probably work out best if he stayed in Hope Springs until he was able to travel. He declined the $125, telling her to use the money to hire a hand to help her with the work of planting and building. Both denied having any interest at all in the possibility of remarriage. However, should circumstances change, they could always say they were widowed and neither would refute the claim. As far as they were both concerned, obtaining a divorce would be a complicated and unnecessary procedure. They joked about how she would soon be referring to him as her dear, departed husband—not dead, just departed.

He regretted that Marjorie was so firm in her refusal to enjoy loving with him. But he had to respect her decision on that.

By late afternoon, Marjorie was regularly peering around

the edge of the leather curtains, looking for familiar landmarks. Leon was getting a little anxious himself for this trip to come to an end. At least they'd not been bothered by road agents or broken axles or any of the countless difficulties that might've slowed them down.

It was early evening before they finally pulled into Hope Springs. When the stage came to a halt, Marjorie piled out first, dragging her valise with her. She set it down, then turned to give him a helping hand. He tried not to put weight on his injured foot, but it was darn near impossible to get out of a stagecoach on one foot and a crutch.

As they were crossing the street to Ruby's Hotel and Boardinghouse, a man wearing a U.S. Deputy Marshal's badge planted himself in front of them.

"Good afternoon," the deputy said, touching the brim of his hat. "Are you Leon McCoy?"

"In the flesh," Leon answered. "What can I do for you?"

"Did you leave a bay stallion over at the livery?" the deputy asked.

"I did," Leon answered, wondering if something had happened to Ulysses. It sounded like he might've been stolen.

"Did you get in a fight with Jake Jarveson three days ago?" he asked.

"I wouldn't call it a fight," said Leon, "but we had words."

What was this all about? Surely they weren't calling in the law to solve each little disagreement folks had. "Listen, if we're going to go over everything that's happened to me the last three days, we're going to have to find a place to sit. There's a lot to cover, and I've got a bum wheel here." He stretched out his foot and nodded toward it.

"You're under arrest," said the deputy marshal.

"What for?" Over the years, he'd been involved in any number of adventures that might've drawn the attention of the law, but he couldn't recall anything he'd done lately that would be of concern.

"For the murder of Jake Jarveson," the lawman announced.

Leon was floored. He hadn't so much as touched the man. It wasn't hard to imagine that someone had been pissed off enough to murder the swaggering son of a bitch, but it wasn't him. Before he had a chance to point that out, Marjorie jumped in.

"Leon didn't murder Jake," she insisted. "He's not capable of murdering anyone. Why, I'm surprised he could find his own socks all by himself."

Now that was a disturbing statement. Did she really have that low an opinion of him, or was she just trying to be helpful? He felt like a fool standing here while Marjorie argued that he was too feather-headed to kill a man.

"What's your involvement here, ma'am?" asked the deputy.

"I'm Mrs. Leon McCoy," she said, slipping her hand through the crook in Leon's arm as if the two of them were out on a Sunday stroll. "We were married recently and we've just returned from our honeymoon trip to Denver."

"Well, Mrs. McCoy, the last time anyone saw Jake Jarveson alive, your husband was arguing with him." The deputy said this as if that fact alone settled the situation in his mind.

Before Leon could get his mouth open, Marjorie had jumped in again.

"Oh, for pity sakes, everyone argued with that man," she said. "He was disagreeable to the bone."

"That may be, ma'am, but not everyone threatened to kill him," he said. "According to an old-timer out there, a man who fits your husband's description did propose to do just that." The man was looking at Leon like he was Jesse James.

"Leon," she said, squinting at him as if she'd caught him in a lie. "You never mentioned you threatened to kill Jake."

"Deputy," said Leon, finally able to get a word in edgewise, "Jarveson was about to draw down on me. All I said was if he pulled that gun out, he was a dead man. It would've been a fair fight. I'll admit I had a poor opinion of the man, but I wouldn't kill him over it."

"You're not from around here, are you?" The lawman hooked his thumbs in the low pockets of his leather vest and gave Leon a narrow-eyed stare.

Leon glanced around. A dozen or so people were standing and nodding along with the deputy, as if to say, "Yeah, what are you doing here, anyway?" He hated this feeling of having to justify himself. Hell, everybody in Hope Springs was a newcomer to the place. Why was he suddenly the outsider?

"I was in Abilene, Kansas last fall, when this Jarveson came up to me and said he liked the way I handled horses. He told me he wanted me to come out in the spring and work his rough string. He made me a pretty fair offer, so I said why not. Then, after I rode all the way here, he said he'd sold his spread and for me to keep on riding. Naturally, we had words. I left directly and came straight to town. You can ask the bartender over at the Lucky Lady. He'll vouch for that."

"You can tell all that to the judge," the lawman said. "My job is to arrest likely suspects, not sort out their sorry stories."

"Let's go tell him then," Leon said.

"Can't. The circuit judge won't be through until the end of the week. I'm afraid I'm going to have to lock you up until he gets here."

"Lock him up where?" Marjorie asked. "We don't have a jail in Hope Springs."

"I guess we'll have to head back to Denver then."

"I'd sooner take a whipping than get back on that stage to Denver," Leon said, and he meant it. "Listen, what if I agree to stay here in Hope Springs until the circuit judge comes through. I couldn't go anywhere the next few days, even if I wanted to. Both my horse and me have pulled up lame."

"Well," the deputy said, clearly considering his offer.

"I didn't shoot the man," Leon said. "And I have no desire to spend the rest of my life being trailed by wanted posters, bounty hunters, and U.S. Marshals. I'll be here when the judge comes through. I give you my word on it."

"Well." The deputy looked Leon up and down, then stared

into his eyes in an attempt to judge the truthfulness of what he'd said.

"I'll vouch for his whereabouts," Marjorie said. "We've filed a homestead claim up where Clear Creek comes down out of the canyon."

"Isn't that where that cowboy got himself strung up over corraling some Lazy J steers?" The deputy's eyes narrowed. He looked back at Leon as if something sounded suspicious here.

"That's the place," she said. "The cowboy never got around to proving up and getting a clear title. When that unfortunate incident occurred, it went back to the government. We filed on it, and we've a great deal of work to do before the snow flies. I assure you Leon will be here when the circuit judge comes through."

"Well, I probably should get some sort of bail money just to be on the safe side," said the deputy. The man was going for it, but not by much.

Leon's hopes sank. Unless the man was willing to take eight dollars and fifty cents, he was out of luck.

"How much do you think you'd need?" he asked, not really wanting to hear what the man was going to say.

"Two hundred dollars ought to do it," answered the deputy.

He might as well have said two thousand. Leon quickly figured that even if he sold his saddle and his horse, seventy-five was about the most he could come up with.

"Naturally, we're not carrying our savings with us," said Marjorie. "If you'll kindly join us for a bite of supper, I'll be glad to get it for you."

Leon couldn't believe it. She was willing to risk better than a year's wages that he wouldn't just ride out of town. He wondered what she'd do for a man she thought highly of.

They picked up their parcels from the stage driver and walked across the street to Ruby's place. He and the lawman waited in the dining room while Marjorie went off to see about the money. It was damn awkward having a woman bail him out of trouble, but Leon didn't see as he had any other choice, so he shut up about it.

The deputy kept a close eye on him until she returned with ten twenty-dollar gold pieces. Marjorie insisted upon a receipt, and he wrote one out.

She told them both to go wash up. There was a pot of beans on the back of the stove, and she'd have it dished out in a minute.

As they started in on their beans and biscuits, Leon asked how Jarveson had come to be killed.

"According to what I was told," said the deputy, "right after the noon meal, Jarveson announced he'd sold the Lazy J to Charles Irwin. This caught his hired hands by surprise."

The lawman paused to take another bite of beans and praise the lightness of the biscuits. Leon wished he'd quit dragging this out and just get on with it.

"But in any case," the deputy finally continued, "he paid off the wages he owed in twenty-dollar gold pieces. Irwin was there. He offered to take on any hands that wanted to work for him, then he rode on back to his ranch. He said that as he was riding out, he passed a drifter on a bay stallion." The deputy finished his biscuit before saying, "I figure that's you."

"Probably was," Leon said. He didn't remember seeing Irwin before that morning at the stage, but there were a lot of men milling around that day. They could've crossed paths.

"While the cowboys were rounding up their gear," the lawman continued, "they overheard you and Jake arguing on the porch and they heard you threaten to kill Jake before you rode out. Everyone figured it was all over until they found out you'd made good on your threat."

"And just how was I supposed to kill someone after I'd already left?" asked Leon. "That doesn't even make sense."

"Turns out, four drovers decided not to sign on with Irwin. It took them a while to get gathered up. They left sometime after you did, yet they beat you to town by a ways. Said they were in the Lucky Lady playing poker when you showed up. I figure you doubled back and did him in."

"I didn't double back. My horse pulled up lame. I stopped by a creek to check his hooves, see if maybe he'd picked up a stone. I let him graze while I had a bite to eat, then I walked him into town. You can ask the blacksmith, I left Ulysses with him."

"That may be. But there's an old-timer who stayed behind to keep an eye on the place, and he swore he didn't see anyone else ride in or out that day except a saddle tramp on a bay stallion, looking for a job. He distinctly remembered this drifter threatening to kill Jarveson. Later, when he brought in Jarveson's dinner, he found him slumped over his desk, dead as yesterday." He stopped to butter another biscuit.

Leon wished his appetite was as good as the deputy's, but his mouth was too dry to chew the biscuits, and the beans plopped like mud to the bottom of his belly.

"What makes you so sure I'm the one that killed him?" Leon asked.

"According to the old codger," said the lawman, crumbs falling from the corners of his mouth, "none of the cowhands cared one way or the other about Jarveson. You were the only one who had a beef with the man."

Why was he always at the wrong place at the wrong time?

"I've had set-tos with a lot of men over the years, but I never shot one in the back," Leon informed him. That was a cowardly act as far as he was concerned.

"Wasn't shot," said the deputy, pausing to take another bite of beans. "His throat was cut, ear to ear."

Leon's stomach turned. He didn't know how the deputy could talk about this and keep eating like he was.

He excused himself to go out back to the privy. As he passed by the kitchen window on his return, he overheard Marjorie and her aunt talking about him.

"Marjorie, you've gone and married a murderer." Her aunt

Ruby said this as if she was telling her niece she'd burned the bacon or let the dog in the house.

"Oh, he's no more a murderer than you are. I'm certain this will all be straightened out in no time." Leon appreciated Marjorie's confidence in him.

"But Charles insists that your husband was the man he saw riding past him on the way to Jake's that day," said Ruby.

"Charles Irwin wouldn't know the truth if you served it to him for supper. I'm surprised the deputy would take his word on any matter at all, let alone something as serious as murder," said Marjorie.

"But what about all the others who heard your husband threaten to kill Jake. They say Jake was never seen alive after that."

"Fiddlesticks. You know as well as I do that if every man who threatened to kill somebody actually did it, there'd be nothing but women left in this world."

He could hear the splash of dishwater and the clatter of pots and pans as they talked.

"Nevertheless, if I were you, I'd think twice before I put my life savings on the line for someone I hardly knew. Good grief, didn't you learn your lesson the last time you did that?" scolded her aunt.

"What was I supposed to do? Let that slow-witted deputy haul Leon all the way back to Denver? Who knows what would've happened then," Marjorie said. "Besides, it's not like he's some stranger. For heaven sakes, I'm married to the man, Aunt Ruby. I should think that entails some responsibilities, don't you?"

"But that's every penny you have in the world. What if he up and leaves?"

"He's not going to run out on me," Marjorie assured her.

"Be sensible. You told me yourself the man's a wanderer," reminded her aunt.

"Oh, I realize he won't be staying around, but I doubt he'll leave owing me money. He's not that kind of man. Besides, this will all be settled shortly. Judge Cunningham is a fair man. He'll straighten this misunderstanding out in no time."

It was odd listening to other people talk about him. Or maybe the odd feeling was having someone come to his defense. In his experience, such conversations always had one person heaping the blame on him and another one piling on more of their own.

He wished he had Marjorie's confidence that this would all blow over. Life was generally more complicated than that.

"Where's Janey?" Marjorie asked.

"I don't even want to think about it," he heard Ruby say. "Hank's going to be hotter than a hornet when he finds out she's keeping company with that Clay Egan again," she said.

"Oh, dear. I thought Clay had gone to work in the gold fields."

"He did, but he's back—broke and lonesome."

Leon thought they'd switched subjects mighty quick and decided he'd best get back in. He wasn't all that interested in who was keeping company with Janey, and the deputy would think it strange if he didn't show up pretty soon.

"How does he intend to provide for her? Where's she supposed to live? Does he expect her to throw her blankets down in a bunkhouse or maybe set up housekeeping in a tent pitched in some gold camp?"

As Leon turned to go, he couldn't help overhearing Ruby's last comment and wincing at the thought of how she could be saying the same thing about him.

"That boy doesn't have the sense God gave a goose," Ruby continued. "And if Hank catches him, his goose is going to be cooked."

Leon decided he'd heard more than enough and walked back around into the dining room.

Over applesauce cake, he and the deputy discussed the weather and the herd of wild horses both of them had spotted on their ride to Hope Springs. Then casually, as if the thought just occurred to him, the lawman said he was heading up north to investigate a string of stagecoach robberies, and did Leon, by chance, know anything about this.

Leon assured him that this was the first he'd heard of any stage holdups. It was discouraging knowing that every time a horse was stolen or a butter churn turned up missing, this deputy would come looking for him.

Hank joined them for coffee, and Leon asked him how Ulysses was making out. He said he'd removed his horse-shoes to trim his hooves and decided that leaving them off for a few days might help him heal up faster. The stallion appeared to be coming along fine, and Hank planned on reshoeing him in a day or two. They agreed that rest was probably the best treatment of all.

The deputy didn't seem to care that he'd told the truth about his horse pulling up lame. He just finished his cake, pushed away from the table, and told them he thought he'd mosey on over to the Lucky Lady and see what was going on. He said he planned on leaving early in the morning, so if he didn't see him before he headed out, he'd see him in a few days when the judge made it to town.

Leon shook his hand and told the lawman he could count on that.

After the deputy left, Hank and Leon went over to the livery to check on Ulysses. Leon found it comforting to have at least one creature on this earth who was glad to see him. Though Ulysses still favored his injured leg, he paced around the stall and generally let it be known that he wanted out. His horse never did like being penned up. Leon could sympathize with that.

Hank and Leon returned to the back porch together. Leon wished Hank would stay and shoot the breeze for a while, but the man was clearly uneasy around him, saying few words and acting anxious to get back inside. Leon didn't know whether it was the marriage or the murder business.

He wanted to tell him he didn't hold a grudge against him over his part in the wedding. It seemed that Hank had been as much of an innocent bystander as Leon himself was in that situation. If it was the murder that had him on edge, he'd like a chance to reassure him that he had nothing to do with that.

"I'll leave you alone with your thoughts," Hank said, heading inside without looking at him.

Leon limped over and sat down in the porch swing. He gazed out into the gathering darkness and wondered how in the hell he'd gotten himself into this mess—married to a woman who didn't want him and accused of murdering a man he'd barely met.

"Thought I'd find you here." He looked up to see Marjorie's shadowy form coming in his direction. She set an enameled basin full of water on the floor, then pulled up a rocking chair and sat down. "Put your foot here in my lap."

"I can do this," he said. "You rest a spell."

"It's no trouble," she said, reaching for his foot. He tried to recall the last woman who'd cared for him. No one came to mind.

She unwound the bandages and eased his foot in the basin of warm water.

"Feels good," he said. "Thank you."

"My pleasure."

She picked up the pile of bandages, walked back into the house, then returned with clean strips of sheeting and a small pan.

"I made up another poultice for you," she said.

"You are too good to me, woman."

"I know that."

"A man could get used to this."

"A man better just appreciate this while it lasts," she advised.

So he did. It didn't sound like it was going to last all that long. He leaned back, stretched out, and closed his eyes. The warm water sure felt good on his foot.

After a time, he thought he heard her murmur, "Wish I were, wish I might, have the wish I wish tonight."

"What did you say?" he asked, looking over toward her.

"I'm wishing on my lucky stars."

He imagined she was dreaming of a snug little cabin with smoke curling out of the chimney. Too bad she wasn't dreaming of him.

"Now you make a wish," she said.

"All right," he agreed, but he didn't know what to wish for. He hadn't made wishes since he was a kid. For all the good it'd done him then, he might as well have been practicing his whistling.

"You're riding your horse and the wind is blowing in your hair and just over the next hill is a grand adventure, right?" she said.

"You're not even close, darlin'," Leon said, closing his eyes.

They had things they needed to discuss. He wasn't sure how to go about it, but he didn't think making wishes was going to do it.

"I've always liked sleeping out under the stars," Leon said after a while. "I feel safer here than I do inside."

"Must have given your mama fits."

"I doubt it," he said, surprised to find the bitter feelings rising in him. He thought he'd left that behind a long time ago.

"Sorry," she said. "I wasn't thinking."

"Marjorie," he said, deciding it was best to just spit it out, "I'm serious about not leaving you with a baby. I know what it's like to grow up unwanted. I wouldn't wish that on any kid."

"Leon, I know children can be troublesome, but I'm sure your mama wanted you."

A soft breeze carried the laughter and squeals of youngsters playing chase. Piano music drifted over from the Lucky Lady, and a dog barked in the distance. The sounds of a small town settling in for the night surrounded them. It seemed a shame to waste a lovely evening like this on depressing topics, so he switched the subject.

"I just wanted you to know that you don't have to worry about me pressuring you none, Margie."

"I appreciate that."

"I'm not saying that if you gave me the go-ahead, I'd hold back," he said.

"I don't believe you need worry about that," she reassured him.

"But as long as you hold the line, I'll behave like a gentleman."

"That's comforting to know."

"Far be it from Leon McCoy to pressure a woman into something she didn't want."

"I'm glad we understand each other on that."

"Of course, if you were to change your mind," he continued.

"You'd be the first one I'd tell," she assured him.

"A wink is as good as a nudge to a blind man."

"Leon, you don't need to concern yourself with me either nudging or winking at you. I'm a grown woman, not some giddy girl. I know my own mind." She was beginning to sound testy.

"It's just that, well, you know, with only the two of us out there and all, you might be worried that, well, that I'd get a notion to, ah, well, you know what I mean."

"What are you talking about?" She sounded genuinely puzzled.

"About it being just the two of us living out there alone in a cabin," he said.

"The two of us aren't going to live out all alone in any cabin," she told him firmly.

"You heard yourself that I can't leave until the judge gets here. Were you expecting me to sleep with my horse?" Surely she'd figured out by now that he had to have someplace to stay.

"No," she said. "I expect that you will stay here at the hotel."

"Living in a hotel is costly, and even with my bum wheel here, I could lend you a hand getting set up."

"I don't think that's a good idea." She shook her head and looked away.

"Why not?"

"Don't you listen to anything I say?" she asked.

"Course I do."

"Then you tell me why I don't want you living out there with me," she demanded.

"Near as I can tell, you're worried that you'll give in to my charming ways and end up with a baby, and I'm telling you—" He stopped talking as the sound of Hank and Ruby arguing caught their attention.

They both turned in the direction of the house when Ruby let out a "No," loud enough to raise the dead. This was followed by a string of muttered curse words from Hank.

They were sure shook up over a fellow calling on their daughter. Maybe most folks were like that.

"My, I wonder what that was all about?" Marjorie said finally.

He shrugged his shoulders. He made it a point to stay out of other people's business. Hank and Ruby lowered their voices, and their murmured conversation blended in with the rest of the evening sounds.

Marjorie picked up his foot, dried it off, packed on the poultice, and began wrapping the bandage strips around it. Even though it felt peculiar having her fool around with his foot, it was sort of a letdown when she was finished.

"There," she said, placing his foot on the porch. She picked up the basin, stood up, and slung the water out in the yard.

As she turned to go, he grabbed onto her arm. "Sit down," he said, then added, "please."

Still clutching the basin, she sat next to him, stiff as a preacher's wife in church.

"Now there's no reason for me not to give you a helping

hand out there," he said. "I told you I'd behave myself, and I meant it."

"Leon, I just think it's best if you stay here, that's all." She reached in her pocket and pulled out a key with a string and a piece of pasteboard tied to it. "You have room number three at the top of the stairs. With everyone out on the roundup, this is a slow time. If you weren't sleeping there, the room would just sit empty."

She stood up. "I've got a lot to do tomorrow. I'd best turn in."

She left him sitting in the swing, wondering where he'd gone wrong. He'd been married three days now and all he had to show for it was a public kiss.

Then there was this Jarveson's murder to consider. He'd best go on over to the Lucky Lady and see if anyone there knew anything about it. He hated to be seen crippling around town, but it beat sitting here talking to himself.

Except for the bartender, the saloon was empty. Without asking, Rooster sat a bottle of whiskey and a glass of water on the bar next to him. "How're things going?" he asked.

"Oh, I'm all right. The world's all wrong," said Leon. That about summed it up for him. He took a sip of whiskey and chased it with a drink of water.

"How's married life treating you, son?" asked Rooster.

"It's not what I always thought it'd be, I'll tell you that." He took another double drink. "How long have you known my wife?" Maybe Rooster could give him an idea on where to go from here.

"Let's see." Rooster drew his lips together and looked up at the ceiling. "They moved here a year or so ago."

"Has she always been like this?"

"Like what?"

How could he describe a gal who tricked a man into marrying her, then wouldn't hardly give him the time of day? What was the word for a woman who had her heart set on homesteading, an undertaking well-known for breaking down strong men?

"Crazy," was what he finally settled on.

"Oh, I don't think Miss Marjorie's crazy," Rooster said. "She does a good job of teaching the little ones, and she's always trying to get a church going."

"Didn't you think it was a mite odd how she got married the way she did?" Leon asked.

"Now that you mention it, that did seem unusual. But love has a way of causing a woman to do unusual things. You're a lucky man, Mr. McCoy." Rooster raised an empty glass in a salute to love or perhaps to luck. Leon wasn't in the mood to celebrate either one.

"You wouldn't believe the troubles I've had lately," Leon said, taking his hat off and running his hand through his hair. "You got any suggestions on how to deal with a skittish woman?"

"How do you deal with a skittish horse?" Rooster asked.

"You take it nice and easy and pretend like you don't mean a thing."

"And then what?"

"Once they calm down, you throw a loop around their neck." The light was starting to come on for Leon.

"I couldn't say for sure, but I suspect the same approach would work with a woman," Rooster said. "Except you already got your loop around her neck, so now you got to just go about your business until she calms down."

Seemed reasonable enough to Leon. He took another double drink. He wasn't certain he wanted to stay, but he sure as hell didn't want to get run off.

"What's this I hear about you killing Jake Jarveson?" Rooster asked, real casual-like.

"Wasn't me," Leon said, leaving no room for misunderstanding. "Not that I have any love lost for the son of a bitch, but I didn't kill him. Heard any talk about who might have?"

"There's some speculation that his wife paid a couple of hired guns to do him in."

"Why in the world would she do that? Seems like it'd be a sight easier just to poison the man's coffee."

"Because she ain't serving him his coffee these days, that's why. She and Jake had a falling-out, and she went home to her family back East right before winter set in." Rooster gave the bar a couple of passes with a wet rag, then looked around and lowered his voice like he was letting Leon in on some inside information. "Rumor has it that her daddy bankrolled Jake on that spread. My guess is that he's none too pleased about the way Jarveson treated his baby girl. He might've sent those two gunmen to put Jake in the ground. The old man probably planned on selling the place so the whole thing wouldn't be a total loss. Could be that was why Jake was in such a rush to sell."

"But you'd think gunmen would shoot Jarveson instead of slitting his throat."

"My guess is they did that to throw the law off their trail."

"Well, it worked."

"Of course, that's just one theory," said Rooster, going back to his normal tone of voice. "Based entirely on the known fact that two of Jarveson's hands spent a lot of their free time practicing their quick draw and shooting at targets."

"Anyone notice them ever try anything with Jarveson?" Leon asked.

"No, they were lying low," said Rooster, "waiting for the right moment. Looks like they waited a little too long."

This wasn't as encouraging as it sounded at first. "Lot of men spend their free time fooling with guns," Leon observed.

"Yeah, but most men don't pack around ivory-handled Colt Lightnings and brag about riding the owlhoot trail with John Wesley Hardin." Rooster bobbed his head as if he'd made his point.

Perhaps there was something to Rooster's suspicions after all. He'd check it out. "Any other rumors?" he asked.

"There are those who think Irwin slipped back and killed him himself."

"Why would he do that? Hadn't he just bought Jarveson out? I heard about the bad blood between the two of them, but why would he kill the man just when he was about to leave anyway?" Leon asked. "That doesn't make much sense."

"A lot of this don't make sense. Of course, Jake's sudden urge to sell might be due to his worries over what his father-in-law had in store for him. But Jarveson wasn't the type to scare easy. What really doesn't add up is where'd that money go?" said Rooster. "Jake insisted on being paid in gold. He used some to square up with his hands, but the rest of that gold's gone."

"So maybe Irwin came back and cut his throat for the gold?" Leon wondered out loud.

"Maybe." Rooster wasn't ready to commit himself. "Hard telling. It could have been any one of those boys who knew about the gold. Five thousand dollars in gold would be awful tempting to a man who makes thirty-five dollars a month." He looked up at Leon as if gauging his reaction to what he had to say next. "Or an ol' boy down on his luck."

"I didn't have the faintest idea how or even if he'd been paid. For all I knew he had a bank draft made out to his mama. Do you think I would be hanging around Hope Springs if I had five thousand dollars in my saddlebags?"

"I guess that don't stand to reason. But you were heard cursing at him."

"Of course, I cussed him out. I rode for close to two weeks because he offered me top dollar to come and work his string of horses. I show up and all he has to say for himself is 'Sorry I sold the place.' You'd be swearing, too." Leon was hot just thinking about it. "But I wasn't mad enough to kill him over it."

"Well, you just stick to that story," Rooster advised him.

"It ain't a story, it's the truth." Leon slammed the glass

down on the bar, grabbed his crutch, and stomped out. What did a man have to do to prove his innocence around here?

"Take it easy," Rooster shouted after him. "I didn't mean nothing by it. I believe you might be in over your head here, son. If I were you, I'd hire myself a Pinkerton detective." But Leon was past listening.

His life was going from bad to worse. Most places, even if the rest of the town was spitting on you, you could count on the bartender being sympathetic to your side of things. Here, even the bartender was all but accusing him of murder.

Lying in bed later, he wondered which room his wife was sleeping in. He was in a hell of a fix. Married to a woman who wouldn't have anything to do with him. Accused of murdering a man he hardly knew to talk to. Down to less than ten dollars and owing two hundred. No way to go to work, what with both him and his horse laid up. Even if he was able-bodied, it wasn't likely that anyone in Hope Springs would hire a man they thought killed one of their own. And he'd given his word he wouldn't leave town.

Way into the night, he turned things over and over in his mind. But try as he might, he couldn't figure any way out of his predicaments. He'd just have to hang on for the ride. He comforted himself with the thought that at least things couldn't get much worse.

The place was quiet except for a low, murmured conversation between Hank and Ruby. He couldn't make out the words, but at times it sounded like an argument. Seemed like they were awful worked up over some boy being sweet on their daughter. Surely they knew that sooner or later someone would come courting. He drifted off, and the next thing he knew, Marjorie was calling him down to breakfast.

Over ham and eggs, she explained that she'd changed her mind about him helping her get set up. She refused to say why, just said that she would be loading up a wagon later this morning and that if he was still willing, she'd appreciate his help.

There was just no telling about women. They'd argue with a gopher until it'd finally give up and climb a tree, then they'd stand underneath and beg that poor little feller to come down out of there before he got hurt.

It wasn't until after breakfast, when he was heading over to check on Ulysses, that he understood what was going on. Passing by the open kitchen window, he heard Marjorie's aunt Ruby warn her about him.

"Marjorie, you are putting yourself in danger taking him out there with you. For all we know, that man may well be a murderer."

"And I'd be putting him in danger leaving him here in town. Just this morning I overheard two men talking about how they ought to hang that stranger that killed Jake. What if more folks get to thinking along those lines?"

Leon swallowed hard. He hadn't thought of that possibility. It looked like things could get worse after all.

"They could just as easily ride out and get him," the aunt pointed out.

"But we could see a group riding out and get ready," she said. "Plus, I strongly suspect that once he's out of sight, most people will just go on about their business and leave matters to the law."

Leon made a mental note to refrain from drinking for the time being. Pain or no pain, he'd best keep his wits about him.

"Can you believe it?" Marjorie asked. "A week ago, hardly anyone in town could stand Jake Jarveson. Now all of a sudden they're ready to form a lynch party to avenge his death."

"It's not so much that it's Jake," explained Ruby. "It's that he's one of ours. People naturally want to protect one of their own against an outsider."

Leon had heard all he cared to. He limped over to the blacksmith shop and stood at the edge of the open barn doors. Inside, Hank was at the forge showing his three boys how to heat an iron ring until it just started to change color. Working together, they used tongs to place the glowing iron band over a wooden wagon wheel and dunk the wheel in a trough of water to cool it off. As the steam billowed out around the four of them, admiration and envy flooded Leon. This was what being a man was all about—doing worthwhile work, teaching your sons a trade.

Hank looked over in his direction. "These are my boys," he said to Leon. "Thomas." A boy about fourteen or so nodded. "Samuel." One about a year younger ducked his head. "And Caleb." Caleb put down his tongs, walked over, and extended his right hand.

"Are you Marjorie's new husband?" he asked.

"I am," he answered, shaking hands with him.

Their conversation was interrupted by the screeching of two little girls running past them. The one in front appeared to be a little older and running just fast enough to keep out of the reach of the younger one, who was going for all she was worth.

"That's Emma and Maggie," Caleb explained. "Emma's the one in front."

"I'll get you for this," shrieked Maggie. She stooped, picked up a horse turd, and threw it at Emma, hitting her in the side of the face. Emma stopped and turned.

"Why, you pig-faced demon," she snarled. The chase was on, this time in reverse.

"Now girls, girls," Hank kept repeating, with no effect whatsoever as far as Leon could tell.

Maggie raced up the ladder leading to the hayloft. Emma was about halfway up when Maggie reached the top, turned around, and pushed it over. It arced across the barn, falling with a clatter and capturing Emma underneath.

It all happened so fast, none of them were able to do anything to stop it. Hank reached the ladder first and lifted it off the little girl, who was shrieking at the top of her lungs. The one up in the hayloft was prancing about loudly repeating, "Ha, ha, you can't catch me. I'm too fast for you, I see."

"They're a handful," Hank said to Leon over the noise.

"Margaret Ann," Hank said, "if you know what's good for you, you'll sit down right this instant and not make another sound."

"But Emma called Mary Beth a crybaby," Maggie shouted in her own defense.

"We'll sort that out later," Hank said. "For now, sit down and hush up."

The boys were laughing and carrying on about how little Maggie had gotten the best of Emma, while Hank helped Emma brush the straw and dirt out of her hair and off her clothes. Despite her loud descriptions of various injuries, nothing appeared to be broken or bleeding.

"You better go lie down and get a cold rag on the forehead," Hank said. "Or you're going to end up with a big knot up there. Caleb, will you take her to the house?"

Emma stumbled off with Caleb, holding her forehead and moaning. Hank warned the boys to stop poking fun at the girls; it wasn't helping matters any.

He and Leon swung the ladder back in place and he called up to Maggie, "Come down here, young lady."

Maggie peeked her head out over the edge, then slowly, rung by rung, came down the ladder. She stood in front of Hank, her lower lip quivering.

"Where is Mary Beth?" he asked.

"She's in with Queenie," Maggie answered. "She didn't mean to pee her pants. She just forgot, and Emma started calling her a—"

"We can straighten that out later. Why don't you and Samuel go see if you can find them," he said. Maggie and Samuel took off in search of her little sister.

"Reckon I'll go see how my horse is doing," Leon said in the lull, and headed toward the stalls. He admired the way Hank handled his kids. He wondered if he was just born that way or if someone showed him how.

After checking on Ulysses, he watched Hank and Thomas put the wheel they'd fixed back on a buckboard wagon.

Hank loaded an ax, a crosscut saw, a pick, and a couple of shovels in the wagon, while Thomas hitched up a calico mare and a buckskin gelding. They climbed in the wagon and Thomas drove the team around to the back of the boarding-house. The kid knew his way around those horses, he had to say that much for him.

Feeling about as useless as a four-card flush, Leon sat on the wagon seat and watched Thomas and Hank load up a trunk. Caleb and Samuel followed with a wooden box. Janey came out of the kitchen with a feather bed bunched up in her arms. It was so big that she could hardly see around it to make her way to the wagon. The little girls carried out buckets and brooms. Marjorie stood in the back of a wagon shifting things around as Hank and his sons kept handing boxes and sacks up to her. Ruby came out of the house with a basket that smelled of fried chicken. Her eyes were all red and puffed up. Leon surmised she'd been crying.

Marjorie shifted the gear all around until she had every-thing right where she wanted it. She sent Samuel and Caleb to saddle her mare, Rosinante, and told Thomas that since he'd done such a fine job handling the horses so far, he might just as well stay at the reins.

Then she told the girls to climb in, they were going on a picnic. Emma, Maggie, and Mary Beth scrambled over one another and the various boxes until they found the spots they wanted. Janey hung back until Ruby pushed her forward, telling her she'd deserved a day off and to have a good time. Janey settled herself in the back with the giggling girls.

Ruby turned to Marjorie. "You sure you're ready for this?" she asked.

"Ready as I'll ever be," Marjorie answered. "I've got but-terflies in my stomach, but I've been looking forward to this day for so long, I can hardly believe that it's finally here."

She situated herself between Leon and Thomas on the buckboard seat. Thomas gave the reins a snap, and they were off.

As far as Leon was concerned, it was a good day to start on an adventure. The sun was shining and the robin's-egg blue sky had a few scattered puffy clouds drifting around. He felt as frisky as Marjorie's horse. She was prancing around with the two boys and kicking up her heels, not enough to cause any worry, just enough to make it exciting for the kids.

Driving through town, Leon couldn't help but see all the collapsed porches and caved-in roofs. Things might have been thriving here once, but Hope Springs had fallen on hard times. Most of the buildings were abandoned and falling into disrepair. The glory days were over.

Marjorie must have noticed him looking around, for she said, "Hope Springs might not be thriving like it once was, but it's a solid little community. Unlike gold prospectors, the farmers and ranchers are here to stay."

She'd know better than he would, but the place sure looked run-down to him.

It didn't help any to see all those pinched-up faces glaring at them as they rode through town. He assumed the unfriend-liness was directed at him as folks waved back and forth with the little girls riding in the rear of the wagon.

Emma tried to push Maggie out of the wagon as payback for the ladder incident, but Marjorie put a stop to that in a hurry. Janey started singing "Oh! Susanna!" and they all joined in at the top of their lungs. This was followed by "Old Dan Tucker" and "From Greenland's Icy Mountain," and be-fore long they were turning off the road onto what could barely be called a trail. It ran alongside a sizable creek and soon opened into an open meadow.

The sight of it all took Leon's breath away. A creek gurgled out of a rocky canyon and wandered along the lower edge of a wide grassy meadow. A painter couldn't have come up with a prettier picture.

He looked over and caught Marjorie's dazed expression as she surveyed the scene. It was clear why she had her heart set

on this place. He was going to have a hard time leaving it be
hind himself.

A log cabin and a small shed stood near the upper edge o
the meadow. Both buildings looked like they'd been throw
up at night by a bunch of boys. The west wall of the cabi
tilted out and the shed looked like a good stiff breeze woul
blow it over.

Even the kids weren't impressed by the shacks. "The
seem so small," Janey said, as Thomas pulled the horses to
halt in front of the cabin.

They all got down and crowded in behind Marjorie as sh
stepped inside. To Leon's way of thinking, the large patche
of sunlight on the packed-dirt floor were not a good sign
There was a window covered in oiled cowhide, but most o
the light was streaming in through the holes in the roof an
the walls. An old rusty metal stove sat in one corner with
table and two rickety chairs nearby. On the opposite side wa
a bed frame strung with a saggy rope net.

"It needs some fixing up," Marjorie said, walking aroun
slowly, running her hands over things.

What it needed was a couple of cowboys to rope a corne
and pull this mess over before it fell in on someone.

"And someday I'd like to put a swing out on the fron
porch," she said.

Here it starts, he thought. *Today she wants a swing, tomorrow it'll be a new outhouse, and the day after that she'l
want me to add on another room.*

The idea didn't seem quite as irritating to him as it had in
the past, but still, he was not altogether comfortable with the
situation. He remembered the chores his stepmas used to have
for his pa. The minute he walked through the door, they'd
have a list as long as your leg of things for him to do. No wonder he'd always been in such a sour mood.

The boys unhitched the team and walked the horses down
to the creek. After leaving the saddle and bridle in the shed,
Samuel went off to stake out Rosinante. Even after the ride,

she was acting up so much that Leon advised him to tie her up away from the others.

While Marjorie, Janey, and the little girls swept the cobwebs from the ceiling and the dust from the shelves and the table, Leon checked around the outside of the cabin. Though it appeared in no danger of collapsing, it wasn't worth putting much effort into either. The shed seemed in better shape up close than it had in the distance.

They were finished sweeping in no time. Marjorie sent the girls down to the creek with buckets and instructions to hurry back.

"Seems like kind of a lonely place," Leon said. He was leaning against the cabin letting his eyes follow the line of foothills to the east. She stood an arm's length away.

"I know," she said. "I am so looking forward to the peace and quiet."

"You'll have plenty of quiet out here, that's for sure," he said. "Don't you worry about being a woman out here all alone?" It was concerning him.

"No more than I worry about it anywhere else," she answered. "If there's another Indian uprising, I'll be no safer in Hope Springs than I would be here, and although a few cowboys may pass by, I doubt this part of the country is frequented by outlaws."

"According to the deputy, there's been some stage robberies up north of here," he warned.

"I guess we should be thankful we weren't robbed," she said.

"That would've been the icing on the cake," he agreed.

They stood gazing off in the distance when a V of Canadian geese veered and flew toward them. Their distant honking blended with the laughter of the children down by the creek.

"I want to be right here when I watch those geese fly south for the last time," she said.

Leon wondered where he'd be when that time came.

"Didn't you ever run across a place that just seemed to suit you?" she asked. "Some place that felt like home, like you belonged there and nowhere else?"

"A few," he answered vaguely. But the truth of the matter was, he never had run across a place that held the same appeal for him that this obviously had for her.

"Well, I hadn't," she said. "Not until I got here. I can't imagine why that cowboy who filed on this homestead spent so little time here."

"What exactly happened to him anyway?" Leon asked.

"He and another man were using the canyon to pen up Lazy J strays. Since this little valley sits between the Lazy J and the Circle I, it was easy enough to do. Jarveson's men caught them at it early this spring and hanged them. I was surprised they didn't hang Charles. Undoubtedly, he was the one that put them up to it. But they didn't."

Leon looked around, letting his eyes follow the creek back up into the canyon.

"It's a shame any man who had a chance at this sweet little spread couldn't think of anything better to do with it than cattle rustling," he said. He wasn't much for putting down roots, but this was a place worth being rooted to, if that's what a man wanted to do. Not that he did, of course.

"Don't get your hopes up," she warned.

"You needn't worry. I'm not cut out for the life of a sodbuster." He pulled a weed stalk and stuck it in the corner of his mouth, imitating a farmer. "As far as I'm concerned, a homestead is the government betting you 160 acres that you'll starve to death in five years. Maybe back East a man can make a living on 160 acres, but not out here."

"I'll have my teaching to fall back on," she said as if she had it all figured out.

"I thought they wouldn't hire you to teach once you were married?"

"That's only if they have to board you around. You can hardly ask a family to take in a teacher and her husband as well. However, since I have my own living arrangements, I doubt there'll be any resistance to my continuing to teach."

"I suppose Hank will give you a hand with the heavy work," he said. Somebody was going to have to.

"Hank isn't going to be around," she said.

"They're leaving?" he asked in amazement. "Why would they leave? He's got a going concern here with the livery, the blacksmith shop, and the boardinghouse."

"They're not leaving—he's leaving," she said.

"He's leaving Ruby and the kids?" He found this even harder to believe. Marjorie must be making this up. "Why would Hank walk away from his family?" he asked, bewildered.

"He's heard there are better opportunities in the Dakotas. He hauled her up and down the Ohio Valley in search of opportunities. After the war, he packed us all out to Denver in search of opportunities." Every time she said the word "opportunities" she sounded more and more bitter.

"Unfortunately, a lot of other blacksmiths had the same idea," she continued. "Hank had a difficult time building up a business, so we moved here. He was certain that with the war over, the gold rush would resume in Colorado, and Hope Springs would return to its former glory. But it appears that's never going to happen. The easy gold's gone, and it's too expensive to go after the rest. Hope Springs is the center of a nice little ranching and farming community, but I doubt it'll ever be more than that. That's fine by Ruby, but Hank's not satisfied with what he calls their hand-to-mouth existence. He's heard about the gold rush in the Black Hills and has decided that there are 'opportunities' just waiting for a good blacksmith in the Dakotas."

"So that's what the arguing was about last night," said Leon, starting to make sense of it all.

"She might as well save her breath. That man's already gone. She'd best just resign herself to it."

"But surely he'll send for them once he's found a place?"

Leon couldn't imagine that Hank would just walk out on all of them. If there was ever a man cut out to raise kids, it was Hank Richmond.

"She told him she's not following this time," said Marjorie with a shrug of her shoulders. "Says she doesn't want to raise her children in the midst of a bunch of outlaws."

"I think those newspaper stories are exaggerated, don't you?"

"I've no idea," she said, "and furthermore, no intention of finding out. I've decided to stay right here in Hope Springs, and so has Ruby."

"Hank'll get it out of his system and be back by fall," he assured her.

"If he's still welcome," Marjorie said. The expression on her face said she wasn't certain he would be. "Ruby says she's waited for him all she's going to wait. Any night he's not sleeping next to her, the spot's up for grabs."

Leon found this hard to believe. What got into women anyway?

With a finger to her lips, Marjorie indicated that they should stop talking about this subject as the girls were coming up from the creek. Leon was just as glad. He needed time to get this all straight in his mind.

"I have to use the necessary," came a little voice. They turned to see Mary Beth dancing from one foot to the other.

"Well, I know what our first job is going to be," Leon said, resigning himself to the situation.

"Come on, cuddle-bug," said Marjorie, taking her hand. "We'll go in the woods for now. It'll be an adventure."

Maggie took her other hand and they set off, followed by Janey and Emma. Leon wondered what had happened to the buckets of water they'd been sent after.

Eventually, the boys brought up the water. When Marjorie and Janey returned, they washed what they could in the cabin.

He and the boys unloaded the wagon, while Marjorie and the girls arranged things inside. When everything was more or less the way she wanted it, Marjorie announced it was time for lunch.

Samuel and Thomas carried the picnic basket down to a stand of cottonwood trees near the creek. Janey carried a blanket and spread it out with plates of fried chicken, biscuits, boiled potatoes, and fried apple fritters.

After his second fritter, Leon leaned back against a cottonwood trunk and said, "Ain't this the life."

"Enjoy it while it lasts, Mr. McCoy," Marjorie sternly advised him.

"I intend to," he said as he pulled his hat down over his eyes and crossed his arms in front of his chest.

A peacefulness settled over them. Occasionally, he'd peek out from under his hat and watch the little girls playing house. They used leaves for dishes and sticks for spoons and knives and did a lot of warning one another to use better manners.

Janey was lying on her belly, dropping twigs in the creek and watching them float away in the current, no doubt thinking about her sweetheart back in town.

The boys were off exploring. He was able to track them by their occasional shouts. He looked up once to see them climbing up the rock cliff at the mouth of the canyon. He watched as they disappeared into a cave about halfway up. He'd asked them to keep an eye out for clay. Maybe they thought they'd find some up there. Who knew?

A soft, warm breeze floated down out of the canyon. It was just enough to keep away the bugs and carry the scent of grass, and trees, and sunshine to him.

From under his hat brim, Leon looked over at Marjorie and watched as she let her eyelids drift down for just a moment. She was a wonder all right. He recalled Rooster's advice to treat her like a skittish mare and he'd eventually be able to tame her. Then a thought hit him like a kick in the gut. Who'd be riding her after he was gone? He knew it was a crude way to think about it, but right now she didn't know what it was like. Once he was gone, and she knew what she was missing, how long before someone else would be warming her bed?

He was glad he wasn't in Hank's boots today. It must be tearing him up thinking about Ruby with someone else. Why wouldn't a woman wait a few months while a man figured out which way he wanted to go. Was that asking too damn much?

He was out of the mood for a peaceful nap now. He pushed his hat back and glanced over at Marjorie. He couldn't believe he'd thought she was on the plain side when he first met her. It must have been the dim light, because she was the most beautiful woman he'd ever laid eyes on. Her cheeks were a peach color that no powder could mimic, and her eyes could cast a spell over a man without her even trying. But it was her mouth he couldn't stop staring at now, the way it kept moving around a little, as if she was thinking about what it might be like to kiss him.

A scream startled him out of his thoughts. With his heart hammering in his chest, he scanned the area, expecting to see that one of the children had fallen out of a tree, or been bitten by a rattlesnake or stepped on by a horse.

He followed the screeching to a nearby slough, where Emma and Maggie were shoving each other around in the mud. Mary Beth was standing on the bank, swinging her little arms back and forth, working up the courage to jump in herself. In a few strides, Leon was next to her and grabbed her around the waist just as she was about to leap. Out of the corner of his eye, he saw Marjorie standing next to him.

"Oh no you don't, punkin," he said, as she squirmed in his arms.

"She pushed me first," yelled Emma.

"Did not, you liar," said Maggie, before giving Emma a good shove which knocked her flat in the mud.

Emma grabbed Maggie's ankles and jerked her down.

Leon tried to keep from laughing at the sight of the two of them wrestling away in the red mud. But he couldn't help himself and burst out howling. Marjorie'd been trying to keep a straight face herself, but this set her off. The girls stopped fighting and started giggling.

They laughed until the tears streamed down their faces, until their sides ached, until they struggled to catch a breath. Leon couldn't recall when he'd laughed this hard or this long. Every time the laughter would start to die down, he'd look over at Marjorie and start all over again. In a chain reaction the girls would follow.

Marjorie was bent double, trying to catch her breath, when Leon was struck by an idea. He set Mary Beth down, unbuckled his gun belt, wrapped it up on itself, and set it aside. Then he swooped Marjorie up, and, before she knew what was happening, he swung her over the edge of the bank. She grabbed on to his shirt, and the momentum carried them both into the mud.

Not to be left behind, Mary Beth joined them. The boys raced back from the canyon and plopped themselves down like cowpies. They began wrestling and kicking mud all over the place. Janey was the only one with the presence of mind to stay out of the mess.

Marjorie and Leon rolled over to the side to avoid the flying feet, knees, and elbows. Then it was like that day at the doc's office, when the rest of the world faded away. Leon wrapped his arms around Marjorie and pulled her in next to him. She buried her face in his neck. Floating in that place between dreaming and awake, where you could hear voices but you couldn't make out the meaning, he cradled her for all he was worth. By her soft sighs, he knew she was floating with him. He was dimly aware of the sun-warmed mud oozing around them, and he closed his eyes, thinking that if that lucky star appeared now, he knew what he'd be wishing for.

All of a sudden Marjorie snapped out of her daze. "Good heavens. Let loose of me."

"Then you let loose of me," he suggested.

She pulled her hands away from his neck and pushed

against his chest. "And in front of the children, yet," she hissed. "Are you out of your mind?"

The mud weighed down her skirt and petticoats, and in a valiant effort to get to her feet, she jerked around and accidentally kneed him in the groin. The pain was immediate. His belly tightened in on him, and he feared he was going to lose his lunch. He doubled up and groaned.

"I'm so sorry," she said, falling back in the mud to avoid stepping on him again. "Is there any way I can help?"

"Maybe later," he gasped, trying to catch his breath. If women only knew what that did to a man, they'd be more cautious.

"Wha' happened?" asked Mary Beth. The children had ceased their frolicking and were staring straight at them.

"You didn't hurt him did you, Aunt Marjorie?" asked Maggie.

"No," said Leon, sucking in air like a winded racehorse. "But your aunt Marjorie sure knows how to wrestle."

"Come on children," Marjorie said, careful to stay clear of him this time in her struggle to stand. "Let's go wash off."

Eventually, Leon found the strength to sit up, but that was about all he could do until the misery passed. To keep his mind occupied, he watched Marjorie holding her soggy skirts in her hands as she herded the children over to where the creek ran fast and clear. The water came up to their knees, and they bent over to splash their faces and arms clean. When he was able to join them, he just sat down in the water and dunked his head under in order to get the mud off. They all followed his example.

The slough ran along the edge of the creek, and the water there was warmed by the sun as it wandered its way slowly through the mud. The creek water, however, came rushing straight out of the snowcapped mountains. Their teeth were chattering and their lips were blue when Marjorie ordered them all up to the bank. She and Janey hung the little girls' dresses on tree branches and let them run around in their shimmies in the sunshine. The boys took off their shirts and boots and walked around in their wet pants, leaving Leon and Marjorie the only ones still dressed in sopping wet clothes.

"I really do apologize," she said, wringing the water out of her hair. "I didn't mean to harm you."

"Forget it," he said grimly. "But I don't believe you'll have any more worries about me getting you in the family way." He shook his hair back and forth, sending drops of water flying in every direction.

"If that technique was effective, I'm sure I'd have heard about it by now," she said. "Perhaps it only works when done daily."

He cringed at the thought of it. That woman had an odd sense of humor. "Say, how would you like to spend the afternoon playing in the mud?" he asked, switching subjects.

"I don't think so," she said. "I believe I've had mud enough for one day. But thanks for the suggestion."

"There was a lot of clay down in that slough," he pointed out. "It's just what we need to chink the cracks between the logs." The cabin wasn't worth putting much work into, but this would keep the bugs out until he could build something better.

"That's not a bad idea," she said. "I'll bet the children would love to help."

As it turned out, they did. The boys brought up buckets of wet clay, the girls gathered dried weeds and grass, and Leon used a shovel to mix it all together in one of the wooden crates. Marjorie brought out the tin plates Ruby had given her and each of them scooped up a plateful of the mixture and used their hands to smear it in between the logs. They had a few mishaps and a couple of mud-slinging contests, but by and all, the work progressed smoothly. By late afternoon, they were all covered in mud again as they stood back to survey their efforts. They'd caulked all the cracks, then forced handfuls of dry moss into the damp clay inside the cabin. Leon and the boys had braced up the leaning wall and used strips of birch bark and slabs of sod to patch the holes in the roof. Together, they'd done a good day's work, and they deserved to be proud of themselves.

"Thank you," Marjorie said, looking from one dirty face to the next. "This will keep out the gnats and mosquitoes this summer and the wind and cold this winter." She turned to look into Leon's eyes. He wondered where he would be this winter and would he ever think of her?

"I'm hungry," said Mary Beth, as she left another muddy handprint on Marjorie's skirt. Marjorie pulled her eyes away from Leon and looked down at her.

"We better get cleaned up then," she said, "and have a bite to eat. I'll race you to the creek."

They were off. Due to his limp, Leon came in last. He might've anyway. He was enjoying watching Marjorie run, her skirts flying and her braid loose in the breeze. More than once during the afternoon, he'd caught himself just standing and staring, looking at her laughing with Janey over some foolishness, watching her easy affection with the little girls, noticing how she gently guided the boys' talk. She was a wonder, no doubt about it. A man would have to go a long way to find another educated woman who liked to play in the mud.

The kicker was what would a fine-looking, good-hearted woman like Marjorie want with a man who traveled with the grass?

After washing off a layer of mud, he headed back up to the cabin, where Marjorie and Janey set out bread, cheese, and hard-boiled eggs on the tailgate of the wagon. With appetites whetted by working all afternoon in the sun, the provisions were quickly consumed. There was a good deal of teasing about what would happen as a result of eating the eggs. In an effort to get Caleb and Samuel to stop telling egg-fart jokes, Marjorie threatened to feed the molasses cookies to the horses.

"If we don't get going soon, it will be dark before we get home," said Janey.

"Can we come back tomorrow?" asked Maggie. "Please, please."

"I don't see why not," said Thomas. "As long as we get our chores done first."

"Good, 'cause I'm going to see if I can bring Mr. Jackson's gold pan," said Caleb as he walked with Thomas toward the staked-out horses.

The boys brought all three horses back and put Rosinante in the shed. Leon helped them straighten the harness lines out and hitch the team up to the wagon. The boys jumped up on the seat. Janey and the girls sat in the back on a blanket.

"Take it slow and easy, Thomas," Marjorie called out as they started down the trail.

Leon considered "slow and easy" to be good advice in general. He vowed to rein himself in so as not to scare Marjorie any more than she already was.

After waving good-bye to the children, they stepped back into the cabin, and Marjorie started setting things to right. He sat down carefully in one of the wobbly chairs, hoping it wouldn't fall apart beneath him, and looked around at how the moss chinking, the quilt-covered feather bed, and the beat-up trunk had turned this dismal cabin into a home. Their wedding photograph was propped up on the shelf and looked out over everything like it belonged. It was a comfortable place.

There didn't seem to be much left to do. He wondered why Marjorie couldn't seem to settle down. She was bustling about the room, moving things an inch this way and then an inch the other like she was expecting company and wanted everything just so before they got here.

"I'll bring up some water," she said, grabbing up a bucket. She darn near tripped over the threshold in her rush to get out the door. Maybe she was just excited about finally having a home of her own.

He started a little fire going in the rusty stove and made a pot of coffee. When the coffee was bubbling, and she still wasn't back, he stepped outside to see what could be keeping her. She was sitting on a stump, watching the sunset and shaking her wet hair out in the breeze. Copper-colored curls fell in waves down her back, rippling and flowing like a Mexican bullfighter's cape. He wanted to run his hands through it, bury his face in it, and he wondered what she'd do if he did. Probably run off in the woods. Or, more likely, bean him on the noggin with one of those water buckets.

He put a hand on her shoulder to let her know he was behind her. She didn't even move. They stayed like that, quiet together, watching the last rosy rays of the sunset fade away.

He was definitely going to have to stay outside tonight, he decided. There was no way he could sleep cooped up in that little cabin with her, not as frisky as he was feeling. Maybe he should just lie down in the creek. The cold water might help him keep his urges under control.

No doubt about it, she was some woman. He wanted her like he'd never wanted anything or anyone before. But she'd made it clear what her terms were, and he couldn't see how he could meet them. Even if he had a mind to stay, there was no way in hell a man could make a living on this 160 acres. Farming was an iffy proposition at best, and he doubted a man could raise enough to feed himself let alone a family here. Not only was the growing season short this high up, but except for this meadow, the land was all covered with rocks. He doubted the whole place could keep a dozen steers alive. Working in Hope Springs was a possibility. If Hank left, they'd be needing a blacksmith. Over the years, he'd shod a few horses and knew his way around a forge. But if Hank couldn't make a go of it, what made him think he could?

All he'd ever done was work around horses and cattle. He might be able to get on as a foreman one of these days, but he doubted it'd be around here. Irwin wasn't likely to hire him on, and he hadn't heard of any other operation large enough that the owners couldn't run it by themselves.

There were some things in life that just weren't meant to
be. This was one of them. No sense wasting time wishing the
world was different.

She leaned back against his thigh, and he felt the dampness
from her hair soak through his britches.

"Look, our wishing stars," he heard her say, and he wished
he had more to offer her than his name on a couple pieces of
paper.

6

*M*arjorie gazed out where the sun had been and knew that if she lived to be a hundred, she'd remember this day. She'd remember the meadow welcoming her this morning with its sprinkling of blue-eyed iris and columbine. She'd remember rolling in the mud and the fun they'd had chinking the cabin together. And she'd remember this man who stood behind her now, his easy teasing ways, his gentle charm.

She's seen how he looked at the kids, at the land, at her. What if he was ready to settle down? Maybe he was tired of roaming from place to place. Maybe this land would hold him.

Leaning back against his leg, she felt the leather gun holster against the side of her cheek and her hopes sank. Leon wasn't some stray dog she could train to stay; he was a wolf. He would be good company for a time, but the minute she turned her back, he'd be long gone.

The worst lies are the ones you tell yourself. Deep inside she knew that though you might be able to harness a wolf up and feed him carrots, he still couldn't plow. There was no sense in fooling herself. Even if she and the land could tame him, she needed a plow horse, not a tame wolf.

The sadness of that settled into a knot and threatened to ruin the end of this splendid day. She was not about to let that happen. She looked up at her stars, closed her eyes, and realized that she didn't know what to ask for anymore. What she'd been wishing for all these years had come true. It was more satisfying than she'd ever imagined.

In the end, she wished that everything would stay just like it was today, that the children would always be healthy and happy, that the breeze would always smell like spring, and that she would always be as content as she was at this moment. Today had been too perfect to last. She knew it was an impossible wish, but then what's the sense of wishing for what was possible? You got that by working.

Joy bubbled up inside of her and it was all she could do to keep from jumping up and whirling madly in circles. But if there was ever a time for keeping a tight rein on one's emotions, this was it. There was no sense in giving Leon ideas. So instead of twirling about, she stood up and walked sedately back to the cabin.

She could hear the swish of his pant legs as he followed her inside, then the clunk of the wooden bar as he dropped it into place across the door. What had seemed like a perfectly reasonable course of action a few days ago was now suddenly foolish and frightening. Her heart was beating a mile a minute as she realized they were locked alone in this cabin, miles from anyone else.

Calm down and stop being so silly. Leon had never treated her with anything but kindness and respect. He'd given no indication that she couldn't continue to expect he would behave like a gentleman.

Being careful not to glance in his direction, Marjorie lit the lantern and surveyed the cabin. She was rather pleased with how things were turning out. Her Lucky Stars quilt spread atop the plump feather bed made that part of the room inviting.

Actually, too inviting. She quickly switched her attention

to the dilapidated stove with its crate of kindling next to it. Her gaze followed up the wall to the shelf with the jars of jam, baking powder, and molasses. Their wedding photograph sat on the end, looking like it'd belonged there all along.

She looked down where he was sitting and realized that though he had a knife and a piece of wood in his hands, he wasn't whittling, he was just staring out, glassy-eyed. She resisted the urge to put a hand on his forehead to see if he had a fever. She hoped he wasn't coming down sick or that his foot hadn't become infected.

"If you'll take those bandages off," she said, turning back to the stove, "I'll fix up your foot."

"You needn't bother," he said. "It's feeling fine."

His voice sounded raspy, like he was having difficulty speaking. Maybe an attack of the ague was coming on.

"Are you not feeling well?" she asked, looking back at him over her shoulder.

He cleared his throat. "I'm feeling fine, why?"

"You sound hoarse, that's all," she said. "Let me take a look at your foot. You've been on it all day, and that mud probably didn't help it any either."

"No," he said, an odd note of panic in his voice. "That won't be necessary."

She turned to stare at him. He was acting so peculiar. "What is the matter with you?" she asked.

"Well, if you must know, I have ticklish fish," he said.

"What?" The conversation had certainly taken a perplexing turn.

"Feet. I have ticklish feet, I mean." If anything, the scratchiness in his voice was getting worse.

"I promise not to tickle them," she assured him. Funny, he'd never mentioned that before, not to her or the doctor. "Now take those bandages off."

Leon leaned over and did as he was told. She wondered what his problem was.

After putting his foot to soak in a basin and pouring them

both a cup of coffee, she offered to read another chapter from *The Last of the Mohicans*. His eyes were drifting shut before the end of the page, so she closed the book early.

She dried off his foot. It appeared to be healing up nicely, for which she was grateful. She was also grateful that he was asleep while she did this. Touching the bony ridges along the top of his foot gave her the most curious sensations. She tried to keep things in perspective by imagining that she was Martha washing Jesus' foot. Then she couldn't remember whether it was Martha or her sister Mary who washed his feet, and in any case she felt more like Mary Magdalene than either of the two virtuous sisters.

Pretending that he was a little boy, she gently played "This Little Piggy" on his toes. She glanced up to make certain he'd not awakened and was watching her behaving so foolishly.

The sight of him sprawled out in the chair took her breath away. This was definitely no little boy, but a full-grown man, and she was playing with fire. She immediately quit fooling with his foot and turned to straining the poultice through a piece of cheesecloth. She placed the damp mixture on his cut and wrapped it all up in clean bandages.

Though her mind was racing from one thought to the next, her body was exhausted. It was time to turn in for the night. She'd asked Ruby if she could borrow a cot, but somehow one had never gotten loaded on the wagon. That was probably just as well given that frightful experience she'd had in Denver. It was fortunate she had a strong heart. Just the memory of being jolted awake, first by that cheap cot collapsing, then by hearing the hammer click back on Leon's pistol, was enough to make her heart skip beats even now. Wouldn't that have been something for the dime novels? Shot by her own husband on their honeymoon. She made a mental note to be sure and waken Leon gently in the morning.

In any case, her plan for this evening was that they would both lie on the feather bed but wrapped in their own blankets.

"Leon," she said, softly shaking his slumped shoulder and

keeping an eye out for any sudden movements. "Why don't you lie down?"

"Going to bunk in the barn," he mumbled, standing up and groping his way in the direction of the door.

"You can do that tomorrow night," she suggested, walking him over to the bed. "Tonight I'd feel safer if you slept here." She pulled the quilt and the blankets down over the trunk and pushed on his shoulders until he sat down.

"Whatever you want, darlin'," he muttered. He lay down fully clothed on the bed and closed his eyes again, or perhaps he'd never opened them in the first place.

Marjorie tugged his other boot off. She unbuckled his gun belt, slid it from under him, and hung it over the bedpost. After tucking a blanket around him, she undressed, put her gray-flannel nightgown on, and blew out the lamp. As she was crawling into bed, she thought she heard Leon say, "Two times two is four. Two times three is six." Why in the world would he be saying his times tables in his sleep?

The feather bed rested on a sagging net of woven ropes. She attempted to stay near the edge, but since it sank in the center, that was impossible. She'd soon slid over next to him. Though they'd slept together in the same bed before, for some reason Marjorie found it most unnerving tonight. Tired as she was, she was too wide-awake to sleep.

She got up, relit the kerosene lamp, and pulled out the pamphlet the woman at the dry-goods store in Denver had given her. Since Leon wold be staying for a few days, perhaps some of Mrs. Shumway's advice would come in handy. Certainly the title, *Guide for the New Bride: Information and Instructions on the Art of Marriage*, sounded encouraging.

The first four pages were devoted to a detailed account of how marriage was a woman's natural destiny, and though there were many joys, there were crosses to bear as well. One of those crosses was the painful and revolting procedure necessary for the procreation of the species and the satisfaction of the lustful urges of men. Without the constraints imposed by women, men would soon dissipate their energies in endless bouts of unchecked passions. References were made to the tragic downfall of the Roman empire.

> Just as it is the woman's role in life to bring order to the management of the household, it is her role in marriage to bring order to the management of the intimacies. Need I say more?

Yes, thought Marjorie. *Just how does one go about managing intimacies.* Mrs. Shumway devoted chapter two to this topic.

> First, postpone the marital initiation as long as possible. Being vaguely "indisposed" will work well for a time. It would be vulgar on his part to ask and indelicate on your part to mention just exactly what you are indisposed about.
>
> This will, of course, only postpone matters for a week or so. Then one must resort to feigning maladies such as headaches, biliousness, dyspepsia, and weariness.

Marjorie didn't think it would be necessary to feign weariness. She imagined most women were weary a great deal of the time.

When the inevitable night occurs, Mrs. Shumway warned that under no circumstances should the wife fall prey to her husband's entreaties about how her active participation would result in enjoyment for her. This is pure fabrication, said Mrs. Shumway. It will only increase his pleasure and thus increase his persistent attentions and is to be avoided at all cost.

This went on with page after page of dire warnings about the importance of refusing to have anything to do with acts too shameful to print in this pamphlet. "Refuse!" admonished Mrs. Shumway time and again. "Your very sanity depends upon it!"

Refuse to do what? Marjorie wished now she'd discussed this matter with her aunt.

In the final few pages, Mrs. Shumway addressed the delicate subject of preventing conception, should the health of the wife or the financial situation of the family require it. Marjorie hoped she would leave the generalities behind and get into some specifics here.

> Abstinence is, of course, the preferred method and 100% effective.
>
> Nursing a child is effective *only* if the babe is nursed around the clock, which means sleeping next to the mother.

Marjorie wondered whether it was the nursing or the constant presence of the child that prevented conception.

> Women of the eastern countries report using a pessary made of camel dung.

Marjorie had no idea what a pessary was, nor did she have ready access to camel dung.

> Withdrawal is an age-old method, but it may be difficult to convince a husband to practice this as many misguided physicians have said it is detrimental to a man's health. While indeed it may be detrimental to their pleasure, it is certainly difficult to imagine that withdrawal would be as detrimental to his health as childbirth could be to yours. In addition, this method has been known to fail.
>
> There are other means of helping your husband reach satisfaction. I won't go into these as no doubt your husband will mention them himself. Use your own discretion in weighing the consequences of perversion versus pregnancy.

Once again, Marjorie wished she had more facts here.

Mrs. Shumway concluded with a few paragraphs on how an intellectual relationship is far more desirable than one based on a few fleeting moments of physical excitement. She urged her readers to nurture these forms of marital intimacies in which marriage partners share conversation, books, and pursuits of the mind.

Goodness, Mrs. Shumway had not said a word about cooking or housekeeping. Marjorie was disappointed in her advice on preventing conception as well. Since she had neither a baby, a pessary, nor camel dung, the only preventative that made sense was abstinence.

Fortunately, she was well prepared to pursue that course of action, but what of the young bride who could not avail herself of that option? Mrs. Shumway needed to either change the title or do more research before she printed up any more copies of her *Guide for the New Bride.*

Marjorie tucked the pamphlet away in her chest, blew out the light, and returned to bed.

She'd already been down to the creek for water and was back at the stove stirring up a pot cornmeal mush when Leon woke up.

"Well, good morning, sleepyhead," she said, dipping out two bowls and setting them on the table. She plopped a dollop of butter in each bowl and a spoonful of sugar.

"Care for coffee?" She was pouring him a cup even as she asked.

"You bet," he said. He sat up on the edge of the bed, still wearing his pants and shirt from yesterday. He placed his foot across his knee, unwrapped the bandage, and examined the cut. "Appears like it's nearly healed up to me."

Marjorie glanced over and agreed that it was at least looking well enough for him to wear both boots today. He put them on and, after a short trip outside, joined her at the table.

The door was wide-open, for even though the cabin had

been aired out yesterday, it didn't take long for the dank-earth smell to return. She much preferred the fresh smell of grass and flowers. The robins had been caroling to one another since sunup, and she could hear the high-pitched calls of the waxwings and the chirps and trills of the sparrows through the open doorway.

It had all the signs of being another glorious day.

After breakfast, Leon took a pan of hot water out to the porch to shave while she cleaned up from breakfast and straightened up the cabin. Marjorie couldn't quite get over the feeling that she was a little girl playing house, where one pretends to be the papa and the other pretends to be the mama. Except Papa had shoulders as broad as a bed and a smile that made Mama's knees wobbly. Playing house had never been like this.

The children must have raced through their chores, because she'd no sooner thrown out the dishwater than she saw the wagon turning up their trail. Leon's horse was tied to the back of the wagon. Perhaps the two of them could go for a ride tonight. Wouldn't that be nice?

It was obvious that Leon was glad to see Ulysses. He examined his stallion's legs and walked him around, talking to him and checking his gait. He appeared to be satisfied. At least he didn't say anything when he returned from staking him down by the creek.

Meanwhile, she and the children unloaded the basket of food Ruby had sent out and the spool of wire, the keg of nails, and the box of tools Leon had asked the boys to bring. They were going to build a privy today.

They picked a spot about halfway between the cabin and the shed, which Leon said would work well because they could stack wood alongside the path and a person could take care of all their morning chores in one trip. He paced off a three-foot square in the grass and Thomas dug up the top layer of sod while he and the younger boys unhitched the team from the wagon. They left the horses' harnesses on and went off to drag logs out of the woods.

While they were doing that, Marjorie and Janey set to digging the dirt out of the hole Thomas had started. Emma, Maggie, and Mary Beth ran back and forth with fruit jars full of cold creek water for everyone to drink.

When they were alone, Janey told Marjorie how envious she was of her and how much she admired her for just up and marrying the man she loved instead of waiting around to see if everyone in the whole entire world approved of her choice.

Marjorie tried to explain things, but it went right past Janey. She was too caught up in her anguish over her parents' disapproval of the young man who'd returned to Hope Springs for the sole purpose of winning her hand in marriage. She went on and on, shovelful after shovelful, about how honorable and kindhearted and hardworking and smart and ambitious Clay Egan was.

"They don't even know him," she kept repeating, until Marjorie was ready to ride to town and reintroduce Hank and Ruby to this paragon of manly virtues.

She attempted to tell Janey that all men are charming when they come calling, but did he have any means of supporting her? That, of course, was what her parents were being so pigheaded about, and Janey was not interested in hearing disparaging remarks about the man she intended to grow old with. Marjorie told her she'd be growing old in a hurry if she married a man who couldn't provide for her. Janey insisted that he had a number of prospects. In fact, today he was awaiting word about a position as a stagecoach driver.

A stagecoach driver? Marjorie was dismayed by this latest development and attempted to convince Janey that this was not a job for a family man. "Not only is it a dangerous and low-paying occupation, but they're gone all the time," she pointed out. Her skeptical comment went in one ear and out the other, as Janey resumed extolling the many fine qualities of her young hero.

Working in a steady rhythm, they soon had a sizable pile of dirt stacked next to the logs the boys were hauling over.

When the sun was directly overhead, Marjorie brought the basket of food up to the edge of the trees where Leon and Thomas were cutting limbs off the logs. She decided that a picnic in the woods would be more convenient for Leon since he had to walk, the easier it would be on his foot. He seemed to be doing fine, however. Though he favored his left leg, he walked about without wincing. He certainly looked better with both boots on.

In fact he was looking better and better to her all the time. Thick, bushy mustaches had always appealed to her. She wondered why men even bothered with those little thin ones. As far as she was concerned, it made them look sneaky. She'd never cared for that skinny mustache Charles cultivated. Thank heavens, they'd not encountered him on their return to Hope Springs. She had so hoped he would find a suitable bride during his winter in Denver. Perhaps with double the number of cattle, men, and land to oversee, Charles wouldn't have time to pester them. If he would just stay away until this business with the circuit judge was settled, she would be grateful.

The kids all groaned in unison at the ham and biscuits Ruby had sent out. They'd been eating ham a lot lately and were tired of it. Leon promised to take them all fishing later on in the afternoon, but Thomas said they had to leave before long as he was supposed to give his pa a hand putting a buggy together.

After filling up on rhubarb muffins, they sat in the cool shade of the trees to give their food time to settle. Two yellow warblers flew around the edge of the clearing singing their bright *sweet, sweet, sweet, I'm so sweet* tune as they flitted from one tree to the next. No doubt the warblers were looking for just the right tree to do some next building themselves.

Leon asked the boys if they'd help him build a stand to saw logs on before they left. Working together, they wired two short poles in a cross pattern, then built a second one and nailed each to either end of another short pole. Once it was upright, he showed them how it would hold a log so that two people using a crosscut saw could cut it to length.

As soon as the stand was finished, they hitched the horses back to the wagon and started on their way home. It seemed empty and quiet without the noisy chatter of the little girls, the boasting of the boys, and the constant recounting of Clay Egan's fine qualities.

"What can I do to help?" Marjorie asked Leon after they'd enjoyed the peace for a moment or two.

"You could use that drawknife to start stripping the bark off those logs," he suggested.

The bark was easy to peel off of the fresh-cut trees. But those that had been dead for a while clung tightly to their outer layer. Marjorie knew it had to be done or the bugs would get underneath and eat away at the wood, but it took considerable effort to pull the strips of bark off some of the tree trunks.

Between the hard work and the afternoon sun, Marjorie's face was soon flushed, and damp strands of hair clung to her cheeks and forehead. She had to unbutton the top two buttons of her dress. It was either that or swoon from heat prostration. Beads of moisture trickled down the front of her, but she was unable to wipe them away as every time she glanced over, Leon was staring straight at her.

He was explaining why he set aside the logs without knots. He would split these later for the roof and the door and for a plank floor in the cabin. It took him forever to get this out. He kept stopping in midsentence and mixing up the words like his mind was off in the clouds.

To make matters worse, Ulysses pulled loose from his tether and began tormenting Rosinante, prancing around her, neighing and nipping at her withers.

Marjorie asked Leon, in a very pleasant manner, to please tie his horse up as he was annoying Rosinante.

"What kind of a name is Rosinante, anyway?" Leon snarled.

For the life of her, Marjorie couldn't figure out what had caused him to become so belligerent. They'd been getting along quite well, having a lovely conversation. Now, all of a sudden, he wanted to argue about what she'd named her horse. Men were quarrelsome creatures.

"Rosinante happens to be the name of Don Quixote's steed," she informed him, finding it difficult to maintain her polite demeanor in the face of his antagonistic attitude.

"Who the hell is Don Quixote?"

"For your information, he's the hero of *Don Quixote de La Mancha*." She wanted to add, "So there," but did not feel that would be helpful.

"Never heard of it," he said, turning away from her.

"It is a book by Cervantes," she said, finding herself becoming a bit cool toward him. "It's believed to be the first novel ever written."

"Well, la-de-da."

"I fail to understand why you're looking down your nose at me. You named your own horse after an ancient Greek warrior," she pointed out.

"I named my horse after General Ulysses S. Grant," he said in no uncertain terms.

By this time, Rosinante had pulled loose from her own tie-down rope and the two horses were tearing across the meadow.

"Do something," she demanded.

"Do what?" he asked. He sounded astounded that she would even make such a request. "I don't believe I'd be able to catch up with them, what with my bum foot and all. Perhaps you'd like to try."

"You are a moody man, Mr. McCoy."

"It's not me that's moody, it's your horse. She's in season, woman."

"Oh," she said softly, covering her mouth with her fingertips. Marjorie didn't know exactly what to say about that. "Is there nothing that can be done?" she asked hesitantly.

"Only one thing I know to do," he said, and stomped off in the direction of the horses. She distinctly heard him say that it was too damn bad that women didn't come into season. She didn't feel a comment like that warranted a reply.

She fully expected him to grab his stallion's halter and tie him back up. Instead he made no effort at all to capture him but headed right down to the creek, laid his gun belt down, shucked off his shirt, pulled off his boots, and stepped out of his pants. Marjorie stared at him in astonishment. Surely he wouldn't pull off his long underwear. But she didn't want to miss it if he did.

He didn't. He still had it on when he jumped right in that cold water and sat down.

This action astounded Marjorie. Now what good was that going to do? Perhaps his foot was causing him discomfort. But were that the case, one would think he'd have stepped a little more lightly on his way to the creek.

She returned to stripping the bark off the logs, with an eye in his direction to see what he would do next. Perhaps he just needed to cool off. She was feeling rather warm herself, and she might go wading later on. However, she doubted she'd get hot enough to strip down to her chemise and sit in the ice-cold creek.

When she saw him emerge from the water, she bent over the log and pretended not to notice what he was up to. But it was difficult not to notice what the horses were up to. She blushed every time they came racing through the meadow, nipping at one another's shoulders. *Good gracious, will they never calm down?*

Ulysses seemed to have recovered completely from his injury. There was not so much as a trace of lameness as he thundered alongside Rosinante. Marjorie cold feel the pounding of their hooves through the log she was sitting on. She only hoped one of them didn't step into a gopher hole during one of their mad dashes.

There was nothing she could do about that now. She decided to concentrate on pulling off strips of bark and deciding whether their next endeavor should be plowing up a garden or building a fence across the mouth of the canyon. Rosinante obviously needed a fenced-in pasture, but with such a short growing season, it was not wise to waste any time getting a crop in. She was so engrossed in her thoughts, she didn't realize Leon had returned until he spoke.

"Will you give me a hand with this?" he asked politely. At least his good temper appeared to have returned.

She stood up and looked at him. *Good heavens. He's left his shirt off.* Probably cooler to work that way. She pretended not to notice as she picked up one end of a log, and the two of them placed it on the stand. He laid the crosscut saw on top and turned it upright. She assumed he meant for her to work one end while he worked the other. She grasped the handle and they began to saw back and forth through the wood.

Her movements were awkward at first, and he suggested that she just follow along and watch him until she got a feel for it.

She didn't believe she would ever catch on that way. Looking at Leon was far too distracting. *Mercy, you could wash clothes on that man's belly.* There were six mounds of muscles, three on each side, and they rippled with his every move.

She tried to pull her gaze up to his shoulders, but the hair on his chest was like an arrow drawing it downward. She had to close her eyes altogether in order to concentrate on the sawing motion.

Then she heard a horrible scream, and her eyes flew open. Just as she'd dreaded, one of the horses must have fallen and broken a leg. She stopped sawing and looked in the direction of the sound. There they both were, near the cottonwoods. Neither appeared injured, but Ulysses was biting Rosinante's neck.

Then it hit Marjorie just exactly what they were doing. She'd never seen anything quite like it in her life. As she stood watching these two powerful animals mate, Marjorie flushed all over and became aware of parts of her body that she generally didn't give so much as a thought to. She felt like she was going to jump right out of her skin. If it was anything like this between people, Mrs. Shumway's intellectual discussions didn't stand a chance.

When it was finally over and Rosinante and Ulysses were walking side by side toward the canyon, she turned to Leon. "Is that what it's like?" she asked in hushed amazement.

"For horses, not for people," he said in a gruff voice. "It's different for people."

"How is it different?" she asked, still amazed at what she'd just witnessed.

"Well, for one, there's not as much biting, and there's a lot less racing around . . . usually."

"Oh," she said, still in a daze.

"Didn't your ma ever explain anything about it?"

She wondered why he was so irritable.

"A little, but she never said anything about it being like that."

"Well it ain't like that. Those are horses, for crying out loud, not people."

He turned and strode off toward the creek, tore off his clothes, and jumped in again.

Leon was certainly a fastidious man. Marjorie had never known a man who bathed as often as he did. Of course, she hadn't known all that many men. But she couldn't recall her uncle Hank or any of the men who lived at the boardinghouse bathing more than once a week, if that often. She never remembered anyone bathing more than once a day, certainly not two or three times a day. It was fortunate they lived near a creek.

She felt fidgety and itchy and hot and sweaty and ready for

a bath herself, but that chilly creek water didn't hold the same appeal for her as it obviously did for Leon.

Even though it would be a while until sunset, she was tired of peeling bark. She decided to stop for the day and put something on for supper. Then, if she could entice Rosinante away from her paramour, she'd go for a ride. That always helped calm her down.

She lit a fire in the stove and put some lentils and ham hocks on to simmer. Then she donned her brown-wool riding skirt and her tan shirtwaist and picked up a zinc bucket with the intention of filling it with oats to entice Rosinante to return.

Apparently, Rosinante had tired of her afternoon frolicking, because she was waiting for Marjorie outside the cabin. Marjorie patted her velvet neck, led her to the shed, and brushed her while the horse ate her bucket of oats.

The tranquillity of last night was gone, replaced by a feeling of restlessness, of uneasiness. It was more than just being annoyed with Leon and his peculiar behavior. She was upset and excited, but she didn't know about what. The land papers were signed. Maybe in five years, when it was time to prove she'd met the homesteading requirements, maybe then she'd be nervous, but not now. She felt like she had right before her first day of teaching. Anticipation of the unknown, she'd called it. But that was over six years ago. She'd had a reason then. She'd been only sixteen years old at the time, and some of her pupils were nearly as old as she was. She was always a little nervous on the first day of school, but nothing like this. Besides, school didn't start again for four months, and she hadn't given teaching a thought all day.

Perhaps it was from worrying about Rosinante. But she was safe now, and still there was this churning at the very core of her. Of course, it was exciting to be living on her land. Perhaps that was the reason. After all the dreaming and planning, she finally had a home of her own.

What she needed was a ride up to the waterfall. She could

launder the clothes she'd been wearing and wash her hair. The hot water would be beneficial to Leon's foot, but she decided she'd just as soon he not know about the place. As much as that man liked to bathe, she never would get him out of there.

As she brushed Rosinante, Marjorie talked to her about the day, and about the ride they'd go on after dinner.

Leon was sitting at the table when she returned. He hardly said a word while they ate. Perhaps he didn't care for the way she fixed lentils. Maybe he was just tired and cranky. Her muscles were certainly aching; his probably were, too. She didn't know what to make of it when he snapped at her over her suggestion that he take his boot off so she could tend to his foot. You'd think a person could be more gracious than that. After all, he'd stepped on a bottle that he broke himself. It wasn't her fault. She'd not injured him.

When he grabbed his bedroll and announced that he was sleeping out under the stars, she was glad to see him go. Maybe he was all out of sorts because he missed seeing the stars at night.

She wrapped her dirty clothes and a towel around a cake of hard soap and a jar of soft soap and walked to the shed. Rosinante stood quietly while she put the bridle and saddle on and mounted up. The trail was easy to follow in the twilight, and they took off at steady lope. She wondered how many times the two horses had been up and down the edge of this creek today.

Within a few minutes, they were at the pool at the base of the waterfall. She slid off Rosinante's back, leaving the reins dangling to the ground. If anything frightened her, she'd take off for the shed. Otherwise, the reins would remind her to stay around.

Marjorie climbed along the edge of the pool until she found the path. Just before ducking under the cascading water, she slipped out of her riding outfit and left it along with her shoes and towel on a rock ledge. Holding her breath, she dashed through the edge of the icy water and into the murky cavern.

She was one big goose bump and wasted no time in immersing herself in the pool of hot water. Her back was sore from digging and bending over the logs all day, and the hot mineral water was wonderfully relaxing. She hadn't realized how much her muscles hurt until she felt their ache begin to melt away. She slid down until only her face was above water and filled her lungs with the warm, moist steam. She'd read where hot springs often smelled like rotten eggs owing to the sulfur dissolved from the rocks, but she could detect no scent other than earth and water here.

She'd been in the cavern once before, when she first explored the canyon. But that had been during the day, and, fearful of being discovered, she'd only dipped her feet in the pool. It was an entirely different experience soaking at night. She let out a whoop and listened to it echo back to her. Then she sang "Greensleeves." It was one of her favorite melodies and sounded even better with her voice echoing in the cave.

The light was fading fast. With only a sliver of a moon out tonight, she knew it would soon be dark in here. *Best wash these clothes while I can still see where the dirt is,* she told herself.

She slipped out of her chemise and stockings and used the hard cake soap to scrub them and the gingham dress she'd worn the last few days. Then she rinsed them out in the overflow stream. That done, she dipped into the jar of soft soap and sudsed up her hair. The lilac scent of the soap infused the air around her, and for a moment she imagined what her cabin would smell like in the spring surrounded by lilac bushes loaded with their lavender blooms.

She held her breath and slid down under the water to rinse out her hair. While the pool was only a little more than waist deep, it was at least ten feet wide. By stretching out flat, she could pretend to be a mermaid, with her hair floating about her.

When she came back up for air, she sensed something was different. She sat up, held quiet, and listened intently to the sounds around her. Other than the slight luminescence of the waterfall, the cave was pitch-black, and she could discern no shapes or movement within it. Nor could she hear anything other than the rushing water.

But something was in this cave. She knew it by the tingling, hair-standing-up-on-the-back-of-her-neck sensation throughout her whole body. Surely a lynx or a mountain lion wouldn't walk through the water. Perhaps a bear had been holed up here through the winter and was coming out of hibernation. She stayed still in hopes that whatever it was would go on its way.

But whatever it was, it was in here with her. Her heart seized to a stop when she felt it grip her hipbones. She struggled for a foothold on the slick rocks and flailed her arms about in a frantic search of something to grab on to.

"Settle down. It's only me."

She stopped moving for a moment. "Leon?"

He answered by pulling her back through the water until she was cradled in his arms. Merciful Mary, he was stark naked. But then so was she. This was shameful, positively shameful.

"Leon, I don't think—"

"Stop thinking, darlin'," he said, and began to kiss the side of her face and down her neck. The feel of his lips and the soft brushing of his mustache against her skin felt wonderful.

Wonderful? Wonderful didn't begin to describe how good this felt. He continued on down until he was suckling on her like a babe. *Mercy. I really ought to call a halt to this.*

Well, maybe in a minute. After all, she was a grown woman, and she had had quite a scare. She deserved a little comforting, didn't she?

She knew this was flimsy reasoning, but she couldn't bring herself to care. She felt safe in his arms—protected and cherished. He may not love her, and she certainly didn't love him, but they enjoyed each other's company, and they'd both been alone for far too long. Even if it was only for the night, how could she stop him now?

She felt his hand begin a gentle kneading motion on the other side. *My, that feels good.* Supported by his body and the warm water, she drifted into a realm of pure physical experience. It was some time before she realized that the pleasurable sensations were echoing in her nether parts as well.

When his hand moved to where it ought not to be, the pressure was such a relief to the aching there that though she knew she should have pushed him away, she didn't. He began a slow circling, and the rest of her body pulsed in tune with the movements of his hands.

At first this felt unbelievably pleasant and relaxing, but gradually the intensity built up until it came close to being unbearable. How much longer could this go on? In frustration, she arched back and sank her teeth into the thick muscle cord that ran across the top of his shoulders.

Then, just when she thought she couldn't stand it one second longer, he stopped. Perhaps the bite had startled him. She kissed that spot on his shoulder. When he remained still, she kissed him on the neck, enjoying the sense of moving her lips in time with the vibrations in her body. She felt like she was looking over the edge of a cliff, light-shouldered and intensely alive.

"Are you ready for more, darlin'?" he whispered.

For heaven sakes, don't stop now.

"Uh, huh," she murmured.

His hands moved to her hips and he shifted her around until she was sitting on his lap facing him. The pressure felt good. Still, she wished he'd go back to what he'd been doing before. That felt better. He murmured something, but for the life of her, she couldn't make out what the words meant. She replied in soft, unintelligible sounds of her own.

Without warning, he grabbed her firmly by the hips and buried himself in her. A sharp, burning pain replaced the hazy humming in her body. She stiffened up immediately.

"Stop that this instant," she cried out.

"It's all right, darlin'," he said, trying to soothe her. "It's all right."

"It is most definitely not all right," she informed him. "This hurts, Leon. I don't believe I'm in the mood for this any longer."

This wasn't at all what she thought it was going to be like. She started struggling to get loose, but he wrapped his arms tightly around her and held her close. The sharp burning pain was easing up, but she was still far from comfortable.

"Just calm down, darlin'," he said. "It'll feel better in a minute."

"Let loose of me." She pushed with both hands against his chest and tried to wiggle out of his grasp. But her strength was no match for his, and, despite all her shoving and squirming, he held her tight to him.

"Please stop moving, sweetheart." A moment later he groaned, and pulled her away from him. Now that he was no longer inside of her, she ceased her struggling and remained still in his arms. She felt his body shudder and heard a moan come from deep in his chest.

"Was that it?" she asked, after a moment.

He pulled her close and pressed her head down on his shoulder. She felt sadly disappointed somehow. No wonder Rosinante had screamed. She felt like screaming herself. Apparently, Mrs. Shumway was right about this business.

"No, darlin'," came his husky reply, "that wasn't 'it' by a long shot."

Leon's mouth brushed against hers, and he began slowly sucking on her bottom lip. His mustache tickled underneath her nose.

"Is this going to hurt?" she asked.

"No, darlin', the hurting part's all over."

For now, she said to herself. *But there will come a time when I'll ache until I can't stand it, wanting this night back again.*

But even if she ran to Rosinante right now, she'd still want this night back. Deciding that she might as well have the memories along with the regrets, she relaxed in his arms.

He kissed her until her toes curled. And he kept it up until her entire body felt just like her feet. He kissed, and petted, and stroked, and teased until she thought she couldn't endure it another moment.

Well, maybe just a little while longer. But surely there was a limit to how much a body could bear before you'd go right out of your mind.

Then she did just that. She couldn't tell, and she didn't care, where she left off and the rest of the world began. She pulsed with the rhythm of the universe, floated on a pillow of stars, then spiraled slowly back to earth.

Her first rational thought was that Mrs. P. Osgood Shumway needed to add another chapter to that pamphlet of hers.

Her second thought was that she'd just accepted heartbreak with open arms. She was hardly a giddy young girl. She knew what she was doing, and she had done it anyway. Now she was doomed to a lifetime of looking out windows. She knew better. Why hadn't she put a stop to it while she still could? *Damn it all to hell.*

Even if it wasn't out loud, she was shocked to find herself swearing like a sailor. But then she'd done a lot of shocking things this evening. She planned on doing more.

She nuzzled Leon's neck. He kissed her behind the ear, and it started all over.

Later, when she had her wits about her again, she offered to shampoo his hair. Groping around the rocks, she found the jar of lilac-scented soap and washed his hair with it. Then he had her stand like a pagan princess in the darkness as he ran handfuls of suds up and down her wet skin. One thing led to another. She knew the smell of lilacs would never affect her in quite the same way again.

"Sweetheart, you are something else," he said later, as they lay in each other's arms near the edge of the pool.

She tried to remember ever being called anything but Marjorie or Miss Bascom. She'd always resented those who attempted to feign a closeness by the use of endearments. However, now that she truly felt like someone's sweetheart, at least for the night, she found that she liked the way it sounded.

He placed a kiss in the hollow of her neck. She knew where this was going to lead, and she followed without hesitation.

Each journey began with a lazy indifference that gradually gave way to a sense of descending, as if falling into a deep feather bed in the dark of night. Drifting, dreaming, deepening into mindless intensity, then back up in a heart-pounding explosion.

Oblivious to anything but the touching and kissing, lost in the feel of her body sliding against his, she wasn't able to hold on to a thought for more than a moment. Would there be anything left of her when this night ended? But even that worry floated away like a feather on a breeze. If tonight lasted forever, it would be all right by her.

But it didn't last forever. The predawn glow gradually replaced the inky intimacy in the cavern and Marjorie remembered that the children were to return today. They would be frightened if the two of them were nowhere to be found when they arrived. As much as she wished they could stay for just a while longer, it was time to go.

If only she had the strength to move. She was sitting on his lap with her back to his chest and her head lying on his shoulder. She turned her head to the side and placed her lips near an ear she'd given considerable attention to just a short while ago. "I can't believe men have to pay women to do this," she whispered.

"Loving ain't always like this," he cautioned her.

They held on to each other and the night for a while longer. Then she pulled away and stepped up on the rocks.

Reluctantly, she picked up her bundle of wet clothes and ducked through the waterfall. The world she stepped back into seemed harsh by comparison to the hidden cave. She felt too raw in the sunlight, and the ease she'd felt with Leon was waning in the light of day.

As she grabbed the towel and began to dry off, she couldn't help but notice his gaze traveling the length of her. Marjorie blushed at his perusal. It was one thing to feel him against her in the dark of night, quite another to stand here naked in the morning with him staring at her.

"Heavenly days, Leon, will you stop gawking?" she said, although in fact she was doing her share of looking herself. Did she put that row of red teeth marks along his shoulders? She didn't remember that. She did remember how she could feel his heart pounding with her fingertips and how her face fit perfectly along the curve of his neck. She dared not look any lower, not the way he was smiling.

"Really, Leon," she said in another attempt to bring some semblance of decorum to what was turning into a rather embarrassing situation. Here they were, both naked as the day they were born, and he was grinning from ear to ear.

"A decent man would turn his back and allow me some privacy," she informed him.

"I don't know about me being a decent man, but you, Marjorie McCoy, are one gorgeous woman," he said, staring for all he was worth.

This was going beyond the bounds. Though she had her pleasant points, she was far from gorgeous. She threw the towel over his head and turned around to slip on her shirtwaist and climb into her riding skirt.

Rosinante let out a welcoming whinny.

"We really shouldn't have left the horses out here all night," she said. Leon acted as if he hadn't heard a word she'd said. She sat down on a rock and pulled her stockings and shoes on. Then she grabbed up her bundle of washed clothes and headed down the path.

Rosinante and Ulysses were standing by the edge of the pond, patiently waiting for them. Either her season was over or else yesterday had exhausted the two of them.

"I bought Rosinante with the money I earned teaching the year we were in Denver," she said, hoping small talk would ease matters between them.

"You don't say."

She glanced up, then looked quickly away. She so wished he would put his shirt on.

"It was a needless extravagance at the time, but I'd always wanted a horse of my own."

It was his turn to say something. When he didn't, she added, "I mucked out stalls to pay for her keep until Uncle Hank bought the livery." She was babbling, just babbling.

He walked up beside her now. "Shall we go?" he asked in a soft, low voice. For a moment, she had the wildest urge to beg him not to go, to stay here with her. *Now, isn't that foolish? A person might as well ask the birds to cease flying from tree to tree, or request the wind to settle down,* she reminded herself.

They mounted up. She kept Rosinante to a slow walk as they made their way to the mouth of the canyon. Her thoughts jumped from one thing to another. What would she feed the children today? How fortunate that nothing unforeseen had happened to the horses left out all night. Did she leave any sourdough sponge out to rise yesterday? Would it be possible to dig a well close to the cabin? Why did last night seem so satisfying while it happened and so shocking while recalling it? Had she really offered herself to him like a loose woman? What must he think of her now? Would he expect a repeat performance tonight? Would she?

Then a realization hit Marjorie like a low branch. What if he left next week? No doubt the circuit judge would make short work of this case when he came through.

If found innocent, Leon would be on his way. She could hardly swallow at the thought of his leaving. What would it be like after a few more nights like this one? Would she end up like her mother, forever checking to see who was coming up the road? How could she stand to spend her life like that?

From his perch on a branch overhead, a gray jay scolded her harshly for her folly.

Then her chest tightened until she could barely breathe. What if the jury found him guilty? Though she was certain he hadn't harmed Jake, the only evidence pointed in Leon's direction. Surely, they'd need something more substantial than a hasty threat to hang a man on. The thought of Leon being rushed off to a makeshift gallows by a group of rowdy men gave her a sudden chill.

"I see you've got a herd of mustangs stopping by your place on their rounds," Leon said from behind her. She looked down at the hoofprints he was pointing to in a stretch of sand. Then she glanced up at him and marveled at the way his wavy wet hair brushed against his broad, square shoulders. Her gaze traveled up to his thick mustache, and she shivered in shame and delight at the memory of where she'd felt it brush against her in the night.

Coming out of the canyon, they rode past log poles scattered here and there. No doubt these poles had formed a fence across the mouth of the canyon before they were torn down by the makeshift posse. She hoped the judge would straighten everything out so there would be no posse this time, and she hoped Leon stayed long enough to get the fence back up.

But what if he wanted to stay longer? What if he wanted to stay forever? Did she dare dream of it? And did she even want that?

Marjorie dug her heels in, and Rosinante broke into a gliding gallop. Gripping with her knees, they flew in rhythm across the meadow. With her hair waving loose all around her, she felt like a pagan princess again.

The air was fresh with the promise of early summer, and the columbines waved their morning greeting. The sound of pounding hooves next to her let her know that Ulysses was no longer content to stay behind. Like Robin Hood and Maid Marian, they thundered alongside one another through the thick grass. Leon threw both arms high in the air and let out howl of exhilaration. Marjorie did the same.

She was so caught up in the moment that she forgot to hang on to the wet clothes, and they fell to the ground. Realizing she'd lost them, she looked behind her. Leon wheeled Ulysses around and, at a full gallop, leaned over and snatched up the bundle in passing. Marjorie's heart was in her throat. What if he'd fallen off?

When he caught up to her, Marjorie was struck by the pure joy that radiated off of this man. How would it be not to have a care in the world?

"Makes you feel good just to be alive, doesn't it?" he said, when they pulled to a halt in front of the cabin. As soon as she slid to the ground, he handed her the bundle of wet clothes, grabbed Rosinante's reins, and took off at a lope.

Although she was certain she would live to regret their night together, Marjorie had to agree with him, it did indeed feel good to be alive.

Leon let out a wild war whoop, and Marjorie answered with a yell of her own before she turned and stepped into the cabin. It seemed so dark and dreary and dank inside that she left the door wide-open as she went about fixing their breakfast. The coffee hadn't even started boiling before she heard the children and looked out to see Thomas stop the team to give Leon a ride back to the cabin. Maggie and Mary Beth were in the wagon, but she didn't see Emma, Samuel, Caleb, or Janey.

She could hear both girls talking at once about the preacher coming this morning and how one of Queenie's puppies had gotten stepped on by a horse and was hurt so bad it had to be put down and how Janey had to stay home and help because their aunt Ruby was sick abed. Maggie expressed the hope that she did not get so sick that she had to be "put down" too. Leon assured her that people were not "put down," only animals. She asked why, and Leon explained it was not fair to make animals suffer. Mary Beth wanted to know why animals were put down when they suffered but people were not. Maggie said Janey was suffering since Uncle Hank had forbidden her to see Clay and Mary Beth wanted to know what forbidden meant and what did suffer mean. When the wagon came to a halt, the girls tumbled out and raced one another into the cabin. Marjorie could see the relief on Leon's face.

"Pancakes!" shrieked Maggie, as she flew through the door. "My favorite."

Thomas told them that Preacher Thompson had sent word he'd be in town this morning to hold church services. Marjorie felt a rush of excitement at showing off her new husband to the folks in Hope Springs.

How things could change. A few days ago she'd have just as soon Leon remained a mystery to her neighbors. Now she wanted them to meet him, wanted them to know him for the peaceable man he was. Once the townspeople got a chance to talk with him, they'd realize there was no way he could have done what he was accused of. There was the slight chance that his appearance would inflame some of the men to consider taking matters into their own hands, but she doubted there'd be any serious talk of lynching on the Lord's day, especially with their wives and children around.

When Leon announced that he would be staying behind to do some chores around the place she was more than annoyed.

"But this would be such a good opportunity to get to know the people in Hope Springs," she said, trying to sound reasonable and keep the irritation out of her voice.

"I'm not interested in getting to know the folks in Hope Springs," he said. "I already know enough people."

"Thomas, why don't you go in with the girls and have some pancakes." It was a direction, not a question. He took it as such and disappeared into the cabin.

"Well, why not?" she asked once they were alone.

"Because about the least exciting thing I can imagine is listening to some preacher give his views on sin. Few are in favor of it, and most drone on and on, long past any interest I've got in listening to them."

"But people are curious about you, and going to church would be a painless way to introduce you to the community," she insisted.

"I've no doubt they're interested in me," he said. "However, I've very little interest in them and no interest at all in going to church."

This was aggravating. "Leon McCoy," she said, "if you have any affection for me, any concern at all about my reputation in this community, you will saddle up your horse and ride to town with me."

"I'll ride to town with you, but I'm not going to church," he said. "That's final."

"Fine," she said, pulling her shoulders back and her head up. "I'll go to church all by myself and explain how my new husband has so little regard for me he won't even accompany me to church services."

"You just do that." He turned away and headed off in the direction of the creek.

A moment of near panic gripped her. Had she pushed him too far? "Where are you going?" she demanded.

"To saddle the horses," he said, without breaking stride.

"What about breakfast?"

"I'm not in the mood to eat."

Why he was being so unreasonable about going to church was beyond her. Few men actually enjoyed going to church, but they accompanied their families for appearance's sake. Perhaps she could change his mind on the ride in.

But he refused to discuss it any further.

They arrived in town to find the boardinghouse in an uproar and smelling of smoke. Janey was trying to scrape burnt potatoes from the bottom of a pan. Emma was wandering around in her stocking feet, discussing where her shoes might be with her rag doll, who sadly nodded her agreement that the boys must have hidden them as a prank. Caleb and Samuel were wrestling in the parlor. Apparently the loser would have to refill the woodbox. Marjorie wondered if the winner would be responsible for tidying the parlor.

Marjorie took one look around and headed into her aunt's bedroom. Judging from the smell, breakfast had not sat well on her stomach. Ruby was curled up under the sheets, moaning softly. Marjorie wished her aunt a cheery good morning, picked up the chamber pot, and carried it out to the privy to empty. After rinsing it out at the washhouse pump, she returned it to the bedroom, picking up a pitcher of warm water on her way through the kitchen.

"How many months along are you, Aunt Ruby?" she asked, not really wanting her fears confirmed. Ruby's last confinement had been a dreadful ordeal. She'd hardly kept a bite down the whole time.

"Nearly two months," her aunt replied wearily. "I expect there will be another little Richmond sometime after the first of the year."

Marjorie wiped a warm washcloth over Ruby's forehead and cheeks and tried to think of something encouraging or at least comforting to say. The best she could come up with was, "It'll be nice to have a baby around again."

"Won't it," her aunt said, but Marjorie could tell she wasn't too enthusiastic about the prospect.

"Does Hank know?"

"He suspects," was all Ruby would say.

This was a fine time for Hank to be leaving. How could he be so thoughtless?

"Would it help if I took the children out with me for the summer?"

"They would love it, but I need Janey and the boys to help run the boardinghouse. You know how busy summers can be."

"Maybe they could come out for the day on a regular basis. I could use the help, and you could use the peace and quiet."

"I'd appreciate that, honey," her aunt said.

"So would I," she said, wringing out the washcloth and hanging it up on the stand. "By any chance, do you know where Emma's shoes are?"

"I hope the dog's not taken them again," she said, sounding discouraged. "You might try under the back stairs." She gave a low moan and curled up on her side. Marjorie decided to leave her in peace.

Indeed, the missing shoes had fallen under the steps. They were all covered in dried mud. Marjorie set Emma down with a brush to clean them and sent the rest of the children off to do their chores. Janey and Marjorie worked together to get the Sunday dinner going. Hank poured himself and Leon a cup of coffee and led the way out to the back porch.

Marjorie realized that despite the earlier burnt potatoes, Janey moved through the kitchen with grace and assurance, adjusting the valves that controlled the air into the firebox, planning the meal so that everything would be ready to eat when they returned. It wouldn't be long until she was doing this in her own kitchen.

Once the food was taken care of, Marjorie sat Mary Beth in a chair so she could fix her hair. Using a brush dipped in water, she started in on the snarled mess.

"Will Clay be in church today?" she asked Janey.

"I don't think so," she said, wiping down the kitchen counter. "He hired on at the Circle I while he's waiting to hear about the stagecoach job, and I doubt they'll let him leave the range during roundup to attend Sunday services."

Once Mary Beth's hair was untangled, Marjorie plaited it into tight French braids along each side. She loved fixing the girls' hair. They always felt so special when their hair was done up, and she enjoyed the foolish chatter as well as the serious discussions that went along with brushing and braiding. It was a time away from the cares of the world. She could still recall sitting on the floor in front of her mother having her own hair braided. Marjorie felt a twinge of regret that she'd probably never have daughters of her own to kneel between her knees while she brushed out their hair and listened to their cares.

In no time at all, she had Mary Beth's, Maggie's, and Emma's hair in sleek plaits. She tied bright red ribbons at the end of each one and sent the girls upstairs to change into their Sunday dresses. They ran off, twisting their heads from side to side to see their beribboned braids fly through the air.

"Let me fix your hair, Janey," said Marjorie.

"You don't have to," she said, pushing some stray strands back under her lopsided bun. She was trying so hard to look grown-up.

"It'll only take a minute," Marjorie said, and led Janey by the hand over to a chair.

Marjorie pulled out the hairpins, parted Janey's hair down the middle, and had her bend her head down so she could braid it on both sides, starting from the nape of her neck. She crossed the blond braids over the top of her head and wound them around until Janey looked like a Viking princess.

It dawned on Marjorie that if it wasn't Clay, it would be somebody else soon enough. She so wished there was some way she could keep Janey young and protected. Or if not that, at least give her some advice that would keep her safe now. But nothing came to mind. After last night, she didn't even know what advice to give to herself, let alone Janey.

The boys came in, damp from washing up, and she gave each of them a quick hair brushing and sent them up to change for church.

While she helped Janey set out the dishes and silverware for later, she thought of how she could be doing this in her home with her children if she'd accepted Charles's proposal. Would she eventually regret the choice she'd made to be a spinster, to remain childless?

What got into her to fret over this matter now? She was hardly a spinster any longer. And after last night, there was at least a fair chance she might not be childless either.

She pushed these thoughts out of her mind as she popped in to check on Ruby. Though her aunt didn't appear as peaked as she had earlier, neither was she feeling up to attending church.

Once the children were gathered in the kitchen, Marjorie reminded them to take a quick trip to the privy before they set out. Janey placed the pot of half-done potatoes on the woodpile. With the lid on, they would continue cooking and be ready to mash when she returned.

As Marjorie crossed the porch, she stopped and asked Leon if he'd changed his mind about attending services with them.

"No, thanks," he replied. "I thought I'd wander on over to the Lucky Lady and sit a spell."

"Then come along with us," Caleb said with a grin. "That's where we're all going."

Together, they trooped around in front of the boarding-house and crossed the street to the Lucky Lady. Thomas, Samuel, and Caleb ran ahead to help carry in the benches that were stacked against the side of the building.

"Hope Springs was built during the gold rush of '59," Hank explained on the way over. "A couple of prospectors found some color on Clear Creek, and people got excited and threw up the town. When the war came, most folks went back home. I always thought the place would pick up after it was over, but it turned out the gold was nearly all played out by then, and those that did return moved on to more enticing places before long."

"Unfortunately," added Marjorie, "the only building they put up that's big enough to hold any number of people was the saloon, and it's a sham, really. Behind that grand two-story false front, there's just the one long narrow room."

"We plan to build a church one of these days," Hank added. "But for now, Rooster shuts his business down on Sunday morning so we can hold services."

Townspeople were making their way from both ends of the street, women in well-washed calico and gingham trying to

keep their children gathered up, men in denim pants and
leather vests nodding to one another.

"You're sure welcome to join us," Hank offered.

"No, thank you," Leon said firmly. "I had my fill of
churching as a kid."

Since he followed them inside anyway, Marjorie wondered
why he'd put up such a fuss. She held on to Maggie and Mary
Beth, and Janey held hands with Emma as they made their
way through the swinging doors. Though the building still
smelled strongly of alcohol, tobacco, and sawdust, it'd been
swept up and aired out. Three tall candles burned on a table
covered with a white tablecloth. This would serve as the pul-
pit. The candles added a nice religious touch as well as making it easier to see the Reverend. Marjorie glanced over to be
certain that the painting of the nearly nude woman over the
bar had been covered with a sheet. It had.

Rooster's piano player, Banjo Bob, was warming up with
"Shall We Gather at the River." The tall, loose-limbed man
seemed to be slightly more sober today than usual, for which
Marjorie was grateful. A month ago, he was drunk as a skunk
and right when everyone had their hymnals opened to "Sweet
Hour of Prayer," he'd burst into a rousing rendition of
"Camptown Races." The men could hardly contain themselves, snickering and snorting as they attempted to keep
straight faces. The women saw very little amusement in the
situation. However, since there was only one other person in
town who could even pick out a tune, and she couldn't pick it
out well enough for people to sing along, they were in somewhat of a bind. There were those in favor of forgoing the
music altogether rather than risk a repeat of this outrageous
behavior. However, they were in the minority.

For weeks, whenever Banjo Bob chanced across a woman,
he apologized profusely for the mix-up. He was terribly sorry
and offered to play the banjo or the fiddle, which he maintained he never got confused on, no matter how much he'd

been drinking. However, most folks felt that neither banjo nor fiddle music would be suitable for the singing of hymns.

He received a number of stern lectures on how he ought to quit drinking altogether. He agreed wholeheartedly, but always pointed out that, "If I weren't a drunkard, do you think I'd still be hanging around this dinky town, playing music for my keep?"

The townspeople allowed that, indeed, if he ever sobered up, he'd probably leave, and they'd be without a piano player. So they let up on the lecturing and the Reverend Thompson gave a fiery sermon on the importance of tolerance and how Christians needed to practice forgiving others for their short-comings. Banjo Bob gave them an opportunity to practice the forgive, if not the forget, part of being a Christian.

As the Reverend had not yet arrived, people milled around the room, catching up on the news. The men and women quickly divided out into their two separate groups, the men to discuss the weather and the finer points of horses and the women to trade recipes and complaints about their husbands. The older boys roughhoused in the back of the room, know-ing just what they could get away with before they incurred the wrath of one or both parents. The older girls sat in hud-dled groups on the benches, giggling and pretending not to notice the boys in the back. Only the young children played with total disregard to gender. They ran and hid behind their mamas in endless games of chase and peek-a-boo.

Marjorie stood alone with Leon near the front of the saloon. She introduced her new husband to the children who, natu-rally, all wanted to know who this man was with their school-marm. To the few adults who approached them, Marjorie mentioned that as soon as things were settled, they would have a cake reception to celebrate their wedding.

Most people preferred to hang back and whisper among themselves. Occasionally, she'd see someone pointing at the two of them and hear snatches of conversation on how Leon'd ridden into town, killed Jake Jarveson, then married the town schoolteacher. Why, people weren't safe in their own beds anymore.

Marjorie answered an inquiry as to the whereabouts of Ruby by saying simply that she'd been feeling poorly in the mornings. They all knew what "feeling poorly in the mornings" meant. Most of the women in the room, at least those between fifteen and fifty, either had a babe on one hip or, from all appearances, would be holding one there before long.

The room was full and still no sign of the Reverend Thompson. Leon asked for something to drink, and Rooster brought him and Marjorie glasses of warm lemonade.

"I wonder what's keeping the Reverend?" Marjorie asked. This situation was becoming decidedly uncomfortable. Who would have thought her neighbors would be so unfriendly at church?

"Oh, he probably got caught up in a poker game and forgot the time," Rooster said.

"I doubt the Reverend is a gambling man," she said, in an attempt to dispel this persistent and, in her opinion, unfounded rumor.

"Any man who goes around in a gambler's getup—long black coat, a boiled white shirt, and a string tie—is doing more than reading the Bible, I tell you," said Rooster, defending his position on the matter. "I, for one, don't fault the man for it. He surely ain't going to keep body and soul together with the piddling amount that shows up in the collection plate."

"Isn't," said Marjorie, automatically correcting Rooster's grammar. "This all started," she said to Leon, "the Sunday the Reverend gave a sermon on gambling, how the Roman soldiers threw dice for Christ's garments, how Saul became king by drawing lots, how life itself was a gamble, especially here in the Territories. But he never once came out in favor of gambling."

"Hard to tell just exactly what that man is in favor of," said Rooster. "The Reverend is a 'shouting Methodist.' He preaches a fiery sermon about free will and such, but he uses words that take some thinking about before a body can decipher their meanings. Sometimes he'll say one thing, then contradict himself in the next sentence. But I distinctly recall that the reverend did come down on the side of gambling."

"Sounds like my kind of preacher," said Leon.

"Oh, really," Marjorie said in exasperation. She'd heard this argument before, and there was no doubt in her mind that the Reverend Thompson had been misunderstood. Why, he would no more uphold gambling than he would preach in favor of the sins of fornication and adultery. Some people just heard what they wanted to.

Marjorie had briefly considered asking the Reverend to marry her, but recalling his views on women being handmaidens to their husbands, she'd dismissed that thought. She'd no interest in traveling the countryside with him. She wanted to settle down on her homestead, undisturbed, and she doubted that would happen were she to wed the Reverend. Besides, the man resembled a mule. He had a gaunt, haggard look to his long face that hinted at the troubles he'd seen, or caused. He preached a good sermon, and that's as much as she knew about him and as much as she wanted to know.

"Regardless of his views on gambling, he sure beats that traveling Baptist preacher that used to come through here," Rooster continued. "Now that man was definitely against gambling. He was also opposed to drinking, dancing, smiling, you name it. In fact, the only thing he seemed to be in favor of was being 'washed in the Blood of the Lamb.' He was forever marching us all down to the creek to wash our sins away by 'immersing us in the cleansing water of our Dear Lord.' It got so I shivered every time Banjo Bob lit into 'Shall We Gather at the River.' "

Marjorie nodded in agreement, recalling how that cleansing water had come straight from the snow-packed mountains.

"It was barely tolerable in the summer," said Rooster, "but

it was downright freezing in the fall. Why, half the town had the croup by Halloween." He pulled out of the conversation long enough to dip out glasses of lemonade and set them in a row on the bar. People knew enough to leave their nickel when they picked up a glass.

"We were fortunate that Rooster called a halt to this foolishness by announcing the Lucky Lady would no longer be available for Sunday morning meetings," said Marjorie. "The Baptist minister was all for meeting down by the creek in God's church, but gave up on that idea when the only one who showed up for Sunday services was Grandma Heltne."

"I recall that," said Rooster, looking back over his shoulder. "She was all bundled up and shouted out right at the beginning that she didn't need to have any sins washed away as she'd not committed any immoral acts since her previous dunking."

Rooster appeared to get a kick out of that memory.

"We never saw him again," Marjorie said. "We weren't able to hold services until earlier this spring when the Reverend Thompson arrived and Rooster generously offered the use of the Lucky Lady again." She smiled and nodded at Rooster.

"It's just good business," Rooster explained. "Having Sunday meetings brings people to town. The women like to get together after dinner, which leaves the men free to enjoy a game of cards and a bit of conversation themselves."

"Now, Rooster," she said. "There's no need to hide your good heart that way. You were willing to put the needs of the town ahead of your own when you stopped allowing services in the fall."

"No one was staying in town anymore," he pointed out. "We were all soaking wet every Sunday. Folks had to go home right after the sermon to change into dry clothes. That Baptist preacher was bad for business, I tell you." After a pause he added, "The angels must have been watching over us when they directed Reverend Thompson down our path."

"I suspect it's the same angel who's picking up his bill over at Ruby's." She looked straight at Rooster to let him know that she was aware of what was going on even if no one else was. He was such a sweet man; too bad he was so short. He'd built a raised floor behind the bar, but even then he didn't quite come to her neck. Without it, he was barely elbow high.

"The good Lord wants us to share," was all he would say.

"We tried to hold meetings without a pastor," Marjorie said, "but it just wasn't the same."

"It surely wasn't," agreed Rooster. "With no one to put a lid on things, the services were nothing but a bunch of old biddies reading Bible scriptures about the shortcomings of others."

"I wonder what could be keeping the Reverend?" said Marjorie in an attempt to switch the subject. She had no desire to spend the entire morning recounting the trials and tribulations they'd endured in bringing this spark of civilization to Hope Springs.

Just then, she noticed Charles standing in the doorway. Now, why would he leave the roundup to attend church? He was probably planning on doing a little campaigning, she decided. She so hoped he wouldn't cause a scene and was relieved when he ignored her altogether and walked over to join the rest of the men.

She wished Hank would come and stand with them. He was well respected in the community, and his associating with Leon wold go a long way toward assuring the townspeople of Leon's good character. Perhaps Hank was making certain the talk didn't veer off in the direction of vigilante action. In any case, he stayed in the back with the other men, leaving her and Leon up front, chatting with the bartender and nodding to people as they glanced their way. The situation was awkward, to say the least. She wished the service would get under way.

Apparently, others were having similar thoughts, because Lucille Herner, Chairman of the Hospitality Committee and President of the Ladies' Bible Study and Needlework Circle was tapping a spoon on a lemonade glass and calling for people to pick up their hymnals and find their seats.

Folks began shuffling around, lining themselves up by families on the row of benches.

"Why don't we sit over here," she said, motioning to the two benches that Hank and the kids were settling into.

"Thanks anyway, but I plan on slipping out when it starts getting hot and heavy," Leon said. "It won't be so noticeable if I stay here by the bar."

"Since the Reverend Thompson," Lucille said in a voice just shy of a shout. She paused and waited for people to settle in their seats. "Since the Reverend Thompson has been unavoidably detained, I thought we would start with the hymns and the committee reports." She now had everyone's attention. She paused again for effect. "Please stand and turn to page 156, 'Sweet Hour of Prayer.' "

Marjorie slid onto the end of the bench next to Mary Beth. She and Hank stood and held the hymnal low so that the little girls between them could see the words. The two of them didn't need it, they knew the words by heart. But it helped the little ones learn to read by following along while they sang.

She turned to look over her shoulder at Leon. Perhaps he'd join them if she invited him with a fetching smile. Her mouth froze midway to a smile as she found herself held captive in his gaze. The room could've been on fire, and she wouldn't have moved. She probably wouldn't even have known it was ablaze. The rest of the world faded, and her thoughts became a jumble of images and sensations. She was aware that his lips shifted slightly, as if sending her a secret kiss. If she could've moved at all, she would have gone to his arms. But her feet felt like they were nailed to the floor, and she didn't have the strength or the will to lift them.

A nudge in the back from Janey pulled her from her reverie. Holy Moses, she'd been staring at him through practically the entire hymn. What would people think? She quickly scanned the hymnal in an attempt to find the verse they were on. She joined in at "and oft escaped the tempter's snare," and wondered how many more times she could escape the snare of her tempter before she'd be lost forever.

"By thy return, sweet hour of prayer." The song ended, and she handed the hymnal to Hank.

Lucille Herner instructed them all to sit down. Then she said that they would now hear the committee reports, starting with the Hospitality Committee. She introduced Evie Sanderson, although everyone there already knew Evie, and said that Evie would be reading a report that the Hospitality Committee had worked many long hours on.

Evie stood and opened her mouth, but before she could get a sound out, Lucille interrupted her to say that the Hospitality Committee took its duties seriously and that they'd examined a number of alternatives but were finally forced to admit that they had no choice but to pursue the course of action that Evie would describe.

Evie cleared her throat and got out an "uh" this time before Lucille cut in. She said that the Hospitality Committee's intention was not to cause any hard feelings, but to ensure the stability and growth of the congregation. She turned to Evie and extended her arm in invitation for her to speak.

Evie said "uh" twice and glanced down at the paper she was holding in her trembling hands. "As assistant to the Chairman of the Hospitality Committee—" she began.

Once more Lucille broke in to announce that a strong congregation was the backbone of a community and that just because some duties were not pleasant did not mean that they were not necessary.

Marjorie wanted to look over at Leon to see what his reaction to this silliness was, but she dared not. What if he caused her to laugh out loud right in church?

Lucille urged Evie to continue. By this time, Evie was trembling all over like a small, nervous dog. Marjorie half expected a little puddle to form at Evie's feet.

Unable to continue, Evie handed the paper to Lucille. "You go ahead," she said in her high-pitched voice.

They fussed a bit, with Lucille insisting, "Now, Evie, it's up to you to read the report," and Evie squeaking, "Oh, I really can't." The paper went back and forth, and people started whispering among themselves.

Marjorie imagined the grin that must be spreading under Leon's mustache, and it was all she could do to keep from glancing back at him.

Finally, Almira Powers, in that ridiculous hat with the bird's nest on the side, snatched the paper away and began to read aloud. "It has come to our attention that certain people are proving to be a divisive force in our congregation."

The congregation quieted down immediately in anticipation of just who would be included on the "divisive force" list.

Lucille tried to grab the paper back, but Almira turned away from her and held the report out of reach. Marjorie wished that Ruby was here. She had a calming effect on people, and that was sure to be needed before long.

"In view of this," continued Almira, while fending Lucille off with one arm, "the Hospitality Committee has compiled a list of those who are no longer welcome at Sunday services." She scanned the list, her face falling into an angry scowl before she'd reached the bottom.

"Well, I'll be!" Almira ripped the paper in two, threw the pieces down, and began grinding them into the floor with her foot. She called Lucille Herner "a meddling old biddy" who ought to have her own name on the list. Lucille reached down in an attempt to snatch the torn paper back. While she was bent over, Almira hauled off and kicked her in the side. Lucille lost her balance and toppled into the people on the front bench.

In their scramble to get out of the way, the first row fell back against the second row, who repeated this maneuver, sending the third row of worshipers into those on the fourth bench. The whole congregation spilled over onto the floor, bench by bench, like a line of dominoes.

Marjorie was caught in the midst of the squalling babies, cursing men, and shrieking women. She struggled to get to her feet, only to be knocked off-balance by those flailing about all around her.

She was relieved to feel a strong arm encircle her waist and pick her up out of the fracas. Leon sat her on the bar, then waded back in the midst of the melee to help Hank pull Janey and the girls out.

Most of the women managed to extricate themselves and their little ones from the heap, but the rest seemed perfectly willing to carry on until the cows came home. The men as well as the boys appeared to be taking an easy enjoyment in the free-for-all, landing a punch here and there and getting their licks in when the opportunity presented itself.

However, the women who remained in the midst of it were going at it like bulldogs, snarling and ripping at each other's hair and clothing. Marjorie had never seen anything quite like it.

"Do something," she begged Rooster.

"What do you want me to do?" he asked in astonishment.

"Stop this brawling."

"Okay, that's enough," he shouted.

As far as Marjorie could tell, this had absolutely no effect. She doubted he'd even been heard above the shouting and swearing of the participants and the cheers of encouragement by the onlookers.

"I think we might have to let the ruckus take its own course," shouted Rooster. "The only thing that seems to be getting busted up are the benches, and they'll be easy enough to nail back together."

Rooster might be willing to stand by and watch this disaster in the making, but she certainly wasn't. She turned to Leon. "Do something," she demanded.

"All right," he said, and pulled his pistol out of his holster.

Good heavens. She hadn't meant for him to shoot anyone. She jumped off the bar and grabbed on to his arm in hopes of averting a catastrophe. Leon wrested his arm out of her grasp, pulled the hammer back, pointed at the ceiling, and squeezed the trigger. The sharp report of the pistol had the effect of stopping the brawlers in midmotion.

The place looked like a giant game of freeze tag. From her years as a teacher, Marjorie knew that once she had their attention, she'd better act fast.

Over the ringing in her ears, she announced, "Anyone who does not stop immediately and go straight home to Sunday dinner will never again be welcome in Ruby's dining room or in my schoolroom."

She let this sink in for a moment. Then, lowering her voice, she emphasized the point with, "And I mean never."

She looked around the room with her that's-enough-of-this-foolishness expression. Would it have the same effect in a saloon as it did in a classroom?

"If we don't leave, are you going to have your husband kill us all in cold blood?" Charles's voice rang out. "I hear he's good at that."

"Are you willing to back up those words, or are you mostly mouth?" Leon said. His hand hung loose at his side, still holding the pistol.

"That's the way you gunfighters do it, isn't it? You egg a workingman into a fight, then claim self-defense," Charles taunted him.

"Irwin, I've about had my fill of you. If you want to settle this once and for all, then step outside. Either that or put a cork in it."

"You'd like that, wouldn't you?" Charles said.

"What I'd *like* is for you to get out my face. If I need to shoot you to do that, then so be it."

"I have no intention of putting these women and children in danger just to satisfy your bloodthirsty approach to problem solving," Charles said, in an obvious attempt to gain the high ground.

"We could always step outside," Leon said.

Marjorie was stunned. There was no doubt in her mind that he meant this. Surely, Leon wouldn't kill Charles just to get him to hush up.

"And risk a stray bullet injuring an innocent bystander. I don't think so," Charles said arrogantly.

"Since you're so concerned about the good people of Hope Springs, I suggest you get out of town before anything unfortunate occurs."

"You've not heard the last of me," Charles warned as he stepped toward the back exit.

"I don't doubt that one bit," said Leon.

The door slammed, ending the shocked silence. Everyone began talking at once.

"Quiet," Marjorie insisted, but the conversation continued to buzz. She put her two pinky fingers to her teeth and gave the shrill whistle she used to call the children in from recess and there was silence again.

"My husband is not a murderer. If you would take the time to get to know him, you'd see that he is one of the kindest, gentlest men you'd ever hope to meet."

"Sounds like the teacher's got herself a pet," someone said. The talk started up again.

"Can I shoot just one of them?" Leon asked Marjorie.

"Absolutely not."

Almira let loose of Lucille and loudly announced that she'd had it with church anyway—bunch of righteous do-gooders. She picked up her hat, smashed and stomped beyond recognition or redemption, grabbed on to her husband's arm, and marched out the door.

One by one, and family by family, most of the rest followed, being careful to keep their distance from Leon. A few cowboys remained behind to help Rooster carry the benches, or what was left of them, around to the side of the saloon.

Marjorie gathered up the children and herded them out the door. The girls were missing their hair ribbons and had a few torn places in their dresses, but the boys' clothes were ripped to shreds. One of Thomas's eyes was swelling shut. Samuel had a split lip and a gash across his cheek. Blood was flowing out of Caleb's nose. She had him pinch his nostrils together as they walked back to the boardinghouse. She hoped it wasn't broken.

She was mortified, absolutely mortified. Leon must think the people of Hope Springs were nothing but a bunch of ninnies. How had things gotten so out of hand?

Worse yet. What must the townspeople think of Leon? First there was that unfortunate incident in front of the stage depot just as they were leaving for Denver, and now this dreadful exchange with Charles. Shooting off his gun in church hadn't helped his image in the least.

It was difficult to imagine a less favorable introduction on both sides. She'd had such high hopes for the day, too.

The yeasty aroma of bread baking surrounded them as they stepped into the kitchen. Marjorie cleaned and slathered ointment on the various cuts and scrapes. Despite her stern disapproval, the boys cheerily recounted their involvement in the brawl as if it were some sort of merry adventure. With Leon's encouragement their tales got wilder and wilder.

"Stop egging them on," she insisted.

Just then, the gaunt Reverend Thompson poked his head in the room. "Did you not receive word that I would be holding services today?" he asked. His eyes went from one boy's face to another, but he didn't comment on their condition.

"We heard," said Hank.

The Reverend looked around the room, taking in the ham on the sideboard and the gravy bubbling on the stove. "Since my arrival was delayed, perhaps it would be better to wait until after dinner to gather up the congregation," he suggested.

Marjorie looked at Leon, then at Hank. Both appeared to be

biting their tongues to keep from laughing out loud. What did those two think was so funny about this deplorable situation?

"We've already gathered," she said. "There was a disagreement that got out of hand." How could she explain what happened without making the whole town sound like a bunch of nincompoops and her own husband like a cold-blooded killer? "I believe it would be best if we let tempers cool down before we get everyone in the same room again."

"Perhaps a sermon on turning the other cheek would be called for here," the Reverend persisted, clearly not wanting to pass up a chance to preach.

"Most of us don't have any cheeks left to turn," said Caleb. He was still holding a wet dishcloth to his nose, but what was visible of the rest of his face was all scraped and scratched.

"I see," said the Reverend. "Perhaps it would be best to let matters settle down."

"We'll be serving dinner in about a half hour if you'd care to join us," Marjorie said.

"I'd be delighted," he said.

"Thomas, please see to the Reverend's horse." She turned to the Reverend. "Would you like to wash up."

Marjorie tied on an apron, set Leon to slicing ham, and directed everyone else, including Hank, to what they could do to help get dinner on the table. As she planned on washing clothes later, she sent Caleb and Samuel out to fill and light a fire under the washtubs.

After pulling the bread out of the oven and putting the cobbler in, she checked on Ruby and was pleased to see that her aunt was sound asleep.

Returning to the kitchen, Marjorie saw Leon trying to remove a loaf from the bread pan by picking it up from the top. She reached across in front of him and, placing her hands over his, showed him how to hold the bread pan by the sides and dump the loaf out onto the cutting board.

Standing next to him, she felt a wave of longing pass through her. So this is what it would be like, this aching want that never quite went away. Even enjoying the simplest pleasure would be tainted by knowing it wouldn't last.

He dumped the other three loaves out and lined them up like sentinels against the hungry hordes.

The children each took a plate and made the rounds, filling them with mashed potatoes, gravy, green beans, and ham and delivering them to the customers in the dining room. Thomas sliced the bread and brought it out, and Janey poured the coffee and collected the seventy-five cents a meal. Samuel carried out a pan of apple cobbler and announced that they were welcome to help themselves to dessert. It was a smooth-running operation, and, within no time, everyone was eating.

The customers could linger as long as they cared to, but Ruby always liked to get Sunday dinner served and out of the way so that they could sit down and eat together as a family. The rest of the week they might grab a plate and sit in the dining room or eat in shifts in the kitchen. But they ate Sunday dinner together.

It was crowded at the kitchen table with the whole family there, and Marjorie noticed that Leon hung back, as if he wasn't quite certain whether he belonged here or not. She put a filled plate at the end opposite Hank and nudged Leon into the chair. The look of relief that flooded his face was enough to break a person's heart. How awful to grow up feeling you were an outsider at your own dinner table. What was the matter with people, anyhow?

She filled another plate and scooted in next to Leon. Hank said a quick blessing, and they began to eat.

After they'd satisfied their initial hunger, the boys began talking about the rope they wanted to tie on a branch so they could swing out over the creek. Caleb mentioned that it was too bad they didn't have a rope dangling there last summer. The Baptist preacher would've loved it.

"Brothers and sisters," he began, his voice hanging on the first syllables in the manner of their former minister. "Catch your sins by surprise. Don't save up until Sunday. Wash them away whenever the spirit moves you."

The girls began giggling, and, just for a moment, Marjorie wished she could let go and join them in their laughter. But someone had to call a halt to this silliness if for no other reason than out of respect for the Reverend Thompson in the other room.

"Caleb, that's enough," she warned. "The Reverend will hear you."

"He would probably think it was funny, too," said Caleb.

"I doubt that," she said.

He began loudly humming "Shall We Gather at the River," which brought on another round of giggling and guffaws, at least among the younger members of the family.

Why isn't their father doing something about the children's misbehavior? Why must I be the responsible one? She decided there was little use in telling her uncle to do something about it, since judging from the amusement on his face, he thought it was as humorous as they did. She glared at Caleb, hoping that would be enough to quell his blatant disregard for propriety, but he avoided looking at her.

"Caleb," she whispered furiously.

"What?" he asked, all wide-eyed innocence.

"Stop that," she insisted.

"All I was doing was humming a hymn. If a body can't hum a hymn on Sunday," he said, standing up and raising his arms with his palms facing inward as if inviting the congregation to stand and join in, "when can we hum a hymn?" He drew out the repetition of "hum a hymn," relishing his own wit and the amusement of his brothers and sisters.

She was grateful that just as Caleb was getting carried away with his impression of the pastor, Leon turned to Hank and said, "I was just wondering, what with the whole town so sure I'm a murderer and all, why do you and Ruby seem so unconcerned about Marjorie being out there all alone with me?"

The mention of murder darkened the mood of the family considerably. With his audience distracted, Caleb stopped in midstream and sat down.

"I admit I had my doubts about you," Hank began. "But Marjorie assured us that you were always the perfect gentleman around her and that if you were going to harm her, you'd had plenty of reason and time enough to do it before you returned from Denver."

"She's right about that," Leon admitted. "I'll be glad when that deputy figures out who actually killed Jarveson."

"I think the deputy has this pinned on you," said Hank.

"I believe so, too," Thomas added. "He always stays here when he's in town, and we haven't seen hide nor hair of him since the day you got back from Denver."

"He lit out after a gang that's robbing stagecoaches up north," said Caleb.

"Did you guys hear anyone mention anything suspicious this morning before church?" Leon asked.

"Jake's two hired guns are working for Irwin now," Hank said.

"Why's that so unusual?" asked Leon.

"Well, even though Charles hired on nearly all the Lazy J hands, what would he be needing with a couple of gunmen?" asked Hank, adding, "Especially now that Jake's gone."

"You've got a point there," Leon said. "Unless maybe they were working for Irwin all along. That might explain a few things."

"I don't suppose you have any idea who might've killed Jarveson?" Hank asked Leon.

"Don't look at me. I don't know a soul here. I just rode into town a few days ago." He paused for a moment, then drawled, "And I've been far too busy to do any detective work, that's for sure."

He looked over at Marjorie, and she felt a hot flush creep from behind her ears. *Good heavens*. They were married and perfectly within their rights to engage in marital relations, but that was hardly a matter to hint about in front of the children.

"Not to mention that you've barely been able to walk," she said pointedly, standing up and turning around. "Anyone care for apple cobbler?" she asked as she walked over to the sideboard. The breeze coming through the window felt good on her overly warm face.

A chorus of "yes, please," filled the room, and she fussed about straightening things up and getting bowls out. Even the sound of his voice had a disquieting effect on her. She knew it wasn't the topic Leon and Hank were discussing now. What did she care about the best way to train a cutting horse and whether having them drag a log around was useful or not?

She turned her mind to all the work that needed to be done before the day was finished. There were dishes to do and supper to fix. The laundry room was piled clear to the ceiling, and the kitchen and dining-room floors could use a good scrubbing. Even though it was Sunday, she didn't believe the Lord would mind if she gave her aunt a helping hand so she could start the week out fresh.

"I could use some help with the wash this afternoon," she announced to the boys.

"Shoot. We was planning on fooling around this afternoon," said Caleb.

"Fishing," said Samuel, nudging his brother hard in the ribs. "We was planning on fishing so that we could have trout for supper."

"Were planning, not was," she corrected him absentmindedly. "And as much as I'd like a nice mess of trout for supper, it's a warm afternoon with a fine breeze. It'd be a good day for hanging out wash."

"It'd be a good day for kite flying," Caleb muttered, almost under his breath.

"I agree. If we all pitch in, there'll be plenty of time for both," said Leon. "What do you say, Hank?"

Leon had obviously caught Hank off guard, but to his

credit, he nodded in reluctant agreement. Marjorie was amazed. Though women often pitched in to help the men out, it rarely worked in reverse. But far be it from her to pass up an offer of assistance.

After dinner, while the girls cleared the dishes, she taught Leon, Hank, and Thomas how to mix the grated soap in the hot water and how to stir the sheets around in the washtub. In anticipation of the muscles they would be developing, Caleb and Samuel offered to crank on the wringer handles.

Marjorie, Janey, and the girls sorted out the piles of laundry from cleanest to dirtiest then turned to hanging out the wash as it came out of the last tub of rinse water. A few items had to be sent through the cycle again, but by and large, they did an adequate job. The sun was still high in the sky when she pegged the last pair of pants up to the clothesline.

After that, Marjorie had them move the tables, benches, and chairs from the kitchen and dining room and stack them on the porch so it'd be easier to scrub down the floors. Holding brooms and mops in their hands, the children all slid and slipped across the wet floor like they were skating on a pond.

Joining in the spirit of things, Leon grabbed Marjorie and spun her around as if they were on a dance floor. It felt good having his arms around her, and, tired as she was, it gave her spirits a lift.

They all enjoyed themselves, the floor got fairly clean, and it wasn't long until the boys were heading off with Leon and Hank to fish away the afternoon. Emma, Maggie, and Mary Beth wanted to play dress-up in the attic and Janey said she was going to call on a friend. Janey didn't volunteer the name of the friend, and Marjorie didn't ask. She hoped it wasn't Clay Egan, but she truly didn't want to know.

The children took their noise and commotion with them, leaving the house sighing quietly and smelling of soap and fresh air.

Marjorie was long past ready to lie down for a nap. It was a struggle to keep her eyelids from drifting shut as she watched the little girls race up the stairs to the attic. Before lying down, she checked in on Ruby and was disheartened to find her aunt sitting on the edge of her bed, rubbing the sides of her forehead.

"I feel like I'm being kicked by a mule," Ruby said. "I hope these horrible headaches don't continue the whole time."

Having no words of comfort to offer, Marjorie suggested a hot bath. It was all she could do to put one foot in front of the other as she went off to check the fire under the hot-water tank. She was thankful that Samuel and Caleb were so energetic about keeping all the tanks and tubs full of water for she surely didn't have the strength to do any pumping now, not after the night and day she'd just had.

While the water was warming, she helped Ruby change the sheets on her bed. It was discouraging. The wash was still hanging on the line, and already the laundry was starting to stack up. Marjorie didn't even want to think about it, or she, too, would be slumped over holding her head in her own hands.

While Ruby gathered up a clean nightgown and undergarments, Marjorie snapped her aunt's nine-patch quilt in the air over the bed and let it settle softly across the length of it. She yawned and wished she could crawl under that quilt and curl up right there in Hank and Ruby's bed. She knew that would never do, but she wasn't certain she had either the strength or the will to keep going.

It turned out she had just enough of both to fill the zinc tub with hot water.

"Thank you, honey," Ruby murmured as she stepped in and sat down to soak.

Marjorie wished there was something more she could do to ease her aunt's pain. She'd suffered through similar bouts nearly the entire time she carried Emma. Marjorie pushed the thought of the ordeal at the end out of her mind. Why did Hank continue to put Ruby's life at risk like this? They already had a houseful of children, and they both knew how hard it was on her.

Then the memory of last night returned, and she realized how persuasive that would be. Even realizing the risk, how could a person say no to that forever?

"Is there anything else I can do for you?" she asked, wondering if she had the fortitude to follow through on her offer.

Fortunately, her aunt said "No," and Marjorie quietly closed the door and shuffled off to her old room. She collapsed on the bed, not even bothering to take her shoes off.

Finally, a few minutes to myself. She lay there thinking how matters had changed between her and Leon. It wasn't just last night, it was today. It was standing next to him in church. It was working alongside him all afternoon. It was laughing in his arms as they whirled around the sudsy floor. Things had definitely changed between them, and she needed some time to consider what it all meant.

But she wasn't going to get that time now. She'd no sooner sunk down in the pillow than she heard a shriek followed by loud wailing, and Mary Beth calling out for her "Auntie, Auntie," at the top of her lungs.

Marjorie waited a minute, hoping against hope that they could work out the situation themselves. When the voices didn't diminish, she swung her feet over the edge of the bed and prayed for strength.

"I'm coming," she shouted. No sense Ruby getting out of the tub. That water wasn't going to stay hot forever.

She plodded up the stairs. Perhaps whatever misfortune had occurred would be resolved by the time she got there.

No such luck. A trunk lid had fallen on Emma while she was bent over the edge. There didn't appear to be any lasting damage, but Emma needed a great deal of comforting as it had been a frightening as well as painful experience. Marjorie suggested that what they all needed after such an exciting day was a nice nap. No one took her up on the offer.

Emma thought she might feel somewhat better if they were

to bake cookies. Seeing that peace was beyond the realm of possibilities, Marjorie agreed and trudged after them, grimly noting Emma's remarkable recovery at the mention of cookies.

They wanted to make cut-out sugar cookies, so Marjorie helped them mix and roll out the dough. The girls fashioned the dough into shapes while she sat with her head on the table, dozing off between disagreements.

She wished she had time to get her thoughts in order. Things had changed between her and Leon. But had they changed enough to make a difference?

7

A wave of wanting passed over Leon as he lay in the high grass and watched Hank and his sons fishing side by side. He wished he'd have grown up with a pa who was around all the time instead of someone who blew into town now and again with a lot of big stories, most of them made up.

But what the heck, he'd turned out all right, hadn't he? If you wanted the truth, he'd turned out a lot like his old man. He found the adventures of life more appealing than the routines.

However, he just might be able to get used to the routine of spending Sunday afternoon fishing, especially in a place like this. Sunbeams worked their way down to him through the holes between the spring leaves. The trees would fill out in a month. By then a man would need the shade. The breeze that seemed to be a steady feature of this whole valley blew the bugs away and kept the air smelling fresh and clean. Through the ripples of Clear Creek he could see trout wiggling back and forth, making their way upstream to spawn.

He figured he was a lot like those fish. It was spring, and it was time to spawn. Now what kind of crude thinking was that? It was one thing to drop a bunch of fish eggs in a stream, quite another to leave behind a kid to fend for himself.

He felt a pang of guilt remembering last night. He'd done everything he could think of to keep from planting his seed in Marjorie. He hoped it'd been enough. He could kick himself for not bringing the preventative he'd gotten from that dry-goods woman in Denver. But how was he to know what the evening had in store? He'd seen her ride off and had followed just to be sure she was safe.

Now be honest, he told himself. As soon as he'd seen her saddle up, he'd had a sneaking suspicion she was off to meet someone, and he wanted to see who it was. For all he knew, it might have been that Irwin fellow. Maybe their wedding was a sham—something she'd made up to make Irwin jealous enough to marry her himself. Perhaps she was seeing the years slip away with nothing but fine talk and promises, and she'd cooked up this whole marriage and homestead business as a way to bring Irwin to heel. Women were devious creatures. He wouldn't put it past one to pull such a stunt.

When he saw her duck under that waterfall, he was certain she was heading to a rendezvous. Why else would she strip down to her shimmy first? He almost rode away right then and there. He would've if he hadn't recalled how innocent she'd seemed watching the horses that afternoon. It struck him as peculiar that an experienced woman would behave the way she did. She acted like she didn't know what was going on with the horses or with him either. Even her own responses seemed a mystery to her.

Things just didn't add up. His curiosity got the best of him, and he'd followed her into the cave. Then he'd heard her singing about someone in a green shirt being all her joy and all her delight and he was a goner. He was buried in her before he so much as gave a thought to what he'd left back in the cabin. It was too late to go back then.

Maybe it was time to settle down. With the exception of that stage ride, the last few days hadn't been all that unpleasant. The townspeople were quarrelsome as all get out, but he imagined he could get used to that.

Settle down and do what though? He'd been around this tree before. The only thing he knew how to do was work with horses and there didn't appear to be a big demand for that around here. If he didn't watch out, he'd be roped and harnessed to a plow before he knew it. What an unsettling thought, to know what every day had in store for you.

No, he'd never cared for routine, for chores, for knowing that tomorrow would be just like today. But right now he was purely envious of this family, their easy laughter with one another and their knowing who was going to wash and who was going to wipe the dishes. Growing up, he never knew from one week to the next who his brothers and sisters were going to be, much less how they were going to divvy up the chores.

That wasn't completely true. He always knew who was going to get the dirtiest jobs. Since the other kids always belonged to somebody, they generally got to pump the water while he was sent to haul out the slop jars. In between stepmothers, he'd lived with a couple of different families, but the situation never changed. Somebody had to weed the garden and milk the goat, and that somebody was usually Leon McCoy.

No sense dwelling on the past, he told himself, *not with a day like this to enjoy.* He'd caught himself a couple fish and now it was time to catch a few winks. He tilted his hat over his eyes and let his thoughts loose.

They went straight to Marjorie. Earlier in the day, he'd seen her standing in the doorway with Mary Beth on her hip. Just for a moment he imagined Mary Beth was their little girl, and the thought had nearly knocked him to his knees. It was right here, all of it, everything a man needed in life. All he had to do was hang on to it.

What would it be like to wake up with this woman in his arms every morning? Would he grow tired of her? Tired of having to answer to her about what he was up to and where he went? Would he live to regret the decision to throw his heart in the ring? What if she didn't want him? What if she only wanted someone to work around her place for a couple months? What if she took a notion to someone else after a while?

Would she wait for him if he was sent to prison?

Prison, hell. They'd probably hang him. There weren't all that many prisons in the territories, and people were generally unwilling to pay the keep for those they judged guilty of crimes. They either horsewhipped or hung 'em, depending on the crime and the mood of the jury.

Maybe he ought to figure his way out of this murder business first and worry about the marriage business later. That's what a sane man would do. A sane man would back off from getting in any deeper than he already was with Marjorie until he found out if it was even possible for him to stay.

He pondered possibilities until he fell asleep. It was close to dusk when Caleb stumbled over him on the way back to the house. The crickets and frogs were going at it, chirping and croaking for all they were worth. The smell of woodsmoke in the air reminded him that it was suppertime, time to be getting home.

Home. That had an appealing ring to it.

On the way back, the boys told him all about the ones that got away in spite of everything they'd done to set their hooks. Leon recalled his own intention of not clamping down on the hook, at least not until he had straightened a few things out first. *That's what a sane man would do*, he reminded himself.

But the minute he saw her standing in the fading afternoon light, gathering sheets up in her arms, he lost any claim to sanity. She was laughing with Mary Beth, who was

walking next to her, holding her skirt up to catch the
clothes-pegs that Marjorie dropped down.

She was beautiful. Her cheeks were blushed with the
breeze, and her smile would have lit up a cave at midnight.
The wind shifted and blew the armload of sheets across her
face. When she reached up and pulled them down, she
turned her head and looked straight into his heart. If she had
told him to drop on all fours and howl at the moon, he'd
have done it. He might do it anyway.

"How was the fishing?" she asked, smiling in his direction.

He would have traded his soul to be tangled up in those
sheets with her right now.

"Did you catch anything?" she asked.

He still couldn't put any words together and was grateful
to hear Caleb announce that they'd not only caught enough
for supper, but enough for breakfast, too.

"As soon as we get the beds made and these clothes
folded, we'll fry up some hushpuppies to go with them.
How does that sound?" Marjorie asked.

If she'd said she was going to boil up some old boots and
serve it over straw, Leon would have nodded in agreement.

Realizing his body as well as his mind was responding to
the sight of her, he turned away and hitched up his britches,
hoping that would make things less apparent. He wanted to
say something about washing up, or giving her a hand
bringing in the laundry, or ask if she needed any wood.
Anything would be better than standing with his tongue
hanging out like an old hound.

He strode off toward the livery, a fishing pole in one
hand and a string of fish in the other.

"Hey," shouted Caleb, running after him. He grabbed the
fish from him. "We don't keep those in the barn."

Leon paid no attention to him. This was never going to
work. He should ride out now while he still stood a chance.
He could promise himself all afternoon that he wasn't

going to touch her, and all it took was one smile to get him so hot and bothered he didn't know whether to whistle or wind his watch.

It hit him that this was why men put up with all the nagging and the endless work. But what about when the excitement wore off, what then? Had that been what happened between his folks? The good times had gone, and he was left behind to be shuffled around to any convenient woman willing to look after him for a time. If he ever saw his old man again, he'd be sure to ask.

Meanwhile, he'd best be on his way before he got snarled up in something he couldn't get loose of.

He set the fishing pole against a wall and strode back through the livery stable to the stall where he'd left his horse that morning. Ulysses stuck his head out over the gate, and Leon patted his neck.

"Going somewhere, or did you just come by to check on your horse?" Hank's voice broke through the quiet in the dim stable.

"Wish I knew," Leon answered.

"Being newlyweds is not as easy as you'd think," Hank continued. "There's a lot to get used to when you first marry." He walked over and leaned against the gate on the opposite stall.

"Let's get this straight—Marjorie and I are not newlyweds," said Leon.

"Sure you are. I saw the ceremony myself," said Hank. "Seemed kind of sudden-like, but it didn't take Ruby and me long before we knew that we were meant for each other. Figured you two made up your minds and decided there was no reason to wait around."

"I hate to disappoint you—" Leon started to explain, then stopped, trying to remember just exactly how he'd gotten to today.

"You won't disappoint me none, I barely know you,"

Hank said. "But my niece Marjorie, now that's another matter entirely."

"Listen, the sooner I get on my way, the better Marjorie is going to like it."

"Did you two have a little squabble?" Hank asked.

Leon couldn't believe it. The man was acting as if a slight disagreement was marring an otherwise blissful love match. Surely he remembered the wedding ceremony. Hank was bound to remember it better than he did. At least Hank had been sober.

"No, we didn't squabble," Leon grimly insisted. "I hardly know the woman."

"I feel the same way about Ruby, even after all these years," Hank sympathized. "Hard telling what goes through their minds."

At least Leon could agree with that. Whatever possessed that woman to be so determined about homesteading was beyond him. Why did she need to move so far out of town for anyway? A woman couldn't live alone out there, not without someone to protect her, and a man who couldn't provide wasn't much of a protector either.

Leon walked over to the tack wall and picked up Ulysses's bridle and reins. "It'd be better all around if I just leave now," he said quietly.

"You're not even going to let her know you're going?" Hank asked.

"She knows I'm leaving," he answered. "Hell, the reason she married me was because I'm a worthless drifter."

"Now, I don't know about that, young man." Hank seemed uncertain. Apparently, he and Ruby had not discussed their niece's marriage arrangement.

"Marjorie's a mighty particular woman," he continued. "I'm certain there was something about you she found appealing."

Did Hank wink at him? There was so little light, it was difficult to tell, but it surely seemed he'd given him one of those winks that would have been followed by a nudge if they'd been any closer.

"What she found appealing is that I wouldn't be staying around."

"There had to be more to it than that," Hank said, but he didn't sound real sure of himself.

"Say, what's with her and this Irwin?" asked Leon.

Hank took a moment before answering. "When we first moved to Hope Springs, he bid twenty-five dollars for her dinner basket at a box social. When he found out she was a schoolteacher, he decided right then and there that she was the woman he needed at his side when he made the run for governor. He's got it in his mind that he needs a practical woman with an education, and he's been calling on her ever since. She tries to discourage him, but he's not an easy man to discourage."

Hank paused. He pulled a piece of straw from a nearby stack and rolled it around with his tongue, taking his time before continuing. Leon didn't push him. He figured Hank would get it out in his own good time.

"You probably know this," Hank said finally, "but Marjorie doesn't have that high an opinion of men."

That was hardly news to Leon. "Well, she did say something about being engaged to a man who made off with her savings."

"I never cared for him or the worthless cuss her sister married," Hank said. "Her pa wasn't much of a provider either."

Leon pulled out a straw for himself and waited for Hank to continue.

"Ruby and I figured that though she was sour on men in general, maybe once she got to know Charles Irwin, she'd change her mind. He seemed like a nice enough sort, and what with his ranch and all, she'd be well cared for."

"Did she ever warm up to him?" Leon didn't want to ask, but felt like he had to know if she'd encouraged the man's attentions.

"I think she tried to be pleasant to him, but as far as I know, she's never mentioned a word about wanting to settle down with the man," said Hank. "Of course, she never mentioned you before either."

Hank straightened out a harness hanging on the wall before going on. "Marjorie's a caution all right. She gets the damnedest notions, but she's got more sand than men twice her size. She'd fight a rattler and give him first bite."

Leon had never heard a woman described quite that way before but he had to admit, it fit his wife to a tee—what he knew of her.

Hank fooled around with a halter and Leon began to wonder if he was ever going to get to the point. "Ruby explained to me how Marjorie tricked you into being her husband so you'd sign those homesteading papers," he said. "I apologize for my part in it."

"It's over now," said Leon, and he truly felt that way.

"You'd be within your rights to just ride on out of here," said Hank. "But I've got sort of a soft spot in my heart for that girl. I wish you'd go say good-bye to her first, tell her you got somewhere you got to be or something you need to do. Let her down easy."

"Hell, I wasn't going to leave her, Hank," Leon said. "I was just going to go nose around a bit, see if I could turn up any information on who done in that Jarveson. Over the years I've taken the punishment for a lot of deeds I didn't do, but I'll be damned if I'll go to prison for a murder I didn't commit."

"Yeah, I'll bet that old codger out at the Lazy J knows more than he's letting on," Hank said. "I imagine a friendly game of cards and a bottle of whiskey would go a long way toward loosening his tongue."

"You read my mind," said Leon.

"You know Marjorie's been with us ever since her mama passed on. Ruby and me, we'd just about given up on her finding someone to build a life with. Glad the two of you seem to be hitting it off."

"I wouldn't get my hopes up if I were you. Once I'd signed those homestead papers, Marjorie's interest in me dwindled considerably."

"Then how come she blushes every time she looks your way?"

"I wouldn't know about that."

"My guess is, you wouldn't have to talk too hard if you were of a mind to settle in with her." Hank was fooling with a rope now. After a short silence, he added, "If that's what you want."

"She's quite a woman, don't get me wrong," Leon assured him. "I'm just not the settling-down type."

"Who the hell is?" Hank asked, turning toward him.

"Then why get the woman's hopes up?" said Leon, with more bitterness than he realized he felt. Much as he liked Hank, he didn't like the idea of the man leaving Ruby and the kids. But it was none of his business, and he ought to just keep his nose out of it.

"I suppose you're referring to my taking off for the Black Hills?"

"I ain't referring to nothing. It's your business," said Leon. "I just think it's a damn shame you leaving her and the kids stranded here, especially with her in the family way and all." He'd said more than he planned on and decided he'd best just shut up about it.

Hank hit the side of the stall with a closed fist, startling the horses with the sound. "What the hell am I supposed to do? I can't make a living here shoeing horses for an 'I owe you one' or a 'I'll catch you the next time I sell a steer.' I don't mind helping Ruby with the laundry now and again, but I don't want to take in wash for a living."

He lowered his head and scuffed straw around with his boots. "Hell, you think I like wandering around, sleeping with a bunch of gnarly old men and eating beans three times a day?"

Leon didn't say a word. In fact, he wished he'd never brought it up. It was hard to see a man hurt like this right in front of your eyes.

"I thought this town was going to grow. I thought the gold mining would pick back up after the war. I thought the Homestead Act would bring in folks, and I could support us with no trouble. Hell, if it weren't for Ruby's contract with the Overland Stage Line, we'd be eating beans three times a day ourselves."

He turned and looked at Leon straight on. "You tell me what I'm supposed to do." He popped the stall another good one. "Hang around here and watch my wife work herself to death feeding and caring for other folks or go find a place prosperous enough to support a good blacksmith?"

"The war screwed things up for all of us," was all Leon could think of to say.

"You got that right."

The man was caught in his own loop, and Leon was regretting that he'd jerked on the rope.

"I'm so henpecked I molt twice a year," Hank said, "but I can't stick around hoping things will get better forever."

"No, I guess not," said Leon. But he wondered how he could walk away from this warm family feeling, everyone pitching in, joking and teasing. Even if he was an outsider, it felt satisfying to be in the midst it. But he had enough troubles of his own to keep himself occupied without nosing into Hank's.

He imagined he could keep a tight rein on himself for one night. Leon picked up his bridle, walked across, and hung it back on the tack wall.

"I guess I can always go check things out tomorrow," Leon said.

"That's what keeps me around," said Hank.

Leon nodded and followed him out through the barn

door. They joined the boys on the back porch cleaning the trout they'd caught. Once they had them gutted and rinsed out, Samuel carried the pail of entrails to the garden to bury while the rest washed up.

Leon noticed how they each grabbed an armload of wood on their way in and dropped it in the woodbox and how Hank went to check on Ruby again. Without even being asked, each boy went about his chores, all the while teasing Caleb about a cutthroat trout that he claimed was at least two feet long but had slipped off the hook before he landed it.

Leon poured himself a cup of coffee and took it to the back of the kitchen, where he sat on the bench and leaned against the wall. The giggling of the little girls floated down the hall and mixed with the smell of coffee and woodsmoke and frying fish.

The scent of lilac water passed over him and he looked up to see Marjorie standing in the doorway. How was he ever going to leave this woman? He felt like his head was playing tug-of-war with his heart.

He needed some time to think things through, and there was absolutely no possibility of that with her standing there looking so dreamy-eyed at him.

After they all ate, Leon suggested that since it was dark already, why didn't they just spend the night in town. He figured it would be a lot easier to keep a lid on things if they were surrounded by a houseful of people.

Marjorie wouldn't hear of it. Exhausted as she was, she insisted he saddle their horses and take her home. She appreciated his concern, but she said she wanted to wake up in her own bed, thank you.

Before they'd even reached the edge of town, she was dozing in the saddle and leaning clear over. For fear she'd fall right off, he'd nudged Ulysses next to Rosinante and lifted Marjorie on in front of him.

As they plodded along he began having serious doubts

about that being a wise idea. With every step, her backside rolled against him, and the situation was getting out of hand. He shifted around and tried to scoot back up on the saddle. She settled in. If possible, it seemed that they were closer than before.

Her head was leaning over on his shoulder, and he could feel her soft breath on his neck. He tried to focus on what they'd had for supper. Those hushpuppies were bite-size bits of heaven, but before he could fully recall their flavor he was recalling what her earlobes tasted like. He decided he'd better think about something else besides food.

He started reciting his times tables, beginning with the threes, when he felt her pitch over to one side. He grabbed her and had her upright before he realized he was holding her by one bosom.

She awoke with a start and pulled his hand off, muttering, "Oh, for heaven sakes, Leon."

If she knew what was happening behind her, she'd have jumped right out of that saddle. Her hair smelled like lilacs and looked like silk in the moonlight. The feel of her body nested into his was driving him out of his mind.

What in the hell was he going to do? If he didn't get away from her, nature was going to take its course.

He looked back to see that Rosinante was still following along and gazed up at the sky. The Big Dipper and the North Star were waiting for him like old friends. A falling star streaked across the edge of the sky. What should he wish for? Did he want this day to become a pleasant memory that he could pull out to keep him company some lonely night? Or did he want this day to last forever?

He'd always prided himself on being a man of adventure. Now all of a sudden, he was imagining things like sitting in a chair at the head of the dinner table instead of on a stump next to a campfire. Would he look down one day and find to his disgust that he was wearing sleeve garters and spats?

A wolf howled in the distance. How many times had he

heard that call and answered with a howl of his own? He'd always considered himself a lone wolf, a man who was content to live on his own, who didn't need and didn't want a lot of people around. But at least a wolf had a mate and some cubs. Maybe that's what he needed. The more he thought about it, the more he was sure that it was time for him to settle in and that the woman in his arms was the one he wanted to settle in with.

Only a week ago he'd been footloose and fancy free, in search of clear skies and warm winds. *Now look at me. Next thing you know, I'll be trading in my saddle for a buggy.*

Well, just what was so good about the life he was leading anyway? Cold and hungry half the time, sleeping next to his horse. What kind of life was that? He'd had some high times, no question about it, but they'd been few and far between.

Maybe he was just getting old. He'd be thirty before long. The thought of coming home every night to Marjorie sounded mighty appealing. He recalled how she looked in the morning with the pillow creases on her cheek and at night when she braided her hair by lamplight. He remembered the way she slapped mud on the cabin, laughing and singing with the girls. He called to mind how nervous and determined she looked that first afternoon in the Lucky Lady and how she kept her shoulders back and her head up even when she was biting her bottom lip and twisting that hankie around. She had the gumption to go after what she wanted even if it meant marrying up with a stranger. And he had to admire a woman for sticking up for her man when, for all she knew, he was a gunfighter and a murderer.

So what if she was on the pushy side? Maybe he needed a nudge now and again.

The longer they rode, the more enticing she became. She was a handful, no doubt about that. But he'd tamed a mustang or two in his day, and he felt certain that he was up to gentling Marjorie.

Then an idea hit him like a sack of rocks. Mustangs. That was the answer to his predicament—mustangs. He could tame mustangs for a living. There was a herd stopping by their place on their rounds. He'd seen the unshod prints near the mouth of the canyon. The hills were probably full of wild ponies just waiting for someone to throw a saddle on them. Though he'd never rounded up a herd on his own before, he didn't see why he couldn't. He'd ridden the rough string for outfits before, and he knew most of the tricks. Only now he'd be doing it for himself. He liked the sound of that.

That took a load off his mind. He'd been knocking back and forth like a cue ball on a billiards table. One minute wanting to stay so bad he could taste it, the next realizing that there was no way in hell he could. Seeing a way out was pure relief.

Once he stopped fighting his feelings for her, he began enjoying the pleasurable sensations of having her next to him. He was surely looking forward to the rest of the evening. And the rest of his life. He'd not given the future much thought before. He generally just wanted to see what would turn up. But it was time. Time to settle down. Marjorie was a good woman. This was good country. What more could a man ask for?

A man could ask for those murder charges to be cleared up, that's what. Three days ago he'd been accused of killing someone, and he hadn't done one thing about it except worry over it. He had to admit that he'd been on the busy side the last few days and that his foot had been giving him fits. But it was healed up enough to put weight on it, and he ought to ride on over to the Lazy J bunkhouse and see what he could find out.

Before he realized it, they were home. Maybe he'd carve out a sign with "McCoy" on it and hang it over where the trail turned into the meadow.

Holding her felt so fine, he hated for it to come to an end.

But Ulysses was standing in front of the cabin and there didn't seem to be any point to sitting on a horse once it'd stopped moving. He swung to the ground and slid Marjorie down in his arms.

She snuggled into his chest but didn't wake up. He carried her into the cabin and laid her on the bed, deciding against taking off her clothes. She could sleep in them. Undressing her would only tempt him to stray from what he needed to do tonight. He did try to take her boots off, but he couldn't get the buttons loose. She probably used some sort of hook, he decided, and he didn't know where she kept that. He tugged the star quilt from under her and covered her up with it.

Gazing down on her, Leon marveled at her innocence and determination. He wondered if he loved her. Women set such store by that word. Sooner or later, she'd be asking whether he did or not, and he'd better think of something to say besides "I dunno, I guess."

His experience with love was limited but from what he'd seen it was something that grew over the years, something you looked back on. You made a commitment and you kept it and then one day you realized that love was a part of that. It didn't just pop up out of nowhere, it grew like a tree. He imagined love could be like a wildflower, shooting up in the spring and frozen dead by fall. But he guessed he'd prefer the tree kind of love. You could hang a family on that—sons to take fishing on Sunday afternoons, daughters in pigtails to ride around on your shoulders.

The more he thought about it, the better he liked the idea of putting down roots here with Marjorie. He could make a living breaking and training horses. He was sure of it.

After lighting a fire to take the evening chill off the cabin, he stood in the doorway and looked out at the new moon hanging over the distant foothills. He felt peaceful in a way he hadn't in years, contented with his lot in life.

But time was passing. He surely wasn't going to get any

information by showing up at the Lazy J in the middle of the night. He picked up his bedroll from the corner where she'd tucked it and, closing the door behind him, stepped back outside.

He put Ulysses up in the shed and threw his saddle over Rosinante. It was unlikely the hands left at the Lazy J knew what the schoolmarm in town rode, but they just might remember what he'd ridden in on. No sense asking for trouble.

Rosinante set off at an easy lope, and Leon turned his mind to the best way to go about uncovering the information he needed.

Announcing that he was Leon McCoy, the man accused of killing their boss, was unlikely to loosen any tongues. But since he'd only talked with one man besides Jake Jarveson, had been riding a different horse, and had a shaggy growth of beard when he'd stopped through a week ago, he figured that he could call himself Will Nickels and no one would be the wiser.

He decided to put on that he was looking for a job and was no more interested than the next man in what had happened to the owner of the place. The cowhands had probably talked this topic to death among themselves and would be glad to have a new audience to test their theories on.

Once he had that figured out, he spent the rest of the ride thinking about Marjorie, dreaming of the life they could build together. It'd been a along time since he'd trusted the world enough to dream. Charlotte had convinced him to give up on that. That gal had sure acted like she wanted him as much as he wanted her. Then, as soon as he was out of sight, she changed up on him.

But Marjorie wasn't that way. First off, she wasn't flirting and teasing all the time. It was unlikely she'd start up just because his back was turned. In any case, he didn't intend to turn his back. A man could keep a woman in mind for years, but a gal couldn't seem to remember from month to month who she was pledged to.

Out of sight, out of mind as far as he could tell. In a way he understood this. A woman needed a man to protect and provide for her. What was she supposed to do while she was waiting for someone to return—hibernate like a bear? Not hardly.

But a man, well a man could get along just fine by himself. What a woman provided could always be bought. His mind wandered to their night at the hot springs. He doubted you could buy that for any amount of money. And he doubted you could buy the way he felt today with everyone joking at the dinner table or working together to get the wash out.

No, this was family. Knowing you belong. Pulling your share of the load. You couldn't buy that, you had to earn it. He wondered if he'd miss his wandering ways, giving up the adventuring and having only himself to answer to. It wasn't such a bad life.

But it seemed a tad on the short side when he stacked it up against waking next to Marjorie every morning.

He looked up at the stars as if expecting to find the answer written there. He saw another falling star streak across the horizon. Must be his lucky night. This time he had no trouble coming up with a wish.

As he turned up the trail leading to the Lazy J, he took out his Colt revolver, spun the cylinder to make sure it was working smoothly, and checked to make certain it was loaded. He didn't anticipate needing it but better to have it and not need it than the other way around. He slid the pistol back into his side holster.

The only light shining at the Lazy J was coming from the bunkhouse. Leon guided Rosinante over to its porch, dismounted, and tied the reins to the corner post. He stomped across the porch to let folks know he was around and rapped on the closed door with the back of his hand.

"Anybody here?" he asked in a loud voice.

"Who the hell wants to know?" came back through the closed door.

"Name's Nickels. Looking for a place to put me and my horse up for the night," Leon answered.

The door swung open and a bent-over old man with a sawed-off shotgun stood in the doorway. The light from a coal-oil lamp fell on the old man's face.

"This ain't no boardinghouse," the old codger said, belligerent as all get out.

"I can see that," Leon told him. "Not looking for a home. Just a place for me and my horse to bed down for the night."

"What are you doing out here?" the old guy demanded to know.

It was a mighty unfriendly greeting, but Leon guessed you didn't get to be an old man by trusting just anyone you met up with.

"Just passing through, thought I'd stop by and see if you might be needing another hand on the roundup."

"Got no idea how they're fixed for hands. Ain't no one here that knows neither."

What a cantankerous old coot. Looked as if his scheme was going to be nipped in the bud.

"Sorry to trouble you," Leon said. "Guess I'll go make a dry camp on down the road." He turned and strode across the wooden porch, stopping to loosen Rosinante's reins. "Thanks for the hospitality," he added.

"Hell, I guess it wouldn't hurt none if you was to spend the night," the old-timer reluctantly offered. "You can turn your horse loose in yonder corral if you've a mind to."

He swung the sawed-off shotgun in the direction of a pole fence.

It wasn't much of a welcome, but it was all Leon was going to get, so he took it.

He walked Rosinante over to the corral, pulled off her

saddle and bridle, and shooed her through the gate. "Behave yourself," he said, giving her a slap on the rump to send her on her way. He didn't see any other horses in the corral. She'd be all right.

He strode back to the bunkhouse, making enough noise on the plank porch to announce his return. Opening the door, he stood for a minute to survey the surroundings.

The place looked like a hundred others he'd been in. Rows of bunks lined all the walls except the corner by the door where the barrel stove was. On the floor next to the stove was a low wooden box full of sand for spitting in. Judging from the brown splotches on the wall, the men living here were still working on their aim. The corners of the room were piled with discarded clothing, worn-out boots, and who knows what all. A few chairs, most in need of repair, took up the remaining space. The old man was sitting in one on the far side of the stove.

The smell was familiar as well, a mixture of coal-oil smoke, old socks, cigarette butts, and sweat that Leon found comforting. He'd spent the best years of his life in such bunkhouses, trading tales and passing around chewing tobacco and cigarette makings.

"You alone?" he asked. Some of the piles of bedding might have a man under them, but it was not likely this soon after sunset, not unless the man was hurt or sick.

"Just me and my Sally." The old man lifted the shotgun up to introduce her to Leon and to show that he could have her ready in no time. "The rest of the hands are over at the Circle I bunkhouse, but they'd come quick enough if they heard a shot. However, at this range, I doubt I'd need any help."

"Don't need to worry about me causing any trouble," Leon assured him.

He tossed his saddle and his bedroll on an empty bunk and dug out a pouch of tobacco, a packet of rolling papers, and a tin of matches. He put them on a stool near the old man and sat down on a chair close enough to reach them, but far enough away that he wasn't crowding the old codger.

"Help yourself," Leon said, leaving the sack open after spreading out a line of tobacco on a rolling paper.

"Don't mind if I do, young man." In spite of his gnarled fingers, he skillfully rolled a tight cigarette, ran his tongue along the edge of the paper, and bent over to get a light from Leon's match before he shook out the flame.

"Who'd you say you were?" the old man asked after they'd both taken a couple of drags on their smokes.

Leon looked over at the old-timer. Did he remember him? Was he giving him a chance to get straight on his story? Somehow he doubted that. Despite his fierce manner, the old man had quickly leaned the shotgun against the wall when offered tobacco.

Besides, he didn't look like he knew come here from sic 'em. His shirttail was hanging out, and the buttons were unevenly matched to the buttonholes. What was left of his gray hair was all tangled up. Probably hadn't run a comb through it since Christmas. Which, judging from the aroma he gave off near the stove, might have been the last time he'd washed up, too. Most of his teeth were missing, as were the two far fingers on his left hand.

"Nickels," said Leon. "Will Nickels."

"They call me Dangerous Dan." He stuck out his right hand and gave Leon a surprisingly firm handshake for as weak as he looked. "I come by the name honestly, but I'd just as soon not go into it."

"Fine by me," Leon said.

They smoked in silence until Dangerous Dan said, "Well, Nickels, if you're looking for a job here, you're fresh out of luck."

"Story of my life," Leon said. He took a slow draw on his smoke.

"Yep, Jake done sold the place," the old man said. He

went into a fit of hacking and throat clearing that was purely disgusting.

Leon didn't know quite how to lead the conversation in the direction of Jake's demise. However, in his experience, bunkhouse conversations ranged far and wide. If he just hung in there, they'd get around to discussing the owner's death.

"You don't say." Leon wanted to keep up his end of the conversation.

"Yep. Charlie Irwin bought the whole place, lock, stock, and barrel."

"Maybe he's looking for a hand," Leon suggested.

"Don't think it'd be worth your time, Nickels," Dangerous Dan said doubtfully. "I hear tell he's got trouble meeting the payroll as it is."

"Oh." Leon tried to sound mildly interested in Irwin's affairs but not overly so. There was no sense in being mistaken for a Pinkerton detective.

"Yep. I reckon it took all his ready cash to buy this spread." He took a deep drag. His cigarette had burned down until he was barely able to hang on to it with his thumb and first finger. He flicked it in the direction of the sandbox and missed. The smoldering butt rolled over next to the door to finish burning.

"Mind if I have another?" he asked.

"Go right ahead," Leon offered.

"Yep, left me behind to keep an eye on things until that woman shows up for her belongings," Dan said as he adjusted a rolling paper just so between the remaining fingers of his left hand.

"What woman?" asked Leon.

"Jakes's wife, of course. I'll tell you that woman was hell for cleaning. She wanted me to sweep this place out every Saturday." He waved his arm about as if he'd been asked to sweep up the prairie once a week.

"She had the nerve to tell me to water it down first." He

ran his tongue along the paper edge in a motion that reminded Leon of a lizard darting after a fly. "Have you ever tried to sweep up mud?" He turned to Leon.

"Can't say as I have," Leon answered.

"Well, I'll tell you it's a damn mess." He gave a quick twist with both hands, producing another tightly rolled one.

Leon struck a match and held it out for him. Dangerous Dan leaned over and sucked in until his roll-your-own glowed a third of the way down.

"If I was a young man like you, I'd just gather my gear and hit the trail." The old coot hawked up a mouthful of phlegm and let fly in the direction of the sandbox but missed. Leon watched in disgust as it slid down the leg of a chair.

Leon imagined that it wouldn't take Dangerous Dan long to gather up his gear. He was probably sitting in most of it right now. But where would he go? Generally, every ranch already had one or two old-timers, too aged and crippled up to be much use beyond making coffee and keeping the stove lit.

"I used to be a hell of a hand in my day," Dangerous Dan started in, as if he'd read Leon's thoughts.

Here it comes—the story of every bronc he ever rode, every steer he's ever throwed, and every fistfight he's ever been part of.

"Too bad about this place being sold," Leon said quickly.

"It's a damn pisser, I tell you." Dangerous Dan took a vicious drag on his cigarette, then tossed the burning butt under a chair.

Leon reminded himself to move his bedroll to a bunk by the door and stay alert for smoke during the night.

"You want a cup of coffee?" Dangerous Dan growled. He stood up and let loose a string of farts so rich you could grow tomatoes on them.

"Don't mind if I do," Leon said, tipping his chair back

and turning his head to the side as if six inches would make any difference.

Old Dan handed him a tin cup filled with a black oily mixture. Leon took a sip. Could have been coffee. Maybe a month ago. Hard telling what the bitter brew was now.

"Ran out of coffee," old Dan said when he noticed Leon hadn't taken a second sip. "Been using roasted dandelion roots. Tastes a lot like that roasted chicory we used to get during the war."

As far as Leon was concerned, it didn't taste like any roasted chicory he'd ever had. But he took another sip just to be sociable.

"One thing nice about having a woman around the place," Leon said, trying to get the conversation back to Jarveson's death, "she probably saw to it that there was a supply of coffee."

"Nah," he said. "Jake's missus wasn't much for cooking. Her family had maids and such to do that. I believe living out here was somewhat of a surprise for her." The old man slurped up a portion of the brew in his tin cup.

"She'll be damned surprised to find out her husband got his throat slit," old Dan said.

"What?" Leon said, trying to sound shocked but not overly so.

"Yep." Dangerous Dan ran a finger across his throat. "Ear to ear it was." He appeared to relish the telling.

"Who done it?" asked Leon.

"I wouldn't know about that." The old guy turned and eyed Leon as if Leon would know about that.

"Don't look at me," Leon said, shrugging and raising his hands in the air. "I just rode up. Remember?"

"You seem mighty interested in things," said Dangerous Dan, squinting at Leon as if accusing him of something.

"Listen, you old coot," Leon said. "I'm only passing the time. Now if you'd rather not talk, I'll just stretch out and catch me some sleep and leave you to your unfriendly thoughts."

"There's no need to get your knickers in a knot," Dan said in that old-man whine of his. "I didn't mean nothing by it."

"Well, quit accusing a man unless you mean it." Leon flipped his cigarette butt in the sand. "I tell you, that gets old after a while."

Dangerous Dan picked up the coffeepot. "Want me to top that off for you?" he offered.

"Nah, I got plenty," said Leon. The stuff was so strong you could tan hides with it.

"Just seems funny you wanting to know so much about Jake and his missus and all."

"Hell, I wouldn't know Jake and his missus if they were dancing on the stove." Leon took another sip of the dreadful brew. "You've got a suspicious nature, old man."

"A man don't get to be my age without keeping his eye on things and when your boss gets killed, it's bound to get a man's suspicions up." He squinted at Leon again.

"Just who are you suspicious of?" Leon asked.

"Well, there was this saddle tramp came riding through," said Dangerous Dan, "and he got into a beef with the boss over a job what had been promised him."

Leon felt the blood leave his face. He was glad the chimney on the coal-oil lamp was covered with soot and giving out so little light. With any luck at all, the old man wouldn't notice how pale he was. Leon swallowed another sip of the counterfeit coffee.

"Did you see him do it?" he asked.

"Nope, but I damn sure heard him threaten to kill Jake," said the old man. "We all did." He let fly a mouthful of spittle. It landed on the stove, and they watched it sizzle into steam. "He rode off and then later that day, Jake turns up cold as a wagon rim. When I brought him his supper, there he was, slumped over his desk with blood running down his arm. That drifter had killed him." Dangerous Dan seemed certain of his story, as if he'd told it hundreds of times, which Leon guessed he had.

"But I thought you said that drifter rode off. Did you see him after that?" Leon asked cautiously.

"Nah, but I figure he snuck back in while we was all in an uproar over Jake selling the place. The boss paid everyone off and then Charlie Irwin offered to take on any of the hands who wanted to work for him. Some of the men didn't cotton to working for anyone as handy with a branding iron as Irwin is. It's bad for a man's health, if you get my drift."

Leon did. He'd seen where the cattle were penned up and he'd heard what'd happened to the men involved. He nodded to let Dangerous Dan know he understood what he was talking about.

"While we was all cussing and gathering up our gear, I figure he snuck in the back way, done the dirty deed, and then rode on out of the country. I doubt they'll ever catch him. But if they do, they'll hang him for sure."

Leon swallowed hard at the mention of hanging.

"Of course, now it could've been those two cowboys Jake hired on a while back. They was always out practicing their quick draw."

"What makes you think they done it?" Leon asked, trying to keep his voice level.

"First off, I been working around cattle my whole life and I ain't never seen no cowhands spending every living minute shooting at tin cans and knotholes. Oh, maybe now and again a couple boys would get in a mood, but bullets is too damn expensive for that sort of foolishness on a steady basis." Dangerous Dan set his empty tin cup down. "Mind if I have another smoke?"

"Go right ahead."

"During my younger years, I rode with a wild bunch, and I can tell you those two were hired guns and that's a fact.

Now why Jake needed a couple of gunfighters around is beyond me. But if he hired them for protection, he got took." Dan rolled another cigarette with a skill that only comes from years of practice.

"Why would he be hiring gunfighters? There isn't a range war going on is there?" Leon tried to sound as if he didn't want to get involved in that sort of mess.

"Not much of one," Dangerous Dan said. "Oh, he and Charley Irwin would get into it now and again, but that'd blow over quick enough. Fact is, I always figured Irwin would be the one to get himself killed. It was a damn shame those two boys was hung over that business with the running iron this spring. I figure they was just doing what they was told." The old codger dropped his voice like he was worried someone might overhear them. Though as far as Leon knew, they were the only ones for miles around. "To my way of thinking, should've hung the man what told 'em to do it."

Then he narrowed his gaze at Leon, checking him out to see if he could be trusted. He must have decided in Leon's favor because he continued talking. "Could be Irwin got tired of stealing Jake's cattle one or two at a time and decided he'd just kill him and take the whole herd. That son of a bitch is so crooked that when he dies, they'll have to screw him into the ground."

Dan leaned over for a light and took a deep drag. Before he could let it out, he began hacking and coughing something horrible. Leon wondered if he should go get him a glass of water or something.

It took Dan a while to get his breathing under control. But when he did, he continued on talking as if nothing had happened. "If Jake didn't hire those gunfighters to scare off Irwin, I bet they had something to do with that wife of his. Her family never did think much of Jake, and I suspect things didn't improve when he beat the stuffing out of her and sent her home."

"Surely they wouldn't have had the man killed for hitting his wife." Beating women wasn't anything Leon approved of, but it happened, and most folks just looked the other way.

"If his wife was going to leave him over it, they damn sure would," said old Dan. "Her daddy bankrolled Jake, you know."

"So you think her family had him killed so they could get the ranch back?"

"It's possible. To my way of thinking, it's just as likely as some saddle tramp killing the boss because he wouldn't give him a job getting his neck broke working the rough string." He sucked in and then let out a stream of smoke. "That don't hardly even make sense, now does it?"

"Not by a long shot." Leon heartily agreed with that line of reasoning.

The old man proceeded to ramble on about what a rounder he was in his younger days. Before they finally turned in, Leon knew about all the broncs he'd ridden, all the men he'd fought, and all the women who'd done him wrong.

The only thing he didn't know was who'd killed the old man's boss. He had some interesting theories, but nothing that came close to being an actual fact.

Dangerous Dan was still sleeping the next morning when Leon left. He thought about waiting around until he woke up to find out if any of the hands were partial to using knives. But then he'd have to drink another cup of that awful coffee, and he didn't know if his stomach could stand it. He must be getting soft.

He kicked Rosinante into a gallop. He couldn't wait to get back home, back to Marjorie. He'd lay it all out for her today. See what she'd say about him staying around.

On second thought, maybe he should put that off until he got this murder charge cleared up. No woman in her right

mind would promise to stick by a man who had something
like that hanging over his head.

He wished he had a clue about how to proceed from here.
The old man hadn't been a lot of help, and he could hardly
ride over to the Circle I and shoot the breeze with the crew
from the Lazy J. Irwin knew what he looked like. There was
no love lost between the two of them, and if Irwin caught
him on his property, he might just gun him down right there
on the spot.

There had to be a better way to go about this. He'd give
it some thought.

But this morning, he had a woman to love, and Leon
McCoy intended to knock her right off her feet with his
charming ways.

8

Marjorie woke up, stretched her arms out on either side of her head, and let out a deep, soul-satisfying yawn. She must've been exhausted last night, for she was still dressed, even down to her shoes. The last thing she remembered was leaning back into Leon, feeling safe and secure in his arms as Ulysses plodded along.

She looked around for Leon and when she didn't see him, she guessed that he was outside taking care of the horses. He probably didn't want to wake her up.

As she started the fire and put the coffeepot on, she thought about what a sweet man Leon was and recalled the effort he'd made yesterday to join in the bantering conversation. He was a hard worker, too. Even with his hurt foot, he'd put in some long days without any shirking or complaining.

The memory of their night in the hidden hot springs brought on a warm glow. What would it be like to look forward to endless nights like that?

But was she willing to pay the price for those nights? Was she willing to endure all the work and worry that went hand in hand with raising children? Was she willing to raise those children alone if need be?

But maybe she wouldn't have to. Maybe Leon was a wan- derer because no one had ever asked him to settle down. She wondered what he would say if she asked him to stay and build a life with her. There was no missing the hunger in his eyes. Maybe he was tired of roaming around like a lost dog.

Though she tried to deny it, living out here alone was a concern to her. Not that she doubted she could take care of herself. Still, she rather liked the idea of Leon protecting her, standing by her side, like he had this morning in church.

Just the thought of that fiasco caused her to knot up inside. What a disgraceful display of brotherly love that had been. How could they call themselves Christians and yet shun him the way they did? Wasn't a man innocent until proven guilty? You'd think that if for no other reason than concern for her feelings, they would've tried to make him feel welcome. In- stead, they stood around whispering and staring like he was a leper.

She had to admit, they didn't treat one another a great deal better. Surely Leon realized that this brawling in church was an extremely unusual occurrence. While the men and boys of Hope Springs were likely to resort to fistfights upon occasion, this was the first time the women had behaved so deplorably. She only hoped it didn't result in permanent damage to their close-knit community. For the most part, people got along and helped each other out. She'd hate to see that destroyed by petty disagreements.

But she wasn't going to let this ruin her day. She threw open the door and filled herself with the chirping and war- bling of the birds in the sweet morning air. Closing her eyes, she counted her blessings—a good man, their own place, and the countless possibilities of the day. *Does life get any better than this?*

When she opened her eyes, she scanned across the meadow and up the creek looking for Leon and the horses, but she didn't see any sign of them. Looking toward the canyon, it hit her that he was probably up soaking in their hidden hot springs. What a grand way to start the day. What a perfect place to ask him to stay.

She let out a whoop that would wake the snakes, picked up her skirts, and ran up the path to the shed. She threw open the door and stopped in her tracks. Ulysses was there, but Rosinante was gone. Leon's saddle was missing as well.

With dismay, she looked out across the meadow. There were no impressions in the grass, no indication that a horse had left the path and crossed to the canyon.

He'd left. He hadn't even said good-bye. He'd just gone.

She felt like a foolish old maid. Here she'd been dreaming of spending the rest of their lives together and he didn't even care enough to say good-bye. He'd just up and left.

The pain was so deep that it hurt to breathe. She sank to the ground and curled her arms around the ache. How could she have been so witless as to think that a few days together would wipe out a lifetime of shiftless behavior? The man was a drifter and a drunkard. He was probably off wrapped around a bottle of whiskey while she stood wondering what she'd done wrong, what had scared him off.

Stop it. He never said anything about staying. That was your preposterous notion, not his. She'd best go on about her business and start referring to him as her "dear departed husband," like she'd planned from the very beginning.

She sat there staring out as if she could conjure him from the morning mist rising off the creek. She needed to gather her wits about her, get her thoughts in order.

When she did, she realized that Leon had not only left, he had left with Rosinante. *Sakes alive, what had possessed the man to steal her horse?* Then she remembered about Ulysses pulling up lame. With the deputy on his trail, maybe Leon figured he had some hard riding to do and Ulysses wasn't up to it.

Anger quickly replaced her sorrow. Of all the low-down, mean, dastardly tricks. She'd have given him Rosinante if he'd asked. But to steal her horse! Now she knew why horse thievery was a hanging offense. She was so mad, she'd gladly pull the rope herself.

She marched back to the cabin and began shoving chunks of kindling into the stove. A long sliver of wood jammed into the palm of her hand, and she jerked it out without feeling so much as a twinge of pain.

"If I never see that man again, it'll be too soon for me," she shouted out as she searched for a rag to wipe the blood on.

"Hello, darlin'." She heard his low voice coming from behind her.

She whirled around. "What are you doing here?" she demanded.

"I live here," he said, acting as if this was a silly question for her to be asking.

"Not anymore you don't. Now get out," she ordered. She grabbed a stick of wood and pointed in the direction of the trail.

Who did he think he was, stealing her horse and then showing his face around here?

"What's the matter, darlin'?" he asked, lowering his voice even more, as if he thought that would soften her mood.

"Don't you stand there calling me 'darlin'' and looking all mystified," she warned him. "You know darn good and well what the matter is." She was not one for cursing, but if there was ever an occasion that called for profanity, this was surely it.

"I have no idea why you're loaded for bear this morning," he assured her. "Last night you cuddled up in my arms sweet as a puppy, and this morning you're ready to hit me over the head with a chunk of firewood."

Her mind was in a turmoil. She was furious, relieved, confused. She turned around so she wouldn't have to see him while she got her thoughts in order. Leon stepped up behind her and put his arms around her. Without thinking, she stomped down on the top of his foot and then raised her leg and gave him a kick in the shins he wouldn't soon forget.

Leon jerked backwards, lost his footing, and fell to the floor. As he was still holding on to Marjorie, she went down with him. She began kicking for all she was worth and rammed her elbow back into his ribs. With no small amount of satisfaction, she heard him let out a whoosh of air.

Scrambling around on the floor, Leon tried to throw his legs over hers and Marjorie kicked and flailed about, struggling to get loose. They slammed against the bedpost, the woodbox, and the walls.

As he was somewhat larger and considerably stronger, it wasn't long before the only part of her body she was able to move was her head, which she repeatedly flung backwards with as much force as she could manage. A spurt of blood arced in front of her as they flopped under the table, and she knew she'd hit her mark.

However, he now had her pinned against the floor, and all she could do was wiggle and twist a bit.

"Arhhh," she cried out in frustration, then went limp while she tried to catch her breath. This was no easy matter with him spread the length of her. From the sound of his panting, he was taking advantage of the opportunity to fill up on air as well.

"Now there's an approach to courtin' I never thought of." Hank's voice caught their attention.

They both turned to look over their shoulders. Hank was standing in the doorway with the boys on either side and the girls peeking through the spaces in between, their eyes wide in amazement.

"But if the two of you find it satisfying," he added, "who am I to say."

"Let me up," she hissed, squirming to get loose.

"Nothing doing," he said. "I don't know if I got it in me to go another round."

"You let me up, or you'll be sorry," she whispered furiously.

"I'm already sorry, and sore to boot."

"I certainly am not going to attack you in front of the children," she said through clenched teeth.

"Well, that's a comfort."

She felt the hot flush of humiliation spread from the back of her neck across her cheeks and up to her forehead. What must they be thinking? There she was, wrestling around on the ground with her skirts up above her knees.

"We'll continue this conversation later," she said. "Now let me up." She pushed against the wall in an attempt to get room to move. Leon held firm.

"Not until you tell me what's going on." He tightened his grip on her.

"I don't want to be butting into your business," Hank said, "but I've got a borrowed plow here on the wagon. If you'll just tell me where you plan on putting in your garden, we'll take it over there and leave the two of you alone to settle your differences."

"Ah, hell, I'll come give you a hand." Leon let go of Marjorie, and the two of them crawled out from under the table.

Marjorie stood and glared at him. Blood was dripping from Leon's nose in a steady stream. She dipped a dishrag in the water bucket, wrung it out, and handed it to him. He held it up to his nose.

"Did she break it, Uncle Leon?" asked Maggie with concern.

He ran his fingers from the bridge to the tip. "Nah, it feels about the same. Come on," he suggested. "Let's go see how a plow works."

They stood aside as Leon walked out the door. Hank followed him, but the children stood staring at Marjorie as she attempted to make herself presentable. It was a task beyond what she could accomplish by tucking in loose strands of hair and brushing the dirt off her skirt. Aside from this morning's scuffle, she'd worked all yesterday and slept through the night in these same clothes.

"Come on, kids," Leon urged from outside. "Let's give your aunt Marjorie some breathing room."

One by one they quit gaping at her and turned away. She heard Thomas mutter, "Madder than a wet hen," as they turned to leave.

Marjorie collapsed in a chair, holding her head in her hands with her elbows braced against her knees. *Good heavens, this fighting and rolling around on the floor is getting to be a regular feature in my life.* How had things gotten so out of hand? Always before, she'd known what to do, how to handle matters. What was she doing married to a horse thief, a drunkard, and—for all she knew—a murderer?

To be honest, she had to cross horse thief off the list. She assumed he'd brought Rosinante back. He'd not been drunk in days, so it was probably unfair to keep accusing him of that. Nor did she believe for a minute that he was a murderer. That deputy was in a rush to get up north and deal with the stage robberies. He'd been hasty in accusing Leon, and Judge Cunningham would straighten it all out once he got into town.

She had to admit that what she was really upset about was how she'd deluded herself into thinking that they would live happily ever after, that all she had to do was ask him to stay. Had she taken leave of her senses? That man would come and go as he pleased without an explanation to her or anyone else. How in the world could she bear a life like that?

It seemed all she did lately was ask herself questions that she couldn't answer. If she kept this up, she'd soon be put in a home, making washcloths and small talk with strangers.

Then a chilling thought occurred to her. What if she couldn't get out of this mess? What if Leon decided to stay? Since he was her legal husband, the law wouldn't be any help, and she doubted that Hank would interfere in her marital difficulties.

Her earlier flush of embarrassment turned stone cold recalling this morning's struggle. This wasn't playing pretend anymore. This was for real. All she knew about the man was that he'd been a scout in the Union army, had been raised by a series of stepmothers, and some woman named Charlotte had given him the mitten. That wasn't enough to base a lifetime on. What had possessed her to even consider it?

She leaned her head back and closed her eyes. *Now what?* She could go back to Ruby and Hank's, lock herself in her room, and forget about this whole sad affair. She doubted Leon would stay around here without her.

But she would most undoubtedly lose this place. The Homestead Act was clear on the necessity of raising a crop and living on the land, and she was certain that federal land clerk wouldn't be making any allowances for extenuating circumstances, not for her at least.

What was a body to do?

Calm down. I'll cross that bridge when I come to it. She had five years for goodness sake. The more immediate problem was what do about being married to a man who took off whenever he pleased and showed up again when the spirit moved him. Even if it was grand when he was around, there was no way she could live like that.

She had to admit, yesterday had been more than wonderful. From greeting the dawn together in their hidden cavern to being wrapped in his arms on the way home last night, yesterday had been magical. She could've done without that fuss at church. But even at that, she recalled the relief of having him pull her from the pile and the strength she'd felt just from having him standing next to her.

She could usually come up with a strategy to deal with any situation. If the first plan didn't work out, then she'd try something else. For the first time in her life she had no idea what to do next.

She could ask him to stay and learn to live with his absences or she could ask him to leave and get it over with. But she wasn't all that certain she wanted him to leave, and even if she did, she wasn't sure he'd go.

In the past, she'd been accused of deciding things too

quickly, not considering all the possibilities. Now it seemed like all she did was consider possibilities.

As much as she hated to admit it, perhaps the best thing would be just to wait and see what happened. There was a lot of work to be done this summer. If he wanted to stick around and help her do it, so be it. No doubt it would be best to put off starting a family until the future was more certain.

She was not at all comfortable with that course of action. In her experience, the surest way for things to get out of control was to sit back and see what happened. But what else was she to do?

Stepping out into the sunshine, her eyes were drawn to where Hank was teaching Leon how to plow. Leon had the reins slung over his back, and Hank was telling him to keep the plow angled down into the ground so that it would turn over the earth rather than just skim along the sod at the top.

She watched the muscles along Leon's shoulders strain and pull at his muslin shirt and recalled the feel of those muscles under her fingertips.

Oh, for crying in the night, think about something worthwhile.

Marjorie turned her eyes away from him and turned her thoughts to the seeds she'd purchased at the dry-goods store in Denver. She hoped putting in a crop of peas was a good idea. Though they grew well during short, cool summers and were supposed to be good for the soil, how much split pea soup could they possibly eat this winter? Naturally, she'd plant carrots, turnips, green beans, squash, potatoes, onions, and cabbage. Ruby could put all the produce to good use. Marjorie had a rhubarb start she intended to plant near the creek, and the boys would help her cut and dry grass for winter hay. That should more than meet the cultivation requirements for this year.

Throughout the day, Leon, Hank, and Thomas took turns behind the plow. Marjorie and the children followed along pitching rocks out of the field and planting rows of seeds. By the time they loaded the plow back in the wagon, a sizable patch of meadow had been turned over and planted. Now all they needed was rain.

Marjorie and Leon stood side by side as they watched Hank and his wagonload of kids turn onto the road. Caleb was leading them in a rousing rendition of "Buffalo Gals." As they disappeared into the trees, "Dance by the light of the moon" hung in the air. For a moment that's exactly what Marjorie wanted to do.

What she really yearned to do was soak her aching back and shoulders in the hot springs, but she dared not go there until she and Leon had settled a few things between them.

Leon's arm rested across her shoulders in an awkward attempt at affection. She knew it would be more comfortable for both of them if she moved closer, but she didn't want to encourage him, so she stayed right where she was.

"Remind me to bake Carl and Almira a cider cake to say thanks for lending us their plow," said Marjorie, continuing to stare out where the wagon had been a few moments before.

"Isn't Almira the one that started that ruckus in church?" he asked.

"I assure you that was very unusual for Almira," said Marjorie, standing stiffly beside him. "I'll admit she's a plainspoken woman, but I've never known her to attack anyone before. In fact, I've never known anything like that to happen in Hope Springs. It's usually a very quiet, neighborly town. I can't imagine what you must think of folks brawling in church like that." She realized she was rambling on, but she couldn't seem to stop herself. "You can be certain that it's not an everyday occurrence."

He turned to her and placed a finger over her lips to quiet her.

"Margie," he said, moving his finger aside to stroke across her cheek, "we need to talk."

"We are talking," she said. "We're talking about that unfortunate incident yesterday, and I was assuring you that you needn't worry about the neighbors being disagreeable, although I can certainly see where you might get that impression." He silenced her by pressing his finger against her lips again.

She knew they needed to discuss matters. She'd thought of little else as she'd worked her way up and down the rows. But she dreaded either decision they'd come to. She couldn't bear it if he left, and she couldn't stand it if he stayed.

Pressing his hand on her shoulder, he turned her around to face him.

"I mean talk about us," he said in his deep, rich voice. Using the knuckle of his closed fist, he smoothed both sides of his mustache, and Marjorie's thoughts wandered to the feel of that mustache against her neck.

"I'm too worn-out for a serious discussion," she said, yawning to emphasize her weariness. "Couldn't this wait until the morning?" She concentrated on the collar of his shirt to keep from looking him in the eye.

"Worn-out doesn't begin to describe how my shoulders feel after bucking that plow through the sod all day," he said. "But we need to get some things straight between us, darlin'."

"Not tonight, Leon," she pleaded softly. "Please not tonight."

He pulled her close to him and kissed the top of her head. "What's worrying you, Margie?" he asked.

"I'm afraid you're going to leave," she said honestly, then added, "and I'm scared you're going to stay."

"That doesn't even make sense, darlin'," he said.

Pressed tight against his chest, she felt him try to hold in a chuckle. Here she was fighting tears, and he was laughing at her. What did he think was so darn funny about the situation? She pulled back and looked him straight in the eye.

"I'll tell you what doesn't make sense," she said. "It doesn't make sense for you to hang around here pretending you want to be a homesteader."

"Maybe I'm not pretending," he said. "Maybe I do want to homestead this place."

"That'll be the day." He might be interested in her, but she seriously doubted he had any interest whatsoever in being a sodbuster. The very word disgusted him. She turned away from him and stared off into the horizon.

"Why don't you just get off your high horse and listen for a minute. Maybe I've been wandering around just looking for a place like this." His hand dropped from her shoulder, and she immediately missed the physical connection to him.

"Ha," she said, folding her arms in front of her.

"Maybe wandering's a young man's game, and it's getting wearisome," he said, slowly stepping up beside her. "Did you ever stop to think that you might not be the only one in this world who wants a place to call their own?"

"Really?" It was difficult to keep the condescending tone out of her voice, and she didn't try all that hard.

"Really," he said. "Is it so odd that I might yearn for the same things you do?" He stepped in front of her, put his hand under her chin, and lifted her face until she was forced to look up at him.

"But what will you do when you hear the wind call your name and the mountains beckon to you?" she demanded, searching his eyes for the truth. "What about then?"

"Then I sleep out under the stars for a couple of nights and I dream about old times. I do what every other family man does when he feels that urge." He cradled her cheek in his huge hand.

"What other family men do," she said, scornfully emphasizing "family men," "is saddle up and go. The women can follow if they're up to it or stay behind if they're not."

His hand dropped to her shoulder and stayed there, as if afraid she would walk away if he didn't anchor her next to him.

"Take my uncle Hank and aunt Ruby," she said, trying to make him understand her concerns. "She's followed him from one end of the earth to the other, and he's still not satisfied. She finally put her foot down and said that she's not leaving Hope Springs, and if he does, she's refilling his spot at the head of the table."

"Seems mighty cold-hearted for such a warm woman."

"Cold-hearted or not, there are thirty-some men for every woman in the Territory," Marjorie pointed out. "I doubt it will take her long to find a replacement."

"With odds like that, even you should've been able to find someone that suited you," he said with a trace of bitterness. He pulled his hand away.

"I did," she said firmly.

"Well, where the hell is he?" he said, sounding downright surly.

"Standing right in front of me," she announced, every bit as cross as he was.

"Hell, lady, I don't suit you. You don't like anything about me." He moved away and lounged back against the porch post.

"You certainly do suit me," she insisted. "I like the fact that you are going to ride out of here any day now and leave me be."

"Maybe I don't feel like riding on. Maybe I plan on settling down right here in this valley."

"You might as well change your plans because that isn't ever going to happen, Leon McCoy," she said in a rush.

"And why not? My name's on the papers, same as yours," he pointed out.

"Because proving up on this place is going to take a lot of hard work, and I don't think you're up to it." Even to her own ears she sounded as if she was trying to provoke him, and she wished she could call the words back.

"Hell, I'm no stranger to hard work," he said. "In case you haven't noticed, Mrs. McCoy, I've been working like a dog ever since I got here trying to show off for you. I even spent Sunday putting out a wash, and me with a bum foot no less."

She had to laugh. Maybe it was because of the way he sounded so like a little boy who was discouraged because he'd tried so hard on his homework and yet it was still a mess. Maybe it was because she was wound up so tight and needed something to loosen her up. Or maybe she was just tired of fighting. Whatever the reason, she burst out laughing.

"I'd like to know what you think is so damned funny," he said. Now he was the cranky one.

Marjorie tried to control herself. She mashed her lips together in an attempt to hold it in, but it just kept bubbling out. It felt so good to laugh after fussing and worrying all day.

"Do you think you're the only one that ever wanted to have a place they could call their own and children they could watch grow up?" he asked, turning away from her so she couldn't see his face. The hurt in his voice put an end to her mirth.

"No," she admitted. "But I just never thought it would be all that appealing to you."

"How do you know what would appeal to me?" he asked, turning back to look at her. "Did you ever consider finding out?"

"I don't want to know what appeals to you, Leon," she said, feeling a sudden sting in her eyes and willing the tears away. "I don't want to know what you dream about when you go to sleep. And I don't want to know what you wish for when you wake up." She knew it sounded callous, but she meant every word of it.

"Why not?" he demanded, resentfully. "Are you just like all the rest? You want to work me like a borrowed mule and then shoo me away when you got no more use for me?"

Her heart went out to him, and she knew she was treading on dangerous ground. "If I know your dreams, Leon," she said finally, trying to keep the catch out of her voice, "how can I bear it when you leave?" Her eyes burned and filled with tears that she didn't bother to blink away or wipe off.

He pulled her into his arms, and she didn't resist. They held tight to each other and rocked back and forth in that slow rhythm known by heart to mothers and lovers alike.

She hoped he didn't promise to stay. He could no more keep that vow than a cat could take up swimming. It just wasn't in his nature. As much as he might mean it today, living on a homestead here in Hope Springs would be too confining for an adventurer, an explorer, a wild man like Leon. He was so much like her papa. She felt her throat tighten at the thought of him.

For some odd reason, she suddenly recalled holding hands with her mama one afternoon as they watched Papa climb up a barn roof to straighten out a weather vane. They both sighed out in relief when he finally got the bent vane set to rights. But instead of climbing back down to the ladder as they'd expected, he turned and ran across the ridge of the roof. Then, right in front of their astonished eyes, he took a flying leap. She doubted she would ever forget the sight of his legs churning in the air. Her fingertips still turned cold at the memory of it.

He landed in a pile of straw. After brushing himself off, he seemed none the worse for the wear. When her mother finally got her voice back enough to ask him why in the world he'd pulled such a stunt, he said he just had to see what it would feel like to fly.

To Marjorie's way of thinking, there were two kinds of people in this world—those who had to feel the danger for themselves and those who were aghast at the very thought of it.

The first kind wanted to taste everything, experience it all, live with a sense of heart-pounding excitement. Those people were constantly testing, exploring, peering into places, wondering what was just around the next corner.

The rest were quite content with their own corner of the world. Though circumstances might force them to skirt around the edge of danger, in their search for the dependable and predictable, they often ignored the peril in situations. It's not that they didn't want to enjoy life, it's just that they found their satisfaction in knowing, not wondering, what tomorrow would bring.

Marjorie was a member of the latter group. What was safe and comforting to her would be tedious and boring to Leon. What kept her sane would drive him crazy.

He'd have to go. He couldn't help it. Nor could she. That's just the way the world was. You could fight it, or you could accept it. Marjorie had learned long ago to accept the things she couldn't change. It didn't mean it wouldn't hurt, but it couldn't break your heart if you didn't let it.

"What if I promised you I wouldn't leave?" he said, putting an end to the long silence between them.

"My mama always said not to make promises you can't keep," she whispered. She rubbed her tears away on his shirt and held on to his waist for all she was worth.

"I'm a man of my word," he assured her. "If I say I'll stay, you can count on it."

"But what about your drinking?" she wanted to know. She was desperate to switch the subject, and this was the first topic that came to mind.

"What about my drinking?" he said, sounding befuddled by either the question or the turn in the conversation.

"I don't want my children raised by a drunkard," she said, realizing she sounded like a prudish schoolmarm. Well, why not, that's what she was.

"Darlin', unless you decide to take up drinking, they're safe," he assured her.

She felt the corners of her mouth pull into a smile and had to remind herself to stay firm. It was that "darlin'" business that always did it. He had a way of drawling out that word in a manner that made her toes twist around in her shoes.

"Ha," she sniffed. "I've only known you a week and you've already gone drinking three times."

"Only twice, and there were unusual circumstances that have to be taken into consideration," he pointed out.

"What about last night?" she asked cautiously. Some men objected if you pried into their business.

"What about last night?" he said, pretending innocence.

"Don't tell me you didn't go off and have a few drinks," she said. "I'm not witless you know." She pulled back and looked up at him.

"You do seem a mite thick from time to time," he teased and then stopped himself with a deep breath. Pulling his shoulders and head back, he continued, "But the fact of the matter is, I didn't go out drinking last night. I rode over to the Lazy J to see if I could get to the bottom of this murder business."

"And did you?"

"No." His shoulders sagged a bit in admitting it. "The only one around the place was an old man, and though he had a lot of 'suspicions,' it didn't appear he had many facts."

"Fiddlesticks." That was disappointing. She knew she should be more concerned about his arrest, and she probably would be if someone had actually seen him harm Jake. But threatening violence was a common enough occurrence between men. Even the boys in her classroom threatened each other with bodily harm over extremely minor slights. She'd seen fistfights break out over a coat hung on the wrong peg or an unkind comment about a horse.

Though he hadn't straightened out the murder, something must have happened to bring about this change of heart over staying.

"So, just what occurred last night that made you decide you wanted to be a sodbuster and a family man?"

"For your information, lady, I've been coming to this decision all week."

"You don't say." It wasn't that she didn't believe him, but she did find it odd that he hadn't mentioned it before now.

"I do say." He pulled her back next to his chest as if that settled it.

She found comfort in the steady beat of his heart and the gentle feel of her cheek nestled against his chest.

"Leon," she said after a while.

"Yeah, darlin'," he answered.

He would be staying, that was apparently settled. How long he would stay was another matter. But while he was here, she had to do something to protect herself if she could.

"Would you mind if we put off marital intimacies for a time?"

"If that's what you want," he said, sounding disappointed. "I take it you didn't care much for the other night?"

"Mercy, that's not it at all," she quickly assured him. "I nearly set my stockings aflame every time I think about it." She imagined he'd be pleased to hear that. "But if we're to spend the rest of our lives together, we need to base it on something more substantial than rolling around in the dark."

And if we are not to spend the rest of our lives together, she thought, *why make the parting any more difficult than it needs to be?* She couldn't begin to imagine what it'd be like to say good-bye after a summer filled with nights spent in each other's arms.

It would be better to devote their evenings to conversations on suitable topics. That way they would both grow intellectually. Later, they might even be able to share some of their common interests via letters. She let that thought leave as soon as it arrived. Leon did not strike her as much of a letter writer. But there was no doubt in her mind that discussions about books and mutual interests could form fond remembrances that could later be pleasantly recalled in a way that memories of lovemaking never could. She only hoped they'd not already begun a babe.

"Just how long were you, ah," he said, stopping to clear his throat, "thinking of?"

"How long have I been thinking of what?" she asked. She'd been lost in her thoughts and was a bit bewildered by the question.

"Thinking of putting off—" he hesitated for a moment, cleared his throat again, and then carefully said, "having relations."

"Until we learn to communicate on an intellectual level," she said with firmness. "I read where an intellectual relationship in which marriage partners discuss books and ideas is far better than one based on a few fleeting moments of excitement."

"I'll bet a woman wrote that," he said, with more than a touch of cynicism.

"Yes, as a matter of fact—a Mrs. P. Osgood Shumway, as I recall. But just because a woman wrote it, doesn't make it untrue."

"You're right. It makes no difference at all who wrote it," he reluctantly agreed. "If that's what you want, that's what you'll get, darlin'. Far be it from me to refuse you your heart's desire." After a pause, he asked, "How will I know when we've had enough 'intellectual communication' to try for a few of those 'fleeting moments of excitement'?"

"I'll let you know," she said primly.

Leon lifted her up in his arms and planted a kiss on her lips that nearly turned her stockings to cinders. Then just as abruptly, he set her down, swatted her on the backside, and said, "I'll see to the horses. You drag out them books, darlin'. We got ourselves some talking to do."

Marjorie stood in a daze as she watched him stride down to the creek. It would probably be best if they postponed the kissing until things were more settled between them. Well, maybe a kiss here or there would be acceptable.

Later, after the horses were put up for the night and Marjorie had stoked the fire and lit the lantern, she and Leon sat across from one another at the table.

"Where are we now?" he said, indicating *The Last of the Mohicans*, which was still sitting on the shelf.

"Chapter three," she said, pulling down the book and opening it to where a lavender ribbon marked where she'd left off.

She wondered if she should reread the first two chapters as he'd slept through a good deal of it. She decided she would fill in with an explanation here and there when it seemed necessary and keep on reading.

> "Before these fields were shorn and tilled,
>> Full to the brim our rivers flowed;
> The melody of water filled
>> The fresh and boundless wood;
> And torrents dashed, and rivulets played,
>> And fountains spouted in the shade."

He appeared attentive. However, midway through the first page she read about "the dull roar of a distant waterfall" and her own attention wandered, recalling the mist, and the spray, and the warmth of the other night.

"While one of these loiterers showed the red skin and the accouterments of a native of the woods," she read, looking up to see if she should explain what accouterments meant.

Good grief, he'd gone to sleep already. She was not going to read one more sentence to a sleeping man. How were they ever going to have any literary discussions if he persisted in falling asleep all the time?

She checked to make sure the latch string was in and the door was barred before blowing out the lamp and walking quietly over to the bed. She pulled off her dress and climbed beneath the covers in her chemise. She didn't even bother to put on her flannel nightgown.

"Get a grip on yourself," she distinctly heard him mutter.

"What was that?" Marjorie asked, pretending she hadn't understood him.

"Just trying to remember where I dropped my bedroll."

"It's in the corner by the woodbox."

"Thank you."

"You're welcome," she said, as sweet as you please.

She listened to him fumble around until he located his

bedroll and spread it out on the floor between the bed and the stove.

"Would you like a pillow?" she asked kindly.

"What I'd like is to snuggle up there next to you, darlin'," he answered.

"You might as well forget that," she informed him, "and I wish you'd stop calling me darlin'."

"What do you want me to call you?" he asked. "How about sweetheart, or honey, or sugar? Do you like any of those better?"

"Why not Marjorie?" she said. "That's my name." Then before he had a chance to reply, she added, "Why is it that men won't call others by their given names. It's always Shorty, or Slim, or Stinky, or whatever."

"Well, Marjorie, I hadn't realized that until you mentioned it."

"Women don't call each other such names," she continued. "Can you just imagine us sitting around a quilting frame calling one other Fleshy, String Bean, or Wrinkles?"

"How about Rooster?" he said this as if he'd caught her in an inconsistency. "Surely that's not his real name."

"I doubt his mother had him christened Rooster, but I have no idea what his real name is."

The conversation ended there, and she could hear him shift around, getting comfortable on the floor. She felt a twinge of regret and was on the verge of offering to share the bed with him if he promised to keep rolled up in his blankets when he said, "Darlin'," and she knew there was no way that was going to work out tonight.

"Darlin'," he said again.

"What?" she demanded. She'd just asked him not to call her that.

"Does this count as an intellectual discussion?" he asked.

"I hardly think anything we've discussed tonight could be called intellectual, not by any stretch of the imagination."

"I thought as much," he said with a sigh of disappointment.

"Do you want a pillow?" she asked.

"Might as well."

She tossed a pillow in his direction.

"Leon?"

"Yes, darlin'."

"I appreciate all your help."

"No problem."

They settled in and listened to the frogs singing their hearts out, calling to one another in a chorus of croaking.

"I wish things were more exciting for you here, Leon," she said after a time.

"Margie, I wouldn't worry about that if I were you. I'm kind of hoping that things will calm down. If the next week is anywhere near as exciting as the last one, I imagine my heart will just flat give out."

She fell asleep with a smile.

The next morning over hotcakes, he told her of his plan to tame wild horses.

"You're just saying that to frighten me, aren't you?" she said. "I thought you were looking for less excitement, not more."

"Taming a horse is nothing to be scared of," he said reassuringly, "not if you know what you're doing."

"And you do?" she said, raising her eyebrows.

"I've gentled a few wild ones in my day," he said modestly. He winked at her, and she knew he was talking about more than horses.

Then he went on to explain that what with all the people heading west, the stage lines, the ranches, and the cattle drives, there was a good market for horses. He was certain that he could get $50 to $75 apiece for the horses running wild in the hills. If he could get sixty or so broke to saddle, that would mean anywhere from $3,000 to $4,000, depending on the market and the quality of the horses. "Not too bad for a summer's work," he said.

This was a preposterous plan as far as Marjorie was concerned. It was absurd to think he would be able to catch even one or two of those horses. She hated to sound discouraging, but if it was all that easy, every cowboy in the country would be doing it.

But he seemed so set on the idea, almost as if he'd stayed up the whole night working out the details. Let him find out for himself, she finally decided. She only hoped he wouldn't be injured in the process. That's all she'd need—him with two broken legs stretched across her bed for the rest of the summer.

After breakfast, he gathered some tools, tied a roll of wire to Ulysses, and left to start fencing off the canyon. At least something good would come out of his silly scheme.

By the time she'd tidied up the cabin, the children had arrived. This time Janey was with them. She jumped out of the wagon and spun around in a circle, with her arms outstretched and her skirts billowing about her.

"I just couldn't bear one more day cooped up in that kitchen," she announced. "Not when I could spend the day out in the sunshine."

Marjorie had never known the girl to be so crazy about sunshine, but she was glad for her company regardless of her reasons for coming out.

The boys unhitched the team and led the horses down to where Leon was hauling the fence poles around. They were scattered every which way, no doubt strewn about when the rustling operation was discovered. Within a short while, they'd towed all the poles and cross posts into piles. But instead of placing them across the mouth of the canyon, they appeared to be creating a fence that extended out from it in either direction, like a funnel.

She and Janey watched their operation as they sat peeling logs for the privy. Emma, Maggie, and Mary Beth helped some but for the most part, they skipped around chasing butterflies and picking bouquets of wildflowers that they brought back in little drooping yellow-and-violet bunches.

Janey certainly seemed taken with the scenery today. She was forever looking this way and the next as if expecting fairies to appear. She was paying so little attention to what she was doing, that Marjorie was not surprised when she nicked her finger on the drawknife.

"I'll be back," Janey said, literally leaping up and racing toward the creek.

Marjorie helped Mary Beth weave dandelions into a circlet to go on her head and comforted Emma when she tripped and skinned her knee. Then they all searched the grass for Maggie's lost necklace. It was some time before Marjorie realized Janey hadn't returned.

After she got the girls going on an alphabet-clapping game, Marjorie set off for the creek. She followed it along as it meandered into a wooded area, stopping when she heard Janey's voice. From the sound of things, Janey was not alone.

It was difficult to decide whether to sneak up on them or give them fair warning. Admitting that she truly did not want to know what they were up to, she shouted out Janey's name.

"Aunt Marjorie?" came the hesitant reply.

Unable to resist, Marjorie followed the path a few more feet. There they were, sitting on a log that spanned the creek, their bare feet dangling side by side in the water. Marjorie was dismayed to see that Janey had removed her shoes and stockings in front of this young man, but she decided to ignore it. After all, she was not her mother.

"What is going on here?" The answer to that was obvious, but it was all she could think of to say.

"We're just talking, Mrs. McCoy," Clay Egan assured her.

Mrs. McCoy. She liked that. Miss Bascom was a prune of a name, reminding one of a dried-up spinster who clucked disapprovingly at children who squirmed in church. Mrs. McCoy sounded like someone who organized quilting bees and always had room for one more at her dinner table.

She watched as Clay helped Janey to her feet and led her across the log back to the bank of the creek. They sat down near one other and began donning their stockings and boots. Mercifully, he did not assist her in putting on her stockings, but from the shy smiles they traded, she assumed that he had helped her take them off.

"So what are your plans?" Marjorie asked as soon as they were fully clothed.

"Plans?" Janey was all innocence. "What plans?"

"Don't try that with me," Marjorie warned. "Clay's grinning like a schoolboy with a frog in his pocket. What are you two up to?"

"Nothing," Janey said in a singsong attempt at innocence.

"Janey," she admonished her gently.

She looked from one to the other, but neither seemed willing to volunteer any information.

"Why aren't you working today, Clay?" she asked.

"Oh, I had the day off," he assured her.

"In the middle of spring roundup?" Marjorie asked skeptically.

"I had to meet the stage," he admitted.

"What for?"

"Clay's trying to get on with the Central Overland Stage, and he was checking to see if they'd sent word yet," Janey said.

"He wants to be a stagecoach driver?" said Marjorie, astounded that they were still considering this ridiculous notion. "It's difficult to imagine why anyone would want such a job, but especially not a young man thinking of marriage."

"No, not a driver." Janey smiled up at Clay. "He wants to run a stage station. He could handle the horses, and I could do the cooking."

Hank and Ruby would have a fit when they found out. "Clay," said Marjorie, "why don't you go help Leon and the boys while Janey and I fix up something for our noon meal?"

"Yes, ma'am," he replied, and started up the path along the creek. Marjorie and Janey walked behind him until they reached the open area and then set off side by side across the meadow.

"Honey, have you thought this through or did it just come up today?" she asked, once Clay was far enough away that he couldn't overhear their conversation.

"We've talked about it some," Janey said.

"But that's such a hard life," Marjorie said. "You'll be stuck clear out in the middle of nowhere."

"No harder than homesteading," Janey pointed out.

"But what if he leaves?" Marjorie asked. How could she convince her to take off her rose-tinted glasses and see life for what it was, see men for what they were capable of?

"You think that just because a couple of men took off that they all will. Well, I don't know about the rest of them, but I know Clay will be there to protect and provide for me as long as he's still breathing. He loves me, Aunt Marjorie."

"What do you know about love?" asked Marjorie, grabbing her shoulder and demanding an answer.

"What do you know about it?" Janey demanded right back. "As soon as a man wants more than a kiss on the porch swing, you run back in the house."

"I'll have you know, young lady, I've done a lot more than kiss on the front porch swing." So there, she thought.

"Well, I have, too," replied Janey, throwing her hand over her mouth as soon as she'd said it. But the cat was already out of the bag.

"Janey!" Marjorie was shocked.

"Only once," she insisted. "Only once."

Only once. All it took was only once. Good heavens, she'd been so caught up in this mess with Leon that she hadn't seen what was going on right under her own nose.

"But I can't wait to do it again," Janey admitted. "I knew you wouldn't understand."

Marjorie understood all right. She understood only too well. However, this hardly seemed the time to discuss that.

"Please don't tell Mama and Papa," begged Janey. She reached out and grabbed Marjorie's hands with both of hers.

"Are you—?" Marjorie asked, not knowing quite how to word the question.

"No." Janey shook her head and looked down at her shoes.

"Are you certain?"

"No," she said quietly. Then looking back up she added, "But I don't know how much longer we can wait. It gets harder and harder to stop each time."

Marjorie didn't want to hear any more on that topic. "You're only fifteen, Janey."

"I'll be sixteen in July," she insisted, as if another month meant the crossing over into adulthood.

"You've got your whole life ahead of you," Marjorie pleaded, with the same earnestness that centuries of adults have pleaded with nearly sixteen-year-old, nearly women. She reached out and took hold of her hands.

"And I want to spend that life with Clay," Janey said. "I want to wake up in his arms. I want to go to sleep holding his babies. I want to grow old looking across the dinner table at him. Is that too much to ask?"

"No, honey, it isn't," Marjorie agreed, biting her lower lip. "I just want life to be easier for you, that's all."

"It isn't easy for anyone," Janey said. "I just want to spend the hard times with Clay." Realizing what she'd said, Janey pulled a hand loose to cover a giggle.

"You're hopeless," Marjorie declared, trying to suppress her own smile.

"I know," Janey said, grinning from ear to ear, "but I'm happy." Then the smile faded and she stared deep into Marjorie's eyes. "And I wish you were, too."

"We'll talk about that some other time," Marjorie said. "Let's get a picnic together."

Half an hour later, they carried two baskets full of food and an old quilt across the meadow to the canyon. When the boys saw them coming, they started to unharness the horses.

While Janey set the food out, Marjorie went with Mary Beth into the woods to relieve herself. On the way back, she overheard Leon's deep voice and stopped to listen.

"Don't care much for this harness business, do you, old boy?" Through the leaves, she watched Leon scratch Ulysses behind the ear and pull the leather straps off. "I don't reckon either one of us cares much for working in harness." Leon let out a heavy sigh. "But it comes with the territory. I imagine we'll get used to it after a while."

Marjorie was annoyed listening to him complain to his horse. The man was acting as if he was in prison, dragging a ball and chain around as he broke up rocks. After all, it was his idea to corral wild horses, not hers. And he was the one saying he wanted to stick around. She'd not insisted upon it. If he was this discouraged within a few days, imagine how wearing his long-suffering attitude would be after a few years.

Leon was a wonderful man—hardworking, easygoing and heart-stopping handsome. There was no denying they were attracted to one another and no denying that he yearned for a home or that she wanted him to stay.

But he was a dreamer. Imagine believing that a person could make $4,000 rounding up mustangs? After this fell through, what would his next scheme be?

No, much as they both might long for him to stay, if he lasted through the summer, she'd be surprised.

9

Leon was glad to have Clay around. The kid was work-wise, didn't have to be told twice to do something, and was excited about the prospect of rounding up wild horses. There was a lot to be said for any one of these three qualities.

He offered the kid his pick of the mustangs if he'd stick around until they were all rough broke but asked him if he was sure he wanted to leave his paying job at the Circle I for that.

Clay assured him that he was little more than a roustabout, spending his days beating the brush for strays or helping the wranglers with the horses. Even though his own horse, Blackjack, was learning to be a pretty fair cutting horse, he never got a chance to work him as they already had a full crew for the branding operation. Plus, he was getting into a row with the foreman every time he came into town to check for messages and that was getting wearisome. If he got his pick of the mustangs, Clay assured him that he'd be making out just fine.

By the middle of the afternoon, they had enough poles and posts rounded up that they were able to build a rough fence on each side of the canyon. If they could ever get the horses headed in that direction, this would funnel them right in. Leon had the younger boys gather up deadwood and stack it in piles across the mouth of the canyon.

Leon asked the boys if they would be interested in spending a few nights out here while they waited for the mustangs to show up. The boys were all eager to get started on the adventure. So, despite their pleas to fish for a while, he had them load into the buckboard and head back to town. They needed to get their gear and make sure it was all right with their folks. They could fish later.

On the way into town, Clay rode alongside Leon and quizzed him about the finer points of rounding up wild horses. Leon didn't want to lie to the kid, but neither did he want to tell him this was the first time he'd ever tried this. It might cause him to lose confidence. So he just kept saying every herd was different and they'd just have to play it by ear. Which was true.

Just as he was about to ask Clay if he'd heard any rumors at the Circle I about who might have killed Jarveson, the kid volunteered the information. Naturally, there'd been plenty of speculation, but no one knew anything for certain. If they did, they were keeping it to themselves. There was a lot of talk about the drifter who'd threatened Jake, but Clay reassured Leon that most of the men figured if he'd wanted to kill him, he could've done it when Jake went for his gun. It would've been a case of pure self-defense. Instead, he'd bluffed Jake into backing down and then rode off. There was no reason for him to sneak back later and murder the man. Their business was done.

What the men did find hard to believe was how he'd rode on into town, married the schoolteacher, and took up homesteading. According to all those who saw him, the tall stranger didn't seem the type.

Clay said there was some talk about how Jake's wife's daddy might have hired those gunslingers to kill him so that he could get his investment back on the ranch.

It seemed to Leon like everyone but the chickens knew

where Jake's start-up money came from. People seemed mighty familiar with each other's business in this valley.

There were lots of raised eyebrows over those two hired guns switching sides so quick. Could be that this was payback time for that hanging earlier in the year. But it wasn't easy to figure out why they would've slit Jake's throat rather than force him into gunplay. Jake was known to have a fast temper and a slow draw. He'd have been easy pickings. Maybe Jake even knew it was coming, and that's why he sold out so sudden-like. There was no doubt that Irwin got a hell of a deal on the ranch. He bought the land and the cattle for about what the cattle were worth.

Although it was comforting to know that the men who'd been there didn't think he'd done it, it worried Leon that there were no better suspects. Things were generally what they seemed, but this appeared to be a muddled mess. He sure hoped the judge could sort it out.

He figured that meanwhile his best course of action was to lie low, keep his ears open, and do his best to be a model citizen. Maybe there'd be some word about the judge when he got to town.

There wasn't. No one had heard any news at all about the judge or the deputy.

Hank thought the mustang roundup would be a good experience for the boys. He wished he could join them, but this was his busiest time of year. Not only did he have the stageline teams to care for, but there was a wagon that needed rebuilding as well as a steady string of horses from the nearby farms and ranches to shoe. He lent Leon a posthole digger and four coils of rope and said he'd be out as soon as he got a spare afternoon.

Worried about their safety, Ruby was reluctant to allow the boys to go with him. They promised to be careful, and Leon said he'd look out for them. She finally agreed on the condition that the boys would not actually ride any of the mustangs until Leon and Clay had them broke to saddle. She packed up more food than they could eat in a week and let them take as many of her dish towels and rags as she could spare. Leon threw them in the wagon along with blankets and a couple saddles.

The boys were champing at the bit to get going, so they set out, leaving Clay behind to say good-bye to Janey. Leon sure hoped things worked out for the two of them, and the sooner the better from the looks of things. Too bad Marjorie didn't moon over him like Janey did Clay.

Just as the road made the curve out of town, who should be riding in but that damn Charles Irwin. It was getting so he couldn't poke his head out of bed without meeting up with that man. Leon pulled his hat down and hoped they could just pass by. He didn't want any trouble, especially not with the boys with him.

Irwin wasn't alone either. He was flanked by two men who looked too dapper to be cowboys. Leon noticed that both had their holsters tied down and Spencer repeating rifles in their scabbards. The one on the right had a droopy eye, and the one on the left had a puckered red scar in the middle of his forehead, like a healed-up bullet hole. That was curious. How could a man survive a bullet in the brain?

"Well, what have we here?" Irwin said, drawing his horse to a halt in front of the buckboard team. "Looks like a little nest of sodbusters, boys."

Leon nudged Ulysses forward until he was in front of and to the right of the team. Irwin and his men had to turn to face him. If there was any trouble, he didn't want the kids to get caught in the crossfire.

"Why don't you just go on about your business?" Leon suggested, watching Irwin but keeping an eye out for any sudden movements of the other two. He supposed these were the gunmen that Clay and old Dangerous Dan had told him about.

"Maybe you are my business, McCoy. We don't like outsiders coming to Hope Springs, shooting up the town, and killing one of our own."

"Well, if I run into anyone like that, I'll let you know," Leon told him.

"I say we string 'em up right here, boss," said the one on the right with the droopy eye. "Who knows how much more trouble he'll cause before the judge gets here."

Leon concentrated on keeping a calm mind. He'd seen men walk away from deadly situations all because they'd kept their wits about them. He intended to be one of them.

"Now, hold on, hold on, boys," said Irwin, raising his hand in the air as if that was going to put a stop to anything. "We're going to do this all nice and legal. I don't want to blow my chances to be governor over some foolishness like this. Even if he is an outlaw, he deserves his day in court."

"I heard the man shot up Sunday services, boss. I say we teach him a few manners," said the one on the left with the puckered scar on his forehead.

From the movement in his shoulders, Leon could see that this one was about to draw down on him.

Leon leaned back, resting his hands near his hips. He figured he stood a fair chance against the three of them. Most horses would jump all over the place once they heard a gun go off. Ulysses wouldn't. The war cured him of that. It sort of evened up the odds.

But having the kids along changed those odds.

"Now, boys," said Irwin. But it was clear from the way he said it that he wasn't ordering them to rein it in, just sort of joshing them along. The one on the left made another move for his gun.

Well, damnit, here it comes.

"I'd hold it right there if I were you." Clay's voice came from the trees behind the three men. "I'll take the one on my right. You go for the one on your right, and then we'll both take down Irwin. That sound good to you, McCoy?"

It sounded damn good to Leon. That kid was the answer to a hundred prayers.

All three men lifted their hands back near their shoulders.

"We was just funning," said the floppy-eyed one on the right.

"Well, go have your fun somewhere else. We got kids here," Leon said. "Don't you have a ranch to run, Irwin? You spend more time in town than the bartender."

"I have a foreman who oversees the day-to-day operations. That leaves me free to attend to business and political matters when necessary," Irwin said. Then he added, "Not that that's any of your concern."

"My concern is how you're in my face every time I turn around," said Leon. "I realize it's bound to be a burden for you to see me and know I married the woman you had your hopes pinned on. But that's over and done with."

"This ain't over between us, McCoy," Irwin warned.

"I don't doubt that, but for the time being, why don't you just go on your way?"

The three men put the spurs to their horses and disappeared around the bend. Clay stepped out of the shadows of the trees.

"Good thing you came along when you did," said Leon. "You're getting to be right handy, kid."

The boys, who had watched the whole set-to in shocked silence, all started talking at once about how if they'd only had guns, they'd have showed that Irwin and his gunfighters a thing or two.

That night, sitting around the campfire, Leon tried to talk about how guns aren't the best way to solve disagreements, but the boys wouldn't hear a word of it. They were more interested in listening to Clay tell about how he'd seen Irwin and his hired guns stop up ahead, so he'd circled around and gotten the drop on them.

Leon finally gave up and began explaining his plans about the fence and the mustangs. They all agreed on who was going to do what when the time came. Marjorie sat next to him for a while. He got up to answer a call of nature and was disappointed to find that she'd slipped back to the cabin while he'd been away.

It was a warm night, with only the barest of breezes coming down out of the canyon. The smell of the pines and the damp earth and the smoke of the campfire had a calming effect on everyone. Rosinante was staked out with the other horses, and their occasional nickering blended in with the gurgling of the creek, the birds bidding one another good night and the frogs calling out that it was time to get up. The steady deep croaking of one old bullfrog reminded Leon of an elderly man who keeps remembering details to a story that no one else has even the slightest interest in.

With their heads on their saddles like real cowboys, the boys stared up at the stars and asked Leon and Clay questions about what it was like riding the range. Most of what they told them was true.

About the time the boys had finally drifted off to sleep, Leon noticed Ulysses restlessly pawing at the ground.

"You hear something, fella?" Leon said under his breath. He sat up and strained to see in the moonlight. Wild herds made regular rounds of their territory, and he'd not seen any fresh hoofprints nearby, so he knew they'd be back before long. He just hadn't thought it would be quite this soon.

But there, lined up at the creek near the mouth of the canyon, was the herd of mustangs. It was hard to make out just how many, but he was pretty sure they were the ones whose tracks he'd seen earlier.

"Shhh," he whispered to Clay, gently shaking his shoulder. He pointed out the herd and reached over to wake Thomas, Samuel, and Caleb. They all slipped on their boots, saddled their horses, and silently mounted up.

It wouldn't take much to spook the mustangs. He was counting on the creek water splashing over the rocks to mask any little noise they might make now. The wind coming down out of the canyon would blow their scent away from instead of toward the horses. Now all they needed was a little luck.

Holding Ulysses down to a walk, he led them across the meadow towards the herd. It would have been quicker to follow the creek, but the sound of an iron horseshoe striking a rock carries quite a distance. He motioned for the boys to spread out. Leon could feel Ulysses quiver beneath him. He knew something was up. If only things would hold for a few more minutes.

But they didn't. A head rose up in the midst of the horses, a high-pitched whinny sounded, and the herd began to move.

"Eeehaw," Leon yelled, feeling a surge of excitement as he dug his heels into Ulysses. The boys let out their own wild whoops, and the chase was on.

It looked as if the horses were going to head straight into the canyon, but just as they reached the opening, they veered to the right and forded the creek.

He guided Ulysses to a narrow, deep section of the creek and gripped tight with his legs as they sailed over. He heard hoofbeats right behind him and hoped it was Clay and not one of the boys. He hoped the herd saw the hastily erected fence before they ran into it. He hoped that this was his lucky night.

Regardless, he was going to give it his best shot. Hollering and waving his hat in the air, he prayed that they didn't stumble into a badger hole or trip up over a log.

The horses didn't appear to be noticing him at all. It was unlikely they could hear him yelling over the thunder of their own hoofbeats, and they probably couldn't see him in all the confusion. In a moment they'd be running right by him. He tore his shirt off over his head and waved it in his outstretched hand. Letting the reins fall around Ulysses's neck, he guided him with the pressure of his heels and knees.

The thrill of the chase was tempered by the thought that he was responsible for these kids. He hoped the boys had sense enough to hang back, but he doubted it. He wasn't holding back, why would they? Looking over his shoulder, he caught a glimpse of Clay. He was right behind him, waving his shirt with one hand and his hat in the other, a-whooping and a-hollering. That kid would make a hand all right.

At the last second, the herd swerved back and ran down alongside the creek, making straight for the canyon with the five of them in hot pursuit. *Must be close to thirty head,* Leon thought as they thundered up the ravine.

He leaped off Ulysses, pulled a tin of matches and a strip of birch bark out of his back pocket.

"Grab some of those sticks," he shouted as he knelt and struck a light to the bark. When it flamed up, he dropped it, scooped up a handful of twigs from the ground and carefully piled them on. He blew on them in huge, openmouthed gusts of air. When the twigs caught fire, he stepped away and let the boys arrange a tepee of dry branches over the flames.

It was working out according to plan. But it was too soon to celebrate.

"Now let's get some more of these going," he said, grabbing a flaming stick. "If those horses come heading back out, you boys jump out of the way, you hear me?" he warned, before heading across the creek with his torch.

Within minutes there was a string of six fires snapping and crackling and lighting up the area. There were buckets and potato sacks in the buckboard in case the flames got away from them. Even with everything spring green, it hadn't rained in a week, and Leon figured it wouldn't hurt to take precautions.

"That ought to keep them back there until we can get a fence up," Leon shouted. Working together, they strung a rope head high across the canyon. As he went along, Thomas and Clay twisted the rope open every few feet and pulled in the corner of a dishtowel or a rag. They dangled like little flags and caught the light of the campfires.

He glanced over and saw that Marjorie had joined them and was helping with the operation. Leon tied the end off to a tree on the far side, picked up another coil of rope, and they repeated the process, this time about chest high.

The stallion would have to convince his mares to jump over the rope fence into the line of fires to get out. Leon doubted they would try, but just in case, he cautioned the boys again to clear out of the way if they heard them coming. There'd always be another time.

"But if we play our cards right," he added, "we won't have to worry about next time."

Playing their cards right meant spending the night erecting the pole fence across the canyon. While Caleb kept the fires going, the rest of them hauled and hoisted poles and wired them to the trees. Marjorie brought around tin cups of hot coffee and helped out when she was needed.

As the dawn signaled the start of a new day, they stood back to survey their work. It wasn't much to look at. Poles were tied off every which way to the trees. But they weren't going anywhere, and that was the essential part.

"She'll hold," Leon declared. Then, looking at each of the boys in turn, he added, "You're some of the best hands I've ever partnered up with."

They ducked their heads and did the aw-shucks shuffle in the dirt. But he could tell from the set of their shoulders that they were proud of themselves. They ought to be. They'd put in some long hours without complaining or slacking off. Hank had done a good job with these boys. He only hoped he could do as well with his own sons. He'd give it his best shot—if he ever got the chance.

After breakfast, they devoted the morning to making the fence sturdier and laying out poles for the corral.

The horses were milling around the far end of the canyon. In addition to a coal black stallion, there were a dozen mares of all colors, a dozen matching colts, and nearly as many yearlings. Clay raised his eyebrows at this counting. Leon said he figured that the stallion must have had a run-in with another stud and taken over his herd. He'd heard that a stallion would kill off the colts that weren't his, but maybe this one just didn't have the heart for it.

After lunch, they all lay down for a nap. When they woke up, he and Clay got out the posthole digger and set to work digging a circle of postholes for the corral. The boys tried to help, but he could see they were dragging so he sent them back to town. As none of them wanted to miss out on any excitement, they were naturally reluctant to go. But Leon pointed out the thunderclouds that were piling in from the west, and they agreed they should probably get on home before it started raining.

By late afternoon, it was coming down in buckets. They crowded Blackjack into the shed with Ulysses and Rosinante and headed for the cabin. Leon and Clay spent the rest of the afternoon discussing the finer points of breaking horses and playing cards at the table. Marjorie sat on the bed silently reading that book with all those peculiar words. About twilight, the sod roof started leaking directly over the table. They put a pan under it and continued shuffling cards.

After dinner, Leon and Clay stepped outside to share a smoke and give Marjorie some privacy to get ready for the night.

Leon told Clay he'd better plan on throwing his bedroll in the cabin as there wasn't room for a rabbit in the shed, what with the three horses in there and all.

"I don't want to put you out none, especially with you two being just married and all," Clay said. "I've slept out in the rain before. I'll just roll up in my slicker."

"Don't worry about it, kid," Leon said. "She'll likely hang up a blanket. We'll make do."

He watched a jagged streak of lightning flare across the sky and counted the seconds until the thunder rolled past them.

"What's it like," asked Clay, "being married and all?"

"It ain't quite what you think, kid," replied Leon. *Not by a long shot.*

"Janey and I are going to tie the knot." The kid sounded hopeful as hell.

"You don't say."

"Just as soon as I can provide for her."

"That's always the sticking point, isn't it?"

"I met this guy from the Overland Stage Company. He said they're opening up new routes, and they're looking for people to run the way stations. He told me he'd let me know in two to three weeks. I expect to hear before long."

"I wouldn't pin my hopes on that kind of promise, kid," Leon advised. But it didn't appear that Clay had even heard him.

"Once I get a good job, I know that her folks'll agree to us getting married." He clenched his fist and jabbed it in the air.

This kid gave a whole new meaning to the word *optimistic*. Even if the man from the Overland Stage remembered him, running a stage station was not what you would call a good job; nor was it a guarantee of approval from Hank and Ruby.

"What's it like?" Clay nudged Leon with his elbow. "You know, every night, just the two of you, all alone out here." It was clear the kid could hardly wait.

"Well, it ain't quite what you'd think," Leon repeated, wondering how to word this. "Women have their peculiarities, you know."

"Like what?" asked Clay, obviously eager to learn all he could on the subject.

"A man can't make generalities. Every woman's different."

"Oh, don't I know that," said Clay. "Whoooee."

Leon looked over to see if steam was coming out the kid's ears. He sounded so excited about the passionate possibilities of marriage that any minute Leon expected him to jump up and click his heels together. Well, why shouldn't he? He was probably getting more affection as a beau than Leon was getting as a husband.

Leon wasn't in the mood for talking anymore. He stared out at the water pouring off the porch overhang, ignoring

Clay's attempts at conversation. He didn't know what to tell the kid about women. A month ago, he'd have said that most of them were faithless and demanding. They'd bleed a man dry, then leave him by the side of the road to latch on to a new one. Best not to expect all that much from them. Enjoy it while it lasted and be ready to move on.

But somehow, moving on didn't sound as appealing as it used to. And while demanding certainly described Margie, faithless didn't fit at all.

He was glad he'd decided to stay. If this mustang business was a bust, maybe he could get on with the stage line training their horses. They sure could use it. Somehow things would work out.

Leon pitched his cigarette butt in a glowing arc out into the darkness. "We better turn in," he told Clay.

He shouted out to Marjorie, asking if she was ready for them. She was.

The lamp was out when they entered, so Leon left the door open to admit a little light while Clay spread his bedroll out on the floor. He barred the door, and they both shucked off their shirts and pants.

When Leon lay down next to Marjorie, he was careful not to touch her. It would be an embarrassment if she kicked him out of bed in front of the kid. But she didn't say anything about him sleeping on the floor, and he sure wasn't going to bring it up.

Later, when he heard Clay's steady snores, he put his arm under her and drew her in close to him. She nestled up like she'd been waiting for him to make the first move. His last coherent thought was that he was going to have to find the time to build another room on this cabin.

The next day started out bright and early with the sound of the boys singing "Oh Susanna, oh don't you cry for me," right outside their door. Leon woke up thinking they must have done their chores in the dark. It wasn't until he was pulling on his pants that he realized they'd slept in until way past daylight.

After a sourdough-pancake breakfast, they all walked down to the fence. There were a couple of places where the ground was all churned up and chunks of wood had been knocked from the poles. However, the fence was still standing and looked like it would continue to do so.

They spent the rest of the day building the corral. It was a slippery mucky mess after last night's rain, but by suppertime there were only a few poles left to put in place.

Clay offered to sleep outside but Marjorie wouldn't hear of it. Not with the ground as wet as it was. Leon thought the ground was dry enough to sleep on, and Clay would be sleeping on the ground in the cabin anyway. But he didn't want to seem inhospitable, so he didn't say anything about it.

They got up earlier the next morning and were drinking coffee when the wagonload of kids pulled in. Janey and the little girls were with them. Clay was glad to see her but disappointed to hear there'd been no message from the Overland Stage.

They finished the corral that morning and built a couple gates, one into the canyon and another out to the meadow. Now that the ground was drier, the work went a little easier.

After lunch, Leon and Clay saddled their horses and rode into the canyon. Marjorie and all the kids watched from the top rail of the corral.

Within a short time, they chased a bay mare with a pure black mane and tail through the open gate into the corral. The stallion had snorted and raced around, but he'd given them no real trouble.

Leon grabbed his bronc belt and cinched the wide strap of leather around his waist. It might look a little funny, but it kept his insides from getting all shook up and it would make it easier on his back when the whipping back and forth commenced. He grabbed a length of cotton rope and a cotton-rope hackamore and rode over to where Clay and his horse

Blackjack were in a standoff with the mare. The sides of both horses were heaving in and out as they tried to get their wind back.

Excitement was in the air. At a nod, Clay and Leon shook out loops in their lariats and edged Blackjack and Ulysses in her direction. She began snorting and circling the corral, frantically looking for a means of escape. They closed in on her, and, before she had a chance to race past them, Clay caught a front leg with his noose, and Leon caught both back legs with his. When their horses dug in, the snubbed ropes pulled the mare to the ground.

Leon could feel the blood surging through him as he stepped off of Ulysses and walked around to the mustang's head. He crouched down, grabbed the mare by her ear and jaw, and twisted her nose up to the sky. Though she was flailing about, trying to get loose of the lariats, he slipped the hackamore over her head on the first try.

Clay took over holding her head and Leon grabbed the other length of soft cotton rope and tied a collar around her neck. He ran the loose end behind her rear leg and up back up through the collar. Pulling her rear leg up close to her belly, he tied the rope off to itself.

Then they both mounted up and shook their loops out. The mare kicked loose of the lariats and struggled to her feet. The rope collar and hobble kept one rear leg from touching the ground and she squealed as she lunged around the corral trying to fight free of it. It might look cruel, but it wouldn't hurt her, and it'd save a lot of wear and tear on both of them.

While she wore herself out, Leon and Clay rode over to the gate. Thomas let them out and quickly closed the gate after them.

"Ever see your pa use a Scotch hobble when he had to shoe a kicker?" Leon asked the boys, who'd been watching wide-eyed from their perch on the top poles. The first time he'd seen someone wrestling down on the ground with a wild horse, he'd been wide-eyed, too. In fact, he still found it a little amazing, even when he was doing it himself.

"I don't believe my pa's ever done anything like that," Samuel answered, staring at him as if Leon had just parted the Red Sea.

A man could get used to being looked at like that.

After unsaddling and staking out their horses, Leon and Clay joined the boys on the rail and watched as the mare fell and scrambled to her feet time and again. Eventually, she gave up fighting the hobble and stood with her nostrils flaring and her sides heaving. Leon slipped down from the fence. He walked over nice and easy, all the while crooning "Shhh, baby, yeah, sweet thing, that's a girl, this is going to be all right, darlin', you'll see, it'll be okay, honey girl," in a low, steady, soft voice.

He stole a quick glance at Marjorie, hoping she didn't remember how he'd used this same tone and almost these exact same words the other night in the hot springs. He only hoped it worked as well on the mare.

It didn't. The minute he picked up the rope trailing from her hackamore, she wheeled away. Leon pulled her head around, forcing the mare to face him. They continued in this fashion for better than an hour. Though she fell regularly, she got right back to her feet, snorting at him like he was a bear. Leon never let on that he was impatient or upset. A long time ago, someone had told him that you've got to control yourself before you can control your horse, and he believed that was true.

He kept pulling her head around to face him and calling her a sweet, spirited horse who was going to be back riding the hills again just as soon as she got used to a saddle and bridle.

Eventually, Leon convinced her, and she stood facing him without lunging, wheeling around, or pulling away.

"Hand me that horse blanket," Leon asked in the same low, steady voice he'd been using to calm her all along. Clay walked around the outside of the corral, picked up the horse blanket, and handed it to him through the poles.

Leon held the horse blanket out so she could get the scent of it. Then he began flipping it all over her body, just lightly here and there. He didn't want to frighten her, just get her used to the feel of it. When she finally submitted to having it across her back, Leon tied her lead rope to a tree that was serving as a fence post. In the same easygoing manner, he asked for his saddle.

She eyed the saddle suspiciously when he eased it onto her back, but otherwise she remained calm until he cinched it down. Then she came loose at the seams, jumping and twisting about in an attempt to dislodge the bothersome weight on her back. She'd become wise to the hobbles and didn't fall this time.

When she'd exhausted herself and was standing still for a moment, Leon stepped into the stirrup, threw his leg over and sat down.

Before she had time to react, he slid off her rump. Pulling out his pocketknife, he trimmed the hair off the end of her long flowing tail until it no longer posed a danger to his eyes. He always enjoyed the astonished expressions on people's faces when he did this. With her one hind leg caught up next to her belly like it was, there was no chance she was going to kick at him. But it looked dangerous.

He went about the tail trimming, all the while talking to her about how he'd leave plenty of hair for her to swat flies and mosquitoes with, just not enough for her to blind him. His soothing words had a calming effect on her, and he kept it up while he walked around, fixing two lengths of rope as reins, one on each side of her hackamore. He untied her from the tree and, still cooing and whispering to her, gathered up the reins, then in one smooth motion was back in the saddle. He unknotted the hobble rope from her neck and threw it to Marjorie.

Either the mare was all tired out or she'd decided fighting

him was useless. In any case, she walked around the corral sweet as you please, even turning to the left and then to the right when he pulled on the reins.

"Can I ride now?" shouted Caleb.

Startled, the mare looked over at Caleb and back at Leon. Then, as if she suddenly realized what she'd been lulled into doing, she threw her back legs in the air, spun in a circle, and crow-hopped one way and then the other, trying to pitch him off. Leon rolled with her movements as if she were still trotting around in circles. He was in his element. The world faded away until it was just the two of them doing this wild dance. He let his body move in response to hers and hung on for the ride.

She finally called a halt to the violent twisting and jerking, and he patted her neck and told her what a beautiful lady she was. He circled her around the corral a few more times, then unsaddled her and turned her loose in the canyon.

He looked over at Marjorie and was pleased to see her staring at him in awe. At least there was something about him that impressed that woman.

That afternoon, he and Clay chased the yearlings into the corral and turned them loose. They needed another year's growth on them, and spring was a good time for them to learn to fend for themselves.

Hank rode up just as they were sitting down to supper. He said a message had come in on the stage, and he figured they'd want to hear about it. Right away Clay got all excited thinking it was for him and was discouraged when he found out it wasn't.

The judge had sent word that he wouldn't be coming through as planned. According to the letter, he'd been involved in a buggy mishap and was laid up with a broken collarbone, a couple of cracked ribs, and a busted leg. He'd be making his rounds as soon as he was up to traveling, but he said not to look for him for a few weeks at least. In the meantime, he advised people to be law-abiding as he was in considerable pain and would be in no mood for foolishness when he got there.

Leon didn't know whether to be disappointed or delighted. He hated having that trial hanging over his head and would rather get it out of the way. But while they were waiting, maybe the murderer would tip his hand. Perhaps that was nothing more than wishful thinking, but it could happen. Given enough time, most people tended to slip up and let their secrets out.

He decided he was no worse off than before, and at least this way he'd be able to work the horses. It'd be a shame to have to just turn them loose after all the effort it had taken to capture them.

The following days were an endless round of gentling one mare after another. The stallion managed to avoid getting in the corral, but his day would come.

Hank rode out now and again to watch. He didn't mention anything more about taking off for the Dakotas, and Leon didn't bring it up. No word arrived for Clay from the Overland Stage.

The kid kept pushing Leon to tell him what was the best method for training horses. Leon finally got him to understand that there was no set pattern, you just worked at winning a horse's confidence and took matters from there.

Neither one of them set much store by bronc fighters— men who believed in beating the orneriness out of a horse. They'd seen these types ride a horse to the ground, slashing the animal with their spurs and whips the whole time. The horse would buck and fight until it was exhausted. Then the bronc fighter would jump off and boast that he'd "showed 'em who was boss."

Aside from the cruelty, which held little appeal to either of them, who would want a mount that'd been taught to distrust and fear riders? It didn't make much sense.

What made a lot of sense was being all hot and dusty and dry and looking up to see Marjorie bringing him cold lemonade and a warm smile. She would always sit on the fence for a while and watch him ride. Leon was on top of the world.

The nights were getting better, too. Clay was sleeping outside, and Leon was still in bed with Marjorie. Though she hadn't wavered from her determination to avoid intimacies, she willingly nestled in his arms each night and had given up on reading him that awful book.

It was a start.

Nearly all the mares were bridle-wise by the time they finally got a halter on the stallion. He was a powerful and bold animal and had tried more than once to break out of the fence. Caleb wanted to name him King, but Janey started calling him Prince Charming, and that was the name that stuck.

Leon found it difficult to keep his calm, patient manner as he went about letting Prince get used to him. There was something about testing your mettle against such a stallion that was pure excitement. He was anxious to get on with it.

Despite all the gentling with the blanket and the Scotch hobble and all, as soon as he threw his leg over that saddle, the stallion turned two ways to Tuesday. He kicked and whirled and pitched and lunged. The bucking jarred Leon's insides and gave his tailbone a fierce beating.

But through it all, Leon never got the impression the horse was mean-spirited, just trying to see how good a rider he was. He wasn't sure how much time had passed before the Prince finally settled down to walking around the corral.

Knowing that it would never again be quite like this first time, Leon didn't want it to end. He turned him to the right and to the left, then put him through the paces. The stallion responded like he'd been doing this since he was a colt.

If Marjorie was watching, he always liked to give her the thumbs-up right about now, just to let her know that he had everything under control.

He looked over to where she usually stood and nearly fell

out of the saddle. There she was, passing the time of day with that damned Charles Irwin. That man was a curse.

Leon decided the ride was over. He leaped down, pulled off the saddle and rope reins, and turned Prince Charming into the canyon pasture. He wondered how long Irwin had been there and what he wanted now.

"Quite a horse you got there," Irwin said sociably.

Leon walked over, climbed the fence, and stood beside Marjorie. The man probably didn't know a horse from his own hind end. Leon eyed him up and down. His boots looked brand-new. So did the pants, the leather vest, and the hat. Leon wondered if the man ever worked. His clothes never seemed worn a bit.

"He'll do," said Leon. "Still a little on the frisky side." Leon felt awkward but figured if friendly conversation was what the man was after, he could keep up his end for a few minutes.

"That's the way I like them," Irwin said. There was still a good deal of arrogance to his manner, but you could see he was trying to be agreeable.

"You don't say." Leon gritted his teeth and looked around to see if the two hired guns were in sight. They weren't. Neither was Clay. He hoped the kid was watching from the cover of the trees.

"Yeah, I like my horses just like my women—frisky," Irwin announced, looking over at Marjorie.

Had he just winked at her? What the hell is going on here?

"Are you out here for some reason other than just to irritate me?" Leon asked. He had his temper under a short rein, but he didn't know how long he could hold it back. The sooner this son of a bitch cleared out of here, the better he'd like it.

"I want to buy that stallion," Irwin said straight out. He stood there with his thumbs hooked in the pockets of his leather vest like he was an overseer on some plantation.

"He's not for sale," Leon informed him.

"I'll give you $150, just like he is," said Irwin, as if he hadn't heard a word.

"I said, he's not for sale," Leon repeated.

"How about $200, cash money?"

"Are you hard-of-hearing or something?"

This man was wearing on his nerves. Leon rested his left arm on Marjorie's shoulder. He kept his right hand near his pistol—not in a threatening way, just ready.

"Three hundred then, and that's my best offer."

"And I still say no." *Lord, he was a persistent man.*

Marjorie put her arm around Leon's waist, and he felt her grip on to him.

"Just why are you so determined to buy my horse?"

"I could use a magnificent animal when I make my run for governor. People out here are inclined to respect a man riding a fine horse, and I doubt they get much finer than that."

"You don't say."

"Charles," said Marjorie, "how did you know about Prince Charming?"

"Who doesn't know about him? Those boys of Hank's have done nothing but talk about this little horse operation you got out here," said Irwin. "I'll have to admit, I am a mite disappointed in your Prince Charming. After listening to those boys tell it, I expected him to be ten feet tall and breathing fire."

"They are prone to exaggeration," said Marjorie.

"I guess you can't fault kids for that," said Irwin.

The man was downright aggravating. Leon wondered if he intended to stand around here all day making chin music. He wished he'd get to the point of his visit. Surely, the man didn't ride out here to bid $300 on a mustang that wasn't even broke.

"Listen, I got work to do," said Leon. "Unless there's something else on your mind, I suggest you get back up on that horse of yours and point him in the other direction."

"Now, don't be so hasty," Irwin said. "Have you heard about the new trail opening up through the Indian Nations?

They're calling it the Chisholm Trail. It's the route ol' Jesse Chisholm traded up and down for years. It runs all the way from Brownsville to Abilene and it's not grazed out like the Shawnee Trail. Just think of all those fat mama cows a man could round up in Texas and sell for top dollar a few months later in Kansas."

Running a herd of wild longhorns through Indian Territory would be some adventure all right. If he wasn't all tied up, Leon might've considered it. But he was, and that was that.

"It's the opportunity of a lifetime," Irwin continued. "They're begging for beef back East, and there're millions of longhorns just running loose in Texas. They've been out wandering around and multiplying all through the war. Now folks are rounding up whole herds of them and driving them up to the railroad head in Kansas. It's all pure profit. Maybe you heard about it."

"I reckon I have," Leon said. Not only had he heard about it, he'd been on one of those trail drives, but he didn't figure it was any of Irwin's business. Besides, he was in no mood to listen to this stupid s.o.b. run off at the mouth, and he couldn't see any benefit to prolonging the conversation.

"It'd be some long, hot days all right, but you'd be in the chips by fall," Irwin said. He sounded like one of those patent-medicine men who stood on their wagon tailgates trying to persuade people to buy their bottles of cure-alls.

"Clean the wax out of your ears and listen to me," Leon said, feeling his anger rising and doing his best to keep it clamped down. "I don't want to herd a bunch of longhorns through the Nations. I don't want to sell my horse to you. And I don't want to listen to any more of your bunkhouse bullshit." He hoped the man would take the hint and leave.

He didn't.

"Five years down the road, you're going to look back at this day and be sorry," Irwin insisted. "This opportunity isn't going to be around forever."

"If you're still here five minutes from now, you're going to be sorry." What in the hell was the matter with this man?

"I was only trying to be friendly, trying to offer you a way to save face and make a little money at the same time. I'd even be willing to put in a good word for you with the judge. Old Joe Cunningham and I go way back."

Shit, just what he needed—a man with a grudge against him being an old friend of the circuit judge.

"How come all of a sudden you're wanting to do me so many favors? You've got to admit, it does seem strange after all the run-ins we've had."

"The truth of the matter is," Irwin told him, "I'm ready to bury the hatchet. I don't have anything personal against you, I just don't want you around. This little place couldn't possibly interest you, and I'd like to help you get on with your journey."

"Well, you can just forget that. I'm not leaving. I'm married now, and we got this homestead going. It may not be much in your eyes, but we like it. Besides, I'm out on bail on a murder charge. If I leave Hope Springs, I get to spend the rest of my life seeing my picture posted on sheriffs' walls and looking over my shoulder for bounty hunters."

"Oh hell—pardon me, Marjorie." Irwin looked over at her. Leon didn't care for that much. "But I told you, that can be fixed."

"I don't want it fixed. I want a judge and jury to say I'm not guilty. What am I going to have to do to get you to leave?" He hated to pull out his gun, but it appeared that shooting at Irwin might be the only way to get rid of him.

"Charles," said Marjorie, "I think it'd be best if you'd just leave."

"Marjorie, you'll regret choosing this saddle tramp over me. It'll turn the whole town against you." He spoke as if he was offering her a friendly piece of advice.

"Am I going to have to shoot you to get you to go?" He felt Marjorie tighten her grip on him.

"I can tell when I'm not wanted," Irwin said.

Leon doubted that. He hadn't ever wanted him around and, as far as he could tell, that hadn't made one bit of difference.

"If you change your mind," said Irwin as he mounted his gray gelding, "you know where to find me."

There was no trick to finding the man. It seemed like all Leon had to do was turn around and there he was. Relief replaced his anger as he watched Irwin ride off down the trail next to the creek.

"That man rubs me the wrong way," he said, without taking his eyes off Irwin.

"But you were interested in what he had to say, weren't you?" Marjorie asked in a sad voice, as if she already knew the answer and it was a burdensome one.

"Don't worry, darlin'," he assured her, pulling her in tight next to him. "I'm getting too old for that kind of life. Cattle outfits need plenty of surefooted cow ponies. We'll make our living supplying those."

"Do you think there was much truth to what he was talking about?" asked Clay, sounding eager as always.

Leon looked around to see the kid step out from behind a stand of willow brush.

"Are there really cattle just running loose for the taking?" Clay continued. "Could a man just round up a bunch of them and drive them to Abilene?"

"Whoa there a minute," Leon said. "Just because there're longhorns on the loose in Texas and people willing to buy them in Abilene doesn't mean it's an easy-money deal. Lot of miles to cover, lot of dusty, hot, hard miles. Longhorns will stampede at the sound of a tin cup hitting the side of a water barrel. Believe you me, there are easier ways to make your way in the world."

Though he'd persuaded Clay it was a foolish venture, the yearning was still there for Leon.

That evening, he stood out under the stars and mulled it over in his mind. Herding cattle up through the Nations would be a thrilling undertaking. There were fortunes to be made and good times to be had. Sure he'd sort of told Marjorie he planned on staying around, but he hadn't promised to be with her every solid minute. A cattle drive would only take a few months. Then he'd be back all moneyed up. They could buy themselves a real ranch instead of trying to scratch and peck out a living on this rocky little piece of ground.

He and Clay could take this string of horses to Texas, working them along the way. All they had to do was find a half a dozen other men who thought the same way they did, and, by fall, they'd all be grazing in sweet clover. He'd have to convince Marjorie not to get all in a lather over his being gone for a few months, but sometimes circumstances forced a man to work away from home. She'd get used to it.

But it would ruin things between them. He knew that as surely as he knew his own name. No matter how he explained it, she'd be hurt, and the hurt would be a wall between them. He'd rather spend the rest of his life scratching in the dirt like an old rooster than to have her turn her heart away from him.

She was still holding the line on physical intimacies, but everything else was free and easy between them. Sometimes they'd start out the day tickling and wrestling around in that bed, and at night they always slept nestled in each other's arms. A lot of times when he was working the mustangs, he'd feel her watching him. He'd look over and there'd she be, worrying that lower lip of hers. For a moment, it'd be just the two of them in the world. He was going to have to be more careful about that. A couple times he'd been paying attention to her instead of to business, and he'd been thrown.

After the noon meal, Clay would usually take the boys off fishing or fooling around. Leon and Marjorie would lie on an old quilt in the cool shade somewhere, and she would rub the soreness out of his muscles. Now that was pure heaven.

More than anything else, he prized that look of awe and wonder and affection that she gave him when she first woke up or when he surprised her while she was working in the garden. What if that was replaced by resentment and hurt every time she saw him? What if she found someone else to look at like that while he was gone? His belly knotted up at the mere thought of it.

Leon was a gambling man, but the odds were against him this time. Much as he wanted to go, he wasn't willing to chance that she'd still feel the same about him when he got back.

Never bet what you can't bear to lose.

Might as well turn in, he decided, *that's that.* Before heading back to the cabin, Leon found the North Star and wished that tonight was the night.

It was getting so he dreaded the evenings. She'd gone back to reading that awful book. He didn't know how much more of it he could take. What was there to say about a story that made absolutely no sense? Every once in a while, there'd be some mention of a fire or a cougar, but most of it was a mystery to him. How did she expect him to hold up his end of a sensible conversation when he'd never even heard most of those words before? Usually, he pretended to nod off. She'd eventually give up on the reading and they'd go to bed.

Bedding down for the night was getting to be pure agony.

How much longer could he endure having her in his arms and yet not be allowed to do anything about it? For the life of him, he didn't understand why she continued to hold him off. He could feel her trembling and sighing and making little moaning noises in the back of her throat. Sometimes, he'd blow on her neck, and she'd whimper and arch into him. But she stopped him right there.

He'd even tried to sweet-talk her into riding around the top of the canyon and climbing down into the hot springs with him. But she refused even to discuss it.

It was getting so just the sight of her got him all worked up. Clay was forever teasing him about how many times a day he took his hat off and ran his fingers through his hair. If something didn't change, he'd be bald by fall.

She was already in bed when he got back to the cabin. He bent down and pressed a kiss on her neck. He could feel her heartbeat on his lips. He grinned a little as he heard her catch her breath. Maybe tonight was the night.

No such luck.

Three things happened as a result of Irwin's visit.

The next morning when they brought Prince Charming up to the corral, Leon jerked off the halter he'd left on yesterday and flipped open the gate. The horse stood looking at him for a minute as if he knew what was on Leon's mind. Then he took off for the hills.

Right before he disappeared up into the trees, the black stallion reared up and let out a cry that echoed across the valley. Leon knew just how he felt.

"What'd you do that for?" Clay asked in amazement.

"Hell if I know," Leon answered. "All of a sudden, it just didn't seem right to keep him penned up." He didn't understand it any more than that. "Maybe he'll gather up another bunch of mares and make us wealthy men."

Then, over the next few evenings, he built a porch swing big enough to hold both him and Marjorie. Somehow it seemed connected to turning the stallion loose. Maybe he was telling himself that he was trading his freedom for something more precious. He generally took things as they came without a lot of philosophizing, but perhaps it was time he started studying on matters.

The next Sunday, he left Marjorie at the Lucky Lady for church services and rode off. She'd tried to persuade him to go with her, but he'd had his fill of the fine citizens of Hope Springs. They were rude as hell to him and barely civil to one another. They needed to hear about "brotherly love" and "do unto others." He already knew that stuff. Anyway, he felt a lot closer to God watching a sunset or riding through the hills than he ever did squashed in with a bunch of small-minded people bickering over who was the friendliest.

Besides, he had something on his mind to do. He rode around the abandoned buildings in Hope Springs until he found two lilac bushes growing next to a tumbledown house at the edge of town. He dug them up, carried them off in gunnysacks tied over the back of his saddle, and planted them near each corner of their front porch. It was his way of telling her that he was putting down roots here. He hoped she understood.

That night, he couldn't get his boot off. No matter what he did, it wouldn't budge an inch. He'd have asked Clay, but the kid was spending the night in town. He was doing a little courting under the watchful eyes of Hank and Ruby.

"You wouldn't happen to have a bootjack, would you?" he asked. "I can't seem to get my boot off."

"Your foot's probably swollen," she said.

It was possible. He'd done a lot of digging today, and even though his foot was healing up fine, maybe he'd busted something loose.

"Here," she said. "Let me try." She stepped over his leg, reached down, grabbed his boot, and tugged. "Push," she said.

Push where? he wondered. Her behind was the only place he could see to push. If he touched her there, like as not he would just forget about the damn boot, throw her skirt up over her head, and frighten her to death.

"Six times six is thirty-six. Six times seven is forty-two. Six times eight is forty-eight," he muttered quickly.

"What are you doing?" She looked back over her shoulder at him.

What'd she think he was doing? He was trying to get his attention on something besides her fanny in his face. Talking about it wasn't going to help matters any.

She gave his boot a couple good jerks and was able to work it the rest of the way off before he got to his nine times.

Then she poured hot water from the kettle into a basin and he slowly eased his foot down into it. He was just beginning to relax when he felt her hands on his ankle and he jerked his foot back.

"Would you mind telling me why you're acting so peculiar?" she asked.

He minded. How could he tell the woman he loved that he'd been horny for so long, even the brush of her fingers got him to thinking things he ought not to.

"Let's just go to bed," he said. The way things were going, he'd have to sleep in the creek to keep his urges under control.

He checked the cut. It looked all right to him, but he probably should get those stitches out. The doc had said a week or so, and it had been almost two.

Apparently, the same thought occurred to Marjorie because without saying a word, she opened the trunk and got out a pair of scissors and a small flask.

"Here," she said, handing him the flask. "I know how you are about pain."

He had half a mind to tell her about the pain he was in now. This living together like brother and sister was for the birds. He planned on staying around and taking care of her, so there was no reason on earth they should be spending their evenings reading books. They could do that later, when they were too old to do anything else.

He didn't even notice her pulling the stitches out. His foot was back in the hot water and she was reaching for that damn book when he realized he needed to do something and do it quick.

He bent over and blew out the light.

"Let's just go to bed," he said.

"But we've not read our chapter tonight," she mildly protested.

"We'll read two tomorrow," he said, drying off his foot in the dark.

"If that's what you want to do," she said, sounding unsure of the situation or perhaps of him.

There was no doubt in his mind what he wanted to do tonight, and listening to her read that ridiculous book wasn't it. As a matter of fact, it wasn't even in the top three.

10

*I*t was a relief when he finally stepped outside. Marjorie
knew it was difficult for Leon to be denied. But it wasn't all
that easy for her either. She just did her best to focus on the
tasks that needed to be done and forget about what it was like
to have his hands run over her hips and down her legs, or feel
his lips pressed against the pulse in her neck, or hear him say,
"Darlin', you comfortable?" in that deep, rich voice of his that
always sent a shiver down her spine.

*Good gracious, think about something else. Don't just
stand here like a nitwit. Put on your nightclothes.* She could
hardly expect Leon to stay out there forever waiting for her to
get ready for bed.

The cool, wet washcloth felt good on her face. It was a
warm night, and then, on top of that, she'd had to wrestle with
that boot.

She found herself standing and staring off into space
again—thinking of how delicious it felt when his feet glided
across hers in the night. *Put that nightgown on and get to bed.*

She opened the trunk and pulled out her gray-flannel gown.
Underneath it was the white-muslin one with the embroidered

lilacs. It looked so cool and appealing that Marjorie decided to wear it instead.

Pulling it on was the most marvelous feeling. It glided across her skin and billowed around her body, sending out a faint scent of lavender as it settled around her legs. Her mother used to tuck dried lavender buds into their belongings whenever they traveled. For a safe journey, she'd say. Usually the fragrance saddened Marjorie, but tonight she found it soothing.

As she slipped under the covers, she wondered what her mother would think of Leon.

"You can come in now," she said, turning over to face the wall. She listened to the door creak on its leather hinges, followed by the thump of the crossbar dropping into place.

Leon began his own nightly routine. In the quiet darkness, she heard the rustle of material as he pulled his shirt off over his head. The chair squeaked when he sat down to pull off his boots. She heard the first one drop and waited for the second one. It was a moment or two before she recalled that he'd taken it off earlier. When she heard the buttons pop open on the front of his pants, she bit down on her pillow and pulled the quilt over her head.

It was agonizing to lie here night after night and listen to him splash water on that broad, hair-covered chest of his. She wondered what else he washed, but she was too shy to look. Not that he would object if she glanced over, or even if she lit the lantern and stared. She couldn't help but notice how he'd been strutting around without his shirt lately, showing off for her. He was forever complaining about how his shoulders hurt from being yanked about on the horses and asking her if she would please give him a shoulder rub. It was heavenly digging her fingers into his deep muscles. Sometimes it was all she could do to keep from sinking her teeth into that thick part along the top.

Get your mind on something worthwhile. You can think about all of this if he's still around in October.

She realized she hadn't said her prayers yet, so she began counting her blessings. She started thanking the Lord for the children, and for her snug little home, and her health. But before long, she was expressing her gratitude for the way Leon's mustache brushed against her neck at night.

This is blasphemous. She was going straight to hell if she didn't get a grip on herself.

She quickly concluded her prayer by asking God to bless and watch over Leon and Mary Beth and Maggie and Emma and Caleb and Leon and Samuel and Thomas and Leon and Ruby and Hank and Clay and Leon, of course. Or had she already mentioned him?

"Amen," she said out loud.

"You can say that again," said Leon as he scooted over next to her.

The bed sank down in the middle under their weight, making sleeping separately impossible. She'd realized that from the first night they'd tried it. But with Clay lying right there on the floor next to them, she could hardly have raised a fuss. That night, and every night since then, she'd turned to the wall so that he didn't get any ideas. He always slipped one arm under her head, kissed her softly on the neck, and conducted himself like a perfect gentleman.

She found sleeping in his arms to be a comfort. As long as he behaved himself, she saw no reason to insist that he move back to the floor.

He curled into the curve of her body, just as he had every night for the past two weeks. She nestled in, using his arm for a pillow. Drawing in a deep breath, she savored his soapy, leathery aroma.

"Darlin', you comfortable?" he asked, resting a hand along her side. His soft breath across her cheek sent a shiver down the length of her.

When he pressed his good-night kiss to the back of her neck, she could feel it all the way to her feet. It felt so heavenly, she had to force her lips together to keep from groaning out loud.

Don't just lie here and moan, do something. So she focused on smoothing the hair on his forearm which, as it turned out, caused him to moan.

Settle down, she said silently, *settle down.* They were always a little tense when they first got in bed, but it passed.

Tense didn't begin to describe how she felt when he casually placed a hand on her bosom. But when his fingertips began tracing gentle circles, her toes curled up so tight that she feared she would have charley horses in both legs if he didn't stop.

Mercy.

She felt the warmth of his body reach out to her through the thin nightgown, and she realized she needed to call a halt to this right now. As enticing as their physical attraction was, she knew it would eventually tear her soul apart, and she had no intention of allowing that to happen. Their night in the hot springs had been a delightful dream that she'd slipped into without weighing the consequences. But tonight was reality. She knew exactly where this was heading, and she had no intention of going there.

While part of her was coolly considering the outcome, the rest of her was already craving what she knew lay ahead. Half ice and half fire, that's how she felt. Even as her mind was trying to pull her back, her body was welcoming desire at the very core of her.

Passion inched through her veins, as he continued his slow assault on her senses. She felt a kiss on the side of her cheek, tender and soft, as if a butterfly had brushed past.

"Stop that," she said listlessly as she floated away with the sensations.

He dropped his hand to stroke along her waist and down her leg. She was keenly aware of the way his touch was muted by the muslin of her nightgown.

"Help me, darlin'," he whispered in her ear as he tugged her gown up.

Help him? If she had any sense at all, she'd get up and go sleep on the floor herself.

"Lift your hips, darlin'." His voice was so husky it hardly sounded like him.

"Stop that," she insisted with as much firmness as she could manage, which, admittedly, was not all that much. But she was able to grasp her nightgown in both hands to keep it down where it belonged.

"Stop what?" he asked. Then he slipped his hand under her gown and started making that circling motion, only slower this time. "Stop that?" he asked, sounding innocent as a babe.

Yes, he should definitely stop that. But before she could get the words out, he wasn't doing that anymore.

"Or stop that?" His voice was soft and low and so was his hand.

Oh my, it was that butter-on-the-back-of-the-stove feeling again. She felt her face heat up and her body start to hum.

Heavenly days. If he'd asked her to get up and dance nude in the moonlight, she'd probably do it without a second thought.

"Leon," she said, desperately trying to keep her wits about her. "I don't think this is such a good idea." She let go of her nightie to press her hands on top of his.

"Then I wouldn't think if I were you, darlin'," he murmured against her ear. "Try feeling. And anytime you feel like calling a halt to this, you just let me know and we will." He kissed her ear and then on down the side of her neck. She felt her hands go limp.

Well, why not? They were married after all. It wasn't like this was the first time either. How much harm could just once more be? She knew darn good and well there were reasons she should say no, but she just couldn't bring herself to say them.

His other arm closed around her. She felt his fingers glide

from the top of her shoulder to the tip of her bosom where they moved back and forth in rhythm with the slow, circling movements of his other hand. The pulsing between the two points drained her of all reason and flooded her with the most exquisite fluttering sensations.

On its own accord, her hand drifted down behind her and touched that part of him that was so different from her. Tossing caution to the winds, she let her fingertips glide along that strange combination of silky solidness.

Leon groaned and tugged again on her gown. In a sensual haze, she pushed up off the bed and allowed him to slide the gown up and over her head. As the muslin slipped across her skin, she realized she was accepting him into her heart and soul. She knew she'd live to regret it, but she couldn't bring herself to care about that now.

His hand searched for pleasure points behind her elbows, in the curve of her knee, inside her legs, sweetly draining all her doubts, her worries, her fears. Gusts of desire shook her and she heard her breath come in long, surrendering moans. Her body melted against his, and her world was filled with him knowing the secret of her. She marveled at the sensations thrumming through her and began longing for what she knew was to come.

"Uhhhhh." The sound came from deep within her as she ran her hands up his back and kneaded his thick, work-hardened muscles.

"Where's the vinegar?" he asked out of the clear blue.

Vinegar? If this didn't beat all. Here she was, about to come apart at the seams, and he wanted something to eat. What got into that man?

She watched in dismay as he pulled away from her, padded across the room, and proceeded to rummage through his saddlebags. Surely he wasn't carrying vinegar in there.

"Leon," she said in frustration, "forget about the vinegar. Come back to bed." *Sweet heaven, I sound like a loose woman.* "Can't that wait until morning?"

"Don't you worry about me coming back to bed, darlin'," he assured her as he walked over to the shelf. "I'll be there in two shakes."

Her breath caught as he passed through a shaft of moonlight coming in around the door. That man was solid muscle from his shoulders to his shins. Marjorie bit the back of her hand to keep from groaning.

Leon uncorked two jugs and sniffed at the tops before finding what he was looking for. It was difficult to tell in the dim light, but it appeared he was washing his hands in vinegar. Whatever for?

She rolled over, closed her eyes, and tried to calm herself down. If she lived to be a hundred, she'd never understand this man. The sharp smell of vinegar accompanied him as he walked back across the room.

"This will be a little chilly at first," he said as he sat down beside her.

She was hot enough to kick off the covers and throw open the door. She would welcome chilly.

"Shhh," he said as he ran his hand up between her legs and pressed something cold and wet against her.

Chilly? I guess it was chilly.

"What's that?" she asked, with a startled jerk.

"It's a preventative," he answered, pushing whatever it was deep up inside of her. "It's a sea sponge. I got it from that drygoods woman in Denver. She said if I soaked it in vinegar, it would keep you from getting in the family way. I don't think that method I used in the hot springs is going to work tonight, darlin'."

Before she had time to consider the matter, she felt his lips where his hand had been, and any thoughts she had flew right out the window. Every pulse pulled her deeper and deeper, until the core of her tightened in like an overwound watch.

Then he began to slow down and the slower he went, the closer she came. Just when she was teetering right on the edge, he stopped altogether.

"Don't stop," she pleaded in dismay.

"Well, make up your mind," he said as he pulled himself up next to her. He turned her away from him and gathered her into his arms as if they were going to drift off to sleep.

Disappointed didn't begin to describe how she felt. To keep from crying out in frustration, she bit down on her pillow.

Before she found the words to tell him that her mind already was made up, she heard him whisper, "Darlin', I promise, I won't stop until we're both too weak to walk."

He planted kisses along the nape of her neck and across the top of her shoulders, his mustache tickling her as he went along.

His hand followed the contours of her hip, then brushed across the center of her before roaming down to explore the back of her knee or up to circle around her belly button.

Just when she was certain she'd had about all she could stand, he cradled her with his body and glided into her. At an unhurried, steady pace, he'd bury himself deep within her, pause for a moment while he caressed her with his fingertips, and then pull nearly all the way out and stop, pressing against her. Adrift in the sensations, she felt the motion of their joining echoed in the movements of his hands—stroking, kneading, moving from one sensitive area to another. It was as if she had a string tied to the core of her and every movement tugged at that string.

She didn't know how much more of this she could bear and urged him with her hips to hurry. He lingered in response, each stroke taking longer than the last.

With every motion, her body clenched and tightened, stronger and deeper until she could scarcely stand the intensity. Though she yearned for the release that remained just out of reach, she didn't want this to end either.

Confused and frustrated, she sank her teeth into the flesh of his arm. He growled in answer, seized the curve of her shoulder in his mouth, and buried himself deep within her.

She hurtled past the point of no return and waves of sensations flowed through her, rippling to the tips of her fingers, the top of her head, the ends of her toes. She floated away on the sweet, gentle pulsing.

It was only later, when she was aware of Leon lying next to her, that she wondered if it had been as grand for him as it'd been for her. She tried to ask, but for some reason she couldn't get the words to come out right. After making a couple incoherent attempts, she just gave up.

"Now that you are too weak to talk," he whispered, "let's get to work on the walking part."

Passion flowed between them like warm honey. They would yield to the numbed sleep of satisfied lovers, only to awaken and start all over.

The birds calling to one another at sunrise roused them from their slumber. She was snug in his arms, blanketed in peace and contentment. He pressed against her back, his belly creating a nest for her, and his legs holding hers captive. She sighed with pleasant exhaustion.

"Sleepyhead," he murmured, nuzzling her neck.

"Mmmm," was the best she could do.

"I'd better go," he said, attempting to untangle himself from her.

A cold knot of fear grabbed her chest and she clung to his arms.

"Not now," she pleaded, as panic replaced the relaxed contentment of a moment ago.

"Darlin', I'm not leaving you," he assured her. "But don't you think we should get up and get dressed before the kids get here?"

She rolled over in his arms and pressed her cheek against his bare chest. It was silly to be so frightened, but she couldn't seem to help it.

"You're right," she said with as much reasonableness as she could manage. "You'd better get going."

"Marie," he said, taking her chin in his hand and pulling

her face up to look at him, "I'll be within whistling distance all day long. Now I know you can whistle."

They both smiled, recalling that Sunday she'd brought the town to attention.

Without a thought, her lips found their way to his. She shivered with the sweet tenderness of their kiss, savoring the moment.

"Go," she whispered finally.

He stood and pulled on his pants. She marveled at his lean, muscular build and blushed at the red scratches her fingernails had left on his back. She was simply going to have to get herself under better control.

She was still staring at him as he tucked his shirttail into his pants and buttoned up. He looked over his shoulder at her and raised his eyebrows. Mercy, she was sitting here stark naked gaping at him. What had gotten into her?

Her white nightgown was draped across the bedpost. She grabbed it, slid under the covers, and wiggled into it. After she heard the door bang shut, she emerged from the bed and placed her feet on the floor. But when she went to stand up, her legs gave way, and she sank back down. As she braced herself for a second attempt, she heard a chuckle and looked up to see that Leon was still there in the room.

He walked over to help her, but she waved him off.

"Just a little tired I guess," she murmured.

"Now remember," he said, as he opened the door and flooded the room with sunshine. "If you need any help walking—" He whistled as he stepped outside.

She wondered if the sponge had been effective last night and if the sharp scent of vinegar would always make her blush. In a halfhearted sort of way, she hoped the sponge hadn't worked. Absentmindedly, she patted her tummy, as if she might be carrying his child already.

Now she knew she'd lost her mind. What was she thinking of? Though she could hardly deny their physical attraction to one another, that wouldn't hold him back once he was ready to go. Not that she thought he was playing her false. Right now he probably had every intention of staying. And he would—for a while. He was in his element training horses and was obviously enjoying all their laughing and teasing and carrying on. But you could hardly build a life around that.

Life was bread rising in the Dutch oven and beans soaking in the pot, a pile of books and a stack of wood that stretched far enough to get you through a cold winter and a chilly spring. It was the day in, day out routines.

Nights like this were pleasant interludes, but they wouldn't bind Leon to her. She knew in her heart that one of these days the pleasure of sleeping in his arms would be replaced by the pain of wondering where he was. How much pain was she willing to trade for?

Even the thought of sleeping without his arms around her tonight brought on an ache she wished she'd never known. How could she bear it this winter?

So now what? Send him packing today instead of waiting for him to leave?

And maybe he was different. Maybe having a home and a family meant more to him than excitement and adventure. Maybe he would stay.

Stay and do what? There were only so many wild horses in these hills. She'd seen the expression on his face when Charles talked of cattle drives and fortunes to be made. Though Leon had refused without hesitation, there was no mistaking the appeal it held for him. How long would he be able to hold out? She knew he cared for her, but he didn't like being harnessed up any better than his horse did.

The reality was that one of these days he'd be taking off. It would probably be just short expeditions in the beginning, a week or so, then a month or two, stretching to longer absences as the years wore on.

It was going to be hard enough to say good-bye now. She could not imagine how difficult it would be once he'd spent the summer in her bed.

For a moment, she fervently wished she'd never known what it was like to spend the night in his arms, never known the aching sweetness of their lovemaking. But that train had already left the station.

The truth of the matter was, if he walked in right now, took her hand in his, and said they were going to spend the rest of the morning making love on the sod roof, she'd climb up there in a heartbeat. Regardless of what her better judgment told her, there was no way she was going to pass up this time with him. She might as well quit worrying about it.

But neither could she stop wondering how long it would last.

That afternoon, following a picnic lunch in the shade, Marjorie lay down next to Leon, closed her eyes, and listened to him talk to Clay and the boys.

He was telling them how the canyon would soon be grazed off and they needed to start staking the mares out during the day. He expected that the stallion would be back to try to chase them off, so they had to be certain the mares were well secured.

He warned them to check around for wild larkspur and locoweed. Horses would bloat on larkspur and that would be trouble enough. But if they got into a patch of locoweed, they might as well shoot them because they'd be no use to anyone anymore. Once a mare got into a patch of locoweed, she'd forget all about going to water, about grass, about anything but nibbling on that weed. It was darn near impossible to break a horse of the habit of grazing on it. She'd keep coming back to nibble on it until her eyes turned glittery and her gait got wild and awkward. If you didn't keep her penned up and away from it, she'd soon be skinny as a rail, stumbling around, trembling, and fighting off anyone that came near her.

Marjorie wondered if it was possible to get crazed like that over a man. As she drifted into dreams, she decided that it was too late. She'd already had a taste of it; she might as well get her fill.

That afternoon, Clay rode back to the town with the boys. The mustang mares had all been ridden once and were staked out to graze, with their colts frolicking about them. She and Leon spent the early evening in their hidden hot springs.

That set the pattern of their days. Clay and the boys rode out every morning and left every afternoon. On sunny days, the little girls came out with them.

They finished the privy and lined the path to it with firewood. They fixed the roof so it didn't leak, and they planked the cabin floor and the front porch, which Marjorie appreciated since the spring rains meant mud. It also meant the garden was bursting with green.

Clay was becoming increasingly frustrated. Ruby never let Janey out of her sight, and he had yet to hear so much as a word from the Overland Stage. Every day he asked Leon if he thought he should ride to Denver to check on the situation.

However, they did hear regularly from the marshal's office. The judge was not recovering well from his injuries. In addition to the broken leg and the cracked ribs, he'd contracted pneumonia, which had settled into a lingering illness. If his condition improved, he would resume his rounds. If he went into a decline, a new judge would be appointed. Meanwhile, everyone awaiting trial was to stay put.

Marjorie knew that this waiting weighed on Leon's mind. There was no evidence whatsoever that he'd killed Jake and no doubt that the judge would clear his name, when or if he ever got to town. But still, it was worrisome having this hanging over their heads.

They rarely went into Hope Springs anymore. Although the lynching talk had died down, the townspeople continued to regard Leon with narrow-eyed suspicion. Marjorie didn't even go to church any longer, as the congregation had split in two and she wasn't about to choose sides. She missed the friendly neighborliness that had made her feel so at home in the community and hoped it wasn't gone for good.

For the time being, it was easier all the way around just to stay home and avoid their unfriendly attitudes and actions.

Staying home had the added benefit of avoiding encounters with Charles and his two gunslingers. Marjorie found it appalling that Charles employed such unsavory individuals.

Though she'd never actually seen them, according to the boys, they'd had run-ins with any number of the local men. They'd even shot Evie Sanderson's husband in the arm after overhearing him say that he considered them dangerous characters and far more likely than Leon to have brought Jake to his untimely demise. Fortunately, it was merely a flesh wound.

Though the two did make Leon look tame by comparison, public opinion had not swayed in his favor either. People were dead set against all three of them.

Leon and Clay worked the horses every day until all but one were gentle enough for the boys to ride. They brushed out their winter coats until they gleamed and took them to town for Hank to shoe.

The day she'd been dreading finally arrived. In a way, it was almost a relief.

As they were getting dressed that morning, Leon mentioned that it was time to take the mares to Denver to sell. For a moment, it felt like all the air had been sucked out of the room. Her fingers turned cold and stiff as they fumbled about fastening the buttons on her dress. More than anything, she wanted to scurry back to bed, pull the covers up, and start the day all over.

But she didn't. Instead, she made breakfast just as she had every other morning. Without a word, she made a triple batch of Dutch-oven biscuits and wrapped up a packet of jerked venison. She tried singing to soothe herself, but it sounded so whiny and pitiful that she stopped.

"I'm not leaving you," he assured her over breakfast.

"That's not your bedroll by the door? Those aren't your

saddlebags stacked on top?" It was difficult keeping the hard edge from her voice, but it was better than sniveling about it.

"Be reasonable, Marjorie," he said, as if whatever he did was sensible and whatever she did was irrational.

"I am. You're leaving, and I'm fixing you food to take with you. What's so unreasonable about that?" Her words sounded as cold as she felt.

He slammed his cup down on the table and coffee slopped over the edge. She reached over and wiped it up without a word.

"We're just taking the mares to Denver to sell," he said, grabbing hold of her wrist. "We'll be back in a week or so. There's no reason to get all worked up over it."

She yanked her arm out of his grasp and moved back to the stove.

He stepped behind her. "Ah, darlin'," he said as he wrapped his arms around her. Marjorie felt his breath across her cheek and then, without warning, the memory of her mother and father standing just like this washed over her. She twisted out of his arms and ran outside. She kept running until she reached the creek. Sobbing and gasping for air, she collapsed to her knees.

The sorrow clawed at her chest. The harder she fought it, the harder it fought back. She covered her ears with her folded arms and pulled at her hair as if the pain would keep out the memories. It wasn't fair it should sneak up on her today. Today was difficult enough already. "Please, not today," she begged over and over.

But the grief had been denied too long, and it wouldn't let her loose. She pressed her hands to her face and hissed out great gulps of air over and over in an attempt to rid herself of the anguish. Rocking back and forth, she tried desperately to think of something, anything, to keep from sinking into that never-ending, bottomless well of sorrow.

Then she felt his arms enfold her, and she couldn't hang on any longer. "Mama," she cried out in despair. "Mama."

Now she had no way to protect herself from the agony. It rolled over her, wave after wave, pounding at her, pulling her under. Years of unshed tears shoved and burned their way to the surface, and she felt her body collapse in on itself. She slid her arms down and grabbed on to her belly as if that might protect her somehow. How could she bear this any longer? She was certain her heart would burst at any moment.

Raging against the pain, she struggled to get him to let go. He responded by tightening his hold on her and murmuring nonsense in her ear. Didn't he know that only made it worse? How could she shut it all out if he wouldn't let her close up?

He held on while she mourned her mother in great, wrenching sobs. She grieved for the sister she missed desperately and the father she barely knew.

When her stomach spewed out its contents, he carried her over to the stream and offered her a drink in his cupped hands. She cried until her throat was raw and her eyes were swollen shut, but the tears continued to burn their way out.

Sorrow stole her away and still he held fast. She was so cold, so cold she couldn't stop trembling. Without a word, he carried her back to the cabin and climbed in bed with her. He warmed the shuddering away with his body. Wrapped in his arms, she sobbed herself to sleep.

She woke up exhausted, drained of all energy and emotion. He was there, surrounding her, keeping her safe.

He kissed her on the eyelids. "Feel better?" he asked gently.

She didn't feel anything, not even numb. It was as if there was nothing left for her to feel with.

"Thank you, Leon," was all she managed to say before drifting off again.

It was late afternoon when she wakened the next time. She was all alone in the cabin. There was stew simmering on the stove. Though she didn't know whether she was hungry or not, she got up and filled a bowl and took it outside. In a groggy daze, she sat down in the swing, held the bowl of stew in her lap, and watched Leon ride the bay mare across the meadow.

"You'd like him, Mama," she said, amazed that there were still tears left in her. Through the watery blur, she watched him guide the mare from a walk to a trot into a lope then a gallop and back down again. His powerful body surged in rhythm with the mustang's, her dark mane and his black hair rising and falling in the same pattern on the wind.

"He loves me, you know." She chatted along as if her mother was sitting on the swing next to her. Two thick, warm tears rolled down her cheeks followed by two more. It was easier to see now. She didn't know why they just kept trickling down, one after the other. She wasn't sad anymore. In fact, she found it rather comforting to sit and talk with her mama after all this time apart.

"I should never have slept with him," she said, but the moment the words were out she knew they were a lie. To think of never knowing what it was like to be wrapped in his arms trading sweet secrets in the dark. No, she wouldn't have missed that for the world. She shivered, recalling the feel of his mustache brushing down her spine. Then she smiled, remembering his attempts to feign interest in their evening literary discussions.

"I'll miss him," she said as she watched him ride up to her. The world blurred up again as two more tears worked their way to the surface.

He dismounted in one fluid motion, and for some reason she was reminded of when she first saw him striding into the Lucky Lady, so at ease in his body, so sure of himself. She wished she felt that way.

"What do you think?" he asked in that deep, rich voice of his.

She thought he was magnificent.

"About the stew?" he said, pointing to the bowl in her lap. "Pretty tasty, huh?"

She glanced down. "Delicious," she said, though she'd not

touched a bite. She saw a drop of moisture plop right in the middle of it and wondered why she hadn't realized it was raining. Then another drop rolled into the corner of her mouth. She tasted it with her tongue and knew from the saltiness that it wasn't a raindrop and she wondered if she would ever stop crying.

He tied the mare's reins to the corner post and sat down next to her.

"Why don't you come along with me on this trip to Denver?" he suggested. He brushed the moisture off her cheeks with his callused fingertips. "We could take Hank's wagon so you wouldn't have to sleep on the ground. Once we sell the horses, we could do a little shopping, maybe take in a night on the town. What do you say, darlin'?"

He sounded so hopeful that she hated to disappoint him, but she wasn't up to the journey. She didn't have enough energy to swat a fly. Making a trek to Denver and back was out of the question.

"I'd just slow you down," she said. It wasn't just that. If this was to be the pattern of their lives, she might as well get used to it now. No sense putting it off.

Besides, Leon was probably planning on letting off a little steam when he got to Denver. How could he do that with her sitting back in a hotel room waiting for him?

"No, I'd rather wait for you right here at home," she said.

"Darlin', I had no idea how upset you'd be about my leaving," he said. "I don't want you to go through that again."

"I guess I'm not very good at good-byes," she said with a weary smile.

"Then come with me," he urged. "You could pick out a cookstove, some windows, who knows what all. I'll be all moneyed up, darlin'. The sky's the limit."

Not trusting her voice to tell him no again, she shook her head and blinked her eyes to help two more tears on their way.

"I know that wasn't all over me," he said as he pulled her

into the shelter of his arms. "But I still hate the thought of you out here by yourself. Will you at least stay in town with Hank and Ruby until I get back?"

Because she didn't have the strength to resist him, she agreed.

As it turned out, they decided to take the wagon anyway. Hank said he had to replenish his stock of horseshoes and pick up supplies for Ruby. The boys begged to join them, insisting that they could help with the horses and that they wanted to see the friends they'd left behind in Denver the year before.

Janey wanted to go, but Ruby said absolutely not. How would it look for her to be taking a trip like this with Clay? Disgraceful, that's what it would be. She had a hard enough time keeping an eye on the two of them in town.

As far as anyone knew, the judge had not been fit enough to start up his rounds again. Just in case, Leon left word for him that he would be checking in with the marshal's office in Denver.

A good night's sleep improved Marjorie's spirits considerably. She gave Leon a detailed explanation of what she wanted in a cookstove—a large oven and a tight firebox, not some leaky thing built for coal that you couldn't control a wood fire in. Those weren't worth hauling home. He was to make certain there was a seal around the firebox door, and if it didn't cost too much extra, a warming oven across the top and a water reservoir at the side would be nice.

Leon had measured for the windows and wanted to measure her as well, but she wouldn't hear of it. She told him straight out not to bother buying anything for her. She already had plenty of dresses and besides, not all styles suited her. She was shocked to look down at breakfast and see him under the table attempting to measure the distance from her knee to her foot and repeated her admonishment not to waste money buying clothes for her. If he was so inclined, she'd appreciate a bolt of goods—blue calico, if they had it. Then she could sew summer dresses for Ruby and the girls as well as for herself. And a length of white muslin, she added. They'd use it and the dress scraps to piece a quilt this winter.

Marjorie tucked a handful of dried lavender buds into the corner of the food basket. She explained to Leon that these were to ensure a safe journey.

It was midmorning before they finally left town. Hank drove the wagon. The boys rode ahead. Leon and Clay followed with a string of horses tied behind each of them and the colts ran alongside the mares.

They'll be back in no time, Marjorie told herself as she stood on the front porch. *There is no reason to be bereft of all hope for the future over such a short absence.* Nonetheless, it was a sad start to the day.

"A whole week with no boys underfoot," said Ruby. "I do believe I've died and gone to heaven."

"I don't see why I couldn't go along," Janey said. She'd been pouting all morning. "I could've cooked and looked after the boys."

"And who would've looked after you, pray tell?" said her mother.

"I can look out after myself. After all, I'm almost sixteen."

Ruby ignored her. They'd been around this tree before. "How are you doing, honey?" she said to Marjorie.

"Fine," she said, feeling forlorn.

"He'll be back before you know it," said Ruby, taking her hand and giving it a squeeze. "Don't you worry."

"I wish he'd just stay gone," she said.

"Oh, honey, you don't mean that," said Ruby.

"I believe I do," said Marjorie. "I have no desire to spend the rest of my life not quite a widow yet not quite a wife. I dread becoming so attached to him that I devote my waking hours to watching the road and my sleeping hours to looking for him in my dreams."

"He'll be back in a week," Janey pointed out.

"For how long?" asked Marjorie. "Will he stay through the winter? Can you just imagine that man sitting and staring out at the snow for six months? I can't."

"But he loves you," Janey said, as if that made all the difference in the world.

"Just because a wolf falls in love, it doesn't mean he's going to give up chasing through the woods and howling at the moon. I—" She realized she'd almost said she loved him. Maybe that was the key. Maybe if she never said the word out loud, it would keep the sad times away. "I care for him, too," was all she'd admit, "but that doesn't blind me to who he is."

The men turned and waved to them just before disappearing around the bend. And as women have since the beginning of time, the three of them waved back and gave a silent prayer for a safe journey.

The wild strawberries were coming on. They took the little girls berry picking that afternoon and put up twelve pints of strawberry preserves that evening. Banjo Bob came over and helped with the horses when the stage arrived. He promised to return when it left in the morning. Ruby sent him back to the Lucky Lady with a pint of preserves and a tea towel full of dinner rolls.

While Ruby was still a bit queasy in the morning, she was fine the rest of the day. She and Janey and Marjorie and the girls worked together scrubbing down and airing out the boardinghouse. On the afternoons it didn't rain, they picked strawberries and put up more preserves. By the end of the week they had seventy-two ruby red jars topped with pale white wax lined up in the pantry.

What they didn't have was any sign of the men. By the second Saturday, they were past glancing out the windows and were sending the girls on regular trips to the edge of town to look for them.

At dusk, they came racing back to report they'd seen a rider. It was probably Clay or Leon riding ahead. They all changed into clean aprons, splashed water on their faces, and tucked loose strands of hair back in their buns.

When it turned out to be the Reverend Thompson, they were all so disappointed it was an effort to be civil to him.

That night, Ruby confided to Marjorie that the longer they were away, the more she worried that Hank had found a job in Denver. Since their disagreement, he'd not said another word about going to the Dakotas. But he'd mentioned a time or two that perhaps they were too hasty in leaving Denver.

Janey expressed her concern countless times that Clay would *not* find a job while he was in Denver. At least not one that her parents would approve of. Their marriage hinged on his obtaining suitable employment, and she questioned her mother endlessly on exactly what sort of job would be suitable. Something with a future was as specific as Ruby would get. Later, she said she was sorry she mentioned that, for it opened up another round of whether this job or that one had enough of a future to it.

At suppertime, the Reverend Thompson asked Marjorie why he hadn't seen her at services lately. She told him that she didn't approve of the town splitting down the middle. People had to depend on one another in times of trouble, and even if they didn't see eye to eye, neighbors should at least be civil. She didn't care for their attitudes toward her husband either, but she decided not to mention that. She did say that she had no intention of attending church services until the congregations were rejoined.

Surprisingly, the Reverend agreed with her. He asked that everyone in the dining room let their neighbors know that there would no longer be separate ten o'clock and noon services. Starting tomorrow, he would preach at eleven, and anyone who cared to join him was welcome.

The next morning, the Lucky Lady was packed at eleven o'clock. Pleased as she was to see this, Marjorie didn't pay a great deal of attention to what the Reverend said and only followed along on the hymns. When she heard hoofbeats out in the street, she was so excited that she bolted from the bench and ran outside.

Her heart nearly came to a halt at the sight of Leon with a two-day beard and an ear-to-ear grin. He nudged Ulysses up next to her, reached over, and lifted her up in his arms. She was so relieved to see him that she didn't think twice about letting him kiss her right there in the middle of the street. All she could think of was how good he smelled, like leather and sweat and Leon. Feeling his hands on her back, she wished she wasn't wearing that thick corset. For that matter, she wished she didn't have a single stitch on. The man brought out the wanton ways in her, no doubt about it.

Lost in the gloriousness of being wrapped in his arms, it was some time before she recalled they weren't alone. She glanced around, and there was Lucille Herner, her face drawn up in a disapproving scowl. Next to her, Evie Sanderson looked shocked. Everyone else had variations on these expressions except for Ruby and the girls, who were watching the road.

Humiliated by her brazen behavior, Marjorie buried her head in the front of Leon's shirt and was grateful to feel Ulysses move beneath her, carrying her away from their suspicious stares and uncharitable remarks.

"It's good to be back, darlin'," he said, and proceeded to kiss the breath right out of her again as they plodded along.

When they finally came up for air, Marjorie realized that they were out of town. Hank was driving the tarp-covered wagon, with Caleb sitting next to him. He reined the team in, and, at a motion from Leon, he and Caleb got down. Leon lifted Marjorie into the front of the wagon and swung in next to her. Hank and Caleb mounted Ulysses and galloped off to town. Though she hadn't seen them, she assumed Samuel and Thomas had ridden in with Clay. Surely, they'd not been inadvertently left behind in Denver.

"I brought you back a little something," Leon said while untying a rope from the back of the seat.

Marjorie hoped it wasn't a dress. Fascinated as that man was by her bosoms, she wouldn't put it past him to buy her a dress with a bodice so low it showed everything but her belly button.

He flipped the tarp back and there, perched on the top of the load, was an oak rocking chair. Its curved back gleamed in the sunlight, and Marjorie couldn't resist climbing up to see if it was as comfortable as it looked. It was. The arms were just the right height, and the seat was low enough that her feet could rest flat on the floor.

"It's beautiful," she said, running her hands over the smooth-grained armrest. She leaned into it and was pleased to discover that the curve in the back fit her perfectly. "So that's what all the measuring was about."

"Built to my lady's specifications," he said. "Got something else for you." He reached into his inside vest pocket, pulled out a folded piece of paper, and handed it to her.

Her heart did come to a halt this time. It was the deed to their place.

Goose bumps rose on her forearms and chills ran down her back. She was so astonished and thrilled she couldn't quite believe it was real.

"How did you . . . ?" was all she could say as she kept reading the lines over and over. There'd be no more uncertainty about whether she'd be able to meet the requirements. Her name was right there next to his on the line for property owners. She'd never have to move again, never have to listen to someone else tell her what she could and couldn't do.

"Turns out that land clerk didn't let on about all there was to know regarding the Homestead Act. In the first place, since you were over twenty-one, you qualified for 160 acres whether you were married or not. Plus, I bet he didn't mention anything about how you could buy the place free and clear for a dollar and a quarter an acre."

Marjorie was stunned. She'd had the $200. She could've bought the place without all this commotion.

But then she wouldn't have had the money to bail Leon out of jail. And, in all likelihood, she wouldn't have had Leon either.

"I figured it was worth the two hundred not to have anything more to do with that mouthy clerk," he said.

Looking up at Leon, she wondered how to thank him for giving her this, her heart's desire. She'd think of something, but for now she stood up, threw her arms around him, and kissed him for all she was worth. She felt the tears roll down her face. It seemed like she wept at the drop of a hat these days.

"Come on woman, you're making a spectacle of yourself," he said, wiping her face with his handkerchief. "Let's go unload. As excited as you are over a piece of paper, I can't wait to see your reaction when you find out what else is in this wagon."

She sat down next to him on the wagon seat and held on to his arm as he drove the team to town.

Ruby and Hank and all the kids were there waiting for them at the livery stable. Clay and Janey were talking excitedly to one another but stopped to help unload the wagon. In addition to crates of horseshoes and sacks of flour, sugar, beans, coffee, and cornmeal, there were ribbons, needles, a bolt of blue calico, and a new pair of scissors.

Within a short time, the only things left on the wagon were the rocking chair, two boxed-up windows, and a crate containing a woodstove.

When the excitement of going through their purchases died down, Hank mentioned that they'd been on the road since before sunup and he could sure use a bite to eat.

They'd just seated themselves around the table when Clay stood and said he had an announcement to make.

"I have some good news," he said with a goofy grin. "One of the fellows who ran that stage station between Hope Springs and Denver got drunk, fell into a horse trough, and drowned."

"I hardly think it's appropriate to be amused at the misfortune of others," said Marjorie as sternly as she could manage given how deliriously happy she was.

"His partner is too discouraged to continue, and the stage master wants me to come back to Denver. He said he wants to talk to me about running that halfway station."

"Well, that is good news," said Hank.

Marjorie wondered why he hadn't told Hank about this on the trip back. Maybe he just wanted to surprise everyone at once.

"He's paying for both Janey and me to come to Denver," Clay continued, his goofy grin fading and a certain amount of hesitancy entering his voice. "Stage fare, hotel room, meals, the works."

"Why in the world would he want to see our Janey?" Ruby asked, looking puzzled.

Marjorie was as bewildered as her aunt. Surely no one would set much store in the opinion of a fifteen-year-old girl about whether Clay could or could not run a stage station. She looked over at Leon. What was this all about? He turned his palms up and shrugged his shoulders to say that he didn't know what was going on either.

"They're looking for two people to run the station. One to work the horses and one to do the cooking. So I told them Janey could cook," Clay explained.

"Did you tell him she was a fifteen-year-old girl?" Ruby asked.

Over the years, Marjorie had heard too many astounding tales from pupils to be overly surprised by this plan of Clay's. But still, he'd seemed more levelheaded than to propose something like this.

"Well, actually, I told him that we were married."

"You what?" Ruby, Hank, and Marjorie all called out at the same time.

"I was pretty sure he wasn't going to let a green kid run the station, so I told him I had a family to support."

"I don't care how desperate you are for a job," Hank said, "Janey's not going to marry you and go off to cook meals at some stage station in the middle of nowhere. You can let loose of that notion right now."

"But Papa, I just have to marry him," pleaded Janey.

"And last year you just had to have a puppy of your own," her father reminded her. "The kid doesn't even have a job, Janey."

"He would have one if you'd let me marry him," she said, giving voice to her desperation and despair over the situation.

"He'd have a meeting about a job, not a job," Hank said, stressing the word "meeting" so they got that clear. "Who is going to hire anyone foolish enough to get married so they'd have a better shot at a job?"

"Mr. Richmond, I love your daughter, and I want to marry her," Clay announced, pulling his shoulders back and standing up straight and tall.

"How are you planning on taking care of her?" Hank asked, making no attempt to hide his increasing irritation with this foolish business.

"The biscuits are getting cold," Ruby reminded everyone in an obvious attempt to calm things down. "And if we don't eat pretty soon I'm going to have to reheat the gravy. Can't we talk about this later?"

Which they did. As soon as everyone filled their plates, Janey begged her parents to change their minds since she was almost sixteen and didn't want to be an old maid. The conversation went around and around, with pleas from Clay and Janey for understanding about how they needed to get married and pleas from Hank and Ruby for understanding about how they needed to be able to support themselves and how an interview for a job was not sufficient grounds to base a marriage on.

They'd just finished eating their strawberry-and-rhubarb cobbler when Janey asked the children if they would please leave the room. Naturally, they didn't want to go just when the conversation was getting good and said as much. But Ruby shooed them out with the promise that they could take the rest of the cobbler to the porch and divide it among themselves.

Once the children were on the other side of the door, all eyes were on Janey.

She took a deep breath and then said, "Job or no job, Clay and I have to get married. Mama isn't the only one who is in the family way."

"Lord a mercy," Ruby exclaimed in a shocked silence.

Hank swore in somewhat rougher language. Leon and Marjorie looked at one another to see if either of them knew anything about this.

"I suppose it's best if you two get married right away then," Ruby said, resigning herself to the situation.

"I guess I got to go along with your ma," Hank said reluctantly. "But I'm disappointed in you, Clay, damn disappointed."

"I'll take good care of her, sir," Clay promised.

"Just like you've taken care of her so far," Hank said bitterly. He pushed his chair back and stomped out of the room.

"Could we get married here, Mama?" Janey asked, filling the silence left by her father's departure.

"I don't see why not." Ruby sighed. "I'll get my wedding dress out, and we'll alter it to fit you. We can use some of the new blue calico to make matching dresses for the girls. I think a barbecue would be nice. I wonder how much a whole beef would cost. Too bad you and Charles had that falling-out, Marjorie. We need to start saving eggs for the cake and—"

"Mama, we don't have time for that," Janey interrupted. "We have to get married this afternoon."

"This afternoon?" Ruby asked, her forehead scrunched together in puzzlement. "Why this afternoon?"

"You don't want us going to Denver together before we're married, do you?" asked Janey.

"Can't you just stay here?" Ruby asked. "We could plan the wedding while Clay's gone."

"Mrs. Richmond," Clay said, "the company is picking up the hotel bill, the meals, and the stage ride. I was kind of hoping this would be our honeymoon. We won't be able to get away once we start running the stage station."

"Weddings are a celebration," said Ruby. "Half the fun is in the planning and anticipation. You young people are in such an awful hurry these days, you hardly even take the time to get dressed." She sounded as if she was ready to burst into tears.

"Mama," Janey said, going over behind her and putting her arms around her mother's shoulders to comfort her, "it'll be all right. Reverend Thompson is right here, and everyone's still dressed up from church. We don't need a big wedding."

Ruby shrugged her arms off and stood up.

"If you are in such a rush, why don't you just jump over a broom." She threw her apron on the table and stomped out of the kitchen.

Marjorie watched as Clay and Janey grimaced at one another. What did they expect? They were lucky Hank hadn't taken a punch at him.

"Clay, you go talk to the Reverend," directed Marjorie. "Leon, will you ask Rooster if we can use the Lucky Lady about six o'clock for a wedding and a dance and ask him to check with Banjo Bob, Pete, and Carl to see if they will play tonight?"

Leon nodded his agreement, scooted back his chair, and left.

She counted off on her fingers to make sure she hadn't forgotten anything. She had. "Leon," she called out to him, "would you ask Rooster if he has a keg of beer we can buy for tonight?"

Caleb and Maggie literally stumbled into the room when Leon'd opened the door. They'd been leaning against it trying to hear what was being said and, no doubt, reporting it to the others.

"Children, as you probably heard, Janey and Clay are getting married. I want you to run around town and invite folks to the wedding tonight at six o'clock at the Lucky Lady. It's not necessary that everyone know every detail about our family's business. If they question why the wedding is so soon, you may tell them that Clay has a job running a stage station and they have to leave tomorrow. But there's no need to tell them anything else," Marjorie instructed them. As they were heading out the door, she added, "And while you're at it, gather up and borrow all the eggs you can. We'll be needing them for the cake."

Once the children were gone, Marjorie turned to her niece and said, "Janey, why don't you go in and ask your mother if she'd help you fix your hair? And try on her wedding dress. Who knows, with a few tucks here and there, it might fit just fine."

Although she certainly understood how distressing it was for Ruby to have Janey married off in such a hurry, there was little anyone could do about it now. Janey and Clay were determined to get on that stage in the morning, and they might as well be married when they did.

As Janey left the room, Marjorie hoped she would remember to ask Leon to ride out to their place and get that white muslin nightgown with the lilacs. The wedding this evening would be for their family and their friends. But tonight, when Janey and Clay made their marriage with one another, she wanted her to be wearing that gown.

The afternoon flew by in a flurry of cake baking. Every time the children would show up with more eggs, she'd mix up another batch of cake batter and bake another layer. She ran out of brandy and raisins before the last two pans were full. She'd put those on the bottom, she decided.

By the middle of the afternoon, the kitchen table was covered with cooling cakes. Marjorie boiled sugar and water into a syrup and poured it in a thin stream over a bowl of foamy egg whites that Samuel and Caleb took turns beating. When it had formed a thick, white, creamy mass, she added a touch of vinegar and pronounced the icing ready.

Then everyone helped carry the cakes across to the Lucky Lady. Caleb followed with the frosting.

While Rooster scrambled to cover the picture of the scantily clad woman, Marjorie assembled the cake on one of the poker tables. After first covering it with a tablecloth and a piece of brown paper, she started stacking on the cakes, using the icing to cement the layers in place. When it was all assembled, the wedding cake was over a foot high, all covered in white frosting.

Leon returned with the white gown while she was spreading the last knife full of icing on the top. She left him and Hank to guard the cake and sent the girls off to pick wildflowers for Janey's bouquet.

She peeked in on Janey, but Ruby was fixing her hair, and she didn't want to interrupt their time together, so she left the gown on Janey's bed with a note wishing her and Clay happiness and joy in their marriage. Then she went off in search of the ingredients for the punch bowl.

She returned to the saloon with a bread bowl and four fruit jars of bush cherries that they'd put up the previous summer. She was pleased to see that the men had moved the benches in and had set up candles along the bar. The Lucky Lady was taking on a rather festive air.

She emptied the cherry juice into the bread bowl and carefully placed the cherries around the edges of the cake. The red cherry dots made a nice contrast to the white frosting.

Mary Beth, Maggie, and Emma returned clutching handfuls of violet and white columbines, pink fairy slippers, and deep blue irises that Marjorie placed in the water-filled fruit jars. She arranged bouquets around the red-dotted cake and stepped back to survey their work. All in all, she was rather pleased with the effect.

The only thing left to do was make the punch. Marjorie

added water to the cherry juice and stirred in ten teacups of sugar. Though the cherry juice gave it a nice pink color, it didn't add much flavor, so she sent the girls home for a jar of citric acid crystals.

Rooster offered to add some sarsaparilla to the punch, and she warned him not to put in anything alcoholic. She'd never found it amusing to offer spiked punch to unsuspecting women. They generally became tipsy without realizing it, and she certainly didn't want Janey's wedding spoiled by someone making a fool of herself.

But it would have been hard to spoil this wedding. Janey beamed with pure happiness as she stood in the doorway in her mama's dress holding her sisters' wildflower bouquet in one hand and her papa's arm in the other. Maggie, Mary Beth, and Emma walked in front of them, clutching their own handfuls of flowers, and Caleb, Samuel, and Thomas stood up with Clay.

They all made such a sweet sight. Banjo Bob played "Jeannie with the Light Brown Hair" on the piano as she walked down the aisle. Even Ruby seemed pleased at the way everything turned out.

Just for a moment, Marjorie wished that she'd waited for this, that she was the one in the white wedding gown, that it was Leon instead of Clay standing there so proud and nervous.

Once the ceremony was over, they pulled back the benches and started dancing. Banjo Bob played his banjo, and Pete and Carl both played their fiddles. When they started in on "The Girl I Left Behind Me," Marjorie pulled Leon out on the floor. Despite protesting that he wasn't much of a dancer, he was surprisingly good at it. Or maybe she was just glad to be in his arms again.

As they danced to "Soldier's Joy," she imagined that this was their wedding party and tonight was their honeymoon. Whirling around the room in his arms, she was carefree, content, and wondrously happy. Maybe the partings would be worth it if it always felt this grand when he got back. She could hardly wait for later tonight.

She stretched up on her toes and leaned into his ear so she could be heard above the music, the dancing, and the laughter. "Does life get any better than this?" she asked him. He bent down and whispered an indecent suggestion about what would make life better as far as he was concerned. She blushed and hid her face against the front of his shirt.

They circled and swung around to "The Old Brass Wagon" before Leon handed her over to Thomas and disappeared into the crowd at the bar. Thomas desperately wanted to ask Almira's oldest daughter, Hannah, to dance, but said he needed to practice with Marjorie first.

After two dances, Thomas worked up his courage to ask Hannah, and Clay stepped up to take Marjorie for a turn around the dance floor. He thanked her for all she'd done to make the day special for Janey.

Over the weeks that he'd been out at their place working with Leon, Marjorie had grown to like this young man. He was smart and hardworking, and he loved Janey beyond reason. She hoped that was enough.

Janey was dancing with her father, and when the music ended she reclaimed her new husband. Marjorie wandered over to the punch bowl and helped herself to a glassful. It was so cool and refreshing, she helped herself to another. She looked around for Leon, but he was nowhere to be found.

Then who should appear at her elbow but Charles. She wondered how he'd even heard of the wedding. He'd not been at church that morning.

Naturally, he asked her to dance right away. She tried to refuse, claiming she was weary. Which she was. But he wouldn't hear of it. After countless choruses of "Blue Tail Fly," she was exhausted, and she insisted they stop and get a glass of punch. She needed to get away from Charles before Leon showed up and caused a scene.

"I really must go," she said. She held her hand up and twisted on her ring to remind him of her marital status.

"I need to ask you something," Charles said, grabbing on to her upper arm.

Here it comes, thought Marjorie. She flashed her blue stone ring in front of his face again in hopes of avoiding that drivel about what a wonderful governor's wife she'd make.

"I'm worried about that old-timer out at the Lazy J. He's been looking after the place until Mrs. Jarveson can collect her belongings. I stopped by this morning to see how he was doing, and he didn't look well at all. I'm afraid he's about to cash in his chips."

"What's the matter with him?" Marjorie asked. She'd seen Dangerous Dan less than a week ago. He was filthy, but he seemed healthy enough.

"He just says he's feeling puny."

They moved aside to let other people to the punch bowl. Marjorie looked around, trying to catch sight of Leon. She decided he must've stepped outside.

"He is getting along in years," Marjorie pointed out. Why was Charles suddenly so worried about an old man feeling puny? That wasn't such an unusual state of affairs.

"But he coughs until he can't keep his food down, and he's weak as worm. It's more than being old. He was old a month ago, and he didn't look like this. I think he's sick."

"Does he have a fever?" she asked.

"How should I know?"

"Well, does he look flushed? Does his forehead feel hot?"

"I didn't feel his forehead," said Charles, acting as if that would've been an odd thing to do. "He's always red-faced from all the hacking and coughing he does, and now his neck's red, too. He says he burnt himself."

"Burnt himself?"

"He wrapped his neck in flannel, but that didn't seem to help, so he cooked up some onions in bacon fat and wrapped them up, too. He should've let it cool down more, I guess."

336 PATRICIA ROY

Marjorie looked around the room for Almira. She'd recently nursed two of her younger boys through the croup. Maybe she'd know what to do. Almira wasn't around.

Neither was Leon.

"I'm real worried," Charles was saying. "He sort of wheezes and squeaks when he breathes, and I don't think that's natural."

Marjorie agreed that it didn't sound good, but she didn't know what she could do about it.

"Plus he rambles on about one thing and another, doesn't make a lick of sense, but says he wants to talk with you and that he's sorry."

"Sorry about what?" Marjorie asked.

"How should I know?"

Just then, Rooster stopped the music so that Janey and Clay could cut the cake. They carried two pieces over to Hank and Ruby. There wasn't a dry eye in the house when Janey hugged her parents and Clay kissed Ruby's cheek and shook Hank's hand.

"I'll do everything in my power to take care of her," he vowed.

Rooster raised his glass of punch, and shouted, "May they always be as happy as they will be tonight."

Everyone joined in the laughter and cheering that followed. The musicians started in again, and Charles grabbed her up and whirled her around so fast, her feet left the floor. She laughed at the pure exhilaration of the moment but insisted he set her down immediately. She was a married woman after all.

Marjorie hurried over to help Ruby serve the cake. No doubt, Leon was out drinking with the men, but surely he would come through the cake line. She hoped he would stay fairly sober. This may not be their wedding celebration, but still, she planned on giving that man a night he'd never forget. Dancing in his arms would be a good way to start it out.

Where on earth was he?

11

Leon was on his third drink, glumly watching his wife spend the evening with another man. She and that Irwin were standing next to one another at the other end of the bar. Their faces were lit by the lantern hanging from the roof. Even from across the room you could tell how interested she was in what he had to say. Probably one of those intellectual discussions she set so much store by.

He knew something she liked to do a damn sight more than talk about books. Maybe he should just mosey on over and remind her. He picked up his drink and started to wind his way through the crowd. He was about halfway there when he nearly bumped into the back of the old biddy that had been booted into the benches that Sunday at church.

"Don't they make a handsome couple, Evie?" she said to her sidekick, who nodded in agreement. Leon assumed they were talking about Janey and Clay, and he had to agree with them.

"It's a shame she had to marry that murderer," the first one continued. "I hear he attacked her right in the hotel, and Hank had no choice but to insist he make an honest woman of her."

Leon stopped. They weren't talking about Janey and Clay, that was for sure.

"You don't say," said her tiny companion.

Leon thought she'd probably been saying it quite a bit as she didn't sound all that shook-up about it.

"He's not even from around here," said the first one. "He's an outsider."

"Hmph," snorted the second one.

Hell, thought Leon, *no one in Hope Springs is from around here. If Marjorie was to marry up with one of the original inhabitants of the area, she'd have to wed a Cheyenne.* He didn't imagine that would sit any better with the two women than he did. But it probably wouldn't be any worse.

"Mark my word, Evie," the larger one said, "those two have been sweet on one another since the day she moved to Hope Springs. They'll get back together once the judge gets to town."

"As it should be," said Evie.

"Judge Cunningham will see to it that Mr. McCoy is properly punished."

"What if he only sends him to prison?" asked Evie.

"That alone should be grounds for divorce, I should think. Surely a woman wouldn't have to stay married to a man in prison for life. The judge always spends a few days out at the Circle I when he makes his rounds. I expect that he will arrange for a quick divorce and a quiet wedding."

"That would probably be for the best," Evie said.

"You know Charles's father is a senator back East."

"You don't say."

"He let it slip out one day. He's quite a catch. He comes from money, he owns that ranch, and he spends every winter in Denver. He has a lot to offer a woman."

"She should've waited for him," said her short friend, "instead of getting tied up with that unsavory gunfighter."

"I understand Charles intends to run for governor one of these days."

"I've heard that."

Who hasn't, thought Leon.

"Marjorie is no charity case either. She's educated and re-fined. She can run a household without a lot of flapdoodle and as good as she is with kids, she'll be a fine mother to his chil-dren. She'll do him proud at his side."

The music stopped and the couples stepped off the dance floor. It made the rest of the room so crowded that short of walking along the bar, there was no way Leon could make his way to Marjorie. Soon folks would be milling around again and he could get over to her.

Clay said something to Hank that Leon couldn't hear, and Rooster lifted his glass in hopes that Janey and Clay would al-ways be as happy as they were tonight. Leon was probably the only one who didn't laugh along with that. His mind was on other things.

When the music started up, Leon saw an opening and moved past the two women just in time to see Irwin swing his wife through the air. She was laughing and having a good old time. He'd intended to go over and claim the next dance, but a man with walnuts for eyes could see who she wanted to dance with tonight.

"Hell's bells," he muttered as he turned around. He paid for a bottle of whiskey and walked out of the saloon with it. If he stayed in there watching the two of them carry on, they would have him up for murder, and this time they'd probably have him dead to rights.

"That you, McCoy?" he heard as he stepped out the door. He looked around, and there was the deputy. It never rained that it didn't pour.

"In the flesh," Leon answered. "What can I do for you?"

"You can tell me what you know about those stage rob-beries up north," said the deputy.

"I don't know a damn thing about them," said Leon. He was disgusted with the world in general and had no interest in carrying on a conversation about stage robberies with that dim-witted deputy. He turned and began walking across the street.

Within a couple of strides, the deputy was walking along-side of him.

"Listen," said Leon, "I'm getting mighty weary of the way you dump everything that happens in this country on my back door."

"I didn't say you had a hand in this," said the lawman in a now-calm-down manner. "But twice now we've followed tracks into the foothills up beyond your place, and I thought maybe you'd seen something when you were out riding around."

"I ain't been out riding around. I got my own place to take care of," he said. Then he added, "Deputy, in your dedication to justice, by chance did you stumble across any information about who might have murdered Jake Jarveson? I'd kind of like to get that cleared up."

"I stopped by to talk to that old codger who claimed you threatened to kill Jarveson. You know who I'm talking about?"

"Yeah, I know."

"Dangerous Dan," said the deputy, like he wanted to be certain Leon understood who they were discussing. "You know how he got that name?"

"Not a clue," he said. Which was about how the deputy was operating in Leon's opinion.

"He used to be a wild one, had himself quite a reputation," the deputy said.

"He tell you that, or did you hear it somewhere else?" asked Leon.

"Oh, I keep my ear to the ground," the lawman told him.

Then he ought to get himself a hearing horn. For a man who just spent the last two months investigating a couple stage robberies and a murder, he didn't seem to know too much.

"Anyway, old Dan can't rightly recall anymore whether it

was the drifter that was going to kill Jake or one of the hands who claimed Jake owed him back wages. Anyhow, the old geezer's nearly blind. He couldn't tell a bull from his big toe. In front of the judge, he'd be just as likely to point me out as you. Besides, the way he's coughing and hacking, he might not last until the judge comes through."

"That's mighty flimsy evidence to accuse a man of murder on," said Leon bitterly.

"Well, I was counting on you taking off," said the deputy. "Then I could mark this down under the solved-crimes column."

Leon didn't care much for the deputy's approach to investigation. "Am I still under arrest?" he asked.

"I guess not," the lawman said.

"Well, then give me my bail money back."

The deputy reached into an inside pocket, pulled out a handful of twenty-dollar gold pieces, and counted out ten of them to Leon.

"What do you know about Irwin's two hired guns?" asked the deputy.

"Don't know a damn thing about them," said Leon. At least nothing worth passing on.

"You three didn't ride together sometime in the past, did you?" asked the deputy, acting real cagey.

"What are you getting at?"

"Talk around town is that maybe they had something to do with Jake's murder."

"Maybe they did. I sure wouldn't know," said Leon, finding himself getting more and more irritated with this deputy. "Is this how you always go about your business, accusing innocent men and asking odd questions?"

"I got my eye on you," said the lawman. "It don't make sense for a man who wears a gun as easy as you do to be hanging around a little place like Hope Springs. There's nothing here for you. At least nothing legal. Maybe you didn't kill Jake Jarveson, but you're up to something. I'll be checking on you real regular, and one of these days you're going to make a slip and I'll be there."

Leon clenched his fist in frustration over this aggravating situation. "You better have something better than an old blind man's maybes before you come after me again."

"You lay a hand on me and I'll have you up for assaulting an officer of the law," the deputy warned, quickly stepping out of reach.

Leon stomped away in disgust. He made his way to the livery stable, where he stood in the dark and poured out his troubles to Ulysses.

"So now every time a dog stays out all night or an apple pie disappears from a windowsill, I'm going to have to answer to that simpleminded son of a bitch." Leon took a long swallow from the bottle in his hand.

Ulysses sympathized with his situation, but he didn't say much.

"And I tell you, I was damned shocked to see Marjorie behave in such a fashion. She seemed so thrilled about me coming home and the deed and all. You'd think she'd at least say 'thank you' before she started loving it up with another man. Maybe she's still mad at me for taking off and this is her way of getting even. What do you think?"

Ulysses didn't rightly know.

"Hell, where did she expect me to sell those horses? Here in Hope Springs? No one here needs any more horses," he said, "or has the money to buy them if they did." He took another drink.

He didn't know quite what to do. He couldn't go back to the dance, and he didn't want to sit over at the boardinghouse and wait around for her like a lost pup. He guessed he'd just wait right there. Sooner or later, she'd come to get Rosinante, and they could talk then.

There was an empty stall next to Ulysses. It was piled full of clean straw, and Leon sat down and proceeded to work his way through most of the bottle. It would be trying, to live with folks thinking he was a murderer who forced Miss Marjorie into marrying beneath her.

He hated the thought of people whispering and staring at him every time he came to town. He wondered if he could talk her into starting over someplace else. That would be the reasonable thing to do.

But Marjorie was not exactly what he would call a reasonable woman. From the first time he'd met her, she'd done the unexpected and stuck to it.

Though he pondered the matter every which way, he fell asleep before he had anything figured out.

He woke up to the sound of voices arguing nearby. He tried to sit up, but his head was pounding, and his belly was rolling and pitching like it was trying to throw the rest of his body off, so he eased back in the straw. He ought to give up drinking.

"I don't care what Charles said last night, you can't just go riding out there by yourself," insisted Ruby.

"My mind's made up," Marjorie said. "That man needs me."

So what if Irwin needs her. I need her, too. The sound of Rosinante's hoofs plodding toward the barn door was enough to make a grown man cry.

Leon lurched to his knees, intending to go after her and explain matters, but he stopped when he realized that reeking of whiskey the way he was, he'd be lucky if she didn't spit in his face.

"What should I do when Leon returns?" Ruby called after her.

"Sober him up with coffee, feed him breakfast, and tell him where I've gone," she hollered back at her aunt.

Then she rode out of his life.

So that was it. She was mad at him for getting drunk, and she was riding out to see Irwin without even giving him a chance to talk some sense into her.

Sitting back down, he wondered just what sense he could

talk her into. Irwin was rich, he was sweet on her, and he could hold up his end of those intellectual discussions she set so much store by. Leon would never be able to offer her more than a hand-to-mouth existence and lucky to do that.

Taming those mustangs beat him half to death. He wasn't sure he had the stamina to do it the rest of the summer, let alone the rest of his life. And even if he was up for it, there was a limit to how many horses were running wild in the hills.

He couldn't imagine what had gone through his mind to think he'd have $4,000 in his pocket by fall. As it was, the summer was half shot and all he had to show for it was $800. It would see him through the winter well enough, but then what?

He'd gotten a good price for the mares and their colts. But then he'd paid a good price for everything he bought, too. The stove and the rocker hadn't been cheap, and he had no idea that calico and lamp oil could cost so much.

And what was he going to do when he ran out of mustangs? It wouldn't take long, the way the land was being settled. He knew he couldn't make a living raising peas. The only thing left to do was to leave town for months at a time and work for wages. He couldn't see that ever working out.

He didn't belong in Hope Springs anyway. There'd always be that you're-not-wanted-here attitude, women pulling their skirts aside when they passed by, men refusing to share a drink with him. Eventually, they'd be giving Marjorie the cold shoulder, too, just for being married to him.

She was a good woman. She deserved better than the life he could offer her in Hope Springs. If he was any kind of man at all, he'd just ride out and leave her be.

The thought of leaving tore at his gut, but he didn't see any other option. It would be all downhill from here. If he could ever manage to get himself situated somewhere, he could send for her. Maybe she'd have her fill of homesteading by then and follow him. Though she'd never come right out and said she loved him, he was pretty sure she did. But who knew how long that'd last.

Once he had his bearings back and was certain that Ruby was gone, Leon got up and reluctantly saddled Ulysses. He sure wasn't looking forward to being hunched over a campfire tonight.

Just thinking about having that smoke in his eyes made them burn and water. He wiped them on his sleeve and was disgusted with himself to realize they were filled to the brim again.

Nothing good ever lasts anyway. Why would this be any different? No sense getting all worked up over it.

He'd walked away from Charlotte and never looked back. It'd hurt his pride all right and made him feel like a fool, but he hadn't felt like bawling about it.

In fact, he hadn't cried since he was a kid. But he damn sure felt like it now. His eyes stung, his chest ached, and his stomach was all tied up in knots. It wasn't due to being hungover. He knew what that felt like, and this wasn't it.

Lord, he hated leaving Marjorie behind. But he couldn't see what else to do. A stubborn man could play out a bad hand of cards if he wanted to, but he wasn't going to win the pot just hoping it would all work out. And he couldn't see spending the rest of his days trying to scratch by, especially with that Irwin always hanging around, flashing his fancy clothes and all. That was already wearisome.

As he was tying his saddlebags closed, he remembered the lilac water he'd stashed away. He was going to give it to her last night once they were alone. Might as well leave it for her, he decided.

He got it out and placed it on the board near Rosinante's stall. Maybe it'd remind her of what she'd thrown over. He might not have been able to offer her a big house with maids and fancy trips to Denver, but she was missing out on being loved by Leon McCoy, and that was nothing to sneeze at.

Well, she wasn't exactly missing out. He expected he'd still love her. He'd just be doing it at a distance from now on.

He stacked the twenty-dollar gold pieces she'd posted for his bail next to the lilac water. They were even.

As he headed out of town, he hoped she was happy.

12

Marjorie slept in fits and starts that night. Not only was she worried about Leon's disappearance, she was concerned about old Dan. He always ate at Ruby's when he came to town, and invariably he'd get into a fuss with someone. More often than not, Marjorie would have to step in and settle him down. He was a cranky old man. Still, it wasn't right to just leave him out there sick all by himself.

With no doctor in Hope Springs, families dealt with illness or injury the best way they could. Though women shared recipes for healing concoctions and neighbors pitched in to help out with chores when someone was laid up, those without family were at a disadvantage. No one had the time to take on nursing a stranger. Then there was always the risk that an illness might be cholera, diphtheria, or some other disease that would put one's own family in danger.

That, more than anything else, was the reason Marjorie had declined Ruby's offer to send Thomas or Samuel out with her. She had a hardy constitution and rarely succumbed to illness, but she was unwilling to expose the boys to anything.

It would do Leon good to find her gone when he sobered

up. Let him realize what it was like to wait around for someone for a change.

She'd looked all over for him last night. At first, she was certain that he was drinking with that bunch of men at the end of the bar, and she'd waited for him to find her rather than going over and embarrassing him. No man liked having his wife drag him away by the ear.

When he didn't come through the cake line, she asked Rooster if he'd seen her husband, and he said Leon had stepped out some time ago. Rooster suggested that more than likely he was waiting for her at the boardinghouse.

That made sense. As unfriendly as people were toward him, he probably decided to spend the evening watching the stars. But if he was there, he was hiding, because she sure wasn't able to find him.

When the reception shifted into a charivari and people set to beating on pots and clanging pan lids together under the hotel windows, she decided Leon had either gone deaf or had passed out in one of the abandoned buildings on the edge of town. She asked Hank to search for him. He came back an hour later, reporting that Leon was nowhere to be found.

Hope Springs was too small to get lost in. Leon must have decided it would be best not to come around her when he'd been drinking and had sought out a place to sleep it off.

It hurt that he would choose to spend his first night back this way. She'd had such high hopes for the evening.

When he hadn't returned by dawn, she decided that as long as she was up, she might as well go out and see what she could do for old Dan. No one else was likely to. By the time she returned, Leon would probably be awake and apologetic. She felt like an old married woman, resentful of her husband's rude behavior but tolerant of it. What choice did she have?

The sunrise ride helped clear her head and put things in perspective. One thoughtless, insensitive act did not mean the man himself was thoughtless and insensitive. Leon had many fine qualities. She needed to focus on them.

Focusing was a challenge this morning. Just as she'd feared, someone had added spirits to the punch bowl. It'd made her giddy and carefree last night and regretful this morning.

When she stepped into the Lazy J bunkhouse, she sniffed the fetid air, took one look at Dan, and decided his lungs needed clearing out. So did the bunkhouse, but that job was more than she was up for.

She told him to get up and get dressed as she was fixing him chicken soup and coffee in the main house. Then she proceeded to do just that. By the time the soup was simmering, she had kettles of water heating on the back of the stove and a zinc tub shoved next to the side of it.

The smell of hot coffee and chicken soup lured the old man into the house. Despite his almost constant coughing and repeated insistence that he was just this close to death, he was able to consume three bowls of soup and five cups of coffee.

Dan swore he was going to die when Marjorie bullied him into the tub of steaming water. For modesty's sake, she allowed him to keep his long underwear on. She threw a blanket over both him and the tub and every time he poked his head out of this steam bath, she made him take another spoonful of hot honey and vinegar. The vinegar would cut the phlegm and the honey should soothe his throat.

She refused to indulge herself in the memories associated with the vinegar's pungent smell. When Leon sobered up, he'd be home. There was no sense worrying about it. For now, she needed to concentrate on the task at hand.

By noon, Dan was clean, breathing halfway normal, and complaining bitterly over her throwing his pouch of tobacco in the firebox. He didn't appear to have a fever or spots any place that she could see. She determined that his smoking was the cause of his cough and his filthy living conditions had brought on the rest of it.

Since he did not appear to be suffering from a dreadful disease that he'd pass around to everyone, she convinced Dan to come to town until he was feeling better. On the ride in, he prattled on about one thing and another and kept vaguely apologizing to Marjorie about something he really didn't want to talk about.

When they got back to the stable, she was surprised to find Ulysses's stall empty. Her first thought was that Leon had left for their cabin without her. But silhouetted in the open doorway were the rocking chair, stove, and windows he'd bought in Denver. A person would think he would've taken those to the cabin with him as long as he was going.

As she went to open the gate to Rosinante's stall, she saw the stack of twenty-dollar gold pieces and the bottle of lilac water.

She was stunned for a moment, unable to think or even move. Then, with a sinking heart, Marjorie realized this must be his final going-away present. He'd given her the deed, the stove, the windows, and the rocker—his way of providing for and protecting her when he wasn't around.

Now he'd paid back the bail money and left her this one impractical gift to say that he cared.

She stood there remembering how her father used to leave little gifts for her mother to find after he'd left. Even though her mother always seemed to find comfort in the tawdry presents, Marjorie never considered that a cheap set of earbobs or a hair comb was much of a substitute for his being around.

But at least her father used to tell them when he was leaving. They didn't have to look high and low before coming to the conclusion he'd taken off.

To hell with Leon and his cheap bottle of lilac water. She threw it as hard as she could and watched as it smashed against the side of her uncle's brick forge. How fitting that their marriage should end with broken glass since that's the way it started out. *Good riddance,* she thought.

She might have thought it, but she wasn't feeling it. She

felt like tossing caution to the winds and riding after him, pleading with him to come back, begging him to give her another chance. How could she make it through the pain she knew was ahead without him here to hold her?

Why would he leave now? Why not in the fall? He enjoyed the excitement of training horses. Why go when he could spend the rest of the summer doing that?

The stone weight on her chest forced her to calm her frantic mind and face reality. The challenge was gone. He'd already proven he could do it. The horses were tamed, and so was she. What more was there left for him to do?

She ached with wanting to curl up around herself, pull the covers over her head, and pretend none of this had ever happened. How could she bear the emptiness and the sadness and the longing that was just beginning. It was all she could do to keep from dropping to the ground where she stood. If not for the old man leaning against the wall, watching her and waiting for her to take care of him, she would have.

In a daze, she put the horses away. Dan's strength was fading, so she pulled his arm over her shoulder and supported him as best she could while they shuffled over to the boardinghouse. Hank got up from the dinner table and carried the old man up the stairs.

She thought how odd it was that she wasn't crying. Had she finally run out of tears? Or was it because she'd known this was coming all along? Leon might've believed he could stay, but she never had. His timing surprised her. His leaving didn't.

She wanted to know if anyone had spoken with Leon this morning, but she just couldn't bring herself to ask.

As she put Dan to bed, she wondered who would care for Leon when he fell sick. Where would he go when he grew old?

He'll be back, she assured herself. *One of these days, when I least expect it, I'll look up and there he'll be with that lop-sided grin of his.* She ached for that moment.

But back for how long? Long enough to break her heart again most likely. Then he'd be off on another wild-goose chase. How could she stand it?

She'd stand it the same way women had always stood it. If Penelope could weave for twenty years waiting for her husband to return from the Trojan War, Marjorie imagined she could find some way to occupy herself until his return. With Janey gone, Ruby could use a helping hand. Getting ready to teach this fall would take a big part of her time. And, of course, there was the homestead.

It was hard to believe that they had the deed to their land already. Homesteading was supposed to be a long, drawn-out process full of hardships and setbacks. Why hadn't she insisted on reading the law herself instead of taking that self-important land clerk's word on it? Had she known about anyone over twenty-one being eligible and the dollar and a quarter an acre business, she could've avoided all this.

But would she have wanted to?

Somehow she got through the next few days. Most of the time she felt like she was somewhere else, watching this woman called Marjorie go through the motions of living.

If it wasn't for the children, she didn't know what she'd have done. During the day, they amused her with their pranks and jokes, and in the evenings, she sat and read to them. Herman Melville's *Moby Dick* captured their attention in a way that the stories in McGuffey's *Eclectic Readers* never had. They'd race through their evening chores in order to listen to as much as possible before bedtime. Marjorie wished Leon was there. He would've enjoyed this book.

She postponed bedtime later and later each night. If she could've avoided going to bed altogether, she would have. She dreamed of Leon constantly and often awoke with a start, certain that he was in the room. She grew more exhausted with each passing day and dreaded spending that first night alone in the cabin.

Old Dan was up and about by the end of the week. He'd acquired more tobacco, which didn't help his cough any. He was spending most of his time over at the Lucky Lady.

On Friday, Rooster offered to let him sleep in a lean-to out back if he'd clean up around the place. Having seen the squalor in which he lived at the Lazy J, Marjorie wondered what Dan could possibly know about cleaning up. But his moving to the Lucky Lady relieved her of the responsibility of caring for him, and she was grateful for that.

On Saturday, Hank said he needed to use the wagon. She was welcome to stay with them as long as she wanted, but he and the boys were going to take her things out to the cabin.

It was foolish to keep putting this off. Sooner or later, she would have to go. At the very least, she should check on the garden.

She rode out with Hank and the children that afternoon. The boys helped drag the rusted barrel stove out behind the cabin and haul the cookstove in. Then they were off to explore the canyon caves. While the girls played with their dolls in the sunshine, Marjorie and her uncle Hank put the cookstove together.

Just as she'd requested, it had a warming oven and water reservoir and the firebox door sealed good and tight. It took up a great deal of room, but it'd be a joy to cook on and would definitely put out enough heat to keep the cabin warm on even the coldest nights.

They pulled off the oiled cowhide and nailed the windows in the two openings. Light flooded the room through the glass and made it look larger. It was purely an illusion, since the rocking chair took up the remaining floor space, leaving barely enough room to walk around.

Coming out to the cabin was every bit as difficult as she thought it would be. Every place she looked held an image of Leon.

In the garden, she saw him struggling and cursing behind the plow.

When she glanced over at the corral, it was almost as if she could still see him flying around on his mustangs, his back arched, his arm flung out, his hat fanning the air.

She almost smiled thinking of him at the table during those evenings when his eyes would glaze over while she read to him.

These memories gave her a peculiar comfort, like moving a sore ankle around to see if it still hurt.

Though she hadn't planned on it, she ended up staying after all. As she sat on the porch swing and watched Hank and the children disappear into the trees, she decided that it would be best if she kept her thoughts occupied with chores and planning for the fall. Dwelling on memories of Leon would just tear at her soul until there'd be nothing left.

It was clear that the call to adventure was stronger than her hold on him in the summer, but things would slow down in the fall. He'd be back before winter set in. She was certain of it.

That night, she sat on their porch swing and watched twilight change to darkness. When her lucky stars appeared, she sent her husband a wish and kiss.

The rest of the summer was filled with the harvesting and preserving of the garden produce. She'd never shelled and dried so many peas in her whole life. No doubt, she'd be eating pea soup on her deathbed.

Most days she rode in and helped Ruby. Hank and the boys came out and cut the high grass for hay.

In August, a letter arrived from the Overland Stage Company asking Hank if he'd consider working on some of their stagecoaches over the winter. They were impressed with the overnight repair job he'd done on a coach that'd been dragged along on its side. As the snow up in the passes began closing down the routes, they'd send the coaches to him. They would freight him the supplies he'd need and send him half the money in the fall and the other half in the spring.

This fortunate turn of events eased matters considerably. For the time being, there'd be no need for Hank to look for work elsewhere.

The second week of September, Lucille Herner and Evie

Sanderson offered to run the boardinghouse for a few days, and they all piled in the wagon and went to visit Janey and Clay.

It was a relief to see that Janey was really as content with her new life as she'd written in her letters. Clay promised that he'd bring her back to Hope Springs as soon as the way station was closed for the winter. According to Ruby's calculations, the baby wasn't due until the first part of February. Nonetheless, they would all feel a great deal better once Janey was home safe with them.

When they returned, Marjorie aired out the old three-room building she'd been using for a schoolhouse. The roof leaked, the wind blew in through the cracks in the walls, and it was impossible to keep heated when the temperature dropped below freezing.

To raise money for a new schoolhouse, they had a box social the last Sunday in September. Charles was out of town, which spared her the onerous task of informing him she had no intention of sharing her picnic basket with him, regardless of what he paid for it. As it turned out, Caleb bid a dollar, beating out some cowboy's offer of seventy-five cents.

It was a depressing event. They only raised thirty-six dollars and forty-two cents and she had to spend the entire afternoon listening to Caleb do bird imitations. He mimicked the jay's loud raucous call almost perfectly, and you couldn't tell his high-pitched, sibilant cedar waxwing from the real thing. He was working on his oriole's song, a series of disjointed whistles and alternating chattering noises. All the other women in town were laughing and sharing secrets with their sweethearts and husbands while she was stuck with an eleven-year-old boy doing birdcalls. Though she appreciated his efforts to cheer her up, she'd had better times.

When the leaves changed from green to gold and started scattering with the winds, she planted tulip bulbs along the edge of the cabin porch. As she dug her hands in the cold, crumbly earth, she thought of how it was already snowing up in the high mountain passes. If Leon didn't come home soon, he wouldn't be back until spring.

Though she tried not to, every time she heard a horse clop pass the schoolhouse, she glanced out the window.

Thanksgiving came and went with no sign of him.

She continued to live out at the cabin. She was warm and snug, and since they'd only had light snowfalls so far, Rosinante didn't have any trouble carrying her to town each day.

It'd been difficult that first night. The memory of Leon lying there with her star quilt pulled up to his chin brought on the first tears.

But after she got the first bout of sadness out of her system, she found she cherished the serenity of reading in her rocking chair or bundling up and sitting out on the swing to wait for the stars to appear. She'd make a wish on her lucky stars and then go back in for the night. It was always the same wish, but she was getting more and more discouraged about it ever coming true.

Just as she was ready to turn in one night, Thomas came galloping up and said she needed to come to town right away. Dangerous Dan's health had taken a turn for the worse, and he was asking for her and the deputy. He said he had something he needed to say to both of them before he passed over.

Thomas saddled Rosinante for her, and on the trip to town he explained that old Dan had been shot in the belly during an altercation at the Lucky Lady. No one seemed to know whether he was even involved in the disagreement, but it was clear that he wasn't going to recover.

According to Thomas, the whole town was abuzz over this. There were those who were sure that old Dan would point the finger at Charles Irwin, or at least his two hired guns, for Jarveson's murder. Most likely, he hadn't said anything before out of fear for his life.

There were others just as certain that Marjorie's husband was the murderer, but that he'd threatened old Dan, causing him to take back what he'd said before. Every speculation ended with, "They never found that money, you know."

As soon as they reached town, they headed straight for the Lucky Lady, where Marjorie found Dan spread out across the bar. Blood was oozing from the bandages wrapped around his middle and even in the yellow lanternlight, he looked terribly pale.

"You came," he said simply, as she took his hand.

"Of course," she said, thinking of what a horrible death lay ahead for this poor man.

"I'm so sorry," he said.

She heard the hushed whispers behind her and wondered whether she should offer him something to drink. His lips seemed parched, but she wasn't certain a person with a hole in his stomach should be drinking, and she didn't want to make matters worse for him.

"You married a good man, Mrs. McCoy," he said, "and I regret pointing the finger of suspicion at him." He launched into a spasm of coughing and hacking that didn't end until Marjorie gave him a sip of water.

That seemed to settle him down without producing any ill effects.

"Mrs. McCoy," he said, "your husband didn't kill Jake. I did."

There was a moment of stunned silence in the room, followed by murmurings of, "What did he say?"

What a kind of thing for old Dan to do, thought Marjorie. He knows *he's dying and is trying to take the blame for something he didn't do so that Leon can start out with a clean slate.*

"I appreciate you trying to clear Leon's name, but the deputy has already dropped the charges against him," said Marjorie.

"He should've, 'cause he didn't do it. I did," he said, loud enough that this time everybody in the saloon heard him.

"I used to have quite a temper, that's how I come by my name. But I never killed no one before, and I wouldn't have done it then if Jake hadn't treated me so poorly. After all the work I done around the place, he was going to turn me out without paying me a dime. Claimed I hadn't done anything worth paying wages for, that I was a charity case."

"That was certainly unkind of Jake, but it hardly seems reason enough to kill him." Marjorie just couldn't bring herself to believe that this harmless old man was capable of murdering anyone. Old Dan was contentious, but he wasn't mean or evil.

"What was I supposed to do, you tell me that?" old Dan asked in a raspy voice. "Irwin said that he couldn't see his way clear to taking on another worthless old-timer. Said he already had two hanging around, and he didn't want three. Where was I going to go? My back was to the wall."

Perhaps he had killed Jake. He certainly sounded serious enough.

"I was a good hand in my day, and I still carry my own weight, but I'll be damned, pardon me, ma'am, if I was going to live out my days begging in a bar somewhere." He indicated he wanted another sip of water.

After a few swallows, he continued. "I thought about it all that afternoon, and the more I thought, the madder I got. By the time I served Jake his supper that night, I was so riled up that instead of handing him the knife for his steak, I just reached over and slit his throat. Right away I was sorry I let my temper get the best of me, but there was no going back. I buried the gold Irwin paid for the ranch. After things blew over, I was going to dig it up and go somewheres else and live out my life in comfort." He raised his head up enough to look down at the blood-soaked bandages. "Guess I won't be needing the gold now."

"Shh," said Marjorie, pressing her hand against his forehead. "You just lie down and take it easy."

"I appreciate your kindness to me, ma'am. I sure don't deserve it, not after the way I sicced the law on your husband. But I didn't realize he was still around. I thought he'd just disappeared on down the road."

Dangerous Dan closed his eyes, and Marjorie looked

around the room. Most of the men had the good grace to look ashamed or at least look away.

Well, they ought to. They'd treated Leon like a criminal over nothing more than a few rash words. She was surprised to see Lucille and Evie standing in the doorway. She guessed the town gossips couldn't wait to hear what a dying man might have to say to the schoolteacher. They'd all thought she was the one who'd been fooled. She hoped they got an earful. Lucille gave a weak smile that Marjorie ignored.

Hank carried Dangerous Dan over to the boardinghouse, where he hung by a thread until the deputy got there the following afternoon. He told the lawman the money was buried out behind the bunkhouse. While the lawman and most of the men in town were out digging it up, Dan passed on to his reward.

The townspeople were shocked by Dan's confession. One by one, they stopped by to apologize to Marjorie for the way they'd treated Leon and vowed to be more neighborly toward him, should he ever return. Though she was gracious about it, she expressed her regret that their apologies hadn't come earlier, when it might've done some good.

Leon had never made a fuss over it, but she knew that the constant snubbing was a thorn in his side. It was a cruel twist of fate that just when he would've belonged, when he would've been accepted, he wasn't around to enjoy it.

She tried not to judge the people of Hope Springs too harshly. For the most part, they were good-hearted, and she could recall any number of times when they'd pitched in to help one another out. She understood that public opinion was the only weapon they had to protect themselves from riffraff and ne'er-do-wells, and she realized that you just couldn't put the welcome mat out for everybody. She just wished they had given Leon the benefit of the doubt.

But if the good folks of Hope Springs were surprised to find out who'd really murdered Jake Jarveson, they were flabbergasted when they discovered that the gold bars they dug up carried the exact same minting stamps as those stolen in the stage robberies up north.

Which, of course, led them directly to Charles Irwin, who quickly claimed that he'd sent his two hired guns to bring the gold back from his bank in Denver. The two gunmen didn't have much to say, which was just as well. Though the deputy wasn't the sharpest tack in the box, even he knew something was fishy with this story. Why would Charles send two of Jake's employees to his own bank to pick up his own money? Now, that didn't even make sense.

The deputy tied them all up, threw them and the gold on the next stage, and with a posse of half a dozen citizens, took the lot of them back to Denver to straighten the matter out.

Marjorie was sorry to see Charles caught up in such an unsavory affair. However, she was thankful that Leon's name was cleared and grateful to have heard the last of Charles's talk of being governor.

They buried Dangerous Dan and things settled down for the winter in Hope Springs.

13

*L*eon leaned over and patted Ulysses on the withers. Their breath formed clouds in the air to match the dusting of snow on the ground. For the last month, he'd been following the stage route, inspecting the way stations and marking down what repairs would be needed in the spring.

He'd parlayed his $800 and his horse-training skills into part ownership in the Overland Stage. He probably could've sent one of the employees to do the inspections, but he didn't mind. He sort of liked checking up on things himself.

Besides, he had some Christmas presents to drop off by Hank and Ruby's, so this would work out well. While he was there, he could talk with Hank about how things were going with the coach repairs.

With any luck at all, he'd get a chance to see Marjorie. Although, if he just wanted to see her, all he had to do was close his eyes. She was right there, waiting for him like she'd been tattooed on the back of his eyelids.

He rode into Hope Springs late in the afternoon and was astounded to see people wave and shout out howdy as he rode by. The two old biddies who'd caused that scuffle at church were out on a front porch pulling taffy, and even they lifted a hand to greet him. Would wonders never cease? He guessed he must resemble some more popular citizen.

Leon left Ulysses in his old stall at the livery, noticing right off that Rosinante's spot was empty. It was both a disappointment and a relief. Though he longed to see Marjorie, he dreaded it as well. What could he say? "Sorry for being such a horse's ass?"

He'd kicked himself a dozen times a day for riding off the way he did. What difference did it make if she danced and chatted the evening away with that Irwin? She was going home with him. Or she would have, if he'd gone home.

But no, he had to go get all liquored up and then decide that $800 wasn't enough, he had to be a big shot. All along she'd believed he didn't have it in him to stay. Why did he have to go and prove she was right?

Even if he'd left so he could build a future for them, he'd walked out on her just like she said he would. He'd regretted that mistake with every breath. As much as he wanted to hold her in his arms, he sure wasn't looking forward to seeing the hurt in her eyes, knowing he had put it there.

Leon headed over to the back porch of the boardinghouse and stood watching through the kitchen window as he worked up the nerve to knock. Ruby and the girls were baking, and Hank, Clay, and the boys were tasting and carrying trays of cookies into the dining room.

It wasn't that he was afraid they wouldn't welcome him. He was pretty sure the friendships they'd developed over the spring would still be there. And it surely wasn't that he didn't want to be surrounded by the love and happiness on the other side of the door.

It was just that for six long months he'd been looking forward to coming back, dreaming of what it would be like. He wanted to savor the moment. Since Marjorie wasn't there, it was a little easier to reach up and knock.

Caleb opened the door and greeted him with one of his big goofy grins. Mary Beth ran flying into his arms, and Emma and Maggie were right on her heels. Hank, Samuel, and Thomas crowded around, and, as soon as there was space, Ruby gave him a smothering hug and Janey planted a kiss on the cheek. He thought Clay never would quit shaking his hand. It was the second-best welcome he'd ever had in his life.

Ruby insisted that he sit right down and have a bowl of chicken and dumplings. He watched her and Janey waddle back and forth, their bellies so big they could hardly get their apron strings tied. He knew it would be indelicate to ask, but he wondered if his wife was in the same condition.

The girls wanted him to try each of the different kinds of cookies they were making for their Christmas Eve baskets. The boys were all anxious to tell him the details of Dangerous Dan's death and Charles Irwin's downfall.

Leon listened as if this was the first he'd heard of it. Months ago, when a stage driver told him about the old-timer killing Jarveson, he'd spit coffee clear across the room. Who would've thought? It was downright gratifying to hear about Irwin being mixed up in that stage-robbery business. That man was as irritating as a needle in an armchair. He hoped his legal problems kept him tied up for years.

Ruby mentioned that Marjorie was living out at their cabin and asked how he'd been doing since he left.

"Oh, I've been doing all right," he said. It wasn't anything like those two months with Marjorie out on their place, but then he doubted anything in his life would ever be that good again.

"What have you been up to?" Hank asked.

"Oh, little of one thing and another," he said. "I bought a part interest in the stage company, and I've been learning the ropes there." He wanted them to know that he wasn't just a drifter, he was a man of substance now, but there was no need to rub his good fortune in their faces. "A man needs a way to earn a living, you know."

"So you're the one I have to thank for arranging for those

stage repairs," Hank said, as if now he understood how that'd come about.

"I put in a good word for you, but it was the way you fixed up that coach that was dragged along on its side that got you the job." Which was true. "How are things going, by the way?"

"Moving along," Hank said. "I think they'll all be in good shape come spring."

"So what are your plans now?" asked Ruby.

"Well, I got a few presents to leave off here, then I thought I'd mosey out and see if my wife will have me back."

"I don't mean to be inhospitable," Ruby said, handing him his coat, "but if you're going you'd best get on your way. It'll be dark before long."

"What's the rush?" he asked. As much as he yearned to see her, he wasn't at all anxious to see the hurt and resentment he'd caused. He hoped that with Christmas coming on, Marjorie would be in a forgiving mood. But there really was no telling with that woman.

"Putting it off isn't going to make it any easier," she reminded him.

He guessed she was right about that.

So he pulled the presents he had for them out of his coat pockets. He'd brought lockets for Ruby, Janey and the girls, and jackknives for everyone else. They all thanked him and there was a round of handshaking and hugs before he was literally shoved out the door.

Since he could hardly leave town without saying hello to Rooster, he stopped by the Lucky Lady to give him his jackknife. Seemed kind of peculiar giving a bartender a Christmas gift, but then it would've been odd not to. Leon guessed that family was where you found it.

Rooster shouted out a welcome that was echoed by every man in the place. You'd have thought he was their long-lost brother the way men kept coming by to slap him on the shoulder and insist on buying him a drink. He told them that he didn't mean to be unfriendly, but he was heading out to see his wife and if he showed up with liquor on his breath, there'd be hell to pay. They all knew about that and said they'd catch him next time.

They were right in the middle of telling him how the stamp on the gold bars had led the deputy to arrest Irwin when Hank stepped into the saloon.

"Ruby thought you'd be here," he said. "She sent me over to tell you that if you don't get on your horse and get going, she'll send Thomas out to bring Marjorie back. So unless you want your reunion to take place right here in the Lucky Lady, I'd suggest you saddle up."

Leon bid Rooster and his newfound friends good-bye and walked with Hank over to the livery. Hank didn't say much, which led Leon to believe that Marjorie might not be as welcoming as the folks in town had been.

Ulysses automatically turned up the trail to the cabin as if he'd been doing it every day of his life. The scattering of snow made the place look different on top, but underneath it was still the same. The creek was frozen over, but the fence was still standing and thin wisps of woodsmoke still curled out of the chimney.

He felt his chest open up at seeing candle flames flickering on a tree in the cabin window.

But it was the sight of her sitting on that swing, all wrapped up like a present in that star quilt, that was enough to raise the dead.

He nudged Ulysses in the flanks. Regardless of how it all worked out, this was one Christmas he wasn't going to watch through a window.

14

*T*his would be her last night in the cabin until spring. She was on borrowed time as it was. Any day, a big snowstorm was bound to hit, and there she'd be—stranded.

She'd read the children the nativity story this afternoon and let them out of school early. They were so excited about Christmas that it was impossible for them to concentrate on their studies anyway. She planned on riding back to town first thing in the morning to open up gifts with Hank and Ruby and the children.

But tonight, she wanted to celebrate Christmas Eve in her own home. She'd put up a little tree with a few candles on the table. It looked perfectly lovely framed by the new window.

Then, bundled in her quilt, she sat on the swing and waited for her lucky stars to come out.

Dusk was just settling into dark when she saw a rider in the distance and quickly crossed her fingers and closed her eyes. "Please let it be Leon," she whispered.

She listened to the soft clop-clop, clop-clop of the horse's hooves until they came to a halt in front of her. What if it wasn't him? What if it was someone out to do her harm?

The mixture of dread and anticipation had her heart pounding so hard she wanted to glance down and see if the front of her gown was moving in and out. But she didn't dare open her eyes.

Well, one of them needed to say something. They couldn't just stay like this all night. Her mouth was too dry to form words, so she tried to whistle. All she could get out was a thin, reedy sound, but it must've been what he was waiting for.

She listened to the creaking of his saddle leather and the crunch of his boots on the frozen grass. Then she heard the words she'd been waiting to hear ever since that dreadful night last summer.

"Darlin', could I have this dance?"

Epilogue

Dear Reader,

There's more to the story, of course. But Leon's waiting for me, so I'd best bring this account to an end.

You may think that some of what I've written is rather explicit, especially for a woman of my age. But I've always thought that Mrs. Shumway was a bit too vague in her marriage guide. To my way of thinking, she left the best parts out. I didn't intend to do that.

In places, I have taken the liberty of filling in what I imagine was going on in my husband's mind. When you live with a man for fifty-one years, you learn a lot of his ways.

I won't try to fool you. Life was not all lilacs and spring breezes after Leon returned that Christmas. We had our share of discouraging, disappointing times ahead of us.

We sold the stock in the Overland Stage and bought the ranch from Charles. He needed the money for his legal defense and offered us a good price and excellent terms. Leon thought it would be a grand adventure, and I hoped he would be satisfied to settle down if he had a ranch to run.

The Rocking M has been one disaster after the next. It

seems that any year there isn't a flood, there's a drought. But somehow we've always made it through.

Prince Charming lived out his days running free. Every once in a while, Leon would go off in the hills and fuss with him. I seriously question whether he ever intended to put a saddle on that stallion again. I suspect he did it more to justify a few nights under the stars and to say hello to a kindred spirit.

Clay found his niche as our foreman, and all the boys worked on the ranch for a time before heading off into the world. I wish they'd have stayed closer to home. I never hear a bird call out that I don't think of Caleb and that silly box social.

One by one, each of the girls left for a time, but they all returned to Hope Springs to raise their families, which pleased Ruby to no end. I certainly miss that dear woman and look forward to visiting with her in the sweet by-and-by. There's no one in the world who could pull together a Christmas celebration like my aunt Ruby.

And no one who enjoyed those get-togethers more than my husband.

It was not easy being married to the governor, and I advised Leon in the strongest terms not to let himself get talked into running. How he kept getting elected, I'll never know. He wasn't a back-slapping, baby-kissing, laugh-at-weak-jokes sort of man.

All I can say is, if you're good with horses and you talk the truth, it counts for a lot in Colorado.

Leon and I never did get around to spending our evenings discussing books. He still wants to save that until we're too old to do anything else with our nights. I tend to agree.

I could go on and on about what a struggle raising five children was and what wonderful people they grew up to be and what gorgeous grandbabies and now great-grandbabies we have, but perhaps another time.

What I want you to remember out of all this is that, upon occasion, married life can be a trial.

But then there will be times when you'll enjoy life beyond belief.

I've had my troubles as well as my joys. But through it all, I spent the best years of my life with the grandest man I ever met.

I wish the same for you, my dear.

Take care,

Marjorie Bascom McCoy

DEAR READER:

So, What do you think? Not bad for a first book, eh? I'll tell you what, it's a dream come true for me.

I've been a reader ever since I can remember, and I've wanted to write books for nearly that long. I am thrilled beyond belief to finally see one of my stories in print.

Over the years, I've dallied at one thing and another, but according to my mother, I've been a storyteller since I first began to talk. (To be truthful, her exact words are, "I never could believe a word that girl said." But close enough, right?)

I grew up way out in the country, and with the exception of a dog named Buster and my two younger sisters (who shall remain anonymous), my companions were imaginary—at least to everyone else. They were quite real to me. My father still tells of how at mealtimes I'd sit on only one half of my chair, leaving the other half for my invisible playmate of the day.

Well, my body might have been stuck on a homestead in Idaho, but thanks to books, my soul was able to roam the earth with fascinating friends. Wrapped in my chenille bedspread, I trudged along on the Bataan Death March. (My mother said I nearly drove her crazy shrieking, "Don't strike me," every time she came into the room. Why I would prefer to be on the Bataan Death March rather than on a nice farm was beyond her.)

With a metal bowl on my head and a rotisserie rod in my hand, I was Don Quixote, off to slay the forces of evil. (Cervantes, the author of *Don Quixote de La Mancha*, wrote, "Too much sanity may be madness, and the maddest of all is to see life as it is and not as it should be." I believe the man was right.)

Eventually, I left home to slay the forces of evil for real. While plugging along toward a master's degree in psychology, I worked at various residential treatment centers for children. It broke my heart. To this day, I can't think of those kids without tears burning their way to the surface.

It gradually dawned on me that what they really needed was someone who believed they were the hottest thing to walk the face of this earth. They needed people who loved them to distraction, not some do-gooder type talking about what was or was not appropriate behavior. (By the way, if you're ever overwhelmed by the need to make a difference in the world, I urge you to sign up to mentor a child. If you'll write me, I promise to put you in touch with the nearest program. Patricia Roy, P.O. Box 3434, Duluth, MN 55803.)

Discouraged, I got out of the social work business and into the ironworker trade. I spent the next six years walking the high iron and listening to "man-talk" in the job shacks. (It's amazing how often men speak of love. They just don't call it that.)

Then I remarried my college sweetheart and we had three kids and one day I woke up and realized that time was awasting. If I was serious about writing down the stories my friends had been whispering to me over the years, I'd better get to it.

So, I pulled up a chair for Marjorie (there's no longer enough room for both of us on the same seat) and started getting her and Leon's story down on pager. Now that we've put the finishing touches to LUCKY STARS, we've pulled up another chair, invited another friend, and started in on another tale.

If you enjoyed Leon and Marjorie's company, you're going to love spending time with Robert and Meg.

Robert's a young, idealistic, English-Canadian Mountie who believes in honesty and honor. Meg's a somewhat older, Irish-American woman who has fallen upon hard times and believes that one does what one can.

En route to his first assignment, Robert visits Bouncing

372

Bess's, a house of ill repute. Though he's embarrassed about being there, what's a fellow supposed to do? It's not like he's saving himself for marriage, it's just that all the girls he knows are.

Meg's dismayed to find herself at Bess's as well. Since leaving home at fifteen, she's embarked on any number of careers with a remarkable lack of success. Now it's come to this.

Midway through their awkward evening, who should show up but Black Jack McCain, her partner on a recent ill-fated riverboat gambling scheme. Meg slips out the back door, steals Robert's horse, and heads north. They meet up on the trail, and against his better judgment, Robert allows Meg to accompany him to his posting.

Though Robert is initially appalled at her outrageous behavior and her criminal tendencies, Meg soon charms her Mountie with her irrepressible high spirits and her willingness to undertake any task no matter how dangerous or difficult.

Meg's equally taken by Robert's courage and his compassion for the people he's vowed to protect. She yearns to accept his offer of marriage.

But Robert's being groomed by his well-to-do uncle for a position of leadership in the Canadian government. An older woman with a shady past would only hold him back, and Meg cares for him far too deeply to ruin his future.

What's a woman to do?

Claire (my editor) tells me that if we want to see WEDDING KNOT in the stores by next June, I'd best get back to writing.

So, until we meet again,

Laugh like this might be your best chance.
Live like what you do makes a difference.
Love like you're still learning how.

Patricia